DOORS WITHOUT NUMBERS

by

CD Neill

Grosvenor House
Publishing Limited

This book is published by
Grosvenor House Publishing Ltd
28-30 High Street, Guildford, Surrey, GU1 3EL.
www.grosvenorhousepublishing.co.uk

A CIP record for this book
is available from the British Library

ISBN 978-1-78148-630-6

"Every man of genius sees the world at a different angle from his fellows, and there is his tragedy."

Henry Havelock Ellis. The Dance of Life 1923

This book is dedicated to all those loved ones whom are out of sight, but never out of mind. x

Prologue

He was tempted to turn back in response to her call, but he knew if he showed the slightest recognition, there would be no turning back. He would have to acknowledge his familiarity with her and be a willing participant to a conversation. Inevitably, she would ask him what he had been doing since they last met. She would be genuinely interested and he knew that it would be impossible to be evasive. He couldn't risk it. So he strode on purposely, bowing his head until he heard her voice calling his name no longer. When he turned the corner, he relaxed in the shadows of the office building. It was unlikely she would pursue him. No doubt she would be confused. He hoped she wouldn't be hurt, but rather question whether it had been him she had seen. After all, it had been at least eighteen years since they had last seen each other. Intimate and intense though their relationship had been, it was still possible that she had mistaken someone else for him.

He stood there for ten minutes, allowing his breathing to become more regular. It was true he had been panicked when he saw her, but also pleasantly surprised. She didn't look any different from those earlier days when they had spent every day together. Her hair had darkened slightly but still retained the reddish tinge that he had admired when it shone brightly in the sun. Her face with its flawless vanilla cream complexion and neck scattered with the freckles that he had once laughingly called breadcrumbs. Her body still lean and willowy under the long coat that she had wrapped tightly against the September chill as she had waited at the pedestrian crossing. He had seen her on the other side, close enough to have recognised her instantly when their eyes had met. Surprise was registered on her face within a second and then delight. The delight he himself had felt before the green man on the pedestrian lights began blinking, and then it had been panic. He had turned away instantly, walking against the tide of people surging towards the pavements edge before the lights turned red. Elbowing himself away as aggressively as he was able, he ignored the angered responses and then walked as fast as he could. Then she had called him. His name rang so clearly and tugged at his conscience but he couldn't have stopped, much as he would have liked too.

He stepped away from the building and entered the park alongside Vicarage Lane, looking furtively around him but also trying to look casual. There was a chance she would have come here, perhaps to clear her head of confusion. Or maybe she had shrugged and forgotten it as quickly as the moment of recognition that had taken place minutes ago. He hoped so but doubted it. She had always been sensitive. It was one of her more enduring qualities, and was instrumental in her being able to show empathy for anyone. He had used to tease her when she cried seeing a dead animal. But another part of him had wished that he was able to care about others as much as she did. Even then, part of him was dead. She had been the one thing that had helped him to feel alive. But that was then. Life was much different now.

He continued his way towards the International Station Arrivals confident she wasn't following him. Seeing her had shaken him but he couldn't allow it to distract him from the purpose of being there. He fingered the photograph in his pocket and tried to memorise every detail of his charges' face. The boy looked younger than twelve which could cause problems with Immigration. However, the child would have a letter from their parents so it was more likely the questioning would take place at Border control in Brussels and wouldn't involve him. Nonetheless, it was important he did not make a mistake when they met. It helped to have information on what clothes they would wear but often this could change at the last moment. One time, the child had wet themselves and had changed during the journey almost causing him to approach the wrong one. Mistaken identity in this job could be detrimental for everyone concerned. The thought made him lick his upper lip nervously. The monitor screen positioned above him showed him that the train from Brussels had arrived. He waited at the coffee bar behind a pillar that obscured him from the CCTV camera watching a family come through the revolving doors and head towards check in. The father, a tall man with a heavy build was trying to push a luggage trolley overburdened with suitcases that wobbled precariously as one of the turned wheels turned back on itself and caused the trolley to stop without warning. The mother, a slim woman in her late twenties held the hand of her young daughter, who chattered excitedly in an undecipherable language, her eyes fixated on the Euro-Disney posters. Occasionally she would point a finger at Mickey Mouse and make skipping movements that shot her forward a step leaving one foot suspended in mid air as she was restrained by her Mother's gait. He watched their flurried activity until they disappeared through passport control, their voices fading away until any memory of them disappeared as quickly as they had arrived. The speakers above him politely reminded all passengers not to leave any baggage unattended and repeated the message in alternate languages. He waited still and silent; the core in a tornado of activity. The alternating rhythms of hurried feet and squeaking trolleys, the laughter in greetings and the quieter farewells. And then the boy arrived. He recognised a small dark face with wide eyes looked searchingly for the man they expected to see. He approached from the side of the turnstiles and made an effort to open his arms in a welcoming embrace so that his mouth was against the boy's ear. "Who saw you off?" He whispered.

The child looked up at him and gestured a lack of understanding. He took the boy's backpack from him and searched through the front pocket until he found his charge's passport. Smiling as if with joy at a reunion, he pocketed the passport in his jeans before handing back the backpack. They headed toward the escalator that lead to the domestic stations entrance, the boy walking silently beside him.

The boy sat quietly looking out of the window of the bus as it navigated its way out of town. He handed the boy a bottle of water and a tablet which he motioned the boy to swallow. The boy did as he was bidden. He guessed the boy had been sedated before his train journey from Brussels but it would be necessary to ensure the boy was co-operative during the handover. Neither talked, the pretence was over now. It wasn't necessary to talk to the boy or act out a relationship for the benefit of other travellers. Experience had taught him that people didn't care one way or other if they saw a child seated next to a single man on a bus, even when the child had been distressed and wailing in foreign languages, it would more likely cause embarrassment to his fellow passengers who would pretend they couldn't hear.

The bus left them at the corner stop six miles away from the town. He gestured again for the boy to follow him as he crossed over a foot-style into a field of long grass still wet from the previous day's downpour. Within minutes of wading through the pasture his jeans and trainers were soaked. The boy followed, still silent despite the discomfort, clutching his small backpack against him as he attempted to match the older man's stride. A gate swung open on rusted hinges as they made their way toward the cottage in the corner of the field ducking underneath two large conifers that brushed against the boy's face as he passed. The boy hadn't uttered a word but seeing the door, he suddenly grabbed his companion's hand and tried to pull him in the opposite direction. This was a common occurrence so he had learnt to ignore the signs of last minute panic. He figured the cottage was to blame for their fear, it looked dark and dingy with the windows boarded up. He pulled his hand away and strode purposely toward the door. He knocked twice, and ignored the boy's frantic attempt to cling to his leg as the door opened. He recognised the elegant woman who hesitantly opened the door and pushed the boy toward her, handing her the passport that he had taken earlier and waited as she compared the photograph to the boy who was now in distress. Without speaking, she ushered the boy in the door and slammed the door shut. He heard the sounds of bolts sliding shut as he retraced his steps back towards the field and the bus home.

It was almost dark by the time he reached his flat in Queens Street. He pushed open the main door with his foot whilst scrambling in his jeans pocket for his door key. But then stopped. His door above the short flight of steps was already open, only a crack, but enough to know someone was there. He stood for a minute, hovering on the top step, confused. Normally his visitor would come to his flat on the first day of every month. The visits would be short; long enough to be handed an envelope with cash for groceries, utility bills and rent and the usual instructions. The plan had never been changed. Until now.

Discreet noises of activity were heard before the shadow of a large figure moved towards the door from inside his flat. He recognised the lumbering movements of his only visitor, but the unusual activity within the flat made him uneasy. At this moment he made a decision and ran back down the stairs two at a time. He sprinted southbound toward Elwick Road, narrowly missing an oncoming car that sounded its horn in indignation. A seagull flew above him, squawking at his recklessness. He continued running until he reached the subway entrance that lead to the train station and then crouched down on his haunches wheezing. His mind was playing tricks on him; maybe he was just being paranoid. Maybe it had been necessary to change his delegated tasks. But if so, why not have slipped the instructions under the door? Why enter the flat?

It was possible that he had mistaken the identity of his surprise guest. It was doubtful burglars had broken in; there was nothing to attract them and certainly nothing to steal. Unless...the unthinkable had happened. He was sure he hadn't been followed from the International Station, he had been careful. Surely, if he had been followed, they would have arrested him after he had delivered the boy? Maybe his visitor was there for an entirely different reason. His use had expired. He shook his head as if to rid himself of such paranoid thoughts and tried to reason with himself. He had been so careful. Every instruction had been fulfilled to the letter, he had never made a mistake, there would be no reason to doubt his value. Without him the whole project would be rendered inoperative.

He slapped his palm flat against his forehead in an attempt to control the thoughts that were flooding into his consciousness. He wished he had kept the tablets; he needed to be still in mind. His fingers scratched at the lining of his pockets in a desperate hope that there would be one nestling in the folds. His search was futile. His consciousness was now overwhelmed by a tsunami of paranoia. He retraced his steps during the day. The only difference between this day and any other was that he had seen her. Was she part of it? Why had he seen her? If only he had spoken to her, had waited for her at the lights. She would have hooked her arm through his just like she used to. The two of them behaving like no time had passed. He whimpered as he rocked himself. He hadn't spoken to her because he was scared, regardless of whether his fear may be unjustified. It was difficult to tell when he had real cause for alarm, his mind played tricks on him all the time. He couldn't cope with change; especially if it was unexpected. For that reason alone, he knew they would have prepared him for a change in plans. Not because they would be compassionate to his situation but because he would be useless otherwise. So why visit him now, without warning? His instinct, clouded though it was, gnawed at him, he suspected he wasn't the first to have received an unexpected visit. The others had warned him this would happen someday. Over the last year he had lost contact with the others. One by one they had faded away, no explanation had been offered, just the order to continue as before. It was possible that they had got away. He envied them, knowing he would never find the courage to do the same.

He became aware of a taxi driver watching him. He met the man's eyes and stared him down. It never occurred to him that the driver was watching him wondering whether he should help the skinny man who was crouched down amongst the pigeon filth, cradling his head in a gesture of despair.

Time had passed unnoticed by the time he had controlled his thoughts and returned to his flat. The light had been switched off and the door closed. He entered the flat and fumbled his way towards the light switch, hoping no-one was waiting for him in the dark. The light blinkered on and focused his attention to the items on the table. An envelope with instructions had been left with a few coins. He read the instructions and frowned. It didn't make sense.

"*Purchase parcel tape with money provided. Retain receipt and change. Wait to be contacted.*"

The residue of his earlier panic bubbled up in the form of a short laugh, he had been paranoid. There was nothing to fear, although the note was ridiculous. Usually the instructions would include a photograph of his proposed charge, their arrival times on a given flight, train or ferry and a delivery address. But this...this was simply a chore. He picked up the coins and left the apartment.

*"Every person of genius is in some degree
at once man, woman and child."*
Henry Havelock Ellis. The Dance of Life 1923.

CHAPTER ONE

Detective Inspector Wallace Hammond's heart felt like it was about to burst out of his chest. Instead of breathing he was gasping for air like a man drowning. He had been jogging for thirty minutes and was now convinced that he was dying. It was his second day on his new healthy lifestyle plan and he felt anything but healthy as a result. Yesterday he had done well resisting the temptation of biscuits with his coffee, had even reduced his sugar down to two spoonfuls instead of the usual three. His evening meal of supermarket bought ready-made three bean casserole had boasted only 430 calories. But now he was craving a bacon sandwich and the muesli he had tentatively eaten two hours ago did nothing but assure him that he deserved better.

He limped towards the park bench and allowed himself to fall back onto it rather than endure the further discomfort of trying to bend his legs first. He allowed his head to fall back and remained slumped. One arm dangling over the side of the bench, the other stretched out sideways on the back rest. He knew he looked ridiculous but at that moment didn't care. The sweat patches under his arms had spread towards an identical stain from under the elasticated waistband of his jogging trousers. His back felt clammy and the sweatshirt clung to his ample body. His greying but thick hair which didn't look great on the best of days was now sticking up at remarkable angles as if it were a bunch of flowers reaching towards the sun. He felt nauseous and decided that jogging was not for him. He had lived fifty two years without choosing to run around a park in the early hours of the morning so he was sure that living the remainder of his years without doing so wouldn't make much of a difference.

The clouds he was staring at were moving fast to make room for the larger grey promise of rain. He decided it was time to move and heaved himself out of the bench. "You sad excuse for a man" he reprimanded himself out loud as he limped towards the park exit.

It was raining heavily by the time Hammond let himself into the house. He kicked his new trainers off dismissively under the coat rack that was over burdened with everything but coats; empty carrier bags, umbrellas of all sizes and colours, clean shirts that were waiting to be ironed, a few tea towels from the occasions when he had answered the door whilst drying up and quickly flung onto the hook before opening the door. A library book, long past its return date teetered precariously between the two hooks on which it rested. He mused, as he shuffled past in his socks, that coat rack hides a multi-tude of sins. Now, like the many other forgotten objects hidden under the bundles, his new trainers will also be lost. Not a bad thing he winced as the newly formed blisters paid homage to the now abandoned footwear.

Hammond paused to check call minder on the phone before climbing the stairs. The tone alternated between high and low tones indicating he had messages. He sat amongst a pile of folded clean laundry on the bottom stair as he dialled 1571. He had three messages, one was from the sports shop on the high-street telling him that his treadmill will be delivered sometime between 10am and six pm on Friday the sixth of December, he noted to call them back and cancel the order. The second message was from Paul, his twenty-four year old son, asking for some money, the third message more surprising. "Wallace, its Lloyd, Lloyd Harris. I would like to talk to you when you are not in the office so give me a call. Perhaps come down to the club. Speak soon." the message beeped to the end. Hammond pressed two to save the last message. Lloyd Harris. He hadn't seen him since his retirement four years previously and there hadn't been much opportunity to talk due to all the many well wishers competing for Harris' attention. The last time he had enjoyed a real conversation with Harris must be at least six years ago, he remembered. Harris had come round for a meal when he was still married to Lyn. It had been around the time when Lyn had moved into the spare room. Hammond wondered if Harris had noticed the tension that hung in the air of the house. It had been a difficult time. He expressed his regrets in a long drawn out sigh and phoned Paul's mobile which rang for several seconds, left a message saying he would transfer money into Paul's account and pulled himself up the stairs towards the bathroom.

By the time Hammond had encouraged his Peugeot Estate through the downpour onto the M20, he had accomplished three of the mornings' objectives. The first, after showering and shaving had been to throw the scales away. His expanding stomach was happier being filled with food that tasted good. If the scales tried to make him feel guilty for allowing himself this luxury, they should go. His second task was to call Harris. They hadn't talked much since the retirement party, so it would be good to catch up. He had arranged to meet his old friend over lunch at the golf club near Maidstone later that day. Thirdly, £400 had been transferred into Paul's account to pay his son's rent for the month. Hammond's conscience nagged him about Paul. He sighed as he clunked the car into fifth gear, Paul had always been a mummy's boy so it had been natural that he had chosen to side with Lyn after the divorce. Not that taking sides had been necessary, Hammond had willingly given Lyn whatever she wanted. There had been no point in trying to dissuade her from leaving. It was obvious she had been unhappy for a long time, she had felt second best next to his career, and anyway, she had never liked overweight men, so sex had dried up as soon as the weight began to pile on. Paul couldn't forgive Hammond for not fighting for the marriage. Hammond remembered the way Paul had confronted him a year ago, "You should have proven that Mum meant more to you than your career, you should have made more of an effort to make yourself attractive". He knew he could have fought to keep Lyn, but he doubted she would have stayed regardless. Lyn and he were too passionate, too head strong. They had acted as catalysts for each other and now he felt too old, too tired for passion. He steered the car onto the slip road towards Folkestone and pushed his foot gently down on the brake pedal. The thoughts in his mind fading as he turned onto the road towards the police station.

Hammond was annoyed to find that there were no biscuits waiting beside his morning coffee in its usual place on his desk. He signalled to his favourite volunteer worker, Emma, who usually worked at the front desk through the glass screen that divided the offices and pointed with a questioning look. She looked at him equally surprised and gestured that she would come to him. Hammond sat himself on the large swivel chair, grimacing slightly as it groaned in protest. Emma came into the office without knocking.

"Morning, Inspector. How is the diet going?"

Hammond looked at her before becoming aware of DS Lois Dunn standing outside the door. "Failed." He answered curtly, hoping that a conversation on the subject wouldn't continue but then remembering his missing biscuits smiled shyly.

Emma leaned her head to one side and sighed. "Typical man" her facial expression said for her and she pointed to the filing cabinet. Following her direction, Hammond got up from his chair and opened the top drawer of the filing cabinet. He found the biscuits lying on top of the printer paper. Emma left him as he opened the packet and pulled out two chocolate digestives with eagerness. He was ravenous already, and it wasn't even mid morning.

"Do you want the bad news or the good news?" Ds Dunn strode into the room after Emma's departure and continued without waiting for an answer.

"The good news is that the boy with the burns is going to make it. The bad news is CPS reckons there is not enough evidence to prosecute the ones who set the warehouse alight."

"What about the witness statement?" Hammond swore with his mouth full of biscuit. This was not good; chances are it would be his neck on the line "Surely they identified the arsonists?"

Dunn looked at him warily "It has been dismissed as being unreliable. The witness has since admitted that they are short sighted and were not wearing glasses at the time."

Hammond had faith in DS Dunn. She had worked with him on and off for two years now and had shown herself to be hardworking and diligent. Hammond would guarantee that if a witness statement was found to be unreliable, it was unlikely to be due to her carelessness.

"Well, continue to question them, it is still possible that they made out the boys carrying a petrol canister or whatever and perhaps we can match any residue on their clothing. In the meantime, I will speak to the team and come up with alternative enquiries." Hammond interrupted their thoughts by requesting that she remind him of an important lunch meeting "For Police Business" he had said as an explanation. He wasn't yet aware of what Harris wanted to talk to him about, but since Harris had been his superior officer twenty years ago, it was still related in some obscure way to work.

Detective Constable Michael Galvin was waiting for Hammond in the Briefing Room. He was perched on the table discussing the politics of football with Detective Constable Tom Edwards but immediately got up from the table and sat on the chair beside it as Hammond greeted them with a nod. Edwards however, continued to mock with sarcastic comments Galvin's sporting ideals despite Hammond's interruption. Hammond slammed the file with the original witness statement onto the table and demanded their full attention. Normally he would have waited, maybe even join in the banter between them but he was hungry and tired from his mornings flirt with a fitness regime.

Galvin looked at Hammond with a raised eyebrow questioning the aggressive placement of the file, and then shifted his attention to the file on the table in front of them.

"I understand that the evidence on the arson case has been rendered useless." Hammond kept his voice level but the team around him knew he was angry, Hammond's temper tantrums were well known in the Major Crime Unit and sometimes not completely justified.

Edwards spoke first. "The witness can't provide a positive id as she led us to originally believe, but to be fair she was accurate in her statement about the clothing they wore, there was enough detail for us to find the lads. One of the victims woke up for a few minutes in hospital and gave us a statement that we have recorded on video. It was enough to make an arrest."

Hammond looked at his team with impatience. The sooner this case was solved, the paperwork examined and ticked off, the more chance the perpetrators would be given the sentences they deserved. A gang of local youths, ranging from fifteen to twenty five, had trapped boys in a disused warehouse and set it alight. Although the two victims were alive, both were in critical care with burns and smoke inhalation. It was important to Hammond that the arsonists not only be identified but apprehended. One mistake could cost a conviction and

he had no intention of allowing the injured parties go forgotten whilst their potential murderers got off scot free on some misdemeanour. There was a knock on the door and DS Lois Dunn stuck her head in. "Inspector. Detective Superintendent Beech wants to talk to you."
Hammond acknowledged her with a raised hand then left the office in search of Beech.

Twenty minutes later, Hammond's raised voice could still be heard from Beech's office. Superintendent Philip Beech, despite being Hammond's superior officer, was sitting at his desk whilst Hammond shouted at him. He seemed unperturbed by the role reversal, he had worked with Hammond for seven years following Hammond's transfer from Maidstone, if he had learnt anything from Hammond's explosive temper, it was because he cared about his job. After receiving numerous commendations for acts of bravery and professionalism over the years, Hammond was a respected colleague. But now Beech's patience was wearing thin. He shouldn't have to justify himself to anyone, least of all his subordinate.
"Wallace, this is being taken out of your hands. That is final, I am not prepared to negotiate this matter further and I certainly shouldn't be expected to justify it."
Hammond was pacing Beech's office, his blistered feet were not appreciating his burst of activity but Hammond's temper was not allowing him to be reasonable to his superior officer or his own physical comfort.
"Fair enough, the witness statement is compromised but it was good enough to help find the boys seen running from the warehouse. We have another video statement from one of the boys in hospital. That is your evidence! Those hooligans deliberately trapped those boys in a

warehouse; they doused the building in petrol, stood back and lit a match. You are telling me that it is not in my control to charge them!"

Beech stood up and walked round his desk, he motioned for Hammond to sit down. Hammond hesitated and then, obeying his sore feet rather than his boss, did so.

"You're a good Detective Wallace. But you are a crap police officer if you can't be objective after thirty years in the profession. I am not justifying their actions Wallace, but it isn't just about those boys who lit the match, it is about whether we have enough evidence to prosecute them, and the CPS does not believe that we do. The only evidence we have is that an accelerant was used to set the warehouse alight. Despite claiming that the attack was in revenge for stolen drugs, No drugs were found at the warehouse or on any of the victims. The witness who claimed seeing the boys running from the scene is short sighted and needs prescription glasses which she was not wearing that day. No canister with any trace of flammable liquid was discovered near the scene, nor were there any traces on the suspects' clothing. The victim's video statement was confused and erratic, it could easily be argued that he was pressured to make the statement whilst being vulnerable and on medication. The other boy refuses to make any statement at all and claims he doesn't remember anything. Without positive identification of their attackers, we have nothing. The forensic evidence is minimal and there is not enough justifiable cause to exceed the budget any further on evidence that is unreliable. Even if the CPS cooperate and make a charge, the jury will laugh us out of the court for being unable to make the charges stick. It is out of our hands."

Hammond had had enough. If Beech wanted him to hand over the case, so be it. It was pointless arguing about it any more. He stood up "I hope that the families of those kids are given a reasonable explanation as to why their boys' attackers are not brought to justice." Hammond slammed the door behind him as he left. Beech sighed, he wasn't subservient to Hammond but he knew it was pointless arguing further. He was the superior officer, not Hammond. His word was final. If Hammond didn't like it, he knew what he could do. Much as he respected Hammond as a man and as a detective, he had no intention of letting Hammond think he could get what he wanted.

Three hours and four rejected CD's later, Hammond felt no happier as he drove towards Maidstone. He had raised the volume during Holst's Jupiter Suite, usually so good at calming his soul, and tried to allow the music to wash over him, but it had failed. He knew it was pointless trying to listen to the radio, the constant talking about absolutely nothing in particular had a greater chance of making him more irritated than ever. It surprised him that the radio stations had any listeners at all and enraged him knowing how much they earned for their verbal dribble. Only last year, he had thrown the Guardian Newspaper down in disgust when Terry Wogan had been reported as earning £800,000 per year. It was ludicrous. His thoughts then turned to the futility of the morning's events, paperwork wanting attention had plagued him, and then there had been the e-mail from a would-be novelist wanting to know what a Detective's role was. He had answered her questions politely but he couldn't help wondering aloud to an amused Emma how many more fictional detectives were going to solve yet more unrealistic murders. He had been tempted to ask the writer whether her story had involved a butler but had thought better of it. His thoughts were becoming muddled. It was easy for a provoked soul to fixate on everything remotely irritating. He slowed the car as if trying to slow his mind. What was he really stressed about? He knew it wasn't really about the radio, or even his altercation with Beech, not entirely anyway. Hammond had been feeling disillusioned for a while now. Despite the efforts of all law enforcers, he couldn't help the nagging thought that crime happened simply because people just didn't care about one another anymore. It was becoming a greedy, self serving world.

As Hammond swung the car into the parking space at the Golf Club, he was feeling self-conscious. There was always a sense of elitism in these places. Hammond was no golfer, and looking around at the people in the parking lot, it was obvious he stood out from the crowd. He dodged his way between puddles toward the main entrance and was reminded by large printed notices on every door that the dress code excluded trainers and jeans. He looked down at his black corduroys with an embarrassed grimace and then stepped forward looking for Lloyd Harris amongst the group of lean men wearing polo shirts and chinos. His eyes drifted over the placement of green upholstered tub chairs and oak coffee tables until he saw the former Detective Chief Inspector at the far side of the room, leaning on the highly polished veneered bar as if he had been there all morning. His head was leaning on an open hand whilst his other hand repeatedly dipped into a bowl of peanuts beside him. He looked up when he heard his name being called and stared blankly at Hammond for a few moments. Hammond felt taken aback at the man's unexpected reaction and offered his hand to his old friend almost shyly. Harris continued munching, his head now alertly raised, his eyes dilated and fixed on Hammond. There was a nervousness apparent in both men and Hammond turned to the bar man relieved at the distraction when he was asked what drink he would like, his hand still outstretched toward Lloyd who suddenly grasped it with both of his own and announced Hammond's name so loudly, it was as he expected applause to follow. Hammond smiled at Harris and tilted his head toward the bar man to offer Harris a drink. Harris accepted with a request for a pint of Guinness and leaned back, looking at Hammond with scrutinising eyes. "So, you are here! I thought for a moment you stood me up!"

"I thought for a moment, you didn't recognise me!" The reply was light-hearted but honest. Hammond paid for the drinks and slid the full pint glass toward Harris whilst accepting his Coke and the change.

"I am an old man, what is your excuse?" Harris bent over the glass of Guinness hooking his top lip over the rim with eagerness. He allowed the stout to slide down his throat with silence as he savoured the moment and then announced his satisfaction with a sigh. Despite the temptation to reply that he was earlier than they had arranged, Hammond gestured towards the chairs beside the glass panelled wall overlooking the course. After the morning's discovery of muscles he never knew existed in his backside, the last thing Hammond wanted was to sit on was an unforgiving stool. They walked towards the panoramic windows and sat down opposite one another giving them to chance to study the other with interest. Hammond was shocked at how Harris had aged since they had last seen each other, but realised that his looks probably hadn't fared any better.

"So, how's Lyn? Is she well and young Paul? How is school?"

The absurdity of the questions directed at him made Hammond pause with his drink in mid air, Harris had seen Paul when he had graduated from secondary school, had celebrated with the family when Paul had passed his GCSE's with A's and B's. It had been nearly eight years ago. The glass of Coke continued its slow journey towards Hammond's lips as he thought about how to reply, and decided to speak honestly without questioning his companion's lapse.

"He's not so young Lloyd. He's twenty-four now, as for Lyn, well, following the divorce, we keep conversation to a minimum. But I hear she's well."

Harris looked stunned for a moment before laughing and leaned toward Hammond.

"Ahh, but in a father's eyes, their son or daughter will always be a child. Look at Kathleen, a grown woman but to me, an innocent girl!" The conversation now recovered, the two men discussed their families with pride and delighted in each other's revelations. Hammond found himself listening eagerly as Harris told him about his daughter Kathleen and part of him was surprised by how pleased he was to hear she had divorced her second husband. He felt himself reddening slightly as he remembered how he had stared at her on their first meeting. It had been in 1992, he and Lyn had been married six years, still happy but over the honeymoon years, with Paul, who was five at the time. A new family excited about their future together when they had invited Harris, then Hammond's superior officer, to dinner. Harris had brought Kathleen which had resulted in Lyn not talking to Hammond until the next evening. It had been obvious, she had said with a trembling lip, that Hammond had fancied Kathleen, so awe struck was he, that he had humiliated Lyn by practically ignoring her throughout the meal. Hammond would be the first to admit that Kathleen was a very attractive woman. Of course, she may have changed over the years, but he remembered her vividly. Kathleen had the skin of the blessed Irish, pale and flawless of imperfection. He remembered her green eyes, her richly coloured auburn hair (out of a bottle Lyn had surmised) that hang loosely down her back. Kathleen, he learnt, during the rare occasions when they had seen each other again, was a woman who made beauty effortless. All the creams and cosmetic products that Lyn had stacked in the bathroom cabinet would have never achieved the natural poise of her imagined rival.

The conversation between the two former colleagues steered toward the years they had spent working together in Medway. Following his promotion to Detective Inspector, Harris had worked on a case of drug-trafficking with CID. During the arrests of the suspects, Harris was knocked unconscious allowing the perpetrator to get away. Police Constable Hammond, who had been assigned to guarding the exits, managed to chase the suspect and arrest him. Due to the fact that the suspect had already attacked a senior officer and threatened to do the same to him, Hammond was awarded a Chief

Constable's commendation for his professionalism and courage. Partly out of appreciation for helping to get the drug traffickers be apprehended and convicted, and partly out of embarrassment for what otherwise could have been seen to be a failure as arresting officer, Harris encouraged Hammond to study for the Police Promotion Exam to earn him the rank of Sergeant. Years later Harris, as Chief Inspector, presided over the newly appointed DS Hammond.

It was for this reason that Hammond was curious as to the real reason why he was here. Harris would not have contacted him for any reason other than an interest in his work. They were friendly; hence the mutual enquiry into family, but criminal investigation was the source of their relationship. Since Hammond's transfer to Folkestone, their only correspondence had been the Christmas cards sent by Lyn until the divorce and then nothing until now.

As if reading Hammond's thoughts, Harris changed the tone of conversation abruptly. "It has been a while since I last saw you Wallace so I doubt you are aware that, until recently, I had been working with the Cold Case Investigation Team?"

Hammond leaned back in his chair somewhat taken aback by Harris' news. Since Harris's retirement, there had been considerable changes within Kent Police. April 2007 had seen collaboration between the police forces and authorities of Kent and Essex which now shared marine services and joint patrols along the Thames Estuary. A joint IT directorate had also been established but what was most significant since Harris's departure from the force was the creation of one of the largest joint serious and organised crime units in the

United Kingdom. The new Serious Crime Directorate, otherwise referred to as the SCD, consisted of six departments focusing on serious crime such as murders and serious sexual assaults across both counties. Another addition was The Cold Case Investigation Team, whose task was to focus on closing unsolved cases, formerly the responsibility of the Major Crime Unit, using the latest technology in DNA profiling. Hammond was aware that the CCIT had been successful in convicting rapists and serious offenders of crimes from twenty years previously. Neither was Hammond ignorant of the fact that the team employed retired detectives as investigation officers but he had no idea that Harris had been one of them. In particular he was surprised that Harris had not told him before now, they had always shared a mutual interest in each other's careers.

Harris ignored Hammond's look of surprise before continuing.

"In 1991, I was involved in an investigation into the disappearance of a nineteen year old girl by the name of Salima Abitboul. She had come from Morocco to fulfil a modelling contract in England. Her flatmate had reported her missing after she failed to return home after a day out. At the time, there was no reason to believe she had been abducted, so we were not concerned for her safety, it was possible that she had run off with a boyfriend. She hadn't taken any personal possessions or any items of clothing with her, although her passport wasn't found at her home, so it was assumed she had taken it with her."

Harris paused suddenly as if he was wanted to choose his words with care. Hammond waited for Harris to sip his drink and remained quiet until his friend resumed his topic of conversation.

"Salima's family were not concerned about her disappearance. Ironically, they were confident that she was safer in the UK than at home so they were not alarmed by her disappearance despite us questioning her whereabouts. They told us that they had received letters from their daughter weeks before telling them that she was going to marry a business man." Harris trailed off as if he were remembering the investigation. Hammond recognised a look of guilt flash across the other man's face, he had a feeling he knew how Harris' story would end. He sat forward in his seat hoping to appear encouraging. "Well, you can understand why we didn't take the disappearance that seriously. The only person who was concerned was Salima's flatmate and it was presumed at the time that the two girls were not confidants; that Salima simply didn't tell her friend of her plans to run off and marry the businessman. On reflection, it was a lapse of judgement not to question the identity of her fiancé or even to investigate further but, like I said, it seemed as if it were no more than a false alarm." Harris paused to sip at his drink, his posture had changed whilst he had been talking and now he sat with his shoulders slumped, the weight of his body leaning onto the arm of the tub chair. "We found her body a week later. She had been strangled." Hammond was curious where the conversation was heading. "You didn't find her killer?"

Harris frowned, making it obvious he didn't approve of Hammond's interruption but he answered quickly.

"A man was charged with her abduction and murder following a confession."

Suddenly Harris leaned forward, his eyes sought Hammond's own with an intensity that Hammond found unnerving.

"The case was closed as far as I was concerned until four months ago. We found traces of Salima's DNA in the apartment of a local man following his suicide."

Hammond appraised Harris for a moment; he wanted to know why Harris was confiding this information in him. "You think this local man was responsible for her death? You got the wrong man convicted?"

Harris ignored the latter question. "The reason I wanted to see you Wallace, was in your capacity as a Senior Investigating Officer. There is something about the case that has been troubling me, more than I cared to admit to the team. I know, but cannot prove, that Salima's abduction is connected to a string of suicides all happening locally within the last eighteen months. The suicides themselves are suspicious enough, it is as if the people concerned compared notes of their proposed suicides before they killed themselves."

Hammond listened to Harris's concerns with mild interest. None of what Harris was saying made much sense; Salima Abitboul's murder had been solved years before so there was no reason to re-open the case. As for the local suicides, he was aware of the latest craze in suicide pacts often founded on the social networking sites that glorified the act of taking their own lives and encouraging others to follow their lead. Despite the ludicrous suggestion of making suicide fashionable, Hammond knew that such websites existed with a dedicated following, especially amongst young, impressionable people. He had seen such a site a few years previously, following the death of a socially inept teenager. A search on the boy's computer discovered he had been taught by such a website how to hang himself. The tutorial included video clippings of other suicides in progress. Instructions on how to measure the rope according to body height and weight, the best knots to use, even examples of the right way to write a suicide note. What Hammond had found particularly sickening was that there was a forum where other members wished each other luck on their future attempts. He suggested this idea to Harris, who shook his head impatiently.

"Have you heard of Fiona Nwasu?"

The name sounded familiar but Hammond couldn't place it. He shook his head slowly and waited for Harris to respond. Harris nodded as if he had expected such an answer.

"She killed herself by jumping off the P and O Ferry at Dover."

Hammond nodded his head as he remembered. There had been a search for Nwasu's body immediately after she had plunged into the water around June last year. The media coverage had been intense.

"Mark Callum, aged thirty-six, was found in his Ashford apartment in September of this year. His head was in a plastic bag that had been tightened around the neck with brown parcel tape. Salima's passport and a hairbrush with Salima's hair were found in a drawer in his apartment. There is no reasonable explanation as to why these items were there but there wasn't enough justifiable cause to investigate it further. Especially since her killer served his sentence and died in 1999 without ever retracting his confession. A suicide note was found on Callum's body, no other foreign hair or fibre samples were found at the scene but I am convinced that it was not a suicide."

Hammond frowned. An investigation conducted four months ago on a non-suspicious death would have been closed by now. Hammond revised the information Harris had just told him, he felt he was missing something. It sounded as if there was little connection between Callum's and Nwasu's deaths, the methods of suicide were entirely different. One suggested an impulsive decision to end a life; another seemed to have been pre-meditated. He was wondering about Harris's involvement. Why the personal interest when the former detective had obviously come across a dead end in his investigation? But instead he allowed himself to reply with practical thought.

"Surely friends and family were questioned?" It was normal procedure after all to question the next of kin, and check medical records when a sudden death occurs.

"Mark Callum had no friends or family. He was a loner. His medical records are backdated to only one year ago. It was as if he didn't exist before then."

"Well, if he was a loner, perhaps he had depression, therefore any psychiatric reports?"

Harris was becoming impatient with Hammond's useless questions.

"Wallace, listen to what I am trying to tell you. Mark Callum's death is not the only one to have occurred in the last year. There have been other very similar deaths all happening concurrently. They were all aged between thirty-three to forty years of age which is unusual considering statistics suggest most suicides occur between the ages of fifteen to thirty-four years. Whilst I am aware of course that each case is different but as far as I know, none of the people were having issues with their sexuality or were in financial crises which you would expect. The pathology reports have indicated suicide; the inquests have supported this but..."

Harris paused, sub-consciously tracing a finger over his top lip as if for reassurance. "..The methods of death are so peculiar. Why a bag over the head? There are quicker ways to die and certainly less painful."

Hammond was listening to Harris intently. There was a chance that Mark Callum had been a missing person before his death, but the autopsy would have confirmed his true identity by dental records or fingerprints if he had changed his name previously.

He wanted to know how this information had found its way to Harris but knew that Harris' thirst for inquiry had always been the driving force behind him, not just in his work, but his life. "No offence Lloyd, but I cannot see what it is you want me to say. From what you have told me there is nothing correlating the cases you have described. The deaths would have been investigated separately surely." Hammond stopped talking. Harris was shaking his head and slapping his hands on his knees with extreme agitation. It was becoming embarrassing.

"These deaths are connected I know it! Everything about them tells me that there is a lot more going on than the police originally thought. The CCIT dismissed the case since Salima Abitboul's murder had been solved in 1991. Despite trying to understand why her hairbrush or her passport were found at Callum's apartment, I found no leads but I trust you will find one where I didn't. If there is nothing to find, I will accept it and forget my suspicions."

Hammond shrugged; he felt he had been backed into a corner.

"I will look into it, Lloyd, I can't promise anything. It could just be a coincidence, but what about the other deaths, you said there were others. How many?"

Harris reached inside his jacket pocket and passed a folded paper across the glass top coffee table to Hammond. "I have done as much research as I can so there is enough to start an independent investigation. I have written a list of names there; just have a look, if only to satisfy my curiosity. Please Wallace, don't fob me off. I am convinced this needs looking into. Promise me you will look at all the details".

Hammond smiled. "Haven't I always? Of course, Lloyd, I will do my best." He put the paper in his pocket patting it as if to ensure if wouldn't run away. "Leave it with me."

*"What we call "progress" is the exchange
of one nuisance for another nuisance".*
Henry Havelock Ellis. The Dance of Life 1923

CHAPTER TWO

It had rained all night causing the mud to thicken and become boggy. Hammond was attempting to sidestep his way along the bank of the path, whilst keeping his boots from being sucked down further into the sticky ground. The mounds of leaves on the banks gave relief to the mud, but occasionally his foot would slide and lose its grip, causing him to compensate by suddenly stretching an arm out to balance himself. At one point this caused him to overbalance so much, he slid into the path of the accompanying officer who was guiding Hammond through the woods on the common approach path designated earlier by the scene examiner.

"It's not far now Sir."

He was reassured by the young officer who had spoken as if reading Hammond's mind. Hammond was grouchy. He had slept fitfully during the night remembering his conversation with Harris. His former colleague had aged so rapidly, it was unnerving. There had been several moments spent in front of the mirror the previous evening whilst he appraised his own features, trying to see how old he looked. He was so disheartened he had gone to bed without brushing his teeth. There was no point if they were soon to be replaced by dentures he had reasoned, somewhat irrationally.

They had been walking nearly ten minutes already, sometimes walking through running water as it spilled down the path toward the rendezvous point at Sandling Road where they had parked the car. Ahead of the trudging men, there was the sound of a dog barking.

"They've brought the dogs in already?"

"No Sir, that is the dog that found the body. We asked the owner to stay here until you arrived." The officer stepped further up the bank to the right of Hammond and gestured towards a clearing that sloped downwards. The slope was carpeted in wet leaves leading to a shallow hole that measured about 5ft in length. It was difficult to see anything else, due the area being surveyed by Scene of Crime Officers who were busy taking photographs and video clips.

Hammond was feeling hot under his paper body suit; he wished he had removed his jacket underneath first. "Has the area been sealed off yet?"

"Not all areas, there are a lot of paths to block. They are working on it as we speak." Hammond turned his head toward a familiar voice. DS Lois Dunn was scraping her blonde hair into a ponytail as she stepped up the bank toward him. This done, she pulled the hood over her head. It made her look more youthful than ever Hammond noted. He smiled a greeting to her and they surveyed the scene in front of them.

The body was partially hidden in the shallow hole. It appeared to be male. He lay half on his side, face down in the dirt. His trousers were partially pulled down, exposing a naked upper left thigh. His right arm was wedged in underneath the weight of his body. The left arm reaching upwards towards the side as if he had fallen into the hole without being able to break his fall. Lying across the back of the legs and back were thick tree branches that had been arranged across the body suggesting a crude attempt to cover the body with woodland debris.

"They're in the process of putting the tent up". Hammond explained. "There's too much water running down from the tree canopy."

Dunn frowned with impatience but stayed where she was whilst the tent was hastily erected. Hammond enquired where the dog owner who reported the find was. Following directions he walked towards a dark haired man. Noting his frail frame, Hammond estimated he was about 80 years of age. The man was seated on a tree stump, talking softly to a Jack Russell Terrier whose nose was blackened by freshly dug soil. The dog was whining and pulling at its lead hoping to return to the cordoned off area. The humming of the generator powering the spotlights interrupted the silence. Hammond introduced himself and crouched down to the man's eye level. It was apparent the man was in shock and looked cold. Hammond introduced himself quietly and reassured him that he would be taken home very soon. The man nodded gratefully and told Hammond his name was William Barnes from New Road, only five minutes' walk away.

"Could you tell me everything that happened this morning, from the moment before you found the body up until when the police arrived?"

Hammond skipped over the word body noticing the man winced at the word.

"I come here most days, Daisy likes the woods." The dog looked up at the mention of her name. She was patted reassuringly whilst the man spoke. "I walk Daisy at the same time every day, morning and afternoon. We usually come here because it is so close to home. Daisy's hip gets stiff if she walks for too long so we only manage short walks." He turned his attention to the dog "We're not getting any younger, are we girl?"

Hammond waited patiently whilst the dog was stroked. The man's gaze remained focused on his dog whilst he continued speaking. "We walk along the path that runs behind the houses, and then turn left onto the main bridal-path which exits near the church. But today, because it was so cold I took a shorter route and walked up the bank where the leaves were. Daisy suddenly took off, for what seemed like no apparent reason. I assumed she had seen a rabbit and ran off to chase it, but when she didn't come back (She usually comes back when I whistle for her) I started to look for her. I came off the path toward the perimeter of the adjoining field...and well...saw him..."

"How long was it before you started to look for her?"

"Not long, about five minutes or so."

Hammond held in a sigh of disappointment. Five minutes wasn't long, but it was plenty of time for a dog to contaminate a crime scene by disturbing evidence.

"Did you see anyone else during your walk? Other dog walkers perhaps?"

"No, I didn't see anyone. I think people go along the bridle-path when it's been raining, the path is less slippery there." The man pointed toward another path that steered east.

"You said you normally walk your dog here every day. Is there anyone you would expect to see during your walk at this time?"

"Sometimes I see runners practising for the Boxing Day Run. They run along the main path but it tends to be later in the day."

It became evident to Hammond that the man could not help them any further, by now he was shivering, and Hammond was concerned for his health. He requested that William Barnes' hand over his clothes and shoes when he got home, explaining it was for elimination purposes and asked an officer to escort the man home, promising to check on him later in the day and handed him his card for future reference.

The suspected crime scene was a hive of activity. With the area now sealed, a thorough search of the area could begin. DS Dunn was stooping within the cramped space of the tent. There were whitened flood lights erected inside on both sides of the shallow grave. From outside, Hammond saw her slim silhouette against the tent sides as she watched the pathologist closely, impatient for information. The pathologist, Dr Ed Henderson was well known to them both, having worked with him numerous times before Hammond knew him as very thorough. Henderson was arrogant and not one to care about making a good impression of himself but he was well respected as being one of the most efficient contributors to the Kent Police. Henderson ignored Dunn but continued looking over the body in silence. It took a few minutes before he stood up, gesturing for Hammond to approach.

"Male Caucasian, I estimate 50 plus years of age. There were a set of keys but no identification or wallet in his pockets. It looks like repeated blunt force trauma to the upper body, but I need to take x-rays. I will let you know for sure after the autopsy. There are several wounds to the arm, here..." He bent down and pointed with a gloved finger at a bruise on the body's left arm where a sleeve had ridden up above the wrist. "...there are also wounds to the thigh; I need to turn the body over to get a look at the face. Can I get some more light down here?" The pathologist shouted to a crime scene officer who hastily offered Henderson a small black case. With apparent impatience, Henderson made a performance of dragging the case to the side of the hole, and opened the case withdrawing a torch, a coloured lens and a pair of goggles. He motioned for Hammond to do the same, completely ignoring Dunn who leant across the pathologist and helped herself to goggles from the case. The ultra violet glare from the torch was directed on the contents of the shallow grave. "There is blood loss but it is unlikely he bled to death, there is not enough here."

Henderson signalled for his assistant to approach closer and pointed to areas that needed photographing.

Hammond turned to Dunn. "We need to trace where each path leads. If the victim was here when he was attacked, we need to understand why he was off the main path. There is nothing here to see, unless he was trying to take a short cut across the field."

Dunn shook her head. "That wouldn't make sense; the barbed wire would have been too much of an inconvenience when there is another path that goes along the edge of the field anyway. If he was trying to take a short cut, this wouldn't be the place."

Hammond turned to Ed Henderson. "Has the white light picked out any footprints?"

Henderson looked up at Hammond; he was now standing with one foot wedged against the body in the recess, balancing his weight on the other leg which was positioned on the upper level as he took the body's temperature.

"There were a few traces of prints, but no complete shoe prints that we can determine. The rain hasn't helped, any DNA evidence will have degraded from the earlier frost and subsequent thaw. The leaves have been disturbed since he has been down there. There are more animal prints, other than the dog that made the discovery this morning, probably foxes."

"Can you tell if the body was moved?"

"There are no drag marks, and nothing to suggest he was brought here any other way other than walking here. We'll compare the soil samples taken here with the soil on the shoes later just in case. There's some soil in his nostrils which suggests he was breathing whilst he lay here so it is likely the death occurred in the spot where he fell."

"He fell? So it may not be foul play?"

Hammond had automatically presumed that the death was the result of an attack. The absence of a wallet suggested a motive of robbery. But now he realised that the torn clothes and blood could have been due to foxes post mortem.

"I won't give you a definite answer, not until I can get the body back for a thorough examination, but I will hazard a guess that this is due to foul play or at least misadventure with another person."

Hammond looked at him with anticipation. "Really?"

"There are traces of semen on his hands".

"So you think maybe the death was accidental, that a sex game went wrong, and his lover panicked and dug a grave?"

If someone had dug the cavity as a grave, they did so quickly and without attention. It wasn't deep enough to conceal a human corpse, being no deeper than two feet deep. If it had happened spontaneously, it was unlikely they had anything to dig with. The only tools being branches to loosen the soil and their hands to scoop out the debris. This would be too time consuming and too risky. Although the site couldn't be seen from the main path, it wasn't far enough from it to be completely hidden, especially if someone wanted to avoid the mud and walk up the bank.

"I can't answer those questions; that is your job. I can only tell you what I find on the body. The hole was undoubtedly already here, there are no fresh soil mounds to suggest it has been recently dug. (Other than where the dog was this morning)."

He tutted and pointed to claw marks that burrowed into the depth of the depression towards the underside of the body. "There is too much insect activity beneath him from what I can tell so it is likely he fell into the hole following a surprise attack."

Hammond thanked him, he knew it was pointless to ask for a time of death at this stage of investigation but wanted an estimate. "Can you give a time of death?"

Hammond was surprised to see Ed Henderson smile.

"There's fixed lividity on the right side of the body and full rigor mortis..."

Henderson's eyes appraised the body in front of him. "The bad weather would have affected the decomposition rate and the temperature of the body but I would guess between twenty to thirty hours ago. Any longer than that and the muscles would have returned to their flaccid state, which isn't apparent here yet. I am not going to give a definite report at this stage. You have an idea to help you start enquiries but be patient. I will call you when I have the full picture."

The watch on Hammond's wrist showed it was now 8am Tuesday, which would mean that the victim had been attacked any time between 2am on Sunday morning and lunchtime on Monday. It had rained heavily throughout the night on Sunday, but had been dry earlier throughout the day. Typical for mid November, it got dark around 4.30pm, an hour later and it would be virtually impossible to see anything in the woods. It would certainly be too dark to attempt to hide a body leaving no trace. It would be too risky, there was a chance that if something had fallen from a pocket of the attacker, or if they had accidently left something behind, there would be no way of reclaiming it at that time. If there had been a meeting in the woods between the victim and a friend, it was logical to assume that it would have occurred during the day of Sunday or Monday morning in daylight. Hammond looked to see if Henderson could give any further clue but Henderson had already turned his back on him and continued his examination. Hammond was dismissed.

Back at the police station, a meeting with the investigative team was scheduled for early evening. It was more practical to use the station rather than set up an incident room in Saltwood since it was so close. Hammond wanted to give SOCO every opportunity to collect evidence from the scene before the briefing later. The autopsy would take longer but he hoped there would be enough information from the external examination back at the morgue to start the investigation.

In the meantime, He wanted to look at the file on Mark Callum and find out as much information about the suicide as he could. The computer database could not promise to offer Hammond any more information than he had already, but Hammond could not take it for granted that Harris had been correct in his assumptions. Harris had behaved oddly, Hammond surmised. The man he had met at the Golf Club had seemed confused and erratic in his thinking. It was more than possible that Harris had seen a connection that wasn't there, but Hammond owed his former colleague the benefit of the doubt. He unfolded the paper that Harris had handed him the day before. The paper was small, but heavily marked with lines and crosses against a list of names. Harris counted five in total. This wasn't much to go on, but it was a start. Of course, Hammond mused, it may be awkward explaining why he wanted to investigate a suicide that was not local to him; after all, the suicide of Mark Callum had occurred nearly four months ago. The inquest had confirmed the manner of death so as far as the police were concerned, it was a closed case. Hammond sighed and hoped, rather ashamedly, that Lloyd Harris was simply being paranoid.

CHAPTER THREE

The coffee handed to him was tepid warm but Hammond sipped it appreciatively. He had spent an hour at the Ashford Police Station looking at the file in front of him. The photographs of Mark Callum's body were detailed and the investigation had been thorough. Hammond knew that a death caused by suffocation would always be treated as suspicious until proven otherwise and the investigating team had left no stone unturned. Mark Callum had been found slumped against a wall. The bag over his head was a strong, clear plastic, like the type wrapped around home delivery parcels. The parcel tape which had been around his neck was excessive. From the photographs it looked like a whole roll had been used with the empty cardboard inner roll left still attached. Hammond considered that a roll of tape usually measured 10 meters. As there had been no tape left elsewhere, it appeared that all of it had been used. This fact alone added credibility that the act of wrapping the tape over the opening of the bag was a sincere attempt to make the seal impenetrable. At the same time, it also added doubt that there would have been enough air to have lasted the several minutes it would have taken to have wound this amount of tape repeatedly.

The photographs showing the apartment were a surprise to Hammond. It was clean and tidy, which was rather uncommon for a man living alone (if Paul and his male friends were anything to go by) but what was so significant was the lack of personality in the room. There was nothing to show who Mark Callum had been. Hammond viewed the map of the apartment drawn up by the scene officers whom had placed a red X in the position where the body had been found. The apartment consisted of a kitchen, a bathroom with a toilet, basin and a small bath and the bedroom. There were only two windows in the flat which explained the dingy light shown in the photographs. One was above the bed in the bedroom in line with the front door. The galley kitchen had a small rectangular window above the sink. A fridge and a small cooker were the only items of furniture in the room with a bare white veneered counter-top. Hammond considered the items in his own kitchen. There were the cooking books that Lyn had left him, stacked up under the boiler (still unread), several tea towels hanging over the oven door, coasters of various shapes and sizes. He remembered that an odd pair of socks were still waiting to be re-homed from their place on the radiator. He had accumulated several magnets over the years and automatically put them on the fridge door, they had no use other to secure the loose postcards he would occasionally receive. The kitchen in the photograph was a stark contrast to his own living conditions. It had no clutter at all. It was bare in all the rooms. The bedroom housed a single bed with a duvet covered in a plain beige sheet and a pillow encased in a matching plain pillow-case. A three drawer chest and a wooden chair in the corner were the only furniture. All rooms were devoid of pictures. There were no posters, no photographs, not even a pin board. Light bulbs hang from the ceiling uncovered. Judging from the photographs Hammond was viewing, Mark Callum hadn't been alive even when his heart had been beating.

He read the pathologist report several times. Dr Karen Leyland had confirmed the cause of death using the evidence of high levels of carbon dioxide in the blood and bloodshot eyes. Hammond peered closer at the autopsy photograph of Callum's neck. There were traces of glue residue from the tape and tracks where the tape had been wound so tight, but there were no finger nail marks or anything to suggest an attempt to remove the tape in a last minute panic.

Hammond leafed through the photographs, taken at different angles of the body. On one photograph, showing the back of Callum, a small scar was visible on the left shoulder-blade. Rulers beside and underneath the scar showed it measured four centimetres across and three centimetres in depth. Although the camera had taken a good clear photograph of the scar, Hammond found himself peering closer to the photograph. The scar was bright pink and looked like a bubble. It had a shape to it, as if it had grown outwards from the centre of the shoulder blade. It would have been noticeable if Callum had been shirtless. In her report Dr Leyland had described the raised area of scar tissue as a hypertrophic scar. A name Hammond had been unaware of until now. She had hypothesised in the report that Callum had sustained an injury to the shoulder blade during childhood that had caused an overgrowth of fibrous tissue.

Footprints of a man's shoe found at the scene had been identified as belonging to the delivery man who had raised the alarm. Hammond read the witness account. The Courier's name was Brad Kelsey, aged 57 years.

His story had been checked by the investigative team who confirmed Kelsey's story. He had been employed by Parcel Force for the last eighteen months. Kelsey had been delegated to deliver a parcel to Callum's neighbours. The neighbours had been away and therefore he had used his common sense to leave the parcel with Callum. He had sworn in his statement that Callum's door had been open which was why he had ventured inside. It was luck that Callum had been found when he did, mere coincidence.

Hammond looked again at the scene photos. Callum had died seated on the floor with legs outstretched, his back leaning against a plain wall, his hands resting with open palms beside him. The skin was devoid of any scratches or defence marks. There wasn't even a graze on the bag to suggest he had attempted to rip open the plastic covering that enveloped his head. Hammond looked over the report numerous times, flicking from one account to another. There had been no foreign fibres found anywhere on the body, the only foreign evidence found in the apartment was a hairbrush found in a drawer with Salima Abitboul's passport. Hammond already knew from his conversation with Harris that the hairs found on the brush were Salima's. He leafed through the pages looking for more information on this but found nothing so instead he returned to the original report. The door to Callum's apartment had been left ajar, which was certainly unusual but perhaps only attributed to Callum's certainty that he wouldn't have visitors. No other fingerprints other than the deceased, the delivery man Kelsey and paramedics had been found in the apartment. This corresponded to the neighbour's accounts that Callum had lived as a recluse.

Forensic graphology had compared samples of Mark Callum's writing with the suicide note found tucked into his sock and confirmed he had written the note with his own hand. Hammond looked at the photograph of the note; "*I have to kill myself before someone else does it for me.*" The words had been written in blue biro, the writing was small but done with a steady hand. Hammond sipped his coffee that was now cold. Although the note suggested Mark Callum had been threatened in some way, he could understand why the verdict of suicide had been reached. There was no other evidence to suggest anything sinister in the cause of Callum's death, only the idea that he had been persuaded to take his own life. That would hint toward murder but it could also be a paranoid interpretation. In his experience, no crime was committed without leaving a trace of guilt. If someone had forced Callum to kill himself, surely they would watch him do it or at least stay close to ensure Callum carried out their instructions. And, if they did, there would be some evidence of their presence at the scene. There would be something, however small, that could correlate the death with someone else's involvement. Hammond considered for a moment that if anyone was forced to take their own life against their will, there would instinctively be rages within them, fighting against the other's will. Surely Callum would have shouted out, done something to point guilt at the assailant, even made a mark on his body to show that his death had been forced. But there was nothing on Callum's body, nothing in his flat to suggest he had had unwanted interaction with anyone else.

Detectives had attempted to substantiate the note's contents by investigating possibilities of someone else being at the flat at the time of his death, they had interviewed neighbours asking if they had ever seen Callum with anyone within the apartment blocks or elsewhere or if anyone had been seen exiting Callum's apartment. No-one had. Hammond eventually admitted defeat with a sigh. In this case, he could find nothing to authenticate Harris's suspicion.

Hammond picked up his empty cup and returned the file to the officer at a nearby desk. At his request, a copy of a photograph of Mark Callum was produced. It was unfortunate that the only photographs they had of Callum were taken post-mortem but it could help with identification later if necessary. The officer smiled at Hammond, and this polite response to his presence encouraged Hammond to speak aloud his curiosity. "Who investigated the suicide of Mark Callum?"

The officer pointed to the file, just returned to him. "Their names are in the report Sir."

"Yes, I know, but I meant are they here? I wouldn't recognise them."

He was directed to a young woman seated at a desk, tentatively tapping at a computer keyboard as if she were intimidated by the technology. She looked at him as he approached and smiled shyly. He introduced himself. "I understand you were part of the investigative team that looked into a suicide a few months ago?"

"I didn't investigate as such; my partner and I were first on the scene."

She identified herself as WPC Manvell. Hammond was familiar with her name as he had read her report only an hour earlier, but he proceeded with his questions regardless. "I've seen the photographs and read the reports but I am curious what your personal reaction was when you first arrived." Hammond was aware his question was unorthodox but he was sensitive to his ex-wife's belief that every room had a story to tell. He had laughed at her when she had said it, but he had since understood what she had meant. Every building had a memory, as if the walls retained energy. He had first felt this when he had entered a house, seemingly normal from the outside, but upon entering, he had inexplicably felt frightened, like a child scared of the dark. He hoped that WPC Manvell would have had the same feeling if something had been amiss.

"My reaction?" The reply was spoken hesitantly but politely.

"If I remember your report correctly. A parcel delivery man knocked at the door of Mark Callum's apartment, the door was open so he looked inside and saw Callum with a plastic bag over his head in the bedroom. He phoned the emergency services and as you were closest to the scene you were the first one to arrive, is that correct?" Hammond continued following an affirmative nod "When you arrived at Mr Callum's flat, did you feel anything was particularly odd?"

She thought for a moment, sub-consciously tilting her head to one side as if waiting for the memory to slide to the forefront of her mind.

"I thought it was depressing, but I didn't really have time to think to be honest. I was just trying to get to the right flat in time, in case the guy wasn't dead. Sometimes a call comes in from someone in a panic saying they have found a dead body and it turns out to be someone unconscious, so I was just desperate to get there as quickly as I could. The paramedics arrived a few minutes after me. We accidently went to the neighbour's flat first because we were told to go to Flat 3b but I went to Flat 3a"

She revised her words as she spoke "I was thinking quickly so was looking for door numbers, but he didn't have a number on his door which is why I missed it at first."

Hammond thanked her and started for the door when he suddenly stopped. A thought had crossed his mind, a thought that was so obvious he was shocked to realise it had only now flashed into his conscience. He returned quickly to the WPC who looked up from her computer with a hint of annoyance.

"The writing paper and pen. Was it moved when you looked at the body?"

The look of puzzlement that was given as a reply made Hammond feel suddenly impatient.

"I don't understand. What writing paper?"

"The note he had written, it had come from a pad, and the pen he used to write the suicide note. Where was the pen?"

At her look of continued bafflement, Hammond quickly excused himself and went back to retrieve the file.

It had taken Hammond another twenty minutes to scour Mark Callum's file again. The contents of Callum's pocket had been catalogued. There had been a receipt for the parcel tape, £2.40 in change and his door key. Nothing else. No paper or pen was evident in any of the photographs or listed in the inventory. This bothered Hammond. He did not like to have any indiscrepancies, and this was an obvious one. Nonetheless, he was not overly concerned. A missing pen and paper could have been moved by the attending paramedics and mistaken for their own and taken away. The Parcel Force courier could have mistakenly picked it up. From what he had read in the file, he was not convinced that there was any reason for Callum's death to be considered suspicious, he needed to think about this logically he told himself. There seemed little point in re-opening a case that had been closed with a satisfactory and rational outcome. If there was future evidence to suggest Callum had been murdered, it would be investigated further by the Serious Case Review Team. Hammond would not find it easy to justify the time and resources spent on rationalising a suspicion of a retired colleague. He would speak to Harris; explain that he couldn't continue the investigation without probable cause. With this decision reached, Hammond allowed his hunger to direct the car to MacDonald's. It hadn't been his intention to stop for lunch, having only minutes earlier phoned William Barnes, arranging to meet him at his home in Saltwood for a few more questions. Now he was here, Hammond was surprised to discover that he automatically chose a chicken burger rather than his preferred beef. He patted his stomach unconsciously as if to reassure his padded friend that it would soon be satisfied and justified his choice of burger as being a healthier option. He wanted to switch his mind off for a few minutes to digest his meal but instead found his mind wandering to Mark Callum's death.

Despite his earlier decision, his conscience told him he owed it to Harris to consider all possibilities. There were four other suicides that Harris had wanted him to look into. Four deaths that Harris believed were related. Hammond shook his head as he argued with himself. Surely, there would be no harm in looking at the other deaths. If he traced a connection as Harris believed and found any suggestion to collaborate Harris' conviction that the deaths were not suicides, or that they were linked in some way to the death of Salima Abitboul, he would hand the information over to Chatham. Let the Cold Case Investigation Team take over the investigation. At least, he would keep his promise to Harris, even though Hammond was not convinced his friend was thinking entirely logically. Discounting the odd behaviour displayed at the Golf Club, Harris had chosen to concern himself with a case that held no personal relevance to him whatsoever. It was this thought alone that confused Hammond more than the discrepancies of the death itself. Using a paper napkin, Hammond wrote down the thoughts floating in his mind. The most obvious source of confusion was why Salima's hairbrush was in Callum's apartment, the next concern was the lack of information on Callum. Harris was correct when he said that Callum had not existed before a year previously. There had been no information on Callum's employment in the file, nothing to suggest he had any financial income other than the fact his bills and rent were paid regularly. Callum did not claim any benefits and according to the report, did not have a bank account. The investigating team had looked into the possibility that Callum had previously lived abroad but this question remained unresolved. A doctor's report had been included in the police file. A local GP had confirmed Mark Callum as being a patient when he prescribed an anti-depressant Tricyclics. It was suggested that Callum had displayed symptoms of extreme anxiety although this was not substantiated by any psychological assessment. No other pre-mortem medical information had been included as the investigation had only been concerned with the cause of the death, and depression had been seen to be a cause for the suicide. Hammond took a large bite from the burger and wrote *Speak to Doctor,* he wanted to know why there were no other medical notes and if possible, get the doctors opinion on his patient's mental health. Depression was a dehabilitating disease but didn't necessarily result in suicide if it was managed. Hammond remembered that the toxicology report had shown no traces of drugs in Callum's body. Is this why he killed himself? Because he hadn't taken his medication, allowing the depression to become overwhelming and cause him to withdraw from society before his suicide? It was possible but Hammond wanted to answer the questions without relying on possibilities. It was unlikely the cause of the depression could be discovered as there were no psychiatric reports, no friends or family to speak to. Yet, this was another indescrepancy. If Mark Callum did not have any contact with any other person, where did he work? Where did his money come from? No money apart from a small amount of change in Callum's jeans pocket had been found at Callum's apartment. How did he survive? The paper napkin was now tattooed in scribbled blue biro, Hammond's curiosity was aroused. He reasoned that there was no harm in asking questions. With this conclusion, Hammond squashed the burger box and threw it from his table into the bin by the door. He congratulated himself on his good aim as he ventured again into the cold air towards his parked car.

William Barnes opened the door to Hammond immediately after the doorbell had been rung giving the impression he had been waiting longer than he had expected for Hammond to arrive. Hammond quickly brushed his hand over his lips in an attempt to wipe off any undiscovered mayonnaise from his impromptu lunch. He offered his hand politely as to signal that he was here on official business and was shown into a small living room heated by an electric fire. After acknowledging Daisy's welcoming wag with a pat on her head, Hammond obeyed Barnes's instruction to make himself comfortable. The two men sat on opposite armchairs upholstered in brown with a large floral design, making Hammond feel as if he had stepped back in time to the 1970's. William Barnes was evidently nervous. He offered Hammond a plate of biscuits which Hammond refused and then feeling guilty for having refused the older man's hospitality, reached out and took two off the plate.

"They combed Daisy." Barnes spoke quietly as he poured two cups of tea from the large teapot on the tray beside him.

Hammond handled the biscuits awkwardly in his hand, looking at Barnes for clarification. "Excuse me?" He took the filled tea cup presented to him, sliding the tea spoon to the side of the saucer allowing his thumb to grip the delicate china.

"They combed Daisy. They stood her on a plastic sheet and combed her, the people in the white body-suits."

"Yes, there may be evidence on her from where she dug around the corpse. I'm sure the Forensic team were gentle with Daisy." Hammond said this as fact rather than as a question, he wanted to keep the interview short so he could get back to the briefing room at Head Quarters.

"She seemed fine. I had to collect her faeces earlier and hand them over."

Hammond nodded, unsure whether to explain the reasoning behind this task and steered the conversation to the dog's morning discovery. "You had a shock this morning; I am hoping that you are feeling better now?" Hammond didn't wait for an answer; the man's affirmative nod was interpreted as such.

"Perhaps now you have had a chance to reflect on the morning's activities, you may have remembered anything that perhaps you may have forgotten earlier?" Hammond realised he sounded patronising but hoped that Barnes had something more to add to his mornings account.

"No, I am sorry, there is nothing more I can think of. I have been thinking all morning of the poor man, lying there in the cold. Do you think he was hurt on purpose?" He was answered by a discreet shrug of Hammond's shoulders.

"We don't know that for sure, but it is necessary to treat the death as suspicious until we can prove otherwise. I have a photograph of the man's face which you would not have seen earlier due to the position he was in. Could I ask you to look at him and see if you recognise him?" Hammond gingerly retrieved a close up photograph of the dead man's face from the inside pocket of his jacket and handed it to the man opposite. William Barnes took the photograph nervously averting his gaze for several seconds before looking at the man in the picture. Hammond was relieved that the dead man's features had not been grotesquely distorted in the aftermath of death. A dried residue was evident around the swollen nostrils and open mouth. The eyes, open and protruding from their sockets, looked the most disturbing. The brown triangular spots covering the corneas were a grim reminder of a lost life, but did not hide the original features entirely. Barnes gulped and shook his head quickly, his hand trembling slightly. For a moment Hammond was concerned the old man was going to be sick but kept the picture within the man's sight. "Are you sure you don't recognise him? Please, look again."

The man did as he was asked; taking deep breaths he studied the photograph, frowning with concentration. Then suddenly his eyebrows shot up and he looked at Hammond with enthusiasm.

"Yes! I recognise him! I don't know his name, but he was often in the woods, just wandered around on his own most of the time. Sometimes he would say hello, when Daisy and I passed him during our walks but I think he was more interested in the bike enthusiasts."

Hammond remembered seeing bike tracks in the woods, he gestured with his hand for Barnes to continue.

"Daisy and I would see him during the summer afternoons or at the weekends during the day. I don't think he knew the boys personally but he would stand there just watching them. They ignored him most of the time, but he didn't seem to mind."

"Do you know the boys on the bikes, enough to recognise them again? Are they local?"

"Yes, I see them around the village a lot, usually milling outside the corner shop before school. I don't know the boys by name, apart from Thomas who lives at the end of this road. His mother cleans for me sometimes."

Hammond noted the details in his jotter and cleared his throat. It was possible that they now had a lead. His heart was hammering inside his chest wanting to get the information to the team as soon as possible. He politely finished his tea with Barnes and got up to leave when his mobile rang. Lois Dunn sounded stressed at the other end.

"You need to get back to station quickly. Detective Superintendant Beech wants you to make a public appeal." Hammond swore under his breath and disconnected the call.

"The world is an unrelated mass of impressions."
Henry Havelock Ellis. The Dance of Life. 1923

CHAPTER FOUR

It was with part fear, part annoyance that Hammond stood amidst the flashing cameras and inquisitive reporters feeling as if he had been thrown into the deep end without a float. He had expected Beech to join them but had been told that his Superintendant was otherwise occupied leaving him with no choice but to answer the repeated questions himself. A press release had been issued but it did little in giving any more detail than what the reporters already knew. An unidentified Caucasian male of medium build in his late fifties had been found dead in woodlands near Hythe. There was nothing much more to tell at this time, Hammond stated. "This is a pretty weak statement, is there any more information you can give us to work on?" The question was thrown from the back of the room; Hammond squinted whilst attempting to address the questioner personally. He recognised the female reporter from the Kentish Gazette Newspaper.

"We are unable to give you any more information at this time but we appeal to anyone who may help us to identify the man. If anyone saw a male of this description either travelling or walking towards Saltwood woods on Sunday, or has any information which they believe can be helpful, we urge them to come forward."

"Is the death being treated as suspicious?"

"The body has yet to be formally indentified and a post mortem will be carried out. Because of the freezing conditions in which the body was found, the results will not be known until tomorrow at the earliest. However, until we can prove otherwise, the death of the man will be treated as suspicious. Therefore any information that can help us will be appreciated." He responded to the questions by repeating himself until the reporters admitted defeat and grumbling amongst themselves left the room. Hammond was horrified to discover he had been sweating throughout the ordeal and made a hasty exit to the bathroom.

It was past 6pm when the team gathered in the briefing room. They were waiting for him with Detective Superintendant Beech seated on a chair at the back. He made an exaggerated gesture of looking at his watch as Hammond entered the room. Hammond ignored him, hoping that his thoughts couldn't be seen in a cartoon bubble above his head. He would surely be fired. He stood at the whiteboard looking at the projected photographs that had been taken that morning. The body had been pictured at all angles, the surrounding area had been searched and noted in several diagrams scattered on the table in the middle of the room.

Hammond took centre position in front of the team.

"We have a lead. The dog owner William Barnes has identified the dead man as being a regular visitor to Saltwood Woods. Apparently, he had an interest in the bike enthusiasts that go there. This gives us two possible scenarios, either he was an avid BMX fan, or he had an entirely different interest; that of young kids. Semen was found on the hands of our victim, which could indicate the latter scenario is the more plausible. We can't rule out robbery as a motive since he had no wallet or identification in his pockets." Hammond switched off the laptop's projector and looked at the faces turned toward him, he gestured for DS Lois Dunn to come forward in response to her upraised hand. She stood confidently in front of her peers, tacking a map to the board.

"This is a map of the woods in Saltwood. I estimate it is about 40 acres. It is owned by Kent County Council and is part of the Saxon Shore Way cross country walks, therefore it is open to the public at all times. This map shows five exits. The exit we used was in Sandling Road, another is at the end of a footpath that leads to Sandling Station, another exit here in New Road, one in Rectory Lane and the North West exit by Saltwood Stables" She dragged her finger over the exits marked in red circles on the map and then pinned a photograph in the centre underneath the map.

"Here is where our body was found, in the southern parts of the woods on ground that dips down away from the path toward farmland. The nearest footpath is parallel although due to the high banks on either side of the footpath, it is not possible to see the area where the body was discovered. This particular path leads toward Sandling Road and is the route for the Boxing Day Run so it is used regularly throughout the day by runners. Directly above this path are other smaller footpaths that lead to the main bridle-path. This bridle way leads from the stables and exits at Rectory Lane adjacent to St Peter and St Paul's Church. There are footpaths all around this area, most lead toward the bridle path. These tracks in yellow..." She was interrupted by Hammond who had stepped forward to take a closer look at the map.

"You said that there is a path directly above the runner's route?"

Dunn hesitated, having lost her flow, then nodded and retraced her finger on the marked footpath in reply.

"Is it possible to see where the body had been hidden from this height?"

She looked at the map and then returned to table where she had been seated moments before. "I've got some photographs here that were taken from the higher footpath, looking down toward the site. As you can see, it is possible to see a little but vision is restricted by the trees."

Hammond studied the photographs. "Did you go up there yourself?" He noted her negative gesture. "It may be worth going there again, try to see a different perspective of the site. You are right, it isn't very visible from where the photograph was taken, but this photograph was taken early morning. There is a chance that later in the day when there is more daylight it is possible to see people standing near the sight. Also, we should do an audio test, check if it is possible to have heard any arguing or raised voices from both positions." Hammond's audience nodded in agreement. Tom Edwards wondered aloud how it had taken thirty hours before the body had been discovered since the woods were in constant use by the local public. He was reminded by Michael Galvin of the cold and wet weather conditions that had undoubtedly compromised the footpaths. A lot could go unnoticed when people are concentrating where they are going without slipping in the mud with their heads bowed Galvin reasoned. Edwards muttered a reply and continued scrutinizing his fingernails.

Dunn waited for several seconds, unsure whether to continue sharing the information she had gathered during the day, then, prompted by Hammond, directed their attention to highlighted yellow lines spreading across the map like a spider's web.

"These tracks highlighted in yellow are the bike tracks. They are designed specifically for dirt tracking stunts and have been built by the bikers themselves, (most likely without the Councils permission). Horse riders trek through the woods using the main bridle path but they are not allowed to venture onto the smaller footpaths." She paused, having lost her train of thought. Galvin spoke up addressing Dunn's report but his eyes focused on Hammond.

"I looked at the bike tracks, there are five separate areas covering 40 by 20 meters, but they all contribute to one play track. Whoever built the track were amateurs but did a good job." He got up from his chair, flashing Dunn a smile as he took her place in front of the whiteboard. He pointed to Dunn's map. "Here, about thirty meters from where the body was found is the start hill. They have used most of the natural resources from the woods by piling up sub soil to create a steep incline here...a platform here...and a slope. Next, there is the table top, which again is a steep incline, a platform and then a decline, before double jump, then the berm which bends downwards towards this area, to a swooping step-up. This part here is designed to be a speed jump."

His finger rested on the red X that showed where the body had been found.

"The hole in which our victim was found was not intended to be a grave. I think it was part of the track, the aim being to jump the bikes over the hole where logs have been placed across."

Hammond listened in silence; He tried to hide the fact that he had only partially understood what Galvin had explained. He had no idea what a swooping step-up was but assumed it had something to do with a mound of soil that was used to perform bike stunts. He was tired and still hungry. It was tempting to call the meeting to a close but he wanted to get the investigation going as soon as possible.

"The next twenty-four hours are crucial. We'll start with door to door enquiries. Is our man local? How did he get to the woods? Was he seen walking or is there a car parked nearby unaccounted for? Until we get a formal identification of our victim we will concentrate on prospective witnesses or people who may have known him. We can assume that the tracks were built by the kids themselves, but it means they would have had access to tools somehow. It must have taken them weeks to design and build the tracks which suggest they plan to continue using it for a while. We need to go back to the woods, try to identify the BMX enthusiasts. Barnes said that our victim would watch them often, in which case they may give us some more information about him. Perhaps he was their coach. It is worth finding out where the kids were between Sunday and Monday morning."

Edward's examination of his fingernails was interrupted for a second whilst he called to Hammond across the room.

"The secondary school is on the other side of Sandling Road, there is a chance they saw our victim on Monday morning on their way to school if they used the woods as a shortcut."

Dunn looked at Edwards with exasperation.

"It's hardly a short cut, especially when it is so muddy. By the time the kids get to school; they'll be dragging half the country-side behind them."

She refrained from patronising Edwards further and turned her attention back to Hammond.

"You think it is worth going to the school?"

There was a good chance that the BMX enthusiasts were pupils at the local school. William Barnes had implied as much. Hammond nodded at Dunn.

"Yes, take Edwards with you in the morning, start with the corner shop opposite New Road, apparently the kids congregate there often, then go to the school; address the kids in assembly, just indicate that we are there for help gathering local information. There is no point in making them panic. They probably already know that a body has been found in the woods since the area has been sealed off, and a small village like Saltwood is bound to have its share of gossip, especially now the media has been informed."

He delegated Galvin to taking another look at the bike tracks in the morning, using the opportunity to interview other dog walkers and runners who frequented the woodland paths. Hammond announced that he would chase up on Forensics. The team arranged to regroup the following afternoon before spilling out the room in undisguised eagerness to get home.

Wallace Hammond sank into a chair allowing himself to digest the day. He stayed there quietly for several minutes hypnotised by the sound of the wall clock ticking until he saw Dunn through the glass door walking down the corridor with a mug in her hand. He called to her, surprised that she hadn't yet left the building like her peers. She responded to his call by walking back to the briefing room, poking her head around the door until she saw him in his crumbled state.

"You are not going home?"

Hammond gave her a lop-sided smile. "I am waiting for my body to get up and move."

Dunn laughed and walked further into the room, still swinging her mug by its handle at her side. "I am going to stay here a few minutes longer, catch up on some e-mails." She saw Hammond's raised eyebrow and blushed slightly. "Well...truth is, I don't want to go home yet. My boyfriend is there, waiting for an answer that I cannot give him."

"Oh." Hammond felt this comment was heading towards unchartered territory. He had only known Dunn professionally for two years; their private lives had never been discussed, until now. He shifted uncomfortably in his seat.

"Don't worry Sir. I am not going to spill my inner soul over the carpet, I just..." She stopped herself from saying anything more with sigh and sat down heavily on a chair next to Hammond, studying her cup as if looking for coffee grounds that could guide her.

"My life is great. I love my job; I've got a great apartment. Everything I ever wanted. I've met this amazing guy and we have fun, but now he wants commitment and everything is ruined."

Hammond looked at her sympathetically. Lois Dunn was still so young; he guessed she was about thirty years of age. It was unusual to know a woman so driven in life without the desperation to be married or have children. He admired her tenacity.

"Do you like being with him?"

Dunn shrugged her shoulders hopelessly.

"Yes, but not enough to want to give up my independence." She looked at Hammond and blushed again, apologising with a wave of her hand as if to wipe away her candour. The two colleagues sat there in silence, lost in their own thoughts before Hammond spoke.

"There is something I have been asked to investigate, something that is not really my responsibility but I feel the need to do it anyway."

He was surprised by his own admittance although now he had spoken aloud of the thoughts that had tormented him throughout the day; it felt as if he were unburdening a heavy load. Dunn looked at him, surprised. She turned her chair so she could face him and listened as Hammond told her about Lloyd Harris's request. She didn't say a word until Hammond relayed the details of Mark Callum's death.

"Well, there are no rules to suicide." She said simply in response to Hammond's questioning the method of suicide. Hammond agreed but then explained his puzzlement over the missing paper and pen, Callum's lack of a social life, the unexplained rent payments. As he spoke, he became aware that Harris's instinct warranted more attention. A detective had no tools of the trade other than their instinct. It couldn't be handed to a young rookie with an id card and a pair of handcuffs, it was instinctual, organic. Hammond shouldn't have doubted Harris's instinct, especially now that his own was beginning to gnaw at him. There was something that wasn't right. Mark Callum's death had been as neat and tidy as his apartment and as such, it bordered on implausible. He shared these thoughts with Dunn as she sat there silently. When he had finished talking, she looked at him intently.

"I know I don't have to remind you that it is going to be practically impossible to justify spending resources on reviewing suicides. Do you want me to help in any way? We could do it in our free time. Galvin will help as well, you know he would do anything for you if you asked him."

Hammond looked at Dunn sharply. He saw she wasn't being sarcastic but was taken aback by her comment. He had noticed Galvin's enthusiasm for the job but had never considered it was in any way related to himself. He waited for Dunn to explain her comment but instead she stood up from her chair.

"Just ask if you need me to check on anything or to help with the investigation in any way."

Hammond thanked her, he was confident it would only be a matter of time before he took her up on her offer.

Hammond was convinced the car was on autopilot, he couldn't remember driving to his house in Stanford yet he arrived outside his front door within twenty minutes after leaving Police Headquarters. He was annoyed to find a battered Volkswagen camper van parked in his usual place, leaving him with no choice but to park further up the road. As he walked toward his house, he noted that the curtains were drawn. He knew that the curtains had been open when he had left that morning. He paused outside his neighbour's house, unsure whether to proceed, his eyes automatically scanning the road for his son's car. It was possible that Paul had come home unexpectedly, but unlikely he would bother to draw the curtains. Hammond considered the possibility and thought again. If Paul didn't have his car, he would have phoned to be collected from the train station and he hadn't heard from Paul. His heart started beating fast in his chest. He crouched down by the wall and considered what to do. If there were burglars, it was likely there would be more than one. He focused on each car parked in close proximity in turn, looking for someone in a car that was a possible look-out. He saw no-one. Whoever was in the house were confident they wouldn't be disturbed. He breathed slowly and crept across to his garden wall, waiting several seconds before skulking across the small front garden to underneath the living room window. He crouched low, confident he was hidden in the darkness. There was a gap in the curtains, he attempted to see through it by raising his head from his crouched position, but could only see the light from the table lamp nearest the window that had been switched on during his absence. For a moment he considered phoning the police, but pride got the better of him and he decided to approach the front door. He rang the doorbell and listened, expecting activity on the other side, there was nothing. Hammond took a deep breath and turned the key in the lock, slamming the door open, causing it to swing dramatically before it concluded its dance with a resounding thud against the wall. Still silence. The house was in darkness apart from the light that was showing from underneath the living room door. He stood with his back against the hallway wall and raised one leg until his foot rested on the door handle. With one push he depressed the door lever and spun into the room with a shout that resembled a tribal war cry. There was a yelp from behind one of the sofas. A black mass of hair slowly raised itself from the other side of the room, followed by two dark rimmed eyes. Hammond swallowed; he was being burgled by a monkey.

"Wally! You frightened the shit out of me!"

The reprimanding voice was accompanied by the petite figure of a young woman dressed in tightly fitted jeans and a black t-shirt with the slogan *"If you can afford me, I'm yours!"* Hammond's face broke into a relieved smile.

"Jenny! I didn't know you would be here." He wasn't sure how to continue. It wasn't every day that his son's best friend visited him uninvited. In fact, he had never officially invited her. Jenny had a habit of doing what she wanted when she wanted regardless of any unspoken protocol.

"It's cool." Jenny continued pulling at the sofa, speaking as if she were accepting an apology from him. "Paul said he had left a message for you. How do you get this sofa to turn into a bed?"

She didn't look at him as she spoke, being so preoccupied with pulling his sofa apart. Her blasé attitude made Hammond feel as if it were he who was intruding into her private domain. He stood there, completely bewildered before walking across the room to assist her unfolding the metal sprung mattress base and rearranged the sofa cushions for her.

"It's bloody freezing in here, Wally"

Jenny looked at him then, and reached her arms around his neck in a tight embrace. The gesture was so unexpected that Hammond, with some embarrassment returned the embrace, patting his hands on her upper back. Then he remembered the front door was still open and returned to the hallway, shutting the door firmly.

Jenny called to him as he returned along the hallway, kicking his shoes off as he passed the coat rack.

"I've made you some dinner, it's in the oven."

He proceeded to the kitchen, questions popping into his thoughts as he did so but decided not to ask, not yet. He headed for the telephone that was mounted on the wall inside the kitchen and dialled 1571 to retrieve his phone messages.

"Hey Dad. I need a favour. Jen's going through a bad time, I told her she could come and stay with you for a while, just until she gets her head sorted. I have given her my keys so don't feel you have to get home early to let her in. I will phone soon." The message ended. It was typical that his son had not thought to ring his mobile rather than the home phone to ensure his message would be retrieved before Jenny had arrived. The female call-minder voice instructed Hammond to save or delete the message by pressing three. He pressed three before replacing the handset and looked around the kitchen. It was unusually tidy despite the faint aroma of burnt toast. He felt un-nerved suddenly and strode back into the living room.

"Jenny, it's lovely to see you of course. I haven't seen you in a while and you look great." He lied; she looked like a small child who had attacked the Halloween face paints. "Although, I have to ask...why the sudden visit? Paul's message said you are going through a tough time. Are you alright?"

He perched on the arm of the chair nearest the door and waited for her to face him. When she did turn, he was taken aback by her response.

"No, Wally. I am not alright. No, I do not want to talk about it, and no, I don't know how long I will be here, but it's probably for a few days, unless you want to be like a typical misogynistic male and kick a vulnerable woman out on the street so you can stay here and be cosy with your smug self?!"

The words were shouted at him with childish aggression, but Hammond stayed where he was, concentrating on keeping his face as neutral as possible. He was unsure how to respond.

"Ok. Where did you say my dinner was?"

*"All human work, under natural conditions,
is a kind of dance."*
Henry Havelock Ellis. The Dance of Life. 1923.

CHAPTER FIVE

The temperature had dropped to several degrees above freezing. The cold air shocked Wallace Hammond awake as he blearily opened his front door. Ideally he would have stayed in bed an extra hour but wanted to get into the office before it got too busy. He stepped out into the cold air and then with second thoughts, returned indoors to retrieve his overcoat. He would have liked to have found his scarf, but the coat rack mountain refused to divulge any clues as to where his scarf could be so he gave up. Wrapping his coat around his shoulders he headed towards his usual parking space forgetting the Volkswagen van was parked there instead. He swore and in his annoyance got out his pen and notebook from his inside pocket and scribbled a hasty message for the car owner. *"To whoever owns this piece of junk. Please note this is residential parking only. Cars will be clamped if parked illegally."*

He knew it was a childish act, but he admitted to himself that it was somewhat enjoyable too. It was unlikely the car owner would trace the message to him. Hammond chuckled quietly to himself as he strolled up to the road to his car, imagining the facial expression of the reader when the message was discovered. He hoped it would give him his car space back.

If there was such a thing as karma, it presented itself to Hammond immediately. The Peugeot's windscreen was covered in a sheet of ice. Hammond remembered too late that he had lost the window scraper last winter and resigned himself to sitting in the front seat with the engine running and the heater on full blast. Minutes past and the windscreen showed no sign of defrosting. Deciding to make his house-guest earn her keep, he called his own home number from his mobile letting it ring repeatedly until he heard a groggy "Who and what?"

Using an encouraging tone, Hammond persuaded Jenny to fill a jug of warm water and bring it up the road to his car. She was not impressed but after reminders that it could be her way of returning a favour she put the phone down. It wasn't long before he saw her unsmiling face, bare of make-up looking down at him through a shower of water. She followed his directions, pouring warmth over all the windows and then walked back towards the house with the empty jug and no word of farewell. As Hammond used his wipers to clear the windscreen of excess moisture, he saw Jenny stop at the Volkswagen van and read his message pinned under the camper-van's wipers. She pulled the note away and looked around at the row of neighbouring houses with a look of agitation. He put the car into first gear and withdrew from his parking space. As he passed his own house, he saw Jenny, seemingly unaware of the icy temperature, dressed only in a Mickey Mouse T-shirt and shorts crouched down in the next door neighbour's porch. It looked as if she was shouting through the letterbox.

The computer was making too much noise for Hammond's liking. He had intended to be discreet and use the empty office to search the names that Harris had given him on the list of suicides, but the way the computer was beeping every time it demanded a password, it was bound to draw attention. Hammond wasn't entirely computer proficient, usually he would ask Emma to help him but he didn't want anyone to know what he was doing. The wall clock told Hammond it was 8am, he had another hour before his presence would be noticed. He searched the list of names included on Harris's note one at a time using the police search network. The first name Hammond searched was Salima Abitboul. She had been found strangled underneath a disused railway bridge near Orpington, and was identified by her flatmate Cheryl Bailey whom had reported her missing days earlier. A Pakistani man had been investigated by police after having been seen going to the site several times before Salima's body was discovered. When he had been arrested, the suspect had a necklace belonging to Salima in his pocket. It wouldn't been enough evidence to convict him had the man not confessed to using an electrical cord to strangle Salima and given police the location of where he had dumped it. This accurate information was enough to convince the jury that he was guilty. Hammond read the report again, he was perplexed as to why the killer had co-operated so fully, he had ultimately convicted himself. This was not the normal behaviour of an offender. In his experience, murderers would be prepared to do anything to escape being convicted. The report stated the man charged had no previous convictions but that didn't mean the man hadn't committed a crime before, just that he hadn't been caught. A guilty conscience could have explained the confession, it wasn't implausible Hammond reasoned. He ensured he had not missed anything in the report on Salima Abitboul's death before referring to the first name on Harris' list of fatalities. Theresa Davenport. The police report stated without doubt that she had killed herself. She had thrown herself off the roof of an apartment block near Cheriton. A neighbour whom had lived the floor below had seen Theresa standing on the edge of the roof several minutes before she had jumped. Despite the neighbour's frantic attempts to talk Theresa off the roof, Theresa had been non-responsive. In desperation the neighbour, 60 year old Anne Walker had run indoors to call the emergency services during which time Theresa had jumped. The autopsy report attributed her shattered limbs as being consistent with concentrated impact force by jumping feet first. The visceral trauma inflicted on the kidneys, spleen and lungs indicated the effects of deceleration forces typical of falling three or more stories. Hammond skimmed the report. Jumping from a height of thirty-six feet would be terrifying, he was curious why Theresa had not been heard screaming before or during her fall. She had not responded to her neighbours attempt to counsel her. Both factors could suggest she had been sedated before her fall although toxicology reports showed there were no drugs in her system. Hammond skimmed the photographs of the scene. There had been trees on either side on the building yet Theresa had chosen an area that had nothing to break her fall. He was surprised to discover that Theresa had eaten a meal of pasta and chicken before she had died. It seemed odd to him that she had eaten a nourishing meal just before killing herself. Her last meal seemed quite simple. Hammond's stomach rumbled at the thought. He imagined that most would choose an indulgent meal before their departure on earth. He knew he would. The police report did not contain much information on Theresa's personal life, it appeared that she had no family. She had left a brief note. *"This is the only choice I have left"*. There was no explanation for her death, neither was the note addressed to anyone in particular which made Hammond wonder why she had written it at all. It was possible that Theresa had wanted to excuse her decision to those who would inevitably have to deal with her body and clear up after her. If so, it gave the impression that she had realised her decision would affect the lives of others. Witnessing a death was traumatic enough, but failing to prevent someone from taking their own lives would undoubtedly create a lifetime of grief, even if the deceased and the witness were strangers. Hammond scanned the rest of the report hoping to find images of her apartment and was disappointed to find none. He would have preferred to have seen what kind of life she had led before she died. The general search engine proved slightly more helpful, listing separate newspaper articles that had reported her death but again, the information on her character or livelihood was limited. Hammond understood the reason for this, having released a press release that included the minimum of information the day previously. An article from a regional newspaper, written in October 2009, described Theresa as a single woman of thirty three who had lived a private, almost reclusive life. She had been employed as a librarian. Hammond closed the tab and scrolled down the listings, eventually clicking on a link that directed him to a Kent Suicide Prevention Plan page. He couldn't find any details about Theresa on the page so tried again, clicking on a link that directed him to a FFASL forum. Hammond scanned the page under Friends and Family Affected By The Suicides of Loved Ones. He skimmed the emotional content of people's personal stories until he found his search entry. It was found under Cherry13's entry to the forum dated March 2010.

"In memory of Theresa Davenport. A girl who did not deserve to die. Her killers are still out there some-where; they know I know...question is what will they do about it?"

Hammond felt excitement reading the entry and leaned closer to the computer monitor, his fingers hovering over the keyboard. He didn't understand why Cherry13 had entered the slightest suggestion of a crime on a suicide forum, but was encouraged by the brief information he had gathered on Theresa Davenport. He read people's replies to Cherry13's entry, hoping to identify a personal response to the implied accusation. Some were sympathetic, having read the entry as the grief-stricken ravings of someone looking to blame for their loved one's death, others condemned the entry as inappropriate, suggesting psychiatric counsel be sought. If only he could identify Cherry13. There was a good possibility they had known Theresa personally, in which case, the note she had left may have been intended for them to read. It was evident that the entry had been specifically worded with the purpose to antagonise and this suggested that Cherry13's identity was not anonymous to the person or people he or she were trying to aggravate.

Eventually his attention concentrated on the deaths of Lucas Dean and Claire Bennet. He couldn't find any mention of either name in any news reports. He tried the police database and retrieved the information on Lucas Dean whom had been charged with numerous drug charges dating from 1992 to 1999 including intent to supply and being in possession of crack cocaine. His death from an overdose of a cocktail of painkillers and alcohol seemed a rational conclusion to a life dominated by drugs. It was evident to Hammond that Lucas Dean had also been a recluse. No concerned friends or family members had reported him missing during the days surrounding his death which may have accounted for the fact that his body had been in the later stages of decomposition when his body was discovered in his apartment. Dean's death may have been left unnoticed for longer had his neighbours not complained about the smell coming from his room. Hammond sighed heavily; he couldn't imagine a life without his son or Lyn being involved somehow. He wondered whether he would have had a similar life to Lucas Dean had he not been blessed with a family. It was Hammond's curiosity that made him look for any mention of Lucas Dean's background. It was mentioned that Dean had been in care during his childhood but there wasn't enough information to create an impression of the man Dean had been. The photographs taken at the scene where his body was found were limited. The scene was dismal with definite indications of suicide rather than foul play. *"It is my time to leave."* The message Dean had written was simple, yet it didn't explain why it had been left or to whom it was addressed. The inclusion of the note was perhaps more significant because Lucas Dean had lived a solitary existence. Unlike Theresa, Dean had not been in any known employment, so his social contacts were more limited, yet he had left a note for someone. Similar to Mark Callum's apartment, his bedsit was frugal and devoid of comfort. Only the bare necessities had been provided for; a single bed positioned near to a wash basin, and a kitchenette was all he had needed. As Hammond studied the photograph, he had a feeling he was missing something obvious but despite double checking every detail in the pictures, he couldn't find anything that would justify the feeling he had. He checked his watch, he could hear movement in the corridors nearby and knew his privacy would be interrupted soon. Quickly he moved onto Claire Bennett. She had been thirty-one years of age when she had slit her wrists in the bath in her one bedroom bungalow in Greatstone. The pathologist whom had examined Claire's body had been Dr Ed Henderson, the same doctor helping Hammond identify the body found in the woods. Hammond wondered whether it was worth questioning Henderson further, but common sense interrupted his consideration. It was better to remain discreet. If he asked a question concerning a sealed enquiry, he would have to justify it and telling Henderson that he was looking into a possible case as a favour to an old colleague wouldn't be good enough. With these thoughts in mind, He returned his attention onto Henderson's autopsy report, reading with interest where Henderson had highlighted several hesitation marks evident on Bennet's wrists before she had inflicted the final, fatal cut which was performed by a razor, found lying on the edge of the bath. She had also written a last message, this time on the bathroom tiles above the bath with her own blood. *"I must do this."*

Wallace Hammond was intrigued. It was as if each death had needed to be justified to an unknown person. However, none of the messages written by their own hands, apart from Mark Callum's, suggested their deaths were coerced. Lois Dunn had said that there were no rules to suicide but it was a common belief, although somewhat misguided, that the process of taking your own life included leaving a message to the world left behind; an acknowledgment that society or circumstances had failed them. It was more difficult to understand the reasoning behind someone wanting to take their own life, but having no family or friends guaranteed a lonely and possibly, miserable existence. Emotional ties to other people often gave a reason to live and vice versa.

Hammond entered the last name on his list into the database. The fifth death was assumed as no body had been found, although witnesses boarding the P&O ferry testified to having seen Fiona Nwasu climb over the upper deck railings and throw herself into the sea whilst the ferry was stationary at Dover Port.

Hammond sat at the computer staring blankly at the screen in front of him, trying to mentally condense all the information he had read. He couldn't understand why his gut was telling him he was missing something, but the feeling was there, a certainty in his belly that he had missed a connection. All five people, including Mark Callum, had died by their own hand. There was nothing to suggest otherwise, so in this respect, he had no problem in concluding that no further investigation into their deaths was warranted. Hammond printed the pages off and quickly retrieved them from the printer tray, folding them carefully and tucked them amongst the folds of his wallet. He felt no more enlightened having researched the notes that Harris had given him. There were no significant correlations between the deaths other than they had occurred at similar ages and within a thirty mile radius. The deceased had all lived solitary lives but there the similarities ended. Hammond deleted his search history and left the computer feeling irritated. He had hoped that the name search would show up further inconsistencies. All he had found were paranoid ravings of a grieving friend on a web forum, and the depressing clarification that there were lonely, desperate people in the world whose only relief from their misery was to end their own lives. He felt he had been force fed a large red herring.

The office was full of activity by 8.58am. Hammond considered getting himself some coffee but decided against it. His stomach felt tender, He wasn't sure if he needed to go to the toilet or fill himself with starchy food. Jenny's offering of baked beans on toast the previous evening had been his second meal of beans within a few days. They must have been working hard cleaning his colon during the night. He grabbed his coat telling anyone within hearing distance he was going out to get some breakfast. It had started to spit with light rain whilst he had been indoors giving the pavement a polished sheen. With head bowed down against the cold air, Hammond walked toward the top end of the high street, his nose following the familiar waft of fried bacon and coffee towards his favourite cafe. He was greeted warmly by the proprietor who was busy serving hot drinks to a queue of customers.

They shouted pleasantries to one another, performing their regular routine of pretending to hear one another over the noise of the spluttering coffee machine by nodding and showing their teeth in friendly grins. He ordered a bacon baguette with ketchup telling himself it would help his stomach settle. As he handed over the exact change to the girl serving him Hammond wondered how old she was, he couldn't tell.

The heavens opened as Hammond left the cafe. A paranoid mind would have interpreted this as a sign that God had waited for him to exit before deliberately drenching him. The paper bag containing his breakfast was kept dry under the breast of his coat as he hot trotted over puddles and flooding drains back to the station. He arrived at the office with soaked hair and frightened a female officer as he removed his coat, realising too late that the tomato sauce in the bacon sandwich had seeped through the paper bag mortally staining his white shirt. He playfully demonstrated that he hadn't been stabbed in the chest by showing a healthy nipple through a gap in the shirt buttons, before going to the bathroom to change his shirt. He was standing at the wash basin half naked when his mobile rang. He answered it quickly, pinning the phone between an ear and his right shoulder as he attempted to slide an arm into the sleeve of the clean light blue shirt.
"Where are you?"
Ed Henderson's voice sounded impatient.
"At the station."
Hammond gave up trying to hold the mobile and dress at the same time. The phone was switched onto loudspeaker and placed on top of the hand drier.

"I've been trying to call you for several minutes. I was told you were out the office."

Hammond couldn't be bothered to explain his whereabouts so asked Henderson the reason for his call, hoping the autopsy of the unidentified man had been concluded.

"I've managed to identify our victim."

"You have? That's great!"

Hammond finished fastening his buttons and tucked the shirt tails into the waistband of his trousers, listening to Henderson's account of his activities.

"I gave the fingerprints to DC Galvin, just in case you had them on file; they matched fingerprints on your database belonging to Graham Roberts, aged 59 from Hythe. Galvin has the details; no doubt he will debrief you. In the meantime, I want to go through my findings with you here at the lab. Can you come over?"

Hammond picked up the phone from its resting place and switched off the loudspeaker.

"Galvin? You gave the fingerprints to Galvin?"

"Sure, he asked me to."

Hammond backed out the bathroom, screwing up his soiled shirt and shoving it amongst discarded paper towels in the bin under the basin.

"Why? He knew I was chasing up the Forensic reports today."

"Brown nosing as usual I expect."

Hammond told Henderson to expect him at the Pathology Lab within the hour and hung up. Two people in the last twelve hours had referred to Galvin as a teacher's pet. Was he the only one who hadn't noticed?

Emma had left a cup of coffee on his desk. He waved to her through the glass as a way of thanks and wrote down his objectives for the day. He wanted to speak to the son of William Barnes' cleaner. Barnes had said that the boy was often practising on his bike in the woods, in which case he would be able to provide the names of his fellow bikers, maybe provide more insight into Graham Robert's attendance at the dirt track. It bothered Hammond that Roberts was on the police database, he hoped the reason wasn't as ominous as he feared. Galvin was occupied dealing with members of the public offering information, DS Dunn and DC Edwards had gone to the school, it was possible they would return with the same information, but Hammond preferred having repetitive information rather than none.

The bacon baguette beckoned Hammond's attention as he sneaked another look at Harris's notes for what seemed like the hundredth time. He still intended to speak to Callum's doctor, even though it could be a waste of time. It wouldn't be possible to check all the medical records on the other people included on Harris' list but he wanted to know as much as possible about Callum, if only to discover a reason how he had acquired a hairbrush from a girl who had been murdered two decades previously. On impulse, he decided to call the doctor whilst he had the opportunity, it would be better to resolve Harris's enquiry before it eat up more time which could be better spent finding Graham Robert's attacker. It took several moments to find the doctor's number. Hammond introduced himself to the surgery receptionist and explained the reason for his call. He was asked to wait several moments whilst she checked to see if the doctor was available to come to the phone. Whilst Hammond waited, he tore a chunk from the sandwich with his teeth, delighting at the salty flavour of the bacon. His greed was abated temporarily when a deep voice came onto the phone and introduced himself as Doctor Kondaveeti. The man spoke slowly giving the impression he had time to spare.

"To be honest, Inspector, I don't really remember Mark Callum. He wasn't one of my regular patients, but I see we have a record on our database. One moment please..."

There was the sound of slow tapping on a computer keyboard.

"You realise of course Inspector, that I am unable to disclose any medical notes."

Hammond explained that it wasn't necessary to protect his patient's confidentiality since Mark Callum had since died and had no family to protect. He purposely tried to sound reasonable and used an expression he usually hated, explaining that he was simply dotting the i's and crossing out all the t's.

"Ah! I see now! Yes, I do remember Mr Callum after all. He came to my surgery a total of three times, the last visit was in July this year complaining of trouble sleeping and wanted sleeping pills which I did not prescribe."

Hammond asked why.

"Well, I remember he had anxiety problems, He was constantly fidgeting and squirming. On his first visit I was persuaded to prescribe him anti-depressants. The second time he complained of trouble sleeping. Again, I prescribed sleeping tablets but during his third visit I was not convinced that the drugs were working or that he needed them as he indicated. He was a very withdrawn man, didn't talk much..."

The tapping sound of the keyboard continued.

"I am reading my notes here which are helping my memory and I recall he wouldn't look me in the eye.

He came across as being quite disturbed. I suspected he may have a drug problem but I couldn't be sure. So, just to play it safe I suggested alternative means like taking more exercise, eating healthily and avoiding stimulants."

"You said you were persuaded to prescribe anti-depressants. May I ask by whom?"

"It doesn't say in my notes but I do remember Mr Callum was accompanied by an older woman on his first visit who I presumed was his mother." There was a pause as if the Doctor suddenly doubted Hammond's earlier reassurance of Callum having no family.

Hammond's heart skipped. "His mother? What gave you that impression?"

"Logic I suppose, Inspector. She was older than him as I said, but she seemed to have some kind of authority over him. She explained Mr Callum's symptoms during the first visit which he confirmed. It was she who asked that I prescribe anti-depressants with the reasoning that nothing else had worked."

"Did you see any medical notes from his previous doctor?"

Hammond knew that the investigation on Mark Callum's death had found no medical history to refer to but it was possible that Doctor Kondaveeti had been given some information when Callum had registered as a new patient.

"No, I was told they were in the post."

Doctor Kondaveeti was trying his best to be helpful. He added that the receptionist couldn't find any record of the previous doctor's name or surgery that Callum had given on his registration form and presumed that it had been a misunderstanding

"No doubt the matter would have been chased further if Mr Callum had not died."

"Did he return after the third visit?"

"No. I guess my advice worked."

It was evident the doctor couldn't help Hammond any further. Hammond gave his thanks to the doctor and ended the call. He took another bite from the sandwich causing tomato ketchup to spurt onto his hand. He licked it away. He hadn't found the conversation with the doctor particularly enlightening, but it had added credibility to the belief that Callum had killed himself. The only question Hammond had now was the identity of the woman whom had accompanied Callum on his first visit to the surgery. There was no doubt that Callum had no family, but it was possible he had an older girlfriend at the time.

His thoughts were interrupted by a tap on the glass. He looked up, licking his lips to see Emma waving a yellow post-it note. He gestured for her to deliver the message.

"There was a message from Mr Ben Dover. He said you could come in the back entrance later."

She looked at Hammond in astonishment when he spluttered chewed food over his chin and rushed over to slap her hand on his back as he sat choking. His face had turned a purple hue. It took several seconds before his coughing fit had subsided. A perplexed Emma returned to her duties after a rather hysterical Hammond had reassured her that he was well enough to be left alone.

CHAPTER SIX

As Hammond drove past the bronze statue of William Harvey at the hospital, he checked the digital clock on the car dashboard. He was late. He parked his vehicle in the staff car park, hoping Henderson had remembered the car registration correctly when he had pre-warned the parking attendants of his impending visit. The last thing Hammond wanted was to have his car clamped. With the last minute decision to play it safe, he leaned back into the car fumbling in the glove compartment and extracted a laminated sign showing the Kent Police emblem. He placed it in full view on the dashboard and depressed the automatic lock button on his key fob. The smell of boiled cabbages from the hospital kitchens suspended itself in the cold air bringing back memories of Hammond's childhood visits to his grandmother.

Dr Ed Henderson stubbornly refused to acknowledge Hammond's presence for several minutes after his arrival; he was studying a cadaver on the stainless steel table, occasionally talking into a small tape recorder. Eventually he paused his examination and walked over to where the Detective Inspector stood patiently. Henderson's sharp gaze took note of the spluttered ketchup stains on Hammond's shirt evident under the open overcoat. He placed his tape recorder down on a table next to where Hammond stood.

"With all the muck we inevitably find ourselves working in, I find it helps to keep clean clothes at the office."

Hammond followed Henderson to the morgue ignoring the comment and waited for Graham's Roberts remains to be uncovered.

"The good news is that there was no difficulty establishing a cause of death. The bad news is that it may be difficult to prove he died as a result of the attack."

The sheet covering Robert's body was pulled back to his waist. Hammond drew in a breath slowly, reminding himself to breathe through the mouth whilst he was there. The body he had seen in the woods had been lying face down. Now the chest and upper body were exposed, he could see that Roberts had not died peacefully and said so, wondering how a beaten corpse could not act as evidence of an attack.

"He had myocardial ischaemic heart disease, or to put it in layman's terms, reduced blood supply to the heart muscle. His coronary arteries had significant fat rich deposits, so much so, that I found a tear in a vessel wall. I doubt it was as a result of any direct trauma, a blood clot had already formed. There is no doubt that he would have suffered symptoms of unstable angina. In short, the question I have to answer, by looking at his injuries is to establish whether he would have died had the physical assault not taken place."

"Was he on medication?"

"I am awaiting blood screening results. Either way, any medication would not have cleared his furred arteries, it would only have controlled his cholesterol levels and blood sugars, reduced the rate of occurrence and severity of his angina attacks. I doubt that any medication he would have taken for the angina would have accounted for such an aggressive trigger as the assault."

Henderson paused whilst he looked pointedly at the clock on the wall above the door. He sighed heavily giving the impression he had better things to do with his time than talk to Hammond and continued pointing with a gloved finger at various points on the corpse lying before them.

"Definite upper body trauma caused by a blunt instrument. I found wood splinters on his clothing so it is likely he was struck by a heavy piece of wood. The extensive subcutaneous damage confirms he took a beating. The internal organs took the force of the attack, there were multiple fractures on the lower left ribs mainly concentrated at the front but the x-rays showed hairline fractures toward the back of the ribcage. There are multiple lacerations to the forearms. Again, the left side has incurred more damage. The spleen was ruptured, probably from the blows to the ribs and abdomen. His heart had continued beating after the attack, hence the blood loss we found at the scene."

Hammond studied the body in front of him and waited for the pathologist to continue. It was obvious that Dr Henderson enjoyed being the source of important information. He wasn't particularly tall, probably no more than five foot eight, but within his own domain, he walked with a straight back and long strides.

"The semen trace found on his palm has yet to be confirmed as being his own but I found no foreign hair around the genitals. It appears he relieved himself of sexual tension whilst he was in the woods." Henderson shrugged with one shoulder "We all have our fetishes I suppose."

Speak for yourself, an inner voice in Hammond replied to Henderson's quip. He pointed towards the legs of the dead victim and enquired with a raised eyebrow if there was anything to report on the lower body. Henderson lifted the sheet off the legs and continued debriefing Hammond with his findings.

"There were several abrasions and bruises evident on the lower limbs, although this one was the most interesting."

Henderson pulled the overhead lamp over to where they were looking, the light beamed down to where Henderson traced a latex gloved finger over a faint bruise evident on the thigh.

"It looked liked there was a pattern to the bruise, so I photographed it with the UV light." Henderson ushered Hammond to the computer in the small room at the side of the morgue. After several clicks on the mouse, Henderson pulled up a photograph onto the screen for Hammond to look at. What had seemed a faint mark on the upper thigh of Roberts was now revealed to be a bruise measuring about three inches in length with a scalloped edge. Hammond studied the picture silently. He couldn't identify the shape of the pattern, even though he knew it was familiar to him. Henderson printed him two copies of the photograph, and the two men returned to their appraisal of Robert's body.

"Did you find any foreign samples?"

The pathologist looked at Hammond sharply and nodded.

"I was just coming to that. Yes, there are two samples of interest. We found a fragment of nail on the shoulder of the victim. It wasn't his own. We found vulpes hairs on the right side of the body, not surprising since he had been laying there for a while. A sensitive nose would have smelled him from quite a way away..."

Hammond interrupted. "A vulpes hair?"

"Latin for fox, I take it you do not remember your school lessons?" Henderson continued talking with a rather smug expression.

"Also, there was a dark stain on the trousers. I gave it to the others for analysis but whilst you are waiting for the results, I am guessing there will be components of something like Barium, Lithium or Sodium Soap."

Henderson coughed, raising a closed fist to his mouth. Too much talking has dried him out, Hammond thought wryly.

"That of course, would explain the patterned bruise on the thigh."

"It would? How?"

Henderson draped the sheet back over Roberts and sealed him away, indicating their meeting was about to conclude.

"Bike grease transferred to the trousers when the bike pedal hit him."

Hammond thanked the pathologist and left him in silence, eager to return to the station and share the findings with the rest of the team. He could taste an imminent arrest and was excited. For a second, he was reminded of why he had loved his job.

It was cold inside the car, but he was thankful it had stopped raining. He switched on the air conditioning, letting the engine run in neutral whilst he unlocked his mobile keypad and searched for Jenny's mobile number. Her phone rang several times before her answer service asked him to leave his message. He lowered his voice and attempted to sound as professional as possible.

"My name is Doctor Yule. B. Sari. I have a message here for Ms Wilma Lecsgro. It is with regret that I must inform you that you will always be short. I apologise for the disappointment this will cause but wish you a good day." He hung up giggling like a schoolboy as he depressed the clutch and slid the gearstick into first gear.

The sounds at headquarters were a melody of intense activity. Various conversations happening at the same time within the enclosed area sounded like a hybrid of pitches and tones. As he swiped his security pass by the door to the headquarter offices. Hammond recognised Dunn's red raincoat that had been left to dry on the back of the chair by the radiator. Soon there would be the exchanging of the information gathered that morning. Hammond was encouraged. If Beech enquired how the investigation was progressing, his positive feedback would be genuine. He saw Edwards at the end of the corridor, talking into a telephone receiver whilst chewing on a bread roll at the same time. Hammond found Edwards rather coarse at times, but he was a good detective and reliable. He held up a hand in greeting as their eyes met. Edwards returned the compliment by taking another bite and turning his back, continuing his conversation on the phone with his mouth full.

"Inspector?" Someone tapped him lightly on his back. He spun around, recognising a woman who worked downstairs in Reception. She smiled at him and informed him that there was someone waiting to see him.

"Who?" It wasn't the best time to receive visitors at the office, the team meeting was due to start in fifteen minutes. "Mrs DiMarco. She has been waiting almost an hour already. She is most keen to talk to you." Wallace

Hammond strained his memory, he didn't recognise the name DiMarco, but he was in a good mood and the name DiMarco suggested a sexy Italian woman. He agreed to follow the receptionist downstairs.

The door lock gave a loud beep as it accepted the pin code, allowing Hammond into the reception area. He looked around, and not seeing anyone, asked the officer behind the reception booth where Mrs DiMarco was. The officer mimicked Hammond's search by half standing from his chair and leaned over his desk allowing his head to aid his peripheral vision by turning it left and right. He shrugged when he was unable to help and then suddenly pointed to the main doors. A woman dressed in a caramel full length coat was smoking outside the door. Her head was shrouded in a black scarf making it difficult for Hammond to distinguish her features. From the back, she was tall and slim, her left arm crossed in front of her, her fingers hooked around her waist. Her right elbow rested on the left forearm as she slowly dragged from her lit cigarette. The smoke she exhaled escaped into the air in a mesmerising ballet. Hammond walked through the main doors, calling her name as she did so. The woman turned and smiled causing her cheeks to dimple around the contours of her mouth. Hammond stopped. It was Kathleen.

"Hello Wallace." She stubbed her cigarette against the building wall and took a step toward him. Overcome by a sudden feeling of self-consciousness, Hammond embraced her gently. His mouth had dried up making it difficult to talk. He found himself staring at her which made the situation worse. Beautiful women unnerved him, Harris's daughter especially. He recovered quickly and guided her back into the reception lobby by placing a hand gently under her elbow.

"I was wondering if I could talk to you in private." Kathleen seemed uncomfortable. The officer in Reception was staring at them inquisitively. Hammond obliged and led her through the security doors until they entered a room used by family liaison officers. The room was comfortably furnished with a cream sofa and a pine coffee table. It wasn't an attractive room but it served its purpose of enabling people to relax.

"It is really great to see you. A surprise, but a great one. You should have phoned, I would have been here earlier." Hammond knew he was gabbling.

Kathleen took off her coat and scarf, flicking her hair loose. It was still long and auburn, darker than he remembered but glossy and soft. She wore a black v-neck sweater and dark trousers with heeled ankle boots. She sat down on the sofa in an expectant manner. Since there was no-where else to sit, Hammond sat beside her, perched on the edge so he could turn his face toward her. They politely exchanged information on how they were and agreed how pleasant it was to see each other again.

"I confess I had no idea your surname was DiMarco, I didn't know it was you."

Kathleen smoothed a crease in her trousers. "It was my married name." It was obvious she wanted to concentrate on the reason why she was there.

"Wallace, I understand that my father saw you recently?"

Hammond answered this was correct. She had spoken as if asking a question rather than confirming fact. He wondered how much Harris had told her.

"He asked for your help?" She continued without waiting for a response, and then turned her body slightly so that she was facing him directly.

"I realise what I will say will appear disloyal to my father but I need to say it." She paused and lowered her eyes to her lap where she had cupped one hand in the other.

After taking a deep breath, she looked back at Hammond until their eyes met.

"I don't know what my Father has told you, but I am asking you, as a friend to us both, to ignore anything he told you when you met the other day. To not do what he may have asked you to do."

Kathleen was speaking in code but Hammond understood that she could know more than she was letting on. Either she was pretending to know more as a way of getting him to speak freely and divulge information or she was trying to determine how much he knew already.

"What is this about Kathleen? It is true your Father asked me to help by looking into something, but he understood it may not be possible or even necessary."

Kathleen listened. "Wallace, I know what my Father asked you to do. He wants you to investigate a suicide that happened recently. Am I right?"

Hammond smiled a reply.

"My father is not well. He gets confused easily, sometimes sees problems where they don't exist. Ever since his retirement, he has felt the need to investigate. He cannot give up the habit of detecting crime, even when there is no crime to detect. I am sorry to say that helping Dad would be a waste of your time."

"What do you mean your Dad's unwell? Is there something I don't know? Forgive me Kathleen but I get the impression you are not telling me everything. If there is something that I should know, please tell me."

Hammond resisted the urge to look at his watch, he didn't want to be late a second time for the team meeting. "Dad has been diagnosed with Alzheimer's. It's still the early stages, but he has good days and some days when he gets so confused, he doesn't make sense. It could be something subtle, like forgetting your name when he talks to you or stopping mid sentence with no idea that you were having a conversation, but there have been occasions when he has gone shopping for groceries and then forgotten the way home."

It was as if Kathleen had punched Hammond in the stomach, the shock of her confession made him feel sick. He felt ashamed that he had had no idea Harris was unwell. Harris had behaved oddly during their recent meeting, but he had no idea of how severe the situation had been. Harris had always been so sure about life, about his work. He found himself swallowing repeatedly. His throat hurt. He looked around the room for the water dispenser. Spying it by the window, he hastily filled a cup with water, throwing the cool liquid down his throat in large gulps. He remembered his manners too late and offered a drink to Kathleen who declined. The silence that hang in the air between them was interrupted by the sound of his mobile phone vibrating in his pocket. He wanted to ignore it, but instead excused himself to Kathleen and answered the call. Lois Dunn spoke efficiently on the other end, telling him the team had assembled in the briefing room. He told her he was on his way and ended the call.

Kathleen understood Hammond's predicament. She stood up and picked up her coat and scarf from the sofa, hanging it loosely over her arm. She approached him as he leaned against the water dispenser, pretending not to notice the moisture in Hammond's eyes.

"I can see this wasn't the best time. How about we make an arrangement to meet another time? Shall I call you?

"No, I will call you."

Hammond straightened up and called to her as she started to leave the room.

"Kathleen, thank you for telling me. I am sorry about your Dad."

She held his gaze for a prolonged moment and then closed the door behind her.

The man had been standing in the cold for over an hour. He had watched her smoking a cigarette outside the police station before a tall grey haired man wearing shabby attire came outside and embraced her. The man hadn't looked like a policeman, he looked more like a vet but the chances of a vet meeting her at a police station were pretty slim he reasoned. He remained at his post across the road, watching with interest as she was ushered into the building. He waited for several moments, then he crossed the road and entered reception. Using the pretext of having recognised the grey haired man but couldn't remember his name was all he needed to get the information he wanted. He thanked the officer at reception before exiting the building and pressed re-dial on his mobile. The voice on the other end of the phone was well spoken and gave the impression of good breeding. Each word delivered with articulation, without inflection. The same way the orders were given, no matter how demanding they were; there was never any doubt what was expected. Standing in the cold and wet was something he had to do often, but it was part of the job and he did it with the hope that it would be followed by a more active role. Watching someone was just the start. Eventually he would know his subject so well that he would be able to think like them, to recognise their habits, their preferences, he would be able to predict their next move. This was an invaluable skill he possessed, in some ways it made him invincible.

"Man lives by imagination."
Henry Havelock Ellis. The Dance of Life. 1923

CHAPTER SEVEN

"I understand we have a name".

Hammond brushed past Michael Galvin who was seated with his back facing the door. He had not noticed Hammond's approach and got up hastily as Hammond passed him. The tone of Hammond's voice was detected as being unusual, but the team were unsure whether it was a positive change in attitude or the opposite. Silent communication between the team members proceeded with stares and facial expressions. With jerks of the head, Galvin and Edwards elected Dunn to speak first.

"Yes we do, Graham Roberts aged 59 years. We have an address in Dymchurch Road. He lived alone, he was a widower, his wife having died from breast cancer in 1998. They had no children. In 2002, he was arrested and charged with driving under the influence of excessive alcohol consumption."

Hammond sipped his tea. His throat still hurt.

"Apparently we have his fingerprints on our database."

This was spoken directly to Galvin.

"Yes, from the drink driving charge but also there was a disturbance a few years back in Hythe High Street.

Roberts was accused of indecently approaching a six year old boy outside the public toilets. The mother of the child caught Roberts exposing himself to the boy and created a scene."

"When was this?"

"2001. No charges were brought against Roberts. He claimed it had been a misunderstanding; that he had used the urinal and hadn't fastened his clothing properly. However, his details were kept on record as a precaution."

It was worth checking with the Public Protection Unit at Canterbury, just to check that Roberts hadn't caught their attention since the incident in 2001.

"What about the mother and child that made the accusation, are they still local?"

Hammond considered interviewing the mother again. Even if the incident had happened nine years ago, there was a strong possibility the mother would remember her child having been in a possibly dangerous situation. His direct manner was making Galvin nervous.

"I don't know, I will check." Galvin stopped short, unsure how to continue. Hammond took another sip of tea and rubbed the back of his neck wearily.

"This is what we have so far. As our Mr Galvin is aware." He ignored the looks passed between Dunn and Edwards. They probably were not aware of Galvin's attempt to earn extra house points by talking to Henderson.

"...we now have an identity for our victim, which means we can ask around, get some background information on him, and question the neighbours. He may be a regular at the local pub, check for any family members. Galvin, that will be your job starting first thing in the morning. We know he was spending time with the kids in the woods, what we don't know is why. Was he there as an invited spectator, as a coach, or simply an interested bystander with nothing else to do on a Saturday or weekday evening? What was Roberts doing the day he died? Look at phone records; check to see if he had arranged to meet anyone in the woods. Dunn, did you have any luck at the school?"

Dunn shook her head.

"We showed an artist sketch of Roberts rather than the post mortem photo, some older children thought they recognised him, but they were very vague. Edwards asked around about the play tracks." Dunn looked at Edwards, willing him to debrief his own findings which Edwards did with a casual manner, he remained seated on his chair, slouched back with one leg resting on the other knee.

"Fourteen year old Robert Freeman is a regular rider at the track. He reckoned there were two or three others that used the track on a regular basis but he didn't know their names or recognise them as students from his school. I checked at the local primary school, but no one could help. I guess they're too young to be allowed to build tracks on their own. I'm going to go to the Grammar School in Folkestone to check there."

"Good. I would like to get information from as many kids as possible. Galvin, you went to Saltwood today, did you have any luck or were you too busy pestering the pathology department?"

Galvin smirked a little." I've got a list of the regulars who compete in the Boxing Day Run. The audio test proved negative. The trees are too dense for sound to carry far. The door to door enquiries were less productive, although one Saltwood resident remembers Graham

Roberts. Her name is Sally Whittaker, she walks her dog through the woods during mid-day. On several occasions she had seen Roberts with a group of boys. The most recent was during the summer holidays, he was laying flexi coil on the tracks. She didn't know the boys who were with him but said they were about fifteen or older."

Ok, so let's look at what we do have. We know that Graham Roberts liked to hang around the play park, the canal and the woods. This could simply be the wanderings of a lonely man, or it could be a deliberate ploy to be near children. Until we can talk to the children he used to hang around with and get more background information on him, we cannot assume he had paedophile tendencies. Therefore it is extremely important that we handle this very sensitively, any indication that this was related to a sex crime, and we will have an uproar."

Hammond made sure this comment was understood. He trusted his team to be discreet but it was important he cautioned them, if only to justify his actions to Beech later on. Hammond repeated the information that Dr Henderson had gathered from the autopsy. "From the injuries Roberts sustained, it appears that he was facing this assailant, possibly with his trousers down, maybe exposing himself when he was first struck. There is evidence that a bike was either thrown at him, or he fell over a bike. But for the sake of argument, let's say a bike was thrown at him, Roberts turns away as if to run, his trousers still undone and he is struck by a blow to the side or to the chest."

"That suggests more than one attacker." Edwards interrupted.

"Yes, it is a possibility, although the scene did not show much evidence of a scuffle. If there had been more than one person beating the crap out of him, the ground would have been disturbed much more." Dunn surmised. "Not necessarily, it had rained a lot, maybe the soil was washed over the disturbed ground." Galvin interjected. "Either way, it looks as if one of the kids are guilty of something." This hypothesis was offered by Edwards. "Or it could be a parent, someone who witnesses Graham Robert's expose himself to the BMX boys and took objection, reacting violently. There are multiple fractures and lacerations. Our victim was battered by a weapon immediately to hand, therefore, it is unlikely it was a premeditated attack, more of a frenzied rage." Hammond realised that they were all presuming Roberts was in some way responsible for his own death, he reminded himself to be objective and consider that Roberts was the victim of a brutal attack. There was still a chance that he was not a sexual deviant but rather a man whom simply enjoyed children's company. He focused on the identity of the assailant. "There is the suggestion that we are looking for someone shorter than Roberts, as the force of the blows were aimed at the chest and lower body. Roberts was six foot two inches. We can concentrate our search for someone around five foot five inches tall who has good upper body strength." Lumps of wood are heavy, if the wood was repeatedly swung, it would have been exhausting Hammond deduced.

Edwards spoke up "What if the attacker was originally on his knees? There were traces of semen, what if Roberts was getting a blowjob before he was struck?" Hammond replied that it was unlikely any DNA would have survived the weather conditions but, presuming that the attacker had reacted after witnessing Roberts getting sexual gratification from another person, there may still be trace evidence. By now Hammond was tired, he needed a hot meal and a good sleep. The day had been an emotional rollercoaster, one minute he had been playing practical jokes with Jenny, the next he was reminded of how vulnerable even the strongest man could be. He swallowed hard, thinking of Harris.

The meeting ended with the conclusion that nothing more could be done until Roberts had been thoroughly checked out, each had their own delegated tasks for the following day. Hammond collected his coat from his chair, he considered distributing the artist sketch of Roberts to the media, appealing for more information, but it would be a gamble. If the media found out about Robert's police record, it could become extremely difficult. Panic would arise amongst the community with the suggestion children had been put at risk. On the other hand, potential witnesses could come forward, family members could be traced, both of which would be essential to learning more about their victim. Hammond sighed heavily, he was too tired to think about it anymore today, tomorrow he would talk to Beech. He had one more task for the day.

There were no vacant parking spaces in New Road, so Hammond resigned to leaving his car outside the pub and walking across to where William Barnes' cleaner lived. Hammond rang the doorbell and looked up towards where Barnes lived four doors away, wondering how the man was faring following his shock earlier that week. The door was opened by a serious looking woman in her mid thirties. She looked enquiringly at Hammond as he introduced himself.

"Mrs Taylor?" he waited for her confirmation before continuing, showing his Id card holding it at shoulder level. "My name is Detective Inspector Hammond from the Major Crimes Unit. I would like to talk with your son Thomas, I have been told he could help me."

Her look was anxious, she stood in the doorway, uncertain whether to invite him in. Seeing her look so concerned, Hammond made an effort to smile with reassurance.

"He is not very well at the moment, perhaps you could talk to him another time."

Hammond promised her he wouldn't take up too much of their time, perhaps he could come into the house and talk with her first, just to explain his visit. Reluctantly she obliged by allowing him to enter. She took Hammond into a small living room to the side of the hallway. The sofa had been placed with its back to the bay window, various electrical leads from a Play-station console snaked on the carpet toward a large television that occupied most of the south facing wall. Mrs Taylor offered to call Thomas to come downstairs, but Hammond shook his head, he would like to talk to her first. She sat down on the edge of the sofa, without inviting him to do the same, so he stood looking down at her, trying to appear friendly.

"I understand from Mr Barnes, your neighbour, that Thomas enjoys BMX bike riding in the woods behind Sandling Road."

"Yes. He is a very sporty boy."

"Was Thomas riding his bike at the weekend?"

"I think so, he spent most of Saturday with his friends, I was working on Sunday, I clean at the nursing home down Bartholomew Lane, He usually goes out with his friends from school or stays here attached to the play-station." She affected a laugh as if to say, you know what young boys are like.

Hammond smiled sharing the joke with her. "I understand there is a regular gathering of BMX enthusiasts in the woods other than your son. Do you know the names of Thomas' friends?"

She didn't. Hammond changed tack and focused his attention on the framed photographs displayed on the window ledge. A boy, presumably Thomas, was beaming with pride as he held up a gold medal hung around his neck. He was dressed in karate gear and looked about ten years of age. Another photograph showed Mrs Taylor and her son with their arms raised, their faces sharing similar expressions of excitement as they rode a rollercoaster. Hammond emitted a small chuckle. Several years ago, on Paul's eighth birthday, he and Lyn had accompanied Paul on a rollercoaster ride during a visit to Legoland. Hammond remembered the day vividly. It had been in summer and Lyn had worn her favourite strapless yellow summer dress. When they had gone to collect their memento photos of the ride, Lyn had adamantly refused to buy it as she thought her arms had looked fat.

Mrs Taylor watched as she saw Hammond bend to look at the pictures. She noticed the smile that played around his mouth and was complimented on his interest. "Thomas has always been a bit of a thrill seeker. He had just won the Open Junior Karate Championship when that photo was taken. It was a great day."

"What grade is he?" Hammond asked the question with genuine interest.

"He had a green belt when the photograph was taken, but he has since been upgraded to Purple."

Even though Hammond was ignorant in the grading of Karate, it sounded impressive and he said so to Mrs Taylor, congratulating her on her son's success. She seemed more relaxed and he used the opportunity to his advantage. "You said Thomas has been feeling unwell, I expect there are lots of bugs going round this time of year." He turned his body away from her indicating he would like to continue his interview with Thomas. She stood up, believing his latter question to be out of polite concern and walked toward the living room door.

"I am not sure what is wrong with him. When I returned home from work on Sunday afternoon he was a little off colour. He has no appetite, just picks at food. I kept him here on Monday but he hated being at home all day on his own. Unfortunately, he is at that age where he refuses to see a doctor."

Hammond laughed as if to say he understood what that was like. She responded in kind and then ascended the stairs calling Thomas. He heard her explaining his visit. After a few minutes, she looked down at Hammond and offered to introduce him to Thomas.

Hammond followed her direction to a room she identified as her son's and entered, purposely leaving the door open. The room was a typical boy's bedroom with a single bed placed under the window, a wardrobe, with its doors hanging slightly off centre. Clean laundry was stacked on top of sports magazines and books. The walls were painted a dark blue making the room feel small and cramped. Hammond recognised the boy from the photographs. He was sitting on a swivel chair kicking his legs that caused the chair to swing from side to side. His fingers flicked with deft speed on the controls of a hand held games console. He was aware of Hammond standing there but was shy and avoided Hammond's gaze.

"How old are you Thomas?" Hammond sat on the bed, leaning forward with his arms resting on his lap, his fingers interlocked.

"Twelve".

"Really? You look older." Hammond hoped that his words would be taken as a compliment. They were. Thomas swung the chair around to face his visitor.

"Do you practise at the bike track in the woods?"

"Yes, I go there as much as I can. I want to be a professional BMX stuntman when I am older. I can do the Barspin, and an Endo, but I still need to practise on my handlebar rides, I have to stop putting my foot down too early."

Hammond made a encouraging noise, guessing the Bar-spin and Endo were BMX tricks. He attempted to guide the conversation towards Thomas's friends. Thomas was now in full stride, he was enjoying impressing a policeman with his skills. He told Hammond that he was involved with a group of boys who were practising for a future Freestyle Competition. He had spent Saturday and Sunday with them, practising in the woods. Hammond was given the names of other boys and wrote them in his notebook. They were older than him, Thomas explained with pride, it wasn't usual for a less experienced boy to be accepted into such an accomplished group. Hammond was pleased with the information Thomas had offered him. He took out the portrait from his pocket and asked Thomas to have a look at the man in the picture, did he recognise him?

Thomas looked down at the sketch of Graham Roberts, and looked away quickly. Hammond noticed Thomas' body tense. The boys demeanour had changed.

"Thomas, I need to know if you have seen him in the woods. We have had several witnesses who have told us this man was involved with building the tracks."
"No, I have never seen him before."
Hammond thanked Thomas for his help and congratulated the boy on his sporting achievements. Thomas smiled weakly in return. On his way back to the front door, Thomas proudly showed Hammond his bike that was housed in the utility room. It was obviously Thomas' pride and joy, having been lovingly maintained. Hammond left with a cheery wave to Mrs Taylor, but once she had closed the front door after him, he sighed heavily. He knew Thomas had lied and it disturbed him.

The next hour was spent with Hammond wandering aimlessly in the supermarket aisles. He was agitated to discover that his usual groceries had been moved to accommodate the Christmas specialties. Instead of finding tomato soup, he found luxury cranberry stuffing mix and Swedish ginger thins instead of his favoured chocolate digestives. He eventually resolved to throwing items in his trolley regardless whether he had use for them. Despite finding bare cupboards infuriating when he was hungry, grocery shopping always seemed like a waste of time. It was Hammonds turn to make dinner for himself and Jenny tonight but he couldn't remember whether Jenny was still a vegetarian or had advanced to vegan. He had to remind himself what vegans could or couldn't eat and wondered whether it was the same as a coeliac diet. Trying to read ingredient labels listed in tiny print proved futile so he resolved to grabbing anything that resembled a vegetable and joined the queue that lead in a orderly fashion down the frozen food aisle.

By the time he had paid and packed the shopping, it was dark. The temperature had dropped dramatically within the last hour and warned that snow was on its way. The car's digital display flashed repeatedly with the warning of possible ice and he asked the car what was the point of cautioning him unless it was going to suggest an alternative way of taking him to his door.

He drove homeward bound, thinking of Thomas and his meeting with Beech tomorrow morning. Earlier Hammond had been pleased that the investigation was making such progress but now he was burdened at the thought that his only suspect so far was a twelve year old boy. He turned into his road and was surprised to see that the Camper van he had mocked that morning was parked on his neighbour's lawn. His usual parking space outside his house had been cordoned off with tape and traffic cones on which a large printed sign was stuck; *"Parking Place Reserved for Mr Hugh Jarse."*

CHAPTER EIGHT

Detective Superintendent Beech was not in the best of moods and it was evident that Hammond was the cause of his distemper. The newspaper that he had thrown onto the desk in front of Hammond offered an explanation. *"Local Man's Killer On The Loose"*. The headline was ridiculous but effective in selling the newspapers, and equally effective in creating panic amongst the small community. Hammond read the front page article with a raised eyebrow, and occasionally scoffed to himself as he read the quotes from local villagers who were apparently concerned they could be the next victims found in the woods. He knew that there would be less interest had the body not have been found so close to Christmas.

"You do realise Wallace, that you have put me in an awkward position?"

Hammond agreed. It was ironic he mused aloud, that he had considered updating the media of their investigation. Beech stood in front of Hammond, looking down at his subordinate with an expression Hammond found difficult to interpret. Eventually Beech sat down in the opposite chair and listened as Hammond debriefed him of the previous days' activities.

"Why didn't you take DS Dunn to the boys house with you? She could have gained their trust, possibly more than you did."

Hammond decided to ignore the question. He knew that Beech would not have understood Hammond's decision to go alone. Hammond's original intention the previous evening was to check a potential witness but instead he had left the Taylor's house having marked Thomas as a plausible suspect. "DS Dunn will be accompanying me later Sir. I am going to check the kids that use the bike tracks, gather any surviving DNA samples and try to find a match it to the nail clipping found on Robert's clothing. I also want to let Forensics look at the boys' bikes. However, I haven't got a motive yet."

"Of course, there is the possibility that one of the kids witnessed the murder. If you are right about Thomas lying to you, perhaps he denied knowing Roberts through fear of discovery. Have you considered that?"

Hammond shrugged with his hands open on either side of him. "Yes, I have considered that possibility. Either way, I will need him to come in for questioning after checking the others."

Beech stretched his legs out in front of him, allowing his body to slump further into the seat of the chair. He looked at Hammond for several moments, considering the best course of action.

"Fine. What about the media?"

"First, I do not want it confirmed that this is a possible murder investigation. It's still possible that the intention was to cause fear to Roberts rather than his death, his attacker may not have realised that Robert's had a weak heart."

"Providing you can prove that there is a close temporal relationship between the attack and Robert's death it is murder, regardless of the perpetrator's intention, Wallace."

Hammond ignored Beech's exclamation that a beaten body was no accident and continued with his reasoning. "We need to get as much information on Roberts as possible. If we release his name, this will help, but we have to be careful. If there is even a sniff that Roberts was once questioned for possible child molestation, we would be opening a can of worms."

Beech nodded slowly before answering Hammond.

"Or it could provide us with a motive. There may be other kids who have had interest from our victim or Graham Roberts may have family members who can dispel the rumours. Either way, the investigation will benefit by appealing to the public. It's possible someone saw him travelling either by foot or bus to Saltwood, it would help to know if he was alone. However, I will answer any questions from the press. It has to be said Wallace, it is unlikely we can do a worse job than your earlier attempt."

Beech left after arranging a time with Hammond for the media briefing. Hammond smiled discreetly to himself as he dipped a chocolate biscuit in his morning coffee, all he would have to do is stand beside Beech looking official. Easy.

Hammond bit off the soggy end of his biscuit, wondering whether to phone his son Paul. He had enjoyed his evening with Jenny and had delighted in her ravenous appreciation of his homemade vegetable lasagne. He had been rather put out when she had rebuked him for using soya milk and cheese, so had questioned her vegetarian preferences. She had responded with her usual shrug and short explanation. "Been there, done that, missed the meat." He smiled as he thought of Jenny, there was no doubt that her presence at home made a pleasant change from eating microwave meals alone in front of the television. However, he was concerned. On several occasions he had seen Jenny lost in thought looking miserable. He picked up the phone and punched in Paul's number with one finger.

"Hey." Paul answered the phone on the first ring, Hammond was surprised and wondered aloud if perhaps Paul had been looking forward to hearing from him.

"No. I was waiting for a call from someone else."

Hammond apologised for the disappointment to his son but explained his predicament with Jenny. He still had no idea how long Jenny was going to stay. How could he help her if he didn't know what was wrong? Paul gave a long sigh at the other end of the telephone. Hammond imagined his son sitting with crossed legs on the sofa, probably still with his shoes on as he usually did despite frequent reprimands for doing so.

"I can't tell you what is wrong with Jen Dad. I promised her I wouldn't say anything."

"Is she in trouble? She's not pregnant is she? She has been eating a lot."

Paul's laughter bounced against Hammond's eardrum before his retort that pregnancy would be the last of Jenny's worries. The conversation drifted toward the subject of Paul's university studies on which he was evasive. Hammond was tempted to ask about Lyn, but knew that Paul's loyalty toward his mother meant he would not divulge any details. He was proud of his son's trustworthy attitude. He missed him and told Paul this, suggesting they meet nearer Christmas. Paul promised to keep in contact and hung up reminding his father that he was expecting another call.

Hammond looked at the wall clock and wondered if it was too early to call Kathleen, decided it wasn't but then replaced the receiver when Tom Edwards walked into the office."I'm about to go to the Grammar School. You want to come along?"

It was luck that Hammond remembered Thomas had given him names of the Folkestone pupils who shared his interest in BMX. He collected his jacket from where he had hung it on the back of the open door and followed Edwards. He had names, all he had to do was to put faces with them and hope that they would be helpful.

The school was only minutes away and it would have been pleasant to have walked the journey. Despite the icy temperatures the night before, the sun was breaking through the clouds making the morning frost sparkle on the wet grass. Dog walkers were out, their hoods pulled over the heads, hands shoved deep in their pockets, most walking briskly whilst their companions trotted beside them, their tails wagging. For a brief moment Hammond thought of William Barnes and Daisy and wondered if they had returned to the woods since their discovery. He thought it was unlikely and sympathised with the elderly man who obviously enjoyed his ramblings with his four legged friend. That could be me in thirty years time, he thought. No-one to share my life with apart from an animal who loves me just for feeding it.

"So, how shall we do this?" Edwards was leaning back in the seat. He had a remarkable ability to relax wherever he was.

"I took some notes last night. There are some names of pupils that go here, have a look if you like, then you are prepared." As Hammond stopped the car at the pedestrian crossing, he passed his notebook over to Edwards who started to thumb through the pages.

"Mark Callum? Is he one of the BMX kids?"

"No! It will be a few pages further up."

Hammond had answered so abruptly, that Edwards stopped turning the pages and looked at Hammond enquiringly. He wanted to ask Hammond if Mark Callum was a potential witness in Saltwood woods, but Hammonds' red face showed him it wasn't advisable. So instead Edwards left the notebook on his lap.

Samuel Lawson was a good looking boy with dark blonde hair swept across his forehead in a pop-star style. He was tall and broad shouldered like a swimmer. Hammond thought reflectively, that if he had looked like that at sixteen years of age, he would have spent most of his adolescence looking in the mirror. Samuel Lawson soon made it apparent he felt the same, his eyes kept wandering onto the door reflection behind Edwards as Hammond questioned him.

"How often do you practise in the woods?"

Lawson's gaze held Hammonds for a second before wandering back to his reflection for another check. "Dunno, most nights after school."

"Why Saltwood? There are woods in Folkestone."

This question was asked by Edwards who had pulled himself up to his full height. He felt Lawson should be reminded who was boss in this situation.

"Saltwood is not too close to home nor too far away either, plus, the ground has good rich soil."

Edwards looked confused, Hammond interjected "Why don't you want to practise nearer home?"

"I don't want anyone to see the competition."

This last comment sounded sarcastic as if Lawson had wanted to include "Dhur!" at the end of his explanation, but he had thought better of it.

"The soil? What has that got to do with it?"

Lawson focused his attention on Edwards whose face flushed.

"If you are going to build a track for BMXing, you need soil that is gritty so it has grip. We couldn't bring in crushed rock sand so that is important. The good thing about the woods in Saltwood is that it has everything to hand naturally; there are expressive obstacles already so it takes less to make a track. Since most of it is already there, it just needs to be exaggerated. Also, the track has to be regularly maintained."

It was obvious to Hammond that Lawson was passionate about this subject. Lawson motioned as if he were moulding the track with his hands.

"After a lot of use, there is settlement in the soil so it needs to be regularly re-dusted and compacted. If we used the woods in Folkestone, chances are that there will be too many people traipsing around the tracks, or taking over it. But Saltwood is quieter. As long as we don't make a nuisance of ourselves people tend to leave us alone."

Edwards twitched the corners of his mouth at Lawson as if thanking him for such a detailed answer, then he turned to Hammond and rolled his eyes in sarcasm. Hammond took over, he handed Lawson the artist sketch of Graham Roberts.

"We have witnesses who saw you with this man laying flexi-coil under the tracks in summer. I understand you saw him regularly at the woods?

Hammond was bluffing slightly. Lawson had not been identified by a witness. The youth looked at the portrait of Roberts and nodded.

"Yes, I knew him. Well, kind of. He used to follow us around like a kid at school wanting to be invited to play. My mate Danny thought he would like to help us build the drainage system so we asked him.." Samuel Lawson was interrupted by Hammond asking for Danny's full name. Hammond looked at his notebook then grunted as he found it, Danny Culver had been identified as a regular at the track by Thomas. Hammond nodded at Lawson, asking him to continue giving information on Graham Roberts.

"I saw him regularly, but not to talk to. He was a bit weird to be honest."

"Weird? In what way?" It occurred to Hammond that maybe Roberts had been simple, not mentally retarded in any way but extraordinarily innocent. It was possible.

"Well, like I said, he would just watch us all the time, or follow us around. Even if we ignored him."

"Did he speak to you?"

"No." Lawson stopped suddenly and looked at the two officers with renewed curiosity.

"Was he murdered? Is that why you are asking all these questions?"

Hammond decided to be honest, it was important that he came across as being mutually cooperative, especially now the press release was about to be updated.

"It looks that way." He said simply.

"Do you know of anyone who wished Mr Roberts harm, or had cause to do so?"

Samuel Lawson looked surprised by the question, but then his face changed as if he had just thought of something.

"Adam Schaffer. He couldn't stand him. Used to call him a freak. One time he pissed in a bottle and threw it at him."
Hammond checked his notes, Schaffer wasn't on the list. He looked at Lawson for more information.
"Where is Adam Schaffer now?"
Lawson laughed, tossing his hair like he was posing for L'Oreal. "You won't find him here. He left school years ago. Spends most of his time fishing at Hythe Canal."
Lawson wasn't able to give more information, he knew Shaffer more as an acquaintance having met the older man near the Castle Inn. Schaffer, he said, wasn't a BMX enthusiast; more of a getting pissed all the time enthusiast.

The two other boys interviewed by Hammond and Edwards were less helpful. Danny Culver remembered Roberts laying the flexi coil with himself and Samuel Lawson but couldn't offer any more information. Neither boy had been in the woods at the time questioned, or had anything more to add to Lawson's account. They did however, know Thomas and described him as "an annoying brat" who wouldn't leave them alone. Gavin Mason, a spotty thirteen year old, was indignant when Hammond referred to Thomas as being a friend of his.
"He is not my friend! He is so annoying, always showing us his stunts on his bike like we are going to be impressed. He hasn't even got a real BMX! Just some cheap ATB bike with pegs on the wheels."

Lois Dunn answered the call on the first ring.
"Dunn, how are you doing?"
Dunn replied that she wasn't doing too badly. So far, she said, she had been checking Graham Robert's family records, bank statements and employment history.

Hammond enquired if she was near a computer at the office, she replied that she was. "Can you do a check on an Adam Schaffer, possibly aged between eighteen to early twenties?" She said she would call him back.

Edwards looked at Hammond quietly, watching Hammond unpeel a Satsuma.

"So, dare I ask who Mark Callum is? You seemed a bit hot under the collar earlier when I mentioned his name."

It was with annoyance that Hammond wanted to tell Edwards to mind his own business, but now, following Kathleen's news on her Dad's deteriorating mental health, continuing the investigation into Mark Callum's death seemed pointless. He repeated to Edwards what he had told Dunn about Lloyd Harris' request, the investigation into Callum's death and the lack of information he had gathered so far. Tom Edwards listened. He was keen to know more and kept interrupting Hammond with questions. Eventually, Hammond finished his tale and allowed the sound of Edwards slurping the remnants of his canned drink to fill the silence.

"How trustworthy is this Kathleen?"

The question surprised Hammond. He responded as such, wondering what relevance Kathleen's character had to do with Lloyd Harris's forwarded investigation.

"Admittedly, I am not an expert on knowing how a woman's mind works. However, it sounds like she is using her charms to get what she wants."

"Which is?"

"To stop your investigation."

Hammond sucked the juice out of his Satsuma segment and then chewed the pith slowly. He remarked that Kathleen had wanted him to stop the investigation because she knew it would be a waste of his time.

"Qui Bono?"

"What are you talking about?" Hammond was starting to think Edwards was being deliberately annoying.

"Who benefits, from the investigation being stopped?"

"Me, obviously."

"So she asked you to stop your own investigation simply because she cares that an officer (whom she hasn't had any contact with for several years) might be wasting his time?" Edwards scoffed and squashed his can with both hands.

"She asked me to stop because she knew it was a waste of time, and perhaps she didn't want her Father to be humiliated."

"Her father has Alzheimer's. Would he know if he was being humiliated? Maybe now he would, but later, he won't remember. What I don't understand is what makes a man who knows he will soon lose his mental faculties call an ex-colleague for help with a case? Why now?"

Hammond didn't reply, he was wondering what Edwards was thinking and wished he would just come out and say it.

"Why now?" Edwards repeated and then answered his own question. "He calls you because he knows he won't be fit enough to continue the investigation himself. He trusts you to do as he asks, out of respect for a man who spent his whole career seeking truth. Harris hasn't forgotten his vocation despite his illness. That should at least tell you that it is worth trusting his instinct to investigate, like he trusted you to carry out his wishes."

Hammond listened to Tom Edwards. Begrudgingly, he admitted that his companion was making sense. He was surprised by Edward's almost compassionate support for Harris whom he had never met. His thoughts were interrupted when his mobile phone rang, he held up a finger to indicate to Edwards to wait whilst he wrote down the address and information Dunn was giving him from the office. After several minutes, Hammond finished scribbling in his notebook, thanked Dunn and ended the call.

"We have an address. He lives in Sandgate." The car left its parking space in the lay-by and headed westerly towards Adam Schaffer's house.

Adam Schaffer had no objection in telling the two officers at his door exactly what he had thought of Graham Roberts. He described the man in the picture Edwards showed him as a "freak" finishing his sentence by spitting on the portrait, narrowly missing Edwards hand who scowled in disgust. Hammond was interested in knowing why. Schaffer looked at Hammond and evaded the question.

"I've just realised why you are working for the pigs, it's 'cos your name's Hammond...get it?" He revelled in his own joke, tossing his head back with an open mouth, displaying several silver fillings in his upper teeth. His breath smelt strongly of liquor. Hammond made an attempt to smile and repeated his question. He was cold standing in Schaffer's porch, but it was obvious the man had no intention of letting them in the house. The way Edwards was wrinkling his nose suggested it was preferable to have fresh air around him.

"Because that man was a pervert that's why."

Schaffer spoke loudly as he answered. Edwards asked him to elaborate, the man in the doorway obliged but answered his question looking at Hammond. "He used to hide in the bushes and watch people whilst having it away with himself." He waited for his audience to take the bait and ask for details but instead Hammond just stood silently, his notebook in his hand whilst Edwards made an attempt to keep his hands warm by rubbing them together.

"I used to work for the council. I was near the library, picking up litter, that sort of thing and THAT freak is there with his ..."

Hammond interrupted, he wanted Schaffer to stick to the facts. "You saw him masturbating?"

The younger man nodded and spat again, this time aiming towards Edwards feet.

"Did you confront him?"

"Yeah, I told him to get the hell away from me."

"But you saw him since that time?"

"Yeah, but he avoided me. I warned them other boys though, the ones at Saltwood that you talked about. I told them to stay out of his way."

Hammond noted this, he wondered why Samuel Lawson hadn't mentioned this earlier. Edwards spoke up. "Did you report Roberts?"

Schaffer admitted he had tried but hadn't been believed.

"You reported it to the Police?"

Schaffer shook his head and groped around in his trouser pocket before withdrawing a packet of cigarettes. He offered the open box to the officers. They both declined the offer and waited patiently whilst the cigarette was lit and Schaffer took a long drag. He exhaled the smoke into the air and watched it disappear. Then he turned back to Hammond. "No. I went into the council offices next to the Library. No offence boys, but I try to keep away from the pigs as much as possible."

Edwards smiled at this last comment, as if to say the feeling was mutual.

"Graham Roberts was found dead in Saltwood Woods earlier this week. Where were you between Sunday and Monday morning?"

Schaffer laughed again causing Edwards to grimace with distaste at the smell that bellowed in his direction.

"I didn't kill him, if that is what you are thinking although I hate perverts. I can prove where I was though, if you want to waste your time checking it up. I was at my Mum's in Seabrook. I stayed there all weekend and returned home on Monday evening."

Hammond thanked Schaffer for his co-operation. Schaffer responded by slamming the door closed.

Detective Sergeant Lois Dunn was waiting with Galvin in the briefing room; she offered Hammond and Edwards's coffee as they walked into the room. Edwards accepted the drink gratefully wrapping his fingers around the mug and savouring the warmth. Hammond declined the coffee, preferring to get the meeting started. The four investigators compared notes on their morning's activities. Galvin had succeeded in interviewing the neighbours and tracing family members of Roberts. Dunn had completed a background search on their victim on the computer. Neither party had found anything to suggest Roberts was antisocial. He had been employed by the Council's environmental services for the last twenty years and had been described by his employer as being a valued and trustworthy employee. The neighbours had also had a good opinion of him. Family members had been traced. Roberts had a sister Eleanor whom he hadn't seen since she moved to The Lake District twelve years ago with her family. She was saddened by her brother's death but refused to travel to Kent to formally identify her brother's body, although the dental records and fingerprints were enough. The parents had died within the last five years. The team took a second to wonder what kind of relationship Roberts had had with his family, there was a suggestion that Eleanor and Graham Roberts were not close, Hammond wondered why. He suggested making a discreet enquiry as to their family background. Michael Galvin had searched Robert's home and found nothing to suggest a motive for his death. No evidence of child pornography had been found or anything to suggest that Roberts had an unhealthy interest in underage boys. Hammond was personally relieved, even though it made their hypothesis of a motive less plausible. It was significant that Robert's wallet had not been found at the house. This substantiated the theory of robbery although it was increasingly evident that the thief would not have been rewarded for his efforts. Dunn produced four bank statements that she wanted to share with them. The contents were worthy of investigation. There had been four separate withdrawals from a savings account within the last six months. One withdrawal was for £800 in cash. A later withdrawal six weeks later was for £250, the third transaction was for £400. The last, also in cash, was for £300. Although the amounts were not excessive, it was noticeable that these four transactions had been the only withdrawals in the eleven years since the account was opened. Before that, the only activity recorded on the account had been a monthly deposit of £150 paid on the first day of every month.

Tom Edwards looked up from the statements that Dunn had laid on the table. "You think Graham Roberts was being blackmailed?"

Hammond stood up from the table and arched his back. His muscles were still healing after their sudden employment from the run in the park a few days earlier."
It could be, but it is worth looking through any receipts we find in Graham Robert's house. Would you say he was an organised man from what you saw at his house? He turned to Michael Galvin as he asked his question who answered with a nod.

"Yes, everything was tidy so it is likely he was the kind of man to keep receipts."

"Fine, we'll have another look. The withdrawals could have a simple explanation. We'll consider the possibility that he was blackmailed when we have ruled out other possibilities. Perhaps check with the sister again, perhaps she was having money troubles and was loaning money from her brother. It would help if she could give us a photograph of Roberts also."

Lois Dunn volunteered to phone the sister later in the day.

They considered Adam Schaffer's story. His mother had confirmed that he had been staying with her at the weekend, helping to renovate her garden. Receipts from the local garden centre showed a bag of compost had been purchased during Sunday afternoon, the checkout girl remembered serving him and a check at Schaffer's mother's property showed evidence of recent work in the garden. It was enough to eliminate him as a suspect. Schaffer had been enraged when he saw Roberts masturbating in the bushes previously. The forensic results proved that the situation had been repeated; only this time, someone else caught him in the act. Hammond and Edwards had successfully managed to obtain non-intimate DNA samples and fingerprints from all the boys interviewed at the Grammar school. Their bikes were to be examined by forensic examiners who would visit the boys' homes later that day. Within the next 36 hours the forensic results would confirm any matches to the nail fragment found on Graham Robert's body. Until they received the results, there wasn't much else to do other than focus on Robert's financial records and find an explanation for the cash withdrawals.

Hammond poured himself a coffee before venturing to his office. He closed the door and dialled Kathleen Di Marco's number.

It was with relief that Hammond walked through his front door later that afternoon. He was looking forward to relaxing in front of the television and allowing his mind to be occupied with other people's fictitious dramas for a change. His shoes were kicked off into their usual place near the door, the door keys slipped into his trouser pocket and the coat was shoved onto the mound of forgotten items on the coat hook. As he headed toward the kitchen, he was greeted by the smell of warmed vanilla. He breathed it in with rapture. It was a long time since he had smelt baking in the house. For a second his mind allowed him the fantastical thought that maybe Lyn had regretted the divorce and was back home, making a cake to celebrate their reunion. He opened the door and stopped in his tracks surprised to see an elderly woman he didn't recognise taking a baking tray out of his oven. Unsure how to react he looked for Jenny and was relieved to see her entering the back door carrying tupper-ware boxes which she heaped onto the kitchen table. She noticed Hammond's look of confusion and approached the woman by tapping her on the shoulder to get her attention. Jenny gestured to the woman by closing her right hand leaving the index and middle fingers visible as she placed them on her forehead before turning her hand so that the half-closed palm was visible at shoulder level in front of her, then she pointed to Hammond and spelt letters with her hands. The woman smiled and nodded at Hammond who stood in the doorway incredulously as he watched the two women communicate in silence. The woman raised her own hand and fluttered her fingers against her nose. Jenny signalled back and the two women laughed at their private joke. Jenny turned to Hammond and eased him out of his confusion.

"Mary wants to know how old you are; I told her you were too old to be her son, but young enough to be her toy-boy."

Hammond smiled awkwardly. He pointed to the biscuits cooling on the wire rack and rubbed his tummy in circular motions in an attempt to demonstrate his approval. Mary placed her fingertips on her chin and moved her hand away from her as a thank you. Then she turned back to Jenny and made rapid gestures, smiling with twinkling eyes. Jenny looked up at Hammond with a look of resignation.

"Mary is surprised you don't recognise her, you have been next door neighbours for over ten years".

This information was a surprise to Hammond, who instantly felt ashamed under Jenny's gaze. His hand reached for a biscuit as he considered what excuse he could give, but Jenny was not easily fooled.

"The biscuits are for the Christmas fair, not for your stomach." Hammond took one anyway and moved around the kitchen unsure what to do or where to stand as Jenny bustled about arranging the food containers. Feeling Hammond watching her she turned around and ushered him away with her hand. "Ok, go now. Leave us in peace." She practically pushed him out of the kitchen and shut the door ignoring his look of bewilderment. Hammond had no idea what had just happened. He shook his head in confusion and muttered to himself about the complexities of the female species before heading to the living room and the television.

It was after 7pm when Hammond's boredom threatened to make him irritable. He fancied another biscuit but didn't want to enter the kitchen in case he was scolded by the female who had taken over his house. It puzzled him how such a petite slip of a girl like Jenny could create so much chaos. He looked out the window and contemplated going to the Fish and Chip shop a mile away but was interrupted in his deliberations by the phone ringing. He answered it grateful for the distraction. "Wallace, that you?" The voice was impatient at the other end.

"Lloyd. I wasn't sure whether to call you or not." Hammond wasn't sure how to relate to his old friend now he knew the man was suffering from the early symptoms of Alzheimer's. It felt as if the man he thought he had known had been replaced by an imposter. Hammond knew this feeling was irrational and unfair but he couldn't trust that Lloyd was contacting him whilst being in his right mind.

"Why not? I was expecting you to call me. How is the investigation going?"

Hammond ran his fingers through his hair as he thought how to answer, he wasn't sure how truthful he could be. He explained he had been preoccupied with another case. He allowed the unsaid to remain hanging in the silence before Harris plunged in

"You've found nothing?"

"No. I looked Lloyd. I am sorry, all I found were a few.." he searched for the appropriate word "..oddities, but I haven't found a shred of evidence that would justify reviewing Mark Callum's death or any of the others. Even if they had consulted advice on how to guarantee their deaths, they died by their own hands. There is nothing to investigate." There was a splutter of agitation; Hammond was asked what efforts he had taken to prove Harris wrong.

"To be fair Lloyd, you didn't give me anything to go on. I checked all the names on the list, the information is limited, despite checking police databases. There are no friends or family to talk to for any of them, if there are, they have chosen not to be forthcoming with any relevant information." Hammond was interrupted sharply by Harris who was now playing the role of a head-teacher scolding a naughty child.

"But I gave you all the information you needed to get you going! Wallace, I thought you were a better detective than this!"

Hammond quietly counted to ten. He was tempted to let Lloyd know that his Alzheimer's diagnoses wasn't a secret and suggesting that his mind was playing tricks on him, but instead of losing his temper he reminded Lloyd that no information had been given to him. There was a prolonged moment of silence for a while before Harris asked Hammond to make sure. Hammond thought back to their meeting at the Golf club. Harris had not provided any enlightening information other than the small crumbled list of names, he said so.

"In that case, I apologise Wallace. Can you come here? I will give you everything I have."

Now he was in two minds how to respond, Hammond wanted to use the excuse of being too occupied with the investigation into Graham Robert's murder. It was true that his time was limited. Instead, he let his conscience do the talking and allowed himself to be persuaded into collecting any further research Harris had collected. It would be easier to wait until the following evening he suggested, since he was due to pick up Kathleen at that time. There was no reply for several seconds and Hammond realised too late that Lloyd Harris was unaware that his daughter and Hammond had been in contact, but the older man hid his surprise and accepted Hammond's idea graciously before ending the call.

As Hammond replaced the receiver, he discovered his hand was shaking slightly. His body was buzzing with nervous energy. Lloyd Harris had sounded perfectly rational on the phone. He had been impatient and persistent, slightly more forceful than Hammond had ever know him to be, but he would never have guessed that Harris's mental health was failing. He remembered what Tom Edwards had said earlier that morning. Harris certainly was persistent with this investigation, there must be a reason for it other than a dogged mind. He looked toward the kitchen door and wondered again what Jenny was doing in there. He hadn't seen anyone leave the kitchen and the smells that wafted down the hall into the living room were sending his senses into overdrive. The phone was picked up again as Hammond's stomach ordered an Indian take-away curry to be delivered to his door.

"The lesser good, our own or that of others,
is merged in a larger good, and that cannot
be without some rendering of the heart."
Henry Havelock Ellis. The Dance of Life.1923

CHAPTER NINE

The car inched its way to Folkestone with Hammond muttering words of encouragement to get it through the snow. His hands were fixed onto the driving wheel, his head bent low as he peered through the flashing windscreen wipers that couldn't clear the large flakes from his window quick enough. The rear brake lights of the cars in front were a constant warning that his journey would be no more than a slow crawl. Grumbling to himself in frustration Hammond contemplated leaving the car and walking to work. He phoned the office and listened to the phone ring unanswered before it was re-directed to switchboard. The unusual wait for the phone to be picked up made him wonder aloud where Dunn, Edwards and Galvin were and hoped they would reach the headquarters safely. The car in front, frustrated by the wait, tried to reverse and turn around. It was a futile attempt, the snow was laying so thick that the wheels couldn't grip and just spun as the car coasted too close for Hammond's liking.

For the third time that morning he checked his mobile phone and contemplated whether to phone Kathleen and cancel their meeting that evening. It had not been his intention to take her to dinner but he had been so surprised, and he admitted to himself, flattered, that he had found himself agreeing to her suggestion with enthusiasm. Now, he wasn't so sure. He didn't have any decent trousers to wear. His black trousers (usually reserved for weddings or funerals) would be too tight. Even if he eat a minimum amount, the skin under the waistband would pinch from the inevitable bloating. He contemplated his current attire that didn't differ much to any other day. Navy corduroys, a plain white shirt and navy tie under a matching jacket was his usual dress, for his expanding waistline limited his choices nowadays. Clothed with comfort in mind with a tie for a professional finish. His quick glance in the side mirror reminded him he needed a haircut.

He checked the clock display and switched on the radio to listen to the hourly local news. Snow had covered most of the South East causing disruptions to all public transport and roads, schools had been closed. Emergency services were advising people to stay at home. Hammond grunted. It never ceased to amaze him how quickly the country ground to a stop at the slightest provocation from Mother Nature. He wondered how Paul was and hoped that London wasn't affected by snow. Paul wouldn't attempt to drive in such weather. He wished the journey to work would be worth the trouble. If he was lucky, murder and mayhem would also slow to a stop and let him leave work early.

When Hammond reached his desk almost two hours later, he was pleasantly surprised to see an A4 envelope from Forensics waiting for him on his desk. The contents were enlarged photographs of bike pedals. The accompanying note had been sent from the forensics team explaining that the pedals on the bikes searched had not matched the patterned bruise found on Graham Robert's thigh. He laid the photographs on the table examining them closely. The pictures had been taken from the bikes belonging to the three boys questioned by himself and DC Tom Edwards the previous day. All the pedals had smooth edges. He sighed with disappointment and left the office to get himself a coffee. Edwards had arrived, he was shaking his head free from the melted flakes that ran down the back of his neck. His hair looked thinner when it was wet and was a reminder of his middle age. He looked up as Hammond approached him from the corridor and joined him on his walk towards the coffee machine. As they walked, Hammond told him about the photographs from Forensics.

"Ah well, it was worth a shot. Just because Roberts had a bruise on his leg from a bike pedal doesn't mean he was attacked by a cyclist."

Hammond agreed, he realised that he had automatically assumed there had only been the one assailant. It was possible that the bike had knocked Roberts accidently hours before the other injuries were incurred. He spoke these thoughts aloud to Edwards who spooned fresh ground coffee into the machine filter whilst listening to Hammond.

"It is unlikely the bruise was caused much earlier than the attack. If the bruising on Robert's thigh was caused by impact from the bike pedal, the blood vessels didn't have a chance to bleed before the heart stopped. Surely that suggests it had just happened?"

Edwards wasn't a eloquent speaker but often the content of his speeches were relevant.

Hammond nodded. "I thought that each bruise is individual, some take longer than others to appear." He hoped that the toxicology report would allow them a better idea of when the impact of the pedal had happened. The medical notes from Robert's G.P had confirmed Roberts had been prescribed a cocktail of medication including Beta-Blockers and Statins but Hammond was unsure whether these could delay the breakdown of haemoglobin which in turn would affect the time scale of a bruise appearing. He vaguely remembered a case he had investigated years ago on a suspicious death. The victim's body was badly bruised and it was suspected that they had suffered a beating contributing to their death. It was later discovered that the time of the suspected attack had been complicated by the victim having taken anti-malaria medication. The consequences were that alibi's given for the victim's attack were given for the wrong time and therefore invalid. It had caused weeks of delays and frustrations before it was discovered the victim's injuries had been incurred hours before his death. Hammond knew that Aspirin could have some influence on the formation of bruises because it was an anticoagulant, but he wouldn't know for sure that Roberts had taken Aspirin until they got the toxicology results. Either way, the bruise on Roberts thigh was relevant because even if it was caused by an innocent party, it meant there were potential witnesses in the woods during the time when Roberts died.

Edwards took a gulp of his coffee and suggested Dr Henderson could help. Hammond hoped that he would volunteer to speak to the coroner but he didn't, instead he told Hammond that DS Dunn was delayed because her car was stuck in snow and Galvin's wife was having pregnancy complications so he was taking her to the doctor before making his way to headquarters.

Hammond was disappointed, he had hoped to discuss any further information Dunn had gathered on Robert's financial status. He ushered Edwards into his office to discuss the pedal comparisons. Each photograph showed what looked like ordinary bike pedals, He wondered aloud whether there was a way of identifying different pedals, but then he had an idea and grabbed the photographs before exiting the office leaving Edwards sitting alone in the office wondering what Hammond was thinking.

It took Hammond ten minutes to identify the police officer whose bicycle was parked in the lobby of the headquarters every day regardless of the weather outside. Constable Mike Andrews was happy to look at the photographs Hammond produced before he started his shift.

"These are platform pedals, typical for the BMX or mountain bikes. They are used to enable the foot to be positioned freely which rests the joints. However, stunt bikers prefer them because they allow the foot to be removed instantly."

A thought struck Hammond suddenly. "If a rider wanted to avoid putting his foot down too much. What pedal would be used then?"

Andrews looked up from the photos. "Not these, you'd probably go for a clip-less pedal. They are usually used with a cycling shoe that has a cleat fitted to the sole, so you'd snap your foot into place on the pedal and it will stay there even in the roughest terrain making it easier to jump over obstacles. Then perform a quick side rotation to release the connection when you wanted to put your foot down." Hammond thanked him and waited for the photographs to be returned. Constable Andrews pointed to the top photograph. "That one's not cheap, you've got a dedicated BMX cyclist owning this! Do they build the bikes themselves?"

Hammond replied he didn't know as he turned to leave, before curiosity got the better of him and he asked how expensive the pedal was.

"Those are made of magnesium with light titanium axles, probably about a hundred quid. It doesn't sound much, but if they're building their own bike, I reckon it's going to be worth a small fortune by the time they've included all the best components."

It was doubtful that any of the boys questioned by himself and Edwards the previous morning had used Clip-less pedals, a young cyclist probably wouldn't bother to change shoes before and after using the tracks, or be able to afford such sophisticated equipment. However, the photographs taken of the bikes owed by Samuel Lawson, Danny Culver and Gavin Mason showed that one of the three boys had expensive taste. Hammond ran his fingers through his hair as if giving his thoughts space to develop. Samuel Lawson and Danny Culver were training for the freestyle competition, there was a chance they were sponsored competitors, in which case their expenses may be shared. Hammond sighed as he dismissed this latter thought. His priority was to identify the bike that had bruised Graham Roberts. So far the information he had gained had been irrelevant. Instead of identifying the type of pedal that had impacted against Roberts, he had eliminated Lawson, Culver and

Mason from being around at the time of the attack on Roberts. A thought struck him. Gavin Mason had mocked Thomas Taylor's bike as being a cheaper imitation of a BMX bike. He quickly retraced his steps to where he had spoken to Andrews and found him heading outside to the car park with a colleague, He called to them to wait whilst he sprinted across the heaped snow ignoring the look of annoyance that crossed the constables' features.

"What would the cheaper alternative be? If a ATM bike was used instead of a BMX?"

Andrews looked perplexed for a moment. "It depends on whether they modify their bike by using BMX components, but if the bike isn't adapted in any way, I would guess a platform pedal, although cage style pedals are used on the cheaper designs because they are economical for the manufacturer."

"Would they work in the same way as a clip-less pedal?"

"Only by making it more difficult to put your foot down quickly. To be honest, cage style pedals are no good for free-styling, they offer less grip than a platform pedal and can cause nasty injuries to the rider if they stop short and lose their footing."

Andrews turned away impatiently and continued his conversation with his colleague as Hammond ventured his way back toward the office where he had left Tom Edwards. He wished he could remember the bike that Thomas had shown him but it had been his intention to question a possible witness rather than look for evidence at the time of his interview with the boy. Hammond sighed heavily, he was angry at his stupidity for visiting Thomas alone, he should have taken Dunn with him.

When he had returned upstairs Hammond saw that Dunn and Galvin had arrived. Galvin looked tired after an evident lack of sleep. Hammond poured him a fresh coffee and handed it to his younger colleague with an understanding slap on the shoulder. He didn't enquire after Galvin's wife, but hoped that Galvin's presence was confirmation of her recovery.

Edwards had discussed the photographs of the bike pedals to the others. They were interested but unsure whether to draw any conclusions until the full forensics report had been completed, it will take longer for any trace evidence to be processed. Hammond found it easier to contribute to the conversation now he had the information provided by Constable Andrews. With refreshed enthusiasm he directed their attention to the computer in the office where he headed an internet search for cage style pedals. It wasn't an easy task but eventually he found what he was looking for. He printed the page off and laid it on the table. They were all silent for several seconds as they compared the autopsy photograph with the image before them. Hammond drew a large question mark under the image before faxing it to Ed Henderson. Whilst they waited for the coroner's reply, Dunn discussed her earlier conversation with Eleanor, Graham Roberts' sister.

"She was adamant that she had not loaned any money from her brother and could not offer an explanation as to why he had made the withdrawals. I got the impression that she didn't take much interest in her brother, she hadn't had much contact with him apart from phoning him on his birthday or at Christmas."

"Did you find any receipts?"

Galvin replied quickly, "I am going to look at the house again, the receipts I have found so far are for electrical goods and the usual household appliances, but none have accounted for the large withdrawals."

Hammond nodded. "We are going to keep looking. It is worth checking his post to see if any invoices arrive."

It took half an hour before they received a reply from Henderson. The conversation that took place between Galvin and the coroner was brief. Galvin replaced the receiver and turned to Hammond. The news was encouraging. The cage pedal had been identified as the pedal that had struck Robert's leg. Now they were one step closer to identifying the bike owner. It didn't mean the person was guilty of assault, but it did mean that they had found a witness whom had been near Graham Roberts at the time of his assault. Hammond dialled the number of the forensic team. It was necessary to look at Thomas Taylor's bike.

Detective Superintendant Beech looked slimmer in his uniform; he sat at the table, leaning towards the microphone as he waited for the hubbub in the room to die down. Hammond felt less self-conscious sitting next to Beech but hoped that the media briefing would be short. Beech welcomed the reporters and photographers warmly, thanking them for attending and apologising for the lapse of judgement in not giving out more detail earlier. Hammond felt his ears burn.

Beech confirmed that Graham Roberts was the man who had died in Saltwood woods following an assault, but was interrupted by a reporter Hammond didn't recognise. "How can you reassure our readers that they are safe?"

Beech smiled, reassuringly. "I am confident that my colleagues will be treating this case with the utmost proficiency. They are dedicated to finding out the circumstances of Mr Roberts' death. I assure your readers and members of the public that the person or people responsible will be apprehended very soon."

"Have you made any arrests?"

"There are people currently helping us with our enquiries."

There were groans from around the room as the media members made it obvious they wanted more. Beech held up his hand and added "I promise to keep you informed of any arrests that we make, but in the meantime, we welcome the public to bring to our attention any information on Mr Roberts that they believe will be of help."

Hammond couldn't believe his ears. A knot formed in his stomach. When the room had cleared, he turned to Beech. "How could you promise that? If my suspicions are correct we may be looking at a child being exposed to public scrutiny."

Beech looked at Hammond with a stance of superiority. "Well, bring him in for questioning and see if you're right. Either way, the media will find out eventually and it is better to look as if we are being as co-operative as possible. Wallace, you do your job, I'll do mine."

The roads had been cleared of snow during the day but DC Michael Galvin drove slowly. Hammond sat in the passenger seat feeling an inexplicable nervousness. From the moment he had received the call from the forensic team he had dreaded reaching the Taylor's house but at the same time hoped that Thomas had returned from school. He checked his watch, it was 3.30pm, the school had finished half an hour earlier. The sooner the boy was brought in for questioning and his bike properly examined, the sooner the loose ends could be tied. For several moments, Hammond tried to think of Paul as he had been at twelve years but then forced himself to stop. He had instructed the car to arrive outside the house quietly, with the intention of being as discreet as possible, but, seeing there were no parking spaces, they were forced to double park outside the house. A uniformed officer accompanied Hammond to the front door whilst Galvin crept toward the back garden in case Thomas attempted to exit out the back door.

Mrs Taylor opened the door looking alarmed. She had obviously seen the car draw up outside the house. She ushered them into the hallway and quickly shut the door behind them. She knew from Hammond's face that he was here on official business and it scared her into submission, her teeth bit down on her fist as she struggled to understand what the uniformed officer was telling her. Thomas appeared from the kitchen and saw Hammond. He started to smile a greeting but then stopped seeing his Mother's fearful reaction. His eyes flicked from his mother to Hammond and then he started to run back into the kitchen. Mrs Taylor yelled his name, she was crying now, but Hammond ignored her attempts to call her son back. He moved quickly toward the kitchen door, slipping on the lino floor as he ventured his way around the door toward the back entrance that lead into the garden. He shouted for Galvin but couldn't see him. Thomas was at the far end of the garden, piling up garden rubbish in a crude attempt to make a step enabling him to climb over the fence. He looked around as Hammond approached him with the police officer close behind. Thomas' nose was running. His eyes large with panic. Hammond slowed to a stop, holding his arm out for the officer to do the same. The two men stood there, waiting as Thomas decided what to do. Not wanting to scare the boy, Hammond spoke quietly to Thomas, explaining that they only wanted to talk to him. He was distracted momentarily by the sound of the garden gate being forced open. Then Galvin stood there as he assessed the scene before him. But now, Thomas was crowded and he wriggled over the fence into the next door neighbour's garden. Hammond ran to the fence, attempting to jump over it, but his arms couldn't support his weight enough to heave himself up. He called to the police officer to pursue Thomas over the fence and exited with Galvin through the gate. They were now by the front of the house, running down New Road after Thomas who kept looking over his shoulder at his pursuers. By now Mrs Taylor had followed them out the side gate, she was shouting for her son to be left alone, but Hammond didn't stop. He needed to talk to Thomas, if only to reassure him. Thomas veered off to the left at the end of the road, he ran alongside the main road before seizing the opportunity to run through a gap in the traffic to get to the other side. Hammond chased, his lungs were now bursting, but he couldn't stop, he ran on the path opposite where Thomas had crossed, the slamming of his feet against the pavement made a thudding sound that filled his head, muffling the noises of chattering school children waiting at the bus stop for their ride home. Hammond looked across to where he had last seen Thomas, wanting to get across the road, but the school traffic was dense with distracted bus drivers and stressed parents wanting to get home before it became dark. He raised his hand to stop the oncoming cars as he attempted to run across but instead was met by angered horns. In the distance he heard a driver shout after him as a car swung around Hammond, not slowing, causing him to step back onto the pavement. Hammond looked over to where he had last seen Thomas, but the boy was now too far away to see. He looked to the right of him in desperation, persistently edging away from the pavement into the road. Eventually the uniformed officer stepped out into the oncoming traffic, forcing the cars to stop. Running to the junction on the other side, Hammond's eyes frantically searched left and right until he saw Thomas heading south down Bartholomew Lane about 200 meters away. A car screeched to a stop beside Hammond, Galvin shouted at him to get inside; he clumsily vaulted over the bonnet and crashed into the passenger seat as he yelled at Galvin to drive on. Thomas's legs were flashing stripes as he ran. By now he was so panicked, he lost all sense of caution and was dodging past oncoming cars as he overtook school children and dog walkers on the pavement. Galvin braked suddenly as he approached parked cars on the left, frustrated by the oncoming cars that refused to give way. He switched on the siren, the noise attracting attention from onlookers as they stopped what they were doing to watch the pursuit of Thomas sprinting southbound. Hammond swayed left and right bracing himself with his hands against the dashboard as Galvin sped after the boy. Hearing the sirens, Thomas turned and then lost his footing, he wobbled and fell sideways. His hands breaking his fall. Galvin pressed his foot hard on the brake to stop. Hammond exited the car. He walked over to where Thomas lay and bent down to the boy, covering him with his jacket and smoothed stray hairs from the boys face, trying his best to calm him.

Thomas eyes were red and swollen but he was no longer crying. He kept wiping his nose on the back of his hand, ignoring his mother who offered him a tissue that she had taken from the box placed beside them on the table. Hammond was doing his best to look relaxed, he was conscious of the video camera set up behind him recording the scene. DS Dunn was seated opposite to Thomas, she was asking the questions, she had a calm, almost melodic voice that made Hammond wonder if she had ever tried hypnosis on anyone.

"Thomas, do you understand why you are here?"

Thomas nodded his head, his eyes suspiciously darting from Hammond to Dunn, then his mother. The accompanying social worker sat quietly on the other side of Thomas but both officers were aware that the woman had sat forward in her seat. Hammond recognised the look of anguish in the boy's eyes as he shifted his body further away from his mother who sat still and quiet beside her son, overwhelmed by the situation she was finding herself in. "You should have protected me." The boy's eyes were screaming at his mother, it was evident she heard it, maybe not in sound, but through maternal empathy, for she winced and looked down at her hands. Mrs Taylor had been warned to be quiet throughout the interview unless any questions were directed at her. She had obeyed this instruction, but only after a warning that if she did not comply, the social worker would take her place.

"Thomas, you do not have to speak to us if you do not want to, but we are hoping you will help us to understand why you lied to Detective Inspector Hammond when you said you didn't recognise Mr Roberts."

Thomas looked up indignantly and questioned Dunn how did she know he had lied. His voice sounded small and weak, he wasn't a proud twelve year old anymore but a frightened boy who felt cornered.

"Thomas, we have spoken to the boys you claimed to have spent the weekend with. They denied being with you." Dunn ignored Thomas's answer that the boys had been lying, instead she continued to maintain eye contact with the boy in front of her.

"We know that Mr Roberts, the man in the picture Inspector Hammond showed you, used to watch the boys practise on their BMX bikes in the woods. We think he liked to watch you too. But at the weekend, you were on your own, weren't you Thomas? Perhaps you were practising your bike stunts so you could impress the boys when you next saw them, to stop them laughing at you maybe."

Thomas eyes widened at the last remark, his face flushed. His eyes flicked to Hammond who kept his face devoid of expression, just listening. Dunn continued, she leaned forward slightly, resting the back of her forearms on the table between them. "We have evidence that we think will prove you were with Mr Roberts at the weekend. It is only a matter of time before the Forensics team trace the evidence back to you. Why don't you tell us everything that happened? We just want to listen to you, Thomas. We don't want to trap you in any way. All we want is for you to tell us what happened at the weekend. You saw Mr Roberts in the woods, didn't you?"

Dunn spoke the last sentence as a fact, rather than a question. Thomas licked his lower lip. His forehead was perspiring; his hands were being wiped repeatedly on the lap of his trousers. Hammond waited, he felt that Thomas was about to break.

"Yes."

It wasn't much, but it was a start. Thomas asked for a drink, Hammond allowed Mrs Taylor to pour water from the dispenser and hand her son the filled paper cup. Thomas took it; he looked at his mother for a long time as he swallowed. It was as if he wanted to rid himself of the burden he had been carrying the last few days.

"I hurt him. Mr Roberts. I didn't mean to, but he was crying and kept asking me to understand, he told me I should feel sorry for him. I wanted him to shut up."

Hammond leaned forward. This was the information he had waited for, but now it was coming out of Thomas' lips, Hammond felt an inexplicable urge to tell him not to say anything further. Instead he took over the questioning.

"Why was Mr Roberts crying Thomas?"

"I caught him...doing things to himself. I didn't mean to, but I wanted to try the jump again so I went back along the track and saw him."

"What kind of things was he doing?"

Mrs Taylor stifled a sob, her hand was over her mouth as she began to realise what her son had been withholding from her. All the years of nurturing her son, trying to keep him safe, making him wear hats in winter, telling him to not lick the knife at mealtimes, and this one time he had needed her protection, she hadn't been there.

"He was having sex with himself."

"What did you do?"

"I tried to go away without him seeing me, but instead he smiled at me and asked me to go closer towards him. He was showing me his...bits...so I shouted at him to leave me alone. I left my bike there and ran away from him."

"What happened then?"

"I ran home, but I wanted to get my bike back. So after a while, I went back, he was there with my bike. When he saw I had come back, he said he would give me my bike if I did something for him first."

There was a long pause. Hammond felt sick to his stomach. He had to allow Thomas to give a spontaneous account, without stopping him recalling significant details freely. Despite his wish to prompt Thomas further, he knew that the boys account had to be said in his own words without any provocation.

"What did he ask you to do Thomas?"

"Touch him...you know...there." His hands pointed to his crotch.

"And did you?"

"No. No. I shouted at him, I called him names and tried to get my bike off him, but he held on and asked me to understand that he couldn't help it. That it wasn't his fault. He was crying like a baby."

"What did you do Thomas?" Hammond spoke very quietly and gently. He could feel Mrs Taylor's fear at what her son was about to divulge.

"I threw the bike back at him, and then I tried to get away but he kept coming towards me and begging me not to go. But I wanted to go away; I wanted him to leave me alone. I hit him."

"What did you hit him with?"

"The wood. There was wood on the ground so I used it to hit him."

It was past 10pm when Hammond left the station. The freezing air bit his face as he opened the door and stepped out where Mother Nature's hostility was waiting for him. The snow had been cleared and heaped on the sides of the main roads to allow the gritters to get through, his feet crunched their way on the rock salt that had been spread across the forecourt. He checked his mobile for any missed calls and considered phoning Paul. He needed to be told that arresting Thomas had been the right thing to do. As a police officer, yes, he had completed his duty, but as a man, as a father, he knew he had condemned a young man and his mother to an uncertain future and it gnawed at his conscience with sharp, unforgiving teeth. Only a week ago, he had been ordered to back down from an investigation into an arson attack on two boys, it wouldn't surprise him if the perpetrators would be offered a lighter sentence in exchange for giving information on the suspected drug trafficking they were involved with. In comparison, Thomas was not a cold blooded killer whom had taken pleasure in causing suffering but he would be answerable to his actions regardless of whether he believed he had acted in self defence. The injustice went against everything that Hammond believed in. It sickened him knowing that he was part of a game that ruled against the vulnerable.

Thomas was young yet he had defended himself with the rage of a grown man. This fact alone disturbed Hammond. Thomas's account did not support the claim of self defence; he gave no indication during his statement that he had been in fear for his life. Roberts hadn't threatened to harm Thomas; he had only tried persuasion which would have been escapable. Hammond believed that Thomas had felt fear when confronted by Graham Roberts, but what he couldn't understand was why the boy had not simply run away and reported the incident. There was no doubt he was proud, it was evident through his persistence in trying to impress the other BMX riders despite their rejection of him. Was it possible that Graham Roberts had been killed in an act of pride? To eliminate the possibility of others knowing about Thomas' humiliation? He wished he had more evidence to prove that Roberts had been a danger to children.

The thoughts in Hammonds mind were consuming and distracting him from his objective to getting to the shelter of his car quickly and escaping the cold. Would it have made a difference if Thomas had a father figure in his life? Hammond wondered. He quickened his pace across the car park, striding purposely, now considering the following day. Hammond knew that he would face the wrath of Beech in the morning; admittedly the arrest had been a shambles. It had attracted too much attention, Thomas's name would be withheld from the media, but it would only be a matter of time before people started gossiping.

His hands were pushed further up the sleeves of his coat as he unlocked his car, wishing he had brought gloves with him and reminded himself to bring them with him the following morning. His wrists ached from where he had stabbed at the computer keyboard with two opposing fingers, but at least the reports had been completed. He sat in the car, not wanting to go home. He needed distraction from his thoughts, perhaps he could see Kathleen tonight despite having cancelled their meeting earlier. He had been partly relieved that he had a good reason to cancel the dinner arrangement but felt ashamed at having disappointed her and Lloyd. He checked the digital display on the car dashboard and considered whether it was worth travelling to Charing where the Harris' lived but then he remembered Jenny was at home and turned the ignition. It would be better to accept Kathleen's gracious offer to wait until another day before meeting her.

He parked the car outside his house and smiled weakly when he saw Jenny seated on the porch step smoking. She looked at him through the fog of smoke and read from his face that he wasn't in the mood to talk. Instead she shuffled her body sideways, enabling his access through the front door. As he passed, Hammond placed a hand on the top of her head and bent to kiss her forehead lightly. "Thank you for not smoking inside the house." He said simply. She stood up, squashing the spent cigarette under her foot and followed him into the house, closing the door with a gentle kick.

"All arguments are meaningless until we gain personal experience."
Henry Havelock Ellis. The Dance of Life. 1923

CHAPTER TEN

Hammond's arm wormed out the bedclothes and fumbled their way across the top of the bedside table until his fingers grasped the mobile that had rung him awake.

"Where are you? Beech is on the warpath!" Dunn was obviously not pleased, Hammond forced his eyes to focus. The sun had intruded into his room through a crack in the curtains and warned him too late that he had overslept. He groaned and sat up in bed.

"I've overslept. I will be there soon."

He hung up and stumbled to the bathroom. He hoped the delay would give Beech a chance to calm down before he saw him, Dunn was good with words maybe she could use her hypnotic voice on his superior officer. A half hour later Hammond's car nosed its way past the melting snow heaps into the Head-quarters car park. The overtired Inspector ambled his way towards the building looking up at the office windows as he did so. There was a chance that Beech would not have seen him arrive, if so, this would allow him an opportunity to sneak in unnoticed.

Emma's face showed him he was in trouble, she held up two crossed fingers to wish him luck as he made his way toward Beech's office. The Detective Superintendant was talking on the phone as Hammond looked through the glass door. Beech signalled to him to come in, his face was red and blotchy. Not a good sign Hammond reckoned, he gingerly sat down on the chair in front of Beech's desk and waited until the telephone was returned to its cradle.

"Good Morning Wallace. How are you? I hope you feel rested?"

Surprisingly devoid of sarcasm, Beech's voice sounded pleasant but he didn't wait for Hammond to respond before coming around the desk and perched on it forcing Hammond to look up at him.

"I apologise for the delay Sir, I left a report from last night's questioning"

Beech nodded an acknowledgement seemingly interested. "I read it. I understand the boy confessed, yet you haven't submitted everything over to CPS."

"The evidence has to be confirmed. I want to go through the forensic reports first before they're notified."

"You have a confession. That should be enough to collaborate the evidence you have gathered so far. Why are you stalling?"

Hammond looked at Beech and without invitation, stood up from his chair and walked behind it, preferring to maintain eye contact from a mutual level.

"We only have evidence that the pedal that caused bruising on Robert's thigh was caused by a similar pedal to the pedals found on Thomas Taylor's bike. Thomas confessed to beating Roberts with a piece of wood. However, despite Forensics examining all the wood they found at the scene, no fingerprints or DNA has yet been identified, possibly from degradation."

"The log was taken from the scene?"

"Possibly, although evidence could have easily been contaminated by the bad weather. Wood splinters were found on Robert's clothing but they can't be matched to one particular piece of wood."

"So, what do you need?" Beech was impatient but willing to listen to Hammond.

Hammond's hands found their way to the warm comfort of his trousers pockets, he stood looking at Beech as he contemplated aloud.

"We still haven't found Robert's wallet. Thomas' bedroom was searched but we haven't found anything yet. The nail clipping is more than likely to be Thomas'; he had a torn nail on his right hand but it still needs to be compared with the DNA sample we took from him. Trace evidence on the pedal needs to be confirmed and I am waiting for the blood screening report. Hopefully we can identify the weapon, but most importantly, we haven't got a motive."

Beech scoffed and was about to interrupt Hammond by reminding him of Thomas's account in his confession but Hammond ploughed through. He had concerns about the case, despite believing Thomas was guilty of the attack on Roberts. Thomas hadn't mentioned covering Robert's body with the branches that were found lying across him when his body was discovered. It was important to identify who had done it because it showed that Roberts was either dying or already dead when someone attempted to hide him, in which case the attack wasn't as spontaneous as Thomas had led him to believe. Collecting enough wood and debris to cover a body took time and some rational thought. It wasn't the actions of someone who had hit out in panic and then run away. Either Thomas had since forgotten covering the body, which could be due to memory loss brought on by trauma or someone had approached Roberts following Thomas' attack whilst Roberts was still alive. Why did they not find Nitrates in Robert's pockets? Surely a patient with unstable Angina would carry Nitrates in case of an attack, yet none were found at the scene. If Roberts had been having an attack, and someone had removed the nitrates as he lay defenceless, that was undoubtedly an act of murderous intent, yet Thomas Taylor had not mentioned removing anything from Roberts, including his wallet and nothing was found at his home.

"There is a suggestion that Roberts had paedophilic tendencies. He was questioned in 2001 for exposing himself to a child and I doubt it is a coincidence that Adam Schaffer caught Roberts loitering near the library which is next to a children's play park. Thomas had reason to believe that he was in danger, perhaps of being sexually molested. However he had the opportunity to run away. His statement doesn't add up, it could be that he said what he thought we wanted to hear. If I could find some concrete evidence that Roberts was a threat to Thomas, to children in particular, it would help to understand why Thomas behaved the way he did."

Beech stood up from his perch on the desk and walked back to his chair. He was irritated by his DI and made no attempt to hide it.

"Thomas's behaviour is not the issue here Wallace. He reacted to a negative situation such as being approached by Roberts with violence. Evaluating why or whether there is a chance he will do so again is not our concern. The psychological evaluation will cover that. You have means; He lied about not recognising Roberts even though Roberts had been identified as being a regular to the woods. You have motive; to stop Robert's advances. Thomas had the opportunity, more than one, since he returned to the scene, and you have evidence. You have a confession, therefore you charge him. When the forensic report comes in, you charge Thomas and get him to court. Stop procrastinating, do your job!"

Beech's voice was louder as he ended his sentence. His attitude angered Hammond. The man was ordering him to effectively back down from another investigation again.

"So, that's it. Case closed?"

Beech looked at Hammond hard, his jaw set. He looked as if he was prepared to have an argument with his subordinate if it was invited, and judging by the way Hammond was now pacing the office, he presumed the invitation was imminent.

"Wallace, let's be frank. You haven't exactly investigated this case with what I would call professionalism so far. Be grateful that you caught the person responsible without making a complete mockery of the Major Crimes Unit. Learn to step away before you end up walking over the edge."

"Let me do my job without blocking me!" Hammond shouted back at Beech. The two men glowered at one another, each refusing to back down. Edwards, Dunn and Galvin had made their way along the corridor on the pretext they were collecting coffee. The raised voices could be heard quite clearly. Edward raised an eyebrow whilst Dunn stood unsure whether to go in to the office.

She felt loyal to her DI, she was equally responsible for the arrest of Thomas, she should be in there with him, taking the fall.

"I am protecting you as well as myself Wallace!" Beech ignored Hammond's attempt to voice his opinion on his latter statement and continued with his reasoning.

"Forgetting the shambolic display of what was meant to be a media briefing, let's focus on your handling of the investigation so far; You charged in and questioned Thomas on your own without notifying your team or your superiors. You questioned William Barnes on his own. You have a highly accomplished team yet you aren't using your resources to their full capacity. You aren't behaving like a team member, let alone a senior officer! To make matters worse, you chase a twelve year old kid out of his house and down several main roads risking his safety. What if he had run out in front of a car because you made him panic? There were witnesses all of whom could testify that Thomas was being pursued recklessly and without due cause. Imagine what that would have done Wallace! You have cocked up big time and I am offering you a chance to step away and let the CPS take it on from here. Don't fight me on this!"

Hammond was very tempted to storm out of the office but he wanted to get his words in first. Beech needed to hear what he wanted to say and the temper he had stirred in Beech was not enough to make him back down.

"We don't have enough! If we turn it over to the Crown Prosecution Service now, two things are likely to happen; either Thomas is sent down as a violent delinquent, which I do not believe him to be, or his aggressive behaviour is swept aside as being justified, which I don't believe it was. Either way, there are questions about this case that must be resolved! You have got to give me more time!"

Beech sighed, he wanted to end this conversation whilst he was capable of acting responsibly. He tried the gentler approach. "Let me be honest Wallace. Your behaviour has been erratic lately. You are not behaving as a Senior officer. You've lost your objectivity. What is going on? Is it your family? Do you need time off?" He paused as if deciding on behalf of Hammond that this was exactly what was needed. "Take some time off, a couple of weeks. God knows a holiday is long overdue. Use it, then come back fresher and stronger. DS Dunn is more than capable of heading an investigation until you get back."

Hammond stood with his mouth open. He was sorely tempted to reply with more than words, instead he turned on his heels and slammed the door so hard he very nearly looked behind him to see if he had broken it.

It hadn't been Hammond's intention to drive to the hair salon in the high street, but he had needed to go somewhere and driving through the town aimlessly did nothing to resolve his agitation. He was angry with Beech for making him feel inadequate. He considered himself to be a good officer, a fair and dedicated law enforcer who simply wanted to do a thorough job. Instead of his efforts being appreciated he had been humiliated and treated as a inexperienced rookie. Ideally a man in his position should return to the office and talk to his team but pride had got the better of him so he decided to stay close to head quarters but away from Beech until his temper calmed.

The sun had melted most of the snow apart from a few shovelled heaps on the kerbs that were turning to a brown coloured slush. He parked the car in a free space just outside the salon and looked through the window. It looked empty apart from an older woman whose hair was being blow-dried by a skinny man wearing tight jeans and a black waistcoat over a white t-shirt. A young girl was seated on a high stool near the door twirling her hair around a finger whilst talking on the phone. She was laughing and bowing her head down to avoid the questioning gaze of a female hair stylist who watched her through the mirror's reflection. It was an impulsive decision to go in the shop but once there, Hammond felt more relaxed. He was anonymous and in the last place anyone would expect him to be. That made him feel free to think about his predicament at work without the pressure of being followed by well meaning colleagues who would no doubt persuade him to go back to Beech with cap in hand.

He sat on the faux leather tub chair nearest the window whilst he waited for the receptionist to finish her conversation on the phone, it was evident the girl was in the throes of a new romance. He watched her and wondered if she was popular with the boys. The girl wasn't pretty but it was obvious she knew how to flirt. In his limited experience, the girls good at flirting were often the ones to avoid, they would surely be bored after the chase. As if reading his mind, the girl looked across and asked if she could help him. He said he would like a haircut. This was, on reflection, he realised, a rather stupid thing to say, after all why else would he be in a hair salon? He was asked whom he would like to cut his hair, he could have Danny or Tony. Hammond looked at the two hair stylists and tried to guess which name belonged to the female stylist. He was inhibited when it came to interacting with camp men and the skinny man looked like he talked a lot. He took a chance and chose Danny which he presumed was a derivative of Danielle. The receptionist called the name aloud and the male stylist looked up and said he would be free in five minutes. He smiled at Hammond and invited him to look at magazines whilst he waited. Inwardly Hammond groaned, he wondered if it would look too prejudiced if he now decided to change his mind and choose Tony instead. He decided it would and resolved to ignoring the fashion magazines completely and looked out the window.

Having decided that it would do no harm to go home early, Hammond found Jenny in the kitchen painting the walls light blue. She looked at his haircut with mute approval as he entered.

"The phone hasn't stopped ringing for the last two hours. I answered the first few calls but ignored the last because I was up the ladder. A woman called; apparently your mobile was switched off. When I asked her who she was she said "I'm Done". I figured it would make sense to you, anyway, she said you must call her back as soon as you get this message."

Hammond looked at the wet paint and wondered why on earth she had chosen light blue for the kitchen. Magnolia had always been his choice. It was a safe colour and more importantly, economical. Now he would have to get matching blue tea towels. Lyn had taught him well enough that the use of colour had to be synchronised for a finished look. He decided to keep quiet about the new decor and instead picked up the kitchen telephone.

Dunn answered her mobile immediately. "Where are you?"

He told her and apologised for his mobile having been on mute, he had forgotten to turn the sound back on after he had left the hair stylists. He listened as she updated him on news at the office. "I spoke to Beech; I told him that we may have new evidence on Roberts. It was almost true; we still need to identify the payments from his savings accounts and check out a mobile number Roberts had called from his landline the previous evening. Beech has agreed to give us another forty-eight hours. Edwards and Galvin are back at Graham Robert's house if you want to join them."

It was a tempting offer but three officers searching a house might seem excessive. Dunn agreed hesitantly and promised to inform him if any invoices were found. He thanked her and promised to keep in touch. He wanted to be updated on any progress, despite Beech's insistence that he take some time off, it would be possible to work behind the scenes without Beech knowing.

The telephone was replaced and then, after a pause, picked up again as Kathleen's number was punched into the keypad. When Kathleen answered, Hammond felt shy. He explained that he had left work early so that it would be possible to see her earlier than planned. They arranged to have a meal at The Oak pub restaurant at seven that evening. As he ended the call, Hammond turned to see Jenny watching him with raised eyebrows. "If you are leaving at half six, that will give you five hours to get ready."

Hammond looked at her with a bewildered expression as she climbed down the ladder and began untying her apron.

"I'll come with you; you'll need new trousers at least. We'll take your car."

Yet again, Hammond found himself thrown into a situation where he was under the control of a girl barely half his age.

The Peugeot crunched its way over the gravel drive leading to the Harris' home. The house was in darkness apart from a splinter of light showing from a window at the top of the house. He approached the door hoping Kathleen wasn't ready, he wanted the opportunity to talk to Lloyd without Kathleen overhearing. It was obvious she didn't want her Father's interest in the suicide investigation to be encouraged and doubtlessly she would hinder their conversation if she were around. Hammond had left earlier than planned. Once he had dressed the adrenaline propelled him to make a move rather than sit around when his mind couldn't concentrate on anything other than what he would or should say to Kathleen. The door had an old fashioned brass knocker that hadn't been polished for a long time. He knocked it gently then waited for several seconds before knocking harder a second time until he heard movement behind the door. Harris' face peered around the partially opened door and gazed at Hammond with a blank expression. Hammond's heart sank. Harris didn't recognise him. He shifted his weight slightly unsure whether to introduce himself or to behave normally as if he didn't know of Harris' affliction, hoping that the older man would gradually remember.
"Hi Lloyd, I am a bit early, I wanted to talk to you before I took Kathleen out" He cleared his throat and stepped forward towards Harris who nodded and opened the door wider.
"Wallace, come in."

Hammond patted his friend on the shoulder as he passed. "Every time I see you, I get the impression you don't know who I am."

"I don't." Harris held out a hand, offering to take Hammond's jacket from him. Unsure what to say in response, Hammond searched Harris's face for a clue and was relieved when Harris smiled.

"The Wallace Hammond I know usually looks like a scruffy fat bastard but you look more like an old gigolo!"

Hammond was aware of heat creeping up his neck to his face, he suddenly felt self-conscious. Had he overdone it? Would Kathleen think it was for her sake that he had dressed smarter than usual? It was for her benefit of course, however he didn't want her to know that. Harris switched on the hallway light and looked up towards the top of the stairs to check if his daughter was within hearing. Satisfied that she wasn't aware of Hammond's arrival, he hung the jacket over the banisters and ushered Hammond into a side room that was easily identified as an office. A small desk lamp illuminated books stacked in neat piles on the floor and any available surface. Glancing at the titles, Hammond noted they ranged from subjects as diverse as psychoanalysis and criminology and included several political biographies. The complete works of Noam Chomsky had been placed still open with the pages face down. The book was well thumbed, the edges of the book stained with use. Hammond was vaguely surprised, he had never considered Harris to have any other intellectual interests which he now realised had been a shallow perception of his former colleague. He continued to take in the room and noticed all photo frames had been placed face down on an old desk littered with newspaper cuttings and scribbled notes. He looked enquiringly at Harris whom was busying himself clearing a space for Hammond to sit down. Lowering himself into a chair by the window, he studied Harris's movements hoping that his former colleague wasn't fading too quickly from the reality in which they shared. Harris finished his fussing and eventually sat near Hammond, perching on a foot stool that he had retrieved from under the desk.

"Kathleen is getting ready. Do you want a drink?"

The offer was declined as the two men sat quietly in the small room. The silence lingered as both men wondered what the other was thinking. Paul would refer to such awkwardness as comparable to seeing a white elephant in the room, all parties could see there was a white elephant, it was impossible to miss but no-one would broach the subject. In this case, the white elephant that Hammond could see was a man slowly losing his memory. It was painful to think about; he had a great deal of respect for Harris and hated to see intelligence such as his be taken away so cruelly.

"I see Kathleen has told you about my Diagnosis." Harris didn't wait for an answer and ignored Hammond's feigned look of ignorance.

"Yes, I am going through the early stages of Alzheimer's but don't you start thinking I am going mad. If you are wondering whether I am fit to make a decision, look at Ronald Regan, he did ok."

Hammond was surprised. "Regan had Alzheimer's?"

Harris smiled suggesting a hint of pride in his answer. "Sure, some of the greats had it; Rita Hayworth was another one and Iris Murdoch. I think Charlton Heston did too."

Hammond felt ashamed that he had been so dismissive of Harris's suspicions after Kathleen had told him about her Father's diagnosis. He owed Harris an apology and offered it quietly.

"Wallace. I know who you are; I remember our years working together which is why I'm confident I have asked the right person to continue where I left off before I forget. Oh stop that..." impatiently, Harris waved a hand in front of his face to dismiss Hammond's attempt to appeal. "You need this..." As he spoke Harris bent down onto his knees and crawled under the armchair on which Hammond sat." No, don't get up, I've got it..." There were sounds of scurrying from underneath Hammond whilst Harris knelt with his head and arms between the chair legs. Hammond prayed silently that Kathleen wouldn't walk into the room at that moment and see the two men in such a compromising position. When Harris reversed himself from his hiding place under the chair, he was dragging a large box file.

"Here you go, there should be all the information you need to get your investigation going." Harris stood up by leaning his weight on the arm of the chair and then bent down to pick up the file before dropping it onto Hammond's lap.

Hammond gasped as he felt the extraordinary weight of the file and opened the lid. There were pages of written notes scribbled in a furious hand, Hammond estimated there must be about a hundred pages worth, underneath the papers were numerous photographs. A quick glance showed him some of the pictures had been taken decades earlier, the colours were slightly faded with a brownish tinge. The edges of the photos were smooth from where they had been handled frequently.

"This is your research?" His reply was a silent nod of Harris's head. Hammond whistled between his teeth, it would take him hours to look through the file contents, he swallowed loudly and looked at Harris enquiringly.

"Lloyd, I wouldn't know where to begin, there is so much here."

Harris had resumed his place squatting on the footstool. He used his arms to brace his upper body as if to ease the pressure on his lower limbs. As Hammond looked at him, he noticed Harris' expression had changed from being an enthusiastic conversationalist to someone deep in thought. It took several moments until Harris spoke again, during which time Hammond simply waited. He didn't know what his friend was going through; how his mind was able to clarify thoughts amongst a dense jungle of confusion that he presumed the Alzheimer's had bestowed upon its carrier, but he guessed that patience from others helped. So he sat quietly and waited for Harris to share his thoughts.

"I joined the police force in 1968, I was nineteen years old and an innocent in every sense of the word. However, I soon discovered that you couldn't be a policeman and remain wet behind the ears for long. Bear in mind Wallace, that the police force had just recovered from two major scandals of police corruption in the late 1950's so the relationship between the public and the police was uneasy."

Hammond was surprised by Harris' choice of subject, but he listened carefully. He was aware that the scandals Harris was referring too had influenced the reform of Britain's police forces in the 1960's. The subsequent 1964 Police Act had removed policing power from local counties by allowing the Central Government to exercise more control over local forces. It had been an issue of debate for his Father whom had argued that such a move exhibited nothing more than a lack of faith in local democracy, and had only achieved to create a weaker structure for law enforcement. Hammond shared these thoughts with Harris who impatiently dismissed Hammond's reply to continue talking. I must keep quiet Hammond thought, if I don't he will lose his train of thought. It was evident that Harris wanted to share something but so far Hammond could not understand the relevance. It must be a need to reminisce, Hammond thought so made an effort to remain silent.

"Of course, the 1970's was different to how it is today. You can't just stop a man and search him because he is Asian or black but in those days, it was the norm. If a man had darker skin, it meant he was up to no good, at least that was the opinion of my colleagues. I guess it is no wonder that the public distrusted us, but we believed we were doing our job. We believed that we were protecting the public. We didn't need what you call 'reasonable suspicion' to bring a man in for questioning. The copper's instinct was the only tool we needed." Harris shook his head and shrugged. Hammond was unsure how to answer, he wasn't sure of the relevance of the subject. What was he trying to say? He listened for any sound of Kathleen's progress but he couldn't hear anything other Harris's breathing. Again, he waited and hoped that by doing so he was being helpful in allowing his friend to share what was troubling him.

"Then of course, the police were the prosecutors, which meant that there was the tendency to focus on a suspect and build a case around them. I admit that there were the odd occasions when we couldn't be entirely sure that evidence leading towards other possible suspects wasn't ignored. The number of acquittals we experienced was from providing weak prosecution preparation so it meant that we relied heavily on confessions in order to secure a conviction. In those days corroborating a suspects' confession with forensic evidence wasn't as important as it is today."

Hammond found himself fidgeting in his chair, he reminded himself to keep quiet and not interrupt Harris' reminiscing even though he wasn't particularly enjoying having a history lesson on policing.

"The pressure on getting results could be crippling, especially on cases with a high public profile, we had to identify a suspect quickly in order to prove we were doing our jobs. Once evidence pointed to one suspect we would focus on it and make damn sure we would get a result that the public expected. We used the philosophy that if a person was found near a scene of a crime or they had a history of committing previous similar offences, it was enough to bring them in for questioning. Police territory could be a very intimidating place, and being interrogated was..well..an intimidating experience."

Harris whistled through his teeth as if he were judging his own past actions. Hammond sat shocked by what Harris was suggesting but at the same time wondered why he was being told such information. Was Harris' confession to clear his conscience? Harris looked at Hammond then and raised the corners of his lips in a thin smile.

"There was coercion. No doubt about that. Of course, there were some good police officers who went by the book but we believed we were doing the right thing for the people we were protecting. But then people started asking questions, the public began to distrust us, and we had to regain their trust so it was necessary to compromise; make ourselves known to be fair. We adopted a trading system where a suspect would give us information in exchange for immunity from prosecution."

Harris was caught up in the flow of his reminiscing, his expressions became animated. Hammond sat listening; he was beginning to feel uneasy wondering where the confession was going to end.

"But then you are faced with the question; Where to draw the line? What started out as compromising became colluding with the commission of offences. There was a lot of perks for officers in the vice squad in particular. I worked alongside Vice at one point in my career. I knew that most of the young girls were being brought over from Europe or as far afield as Africa for prostitution but the girls were looked after and treated well. We looked after them and protected them from nasty punters in exchange for a free ride so to speak. It worked well; the girls trusted us and would often allow themselves to be used to get information from their contacts. There was mutual trust from both sides. I became friends with one of the girls there, she called herself Pattie..." There was a sound of a door closing from upstairs, Harris sat up and left the room leaving Hammond sitting on the chair perplexed. He was about to move and join Harris in the hallway when the older man returned to the office and shut the door.

"Don't worry, she'll be ages yet...where were we? He stood looking at Hammond who started to remind Harris about the girl called Pattie before Harris remembered and resumed his position on the stool.

"Anyway, it became apparent that there were too many bribes being taken in the Vice Squad and rumours were spreading like wild fire of collusion between armed robbery gangs and high ranking officers in specialised units such as the regional Crime Squad and Criminal Intelligence..."

Hammond interrupted, He realised what Harris was telling him about.

"You are referring to Operation Countryman?"

Harris looked annoyed by Hammond's interruption but he nodded with affirmation.

"Yes, exactly. Originally it was established following suspicion of corruption within the City of London Police but it became apparent that the Metropolitan Police were also under investigation. I hadn't been discreet regarding my affair with Pattie, whom by then had established herself as a madam with girls working under her, but I knew it couldn't be proven that I was involved in taking bribes. The worst I could be accused of would be to have turned a blind eye to their involvements with organised crime and coercing confessions and the like. So, I was offered a deal; any enquiry against me would be forgotten if I agreed to co-operate. I became an informant for the Home Office."

Hammond was dumbstruck. He had joined the Police force three years following the closure of the major wide-ranging investigation into police corruption, but the aftermath of what had been called 'Operation Countryman' had been in existence during his early years as a police constable. Over 400 police officers had been dismissed from the force either during or after the investigation by the Home Office. Distrust between officers had been well documented following allegations, some unfounded, that officers had betrayed their colleagues during the investigation. Despite spending £4 Million during the six year investigation, no criminal charges were made despite the belief that over 300 officers had been involved in criminal dealings.

"This was why you were transferred to Medway?"

Harris nodded. "It had something to do with it I am sure. Working undercover and reporting the people I had respected as friends as well as colleagues wasn't something I enjoyed. But you see, I was young and selfish and I wanted to protect my own interests."

"You mean Pattie, the girl you were having an affair with?" Hammond wondered what influence Pattie had had over Harris, he suspected that there was more to the story than Harris was telling him. If Pattie had been working as a madam, it was possible that Harris was protecting her from investigation as well as himself. Certainly it would not have looked good if it had been made public that a police officer was associating with prostitutes but at the same time, it may not have warranted a dismissal. There must be more to this than Harris is telling me Hammond thought. He watched his friend closely, hoping for signs that Harris was going to tell him more.

"I kept some information back. It wasn't in my best interests or Pattie's either to tell everything. So I withheld details that I felt would make no difference to their investigation. Some of the information I collected is in that box." Harris pointed to the box file on Hammond's lap. For a moment Hammond looked down at the box, he tried to understand what relevance it had to the investigation Harris had delegated him to do.

"You mean it is connected somehow with the murder of Salima Abitboul?"

Harris gave a short nod of his head but his eyes remained fixed on the floor.

"How?"

"I am ninety-nine percent sure that Salima was one of Pattie's girls."

Suddenly Hammond realised what Harris was trying to tell him.

"The man who confessed to murdering Salima Abitboul was innocent?"

Harris looked up slowly, and looked Hammond in the eye.

"Yes, I think so, but I didn't know at the time. A Pakistani man had been seen visiting the site where her body was found, he was found with her possessions. I believed he was guilty. I guess it was the racist in me that made me so damn sure but I didn't have enough evidence, so it took some persuasion."

"Why now? Why didn't you present this..." Hammond swept his hand over the box file in an agitated fashion "...this possible evidence and get the man freed if you believe he was innocent after all?"

"He died from cancer in prison years ago. What good would it have done? I believed he was guilty. We had some evidence, the confession just secured it. It is only now that I wonder whether we made a mistake."

"So, you want me to find out if Mark Callum was guilty of her murder? Is it possible that he had known her during his childhood hence him having her possessions?

"I cannot say for sure, but I do recommend that you consider what I have told you when you investigate."

Hammond sighed, he felt that time was running out for the two men. Kathleen could appear at any moment and he felt he was making progress.

"Lloyd. If there is more, tell me, tell me as much as you can. I feel as if I am walking blind here."

Harris put his hand on Hammond's shoulder. "I trust you Wallace, only you. Like I said before give it your best shot please. It sounds disloyal to say it but it is important that you do not show any of this to Kathleen. I don't know whether you are friends now nor do I care what your relationship is, but do not share any of this information with her. Promise me Wallace."

Hammond considered that the promise would be useless since Kathleen would surely ask why he was carrying a large box file out of her home, and worse still, would want to know the contents. Hammond wasn't good at lying, it wouldn't take a genius to guess the truth he argued. In reply, Harris suggested he distract Kathleen whilst Hammond hid the file in his car. Feeling it was a unnecessary precaution, he shoved the file under the driver's seat before returning indoors.

The man had stood hidden in the shadows of the overgrown garden. From his position he could see the front door open and the Detective come outside carrying a parcel. He stepped further back hoping the light seeping outside from the house wouldn't compromise his hiding place and watched as the policeman opened his car door and placed the parcel inside before quietly closing the door. The car's headlights blinked as the car was locked by the remote control before the front door was shut again. The man waited for a minute, before stepping lightly across the gravel towards where the policeman's car was parked. He skirted around the car, looking in the window, hoping to see where the parcel had been placed but it was too dark to see inside. He looked toward the house again and reconsidered his plan of action. He looked up at the light coming from the top window and waited until it went dark, then he crept his way back down towards the drive and returned to his car parked discreetly along the lane. He waited.

The conversation in the car was stilted. The newly styled Inspector Hammond was feeling absurdly self-conscious, he was painfully aware that this was his first social meeting with a woman he didn't work with. He felt out of practise and hoped that Kathleen would encourage a topic of conversation. Instead, she looked out of the window during the five minute drive and simply nodded when he remarked how well her father had looked.

As he parked the car behind the pub, Kathleen asked if she could be excused for a moment; she had to visit the ladies room. She left the car quickly, shutting the door with a careless manner before she hurried to the main entrance of the restaurant. Her behaviour was rather odd since she had only just left home, but Hammond contemplated the possibility that she was also nervous. Perhaps like him it was the first opportunity to be alone with a single man since her divorce. He sat in the car for several seconds, wondering how he could steer the conversation onto her Father. After all, that was why he had wanted to meet her. The box file underneath his seat beckoned his attention. He thought that Harris' warning was rather extreme but it wouldn't hurt to take it indoors with him. Kathleen wouldn't be interested in the contents if she thought it was connected to his work. Whilst he was waiting for her, he could have another peek at the contents in the light of the restaurant.

Kathleen was sat waiting at a table as he ambled his way into the entrance, he gave his name to front of house and was about to be accompanied to where she sat before he changed his mind. It had been a stupid idea to bring in the box file with him. He was about to eat a meal, it wasn't as if he could spread the contents over the table and shovel a fork with one hand like he did at the breakfast table. He asked the maître d' if they could look after the file on his behalf. They were happy to put it in their office where it would be safe he was assured. Gratefully, he accepted and reprimanded himself mentally on forgetting his manners.

"I should tell you Wallace, how dashing you look. I do like the hair cut." Kathleen showed off her dimples as she smiled. Her attitude had changed dramatically from when she had been in the car and he was encouraged by her willingness to converse. The drink menus were offered. Despite the temptation to have beer, he ordered the safer option of mineral water but Kathleen quickly rebuffed his choice.

"Oh Wallace, this is a friendly re-union! Let's be a little more adventurous!" She ordered a bottle of Burgundy dismissing his preference to be teetotal.

"Oh come on, we have so much to talk about. You can order a taxi if necessary. I'll pay!" She pouted her lips playfully and rested her hand on his in an attempt to persuade him. The ploy worked. Hammond had not had the best day and if Beech had his way, there was no need to worry about going to work early in the morning so he raised his glass to toast a relaxed evening.

The conversation, aided by the wine, was soon flowing. Harris must have felt his ears burning as his daughter and former colleague discussed his mental state.

"He admitted to me that he had been diagnosed but to be honest he seems ...well.. if you pardon the expression... normal. He was as rational as ever. Are you sure your

Father's symptoms are as advanced as you fear them to be?"

"Like I said Wallace, there are good days and some bad days. I guess you were lucky tonight. Two days ago, he was in a terrible state; I came home just after seven to find him wandering around the village with no shoes on. It was freezing! By the time I had persuaded him to get in the car and come home, he was so agitated that I had to call the GP to sedate him."

Hammond stopped chewing his pork loin and looked at her with astonishment.

"He is that bad? What about drug therapy?"

Kathleen poked her Haddock with her fork, lost in thought.

"The inhibitors help to slow down the degeneration but there are times when he gets so confused. If I am not there every day morning and night handing out the medication, he won't take the tablets or forgets the dosage." She raised one shoulder as if to express her acceptance of the situation rather than questioning it.

"So he forgets to care for himself yet he remembers details of us working together. It's crazy."

Kathleen looked sharply at Hammond.

"Are you suggesting I am exaggerating?"

"No! Not at all, I guess I am just so perplexed how the human mind works! It is all beyond me, yet your Father seems to have accepted his fate. I saw all the books of Psychology; he must be a learned man."

He felt himself being scrutinised suddenly. Kathleen had put down her fork to pick up her glass, sipping slowly as she looked at him over the rim.

"You saw his office? You are honoured; normally it is out of bounds. I am not allowed in there."

"I didn't see much to be honest, just books." It was a good time to change the subject, but Kathleen seemed less keen in ending the topic of conversation.

"Yes, but you were there long enough to see what kind of books there were. Like I said, you are honoured. I expect he wanted to show off his research. He spends a lot of time in that room scribbling away on goodness knows what. Did he seem obsessive to you?"

Kathleen's question was innocent. Hammond owed her the truth, she was concerned about her father, it was cruel to deliberately keep information from her.

"Perhaps a little. He has been very keen to show me the information he has gathered regarding local suicides."

"And did he?"

"Yes, I had a glance at what he had collected. However, a glance was all I could afford, he had completed a file worth at least. I don't know what the file contains though."

"So that is what he gave you?"

Kathleen's perception had to be honoured, he nodded but gave no more details. So far Hammond was telling Kathleen the truth even though he had the intention of studying the file contents later. He hoped that he appeared to be cooperative and sympathetic to her situation. She was trying hard to protect her Father's reputation, whilst Harris was trying to protect her innocence. Hammond was stuck in the middle, but he owed it to Harris to keep his promise, more than he owed loyalty to Harris' daughter.

Kathleen changed tack, she was curious to learn of Hammonds parents. He was rather reluctant to focus attention onto himself but he was grateful for the change in subject and answered her questions openly.

He accepted a top up from the second bottle of wine and sipped it, enjoying the acidity after his rich meal.

"My mother was the typical home maker, always making jams and homemade breads. She used to refer to herself as a housewife but in reality she was a bit of everything, cook, seamstress, gardener, you name it, she'd do it!"

Kathleen watched him as he recounted stories of his youth. She didn't interrupt and seemed to enjoy hearing of his childhood exploits.

"Many a time I would bring home frogs, newts that kind of thing, I would shove them in my pocket and hide them in my room. I remember when I was about ten, I befriended a mouse. My mother hated mice. She was absolutely terrified of them, but one day I came home and found her hand feeding it scraps of meat that she had saved from my Dad's supper. She was angry with me for not leaving it any food or water whilst I was at school. I think that was the last pet I ever had!"

Kathleen laughed as she imagined a young mischievous Wallace and abruptly changed the subject.

"Has there been anyone since the divorce?"

"No. I haven't had much of a social life to be honest, work tends to take up most of my time. I think that is why Lyn left. I couldn't prioritise our relationship over my work commitments. Women tend not to be interested in a work-a-holic divorcee. Either that or I have been walking around like a jam jar with the warning. '*Reject if depressed*' written on my forehead."

Kathleen attempted a smile making it obvious she didn't appreciate his humour. He reminded himself to keep the jokes to a minimum.

"Why did you become a policeman?"

"Blame my father for that. He loved watching a television series called 'Fabian of the Yard'. I wasn't born when the series was broadcast but he used to tell me how each episode had been a dramatisation of a genuine crime that had happened around London. He loved recounting the investigations and I guess I grew up doing what most kids do; wanting their father's approval."

"Did he approve?"

"He died of a heart attack before I enrolled, but yes, I think he would have."

"What about your mother?"

"When my dad died, mum just faded out of her own life. She ended up in a nursing home when she was only fifty- five. I had just met Lyn and I guess my head was elsewhere, it never occurred to me how young my Mum was or how much she needed me at that time. She died two years later but by then I was married and about to be a father." Talking about his mother made him sad, he was embarrassed that he had given so much of himself away and distracted himself from his musing by finishing his wine.

Kathleen was giving him her full attention. He rather liked it, although he was hoping she would talk about herself. He was curious about her husband but she simply shook her head when he asked. The desert menu was brought over and two diners contemplated their choices quietly.

The atmosphere had changed slightly, it was as if Kathleen had clammed up again, she studied her coffee thoughtfully. Eventually she pushed the coffee cup to the side dismissively and leaned forward.

"I think we should have an affair."

The cheesecake about to enter Hammond's mouth paused mid flight. He met her eyes and realised she was serious.

"Oh." The fork was returned to its plate as he struggled to know what to say and realised he couldn't say anything. There was a bubble of hysteria forming in his stomach, he had the dreadful feeling he was about to start giggling. Was she kidding? She was way out of his league!

"They have rooms here. A double is vacant if you are interested." Kathleen's foot travelled to Hammond's leg under the table. He felt rather uncomfortable by her brazenness, checking the room availability meant her flirtation was premeditated. He replied quickly before he could change his mind.

"Kathleen, I am flattered but I am not really..." His voice trailed off unsure what reason to give. To decline such an offer was something bordering on crazy. Yet it felt wrong. Perhaps it was the wine but all he really wanted was to go home. He apologised for his lack of energy. Taking the hint Kathleen gestured to the waiter to bring the bill. Hammond felt ashamed, he wasn't behaving like a gentleman but then she wasn't behaving much like a lady either. He paid the bill on his credit card and left a generous tip with the promise his car would be collected from the car park when he was sober. As they waited for the taxi, Hammond took her hand and turned her around to face him. "Please do not think that I do not want you, Kathleen, you are a very attractive woman. I respect you and I like you."

"There is no need to apologise Wallace, although I would be grateful if you could escort me home in the taxi."

It was during the journey home that Hammond suddenly remembered he had left the box file at the restaurant. He slapped his forehead punishing his absent-mindedness and phoned The Oak asking them to keep the file in a safe place until he came to collect his car. Once reassured, Hammond allowed his head to loll back on the headrest as the taxi sped homebound.

"A man must not swallow more beliefs than he can digest"
Henry Havelock Ellis. The Dance of Life. 1923

CHAPTER ELEVEN

Overnight a rain shower had moved in from the North coast. Hammond watched as it rinsed all residue of rock salt and sludge away. The wet roads reflected the glare of the street lights sending white beams into the darkened room. He was sitting in the armchair looking out the window. A silver car passed by slowly, it's sweeping lights disturbed a black cat that was resting on the wall at the end of the garden. It sat under the cover of an overhanging shrub watching the rain descend and tried to catch the droplets with a paw before licking itself clean. Occasionally Hammond would take sips of brandy before tilting the glass gently from side to side. The liquid swirled in waves that lapped against the side of the glass before it sloshed back into the brown pool. He had no idea what the time was, possibly early morning. It was as if time had slowed to a stop, causing his thoughts to linger unresolved.

Beside him Jenny stirred in her sleep, intermittently murmuring words that were incomprehensible. She was huddled under the duvet, hidden apart from one arm hanging over the edge of the sofa bed. He watched her in her slumber, wondering what it was that troubled her. Hammond wished she would trust him to help her, but maybe she could see what he feared, that he had lost his ability to see things clearly. To act with logical thought rather than over analysing situations that warranted no reasoning. *Why can't I just accept that crap happens?* He thought about Lloyd Harris and wondered if he had been as corrupt as he had suggested. He was shocked that his former colleague had acted with such prejudice in his early years as an officer but at the same time, he wondered how possible it would have been to refuse to co-operate with what was seen to be normal practise. He remembered a television programme he had watched with his Father about corruption within the New York City Police. An investigation in the 1970's had divided corrupt officers into two types; There were the *'meat-eaters'* who misused their position of authority for personal gain, and the *'grass-eaters'* who accepted such corruption existed and were willing to accept payoffs. He couldn't know for sure which category Harris belonged to. Either way, Hammond knew he wouldn't get rid of the disappointment he had felt as Harris told him. Hammond had admired his former DCI but now he wondered whether such admiration had been warranted. The sigh he emitted was heavy as he wondered if Beech was right, that he had lost his objectivity. He berated himself out loud and immediately regretted it, seeing Jenny twitch suddenly under the covers. He winced guilty that he had disturbed her as she poked her head from under the duvet. Her eyes squinted as they adjusted to the light that beamed through the window. He mumbled an apology and made a move to get up from his chair telling her to get back to sleep. Instead she sat up, pulling the duvet around her shoulders and held out a hand to take the Brandy glass from him. After draining his glass with what looked like expertise in slugging back liquor, she looked at him "Why aren't you in bed?"

He expected a sarcastic remark, a suggestion that an old man like him needed recharging, but she simply waited for him to answer her question. He got up out of the armchair and moved beside her on the sofa bed, stretching his legs out to the length of the mattress and gave a grunt as it squeaked under the strain of his weight. He slid an arm behind her neck, offering his shoulder to her in a paternal manner. She accepted and they sat there in an embrace for several minutes not talking, enjoying the stillness.

"I have been an idiot, Wally." Jenny spoke quietly. Her voice was muffled as her head lay against him. Hammond waited for her to continue; not wanting to interrupt what he hoped would be a moment of confidence.

"I fell in love. How crazy is that? After all the years of convincing people I was unlovable and didn't give a damn, and then I go and let myself fall in love with someone who *really* didn't care one way or other!" Jenny gave a short laugh, though her voice was devoid of good humour. Hammond glanced down and gave her shoulder a gentle squeeze with his hand to welcome her into the broken hearts club. He felt dampness on his left shoulder and realised Jenny was weeping. It shocked him, he had never seen Jenny cry before. She always seemed so strong. Instead of replying, he allowed Jenny to talk. His willingness to listen was a surprise to him. Emotional outbursts were usually something he avoided and if he couldn't avoid them, he would mimic the act of listening to the other's cause of concern with deaf ears. But this was different. Jenny was an enigma to Hammond and he wanted to understand her. Since Paul had introduced Jenny two years ago, information about her had been withheld as if Jenny presumed people would accept her the way she was without knowing her background. She never mentioned her parents, her friends or her history. Jenny was a person of the moment, her past was irrelevant to her present. Despite Hammond's curiosity, he had never asked Jenny about her family, it would have caused too much embarrassment to the both of them. She had been accepted into the family simply by stepping into it and declaring it as her adopted home.

"It's the humiliation I can't cope with. The fact that I was just Angela's sexual experiment. If she were a lesbian, there was always a chance she would come back to me, but now she decides she isn't, it makes everything seem so final."

Hammond moved her so he could get the brandy bottle, and returned to the bed refusing the glass she held out to be filled, instead passing her the bottle. She grasped the bottle firmly and took a swig before nestling again against his chest.

"How do I breathe? It feels as if my chest has imploded, I can't rid myself of this weight. I want to forget her, to move on, but this pain..." Jenny thumped her chest with a closed fist "It won't shift. My body is going through all the motions of surviving, but inside I feel so empty. Wally, how can I go back there, knowing I will see her with him?"

Hammond felt his throat tighten as she expelled her heartache and found himself thinking of Lyn. He emphasised with Jenny's grief. For several days after Lyn had walked out he had woken in the morning believing it had been a bad dream. When she had filed for divorce it made everything seem so final. There would be no second chances. He had failed. The anguish he had felt with the realisation that his nightmare was reality had engulfed him in a despair he had found impossible to shift. Over time he had learnt to bury his grief under his work but now Jenny was re-living his moment of agony.

"Jenny, you will carry on because you are a survivor. You will wake, eat and sleep one day at a time until gradually the pain becomes less and less. Eventually, you will wake up and realise that Angela had the biggest loss. She had a cool, hot chick girlfriend who has a wicked sense of humour, who makes the best baked beans on toast and who knows how to drink like a man. She will be the one humiliated for not knowing a good thing when she had it." Hammond spoke the words without humour, he was serious. Lyn used to say all the time that all she wanted in a man was capability, humour and kindness. Jenny had all three. "You are a better man than me, that's for sure!"

Jenny wiped her eyes on his shirt sleeve. "Thanks Wally, although you are not too bad, for an old fat man anyway!" They took turns to swig the brandy. Hammond looked out the window. It had stopped raining; the sky was white with pink patches on the horizon. The day was approaching, but Hammond wasn't ready to sleep. Jenny sat up and leaned against the back of the sofa enjoying the hazy warmth the brandy had bestowed upon her.

Hammonds' stomach gurgled, he smiled noting Jenny had pretended not to hear it.

"Have you got any of those delicious cookies left?"

"No! Mary took them home with her to give to the cake stall. Greedy pig, you would have eaten most of her efforts!"

Jenny's confession had allowed the rare opportunity for him to broach the subject which had reawakened his curiosity. He shifted his weight as he moved his legs to a more comfortable position, noting that his back muscles were stiff after his earlier chase.

"What is the story between you and Mary?"

Jenny looked at him sideways and shrugged as she examined the brandy bottle for drips.

"There isn't a story. I owed Mary a favour for letting me park my van on her lawn. She took pity on me after I showed her the note you left."

"Ah." There wasn't much more to say to this, Hammond felt rather embarrassed at having been found out, it had been easier accepting her counter attack message that she had left with Emma rather than risking a direct confrontation.

Jenny grinned at him before snorting with laughter as she recounted her presumption that it had been the neighbour who had insulted her vehicle. "Poor Mary, I woke her up from the vibrations caused by me banging on the door, I was shouting at her for ages before I realised she was staring at my lips. If she had been younger, I would have presumed she fancied me!"

"The sign language, how did you learn it?"

Jenny's laughing eased, She offered Hammond the almost empty bottle.

"You'd better get some sleep. Thank you for listening to my woes."

He took the hint and moved off the sofa bed, noting that the bed frame shifted as he shuffled himself to the edge to stand up. He looked at Jenny and asked if she had found the bed comfortable. It served the purpose she replied. Hammond suggested that she use the bed in Paul's room. It wasn't as if Paul needed it anyway, he was rather ashamed that he hadn't thought of the idea earlier. Jenny accepted his offer and seemed pleased although he was aware she wanted him to leave her in peace. He bid her a restful sleep and walked to the kitchen where he placed the bottle on the worktop and left his glass in the sink. It was at that moment he remembered Harris' call telling him about the file. It had been two days ago, the time when Kathleen had said Harris had been found confused wandering the streets. Either she had been dishonest or Harris had left the house with a sudden attack of dementia within minutes of phoning him. He doubted the plausibility of the latter scenario and wondered why Kathleen had lied to him.

Rather cowardly Hammond informed Dunn of his intended day of absence by SMS text. It wouldn't come as a surprise to her he reasoned. Beech was unlikely to welcome Hammond back into the office until he could show he was fit enough to continue an investigation. Hammond knew he was perfectly fine but after a sleepless night, he was going to exploit the situation and stay in bed a little longer.

Hammond's feet were cold; the duvet had been pulled over the wrong side of the bed and was now dangling towards the floor rather than covering him. He adjusted the covers and lay back on the pillows, staring at the ceiling of his bedroom. He hadn't noticed before how badly it needed to be painted, his eyes scanned the walls and saw that the decor had aged without him noticing.

The north wall was looking damp; he reached his hand out as far as he could and felt the wall with the back of his hand. How could I not have noticed rising damp on the walls he thought. He scoffed at himself realising that inadvertently he had proven Beech was right; Hammond wasn't seeing what was right in front of him. His hand returned to the warmth of the bed and he lay listening to the muffled sound of Jenny singing in the shower. He reflected on her situation confessed to him only hours earlier. She was more sensitive than he had supposed. He hadn't been very considerate towards her, but at least he knew she would be more comfortable in Paul's room. He knew Paul wouldn't object since he hadn't been home for months, too busy getting on with his own life Hammond considered and decided to phone his son later.

By the time Jenny appeared downstairs, the tea was poured, bread toasted and an array of jams were spread out on the table. Hammond was surprised at how many conserves there were, he didn't remember buying any of them. She looked surprised to see him sitting at the kitchen table in his pyjamas and stopped short.

"Sit down Jenny, have some breakfast."

She eyed him suspiciously. "Ok, what have I done? You want me to leave?" It was a rhetorical question, she continued speaking without allowing him to explain he was simply trying to show her he cared.

"I knew it was too good to be true. I suppose it is because I am not doing anything all day, is that it? I should be paying rent or something." She sighed heavily and sat on the chair opposite him, grabbing a slice of toast with a sulky expression.

"Why? Do you want to move in? How long do you intend to stay?"

"I don't know! How should I know? How long does it take for a broken heart to mend?" she replied sarcastically. Hammond was amused by her answer, he tried not to smile but instead held her gaze with what he hoped was a kind but firm expression.

"You are welcome to stay for as long as you need too Jenny, but I don't think it is healthy for you to stay here all day dwelling. We need to find something for you to do."

"So that is why you stayed home today? To take me job hunting?"

"No, I am at home because my boss thinks I am unfit and need time off."

She stared at him in disbelief.

"What a bastard. I hope you told him where to go?" She bit into her toast, resembling a dog tearing at meat.

Hammond changed the subject. "I thought perhaps you and I could do something together, take a walk or something."

"Have you seen outside? Don't be an idiot Wally, it's bloody freezing out there!"

Jenny poured herself tea, and blew into the mug before tasting it. She grimaced before adding milk and several heaps of sugar.

"This is what we will do Wally. First you tell me how your date went last night, then you are going to tell me what has been on your mind lately. Ever since I have been here, you have been walking around with your head in the clouds."

Startled, Hammond looked at her. "I have?"

"Yep, It's not a woman, I know that much. You get this look across your face as if you are thinking hard."

"Oh."

"The date, how did it go?"

Hammond remembered Kathleen's proposition and blushed slightly, not replying.

"Aha! You got laid!"

It took a second to set her straight. Jenny stared as if she couldn't believe what he was saying. It was a mystery to her how Hammond could have possibly refused Kathleen's offer. Hammond had thought the same, but then he was reminded of the nagging doubt he had about Kathleen. Tom Edward's words kept floating to the forefront of his mind. "How trustworthy is Kathleen?" he had said. At the time Hammond had thought Edwards was simply imagining a conspiracy for the sake of being awkward, but since then Kathleen had lied to him and he didn't understand why.

"It could be perfectly innocent, she might have simply got her dates wrong or maybe she wanted you to feel sorry for her. Some women are like that you know, they like to be seen to be hard done by and need a hero to rescue them."

Hammond wasn't sure. He couldn't rid himself of doubt that Harris was not as confused as Kathleen would like him to believe, but why would she want to mislead him? So that he wouldn't help his friend? If Harris had been working on his own investigation before he was diagnosed surely Kathleen would appreciate her father having an interest that distracted him from the thought of his own mortality? He felt uneasy about the way she had suddenly tried to seduce him. He hadn't seen her for years, why take an interest in him now?

Jenny had more faith in his ability to attract women than he did. "Perhaps she has fancied you for ages but didn't make a move because you were married."

Hammond's facial expression suggested he was considering the idea although his instincts told him otherwise. The policeman's motto rang in his head "Assume anything, believe nothing, challenge everything." It was a sad state of affairs when he couldn't trust a former police officer's daughter. It was Hammond's turn to confide in Jenny. He moved on to the subject of Lloyd Harris, telling Jenny about the request Harris had made, but deliberately omitted his involvement with The Home Office investigation during the 1980's. Kathleen had contacted Hammond after Harris had asked him to look into the case, it was too much of a coincidence for Hammond's liking.

"So, this file, take a look at it. You don't have to go into work, so how about we both look into it? I can help you."

Jenny seemed enthusiastic. Pleased to have found her a distraction from her heartache he agreed and collected the little information he had gathered so far. The two heads bent over the papers he had printed off the internet a few days previously. Jenny's interest was focused on the FFASL forum pages. She read the last entry circled by Hammond. *"In memory of Theresa Davenport. A girl who did not deserve to die. Her killers are still out there somewhere, they know I know...question is what will they do about it?"*

"Did you reply to Cherry13?"

Hammond replied that the original comment by Cherry13 had been entered several months before.

"It's worth trying, just to see if you get a response, you know, throw some bait and reel them in." Hammond was confused; Jenny made it all sound so easy, he doubted that Cherry13 would fall for such a ploy and said as much, adding that he didn't know what results he hoped to achieve.

"Well, for a start you may find out their identity, secondly, if you can get Cherry13 to reply to your e-mail somehow, you can get their IP address and trace from where the e-mail was sent."

Hammond confessed he hadn't thought of this. The difficulty would be in encouraging Cherry13 to send a personal e-mail. The forum could be protected by confidentiality rules which meant that the only way of gaining access to this material would be by exposing his true identity and worse still, making his investigation official. Even if he did succeed in getting Cherry13 to reply personally, it would be foolish to assume that Cherry13 had used a computer at their home, the IP trace could lead to a public computer. He spoke these thoughts aloud to Jenny.

"If Cherry13 used a public computer, there may be CCTV; all you'd have to do is check the time of the entry."

"To access the CCTV footage, I would need to make an official request, I don't want to do that unless I am sure there is a crime to investigate."

"You may not need to do it officially, it depends on the settings of the forum, sometimes you can share your details when you register, make your e-mail address public, or there may be a facility that sends you an e-mail every time someone has made an update on the forum page."

Hammond felt encouraged. For the first time he wished he had a computer at home, and said so to Jenny who suggested borrowing Mary's. She returned from their next door neighbours house carrying a laptop and set it up on the kitchen table. Jenny's fingers tapped lightly over the keyboard. Using Mary's wireless signal, they managed to get onto the internet and find the forum page where Cherry13 had written her entry..

Using a new e-mail account set up specifically for the purpose, Jenny registered an alias onto the FFASL forum and highlighted Cherry13's icon. A new tab was opened with an option to contact Cherry13. With a broad smile, Jenny passed the keyboard to Hammond and encouraged him to write a message. Pleased though he was by their progress, he suddenly felt hesitant and questioned his methods. He was beginning to behave like a private detective which was the last thing he wanted to do. He sat there in silence, not knowing what to write. He decided to be honest but keep the message simple. "I would like to know more about Theresa Davenport. Why do you think she was killed?" He clicked send and then questioned aloud what was supposed to happen next. There was no activity for a while during which time, Hammond had drunk three cups of coffee and Jenny had ventured outside the front door to smoke the last of her cigarettes. Eventually their patience was rewarded by a tab appearing on the bottom right corner of the screen. Cherry13 was online, he was invited to enter a chat room, he accepted. The reply by Cherry13 asked why they were interested. With tact and diplomacy Hammond replied, he was unsure whether to include too much information but knew he needed something to make Cherry13 realise his interest exceeded beyond mere curiosity.

"If Theresa was killed like you say, then I want the guilty identified."

The reply was immediate. "Why should I trust you?"

His answer was typed before he had a chance to think about what he wanted to say.

"Because Theresa may not be the only one. There may be others."

There was no reply, Cherry13 went off-line. Hammond swore loudly, he had blown it.

"A very little bundle of instincts and impulses is indispensable to a man on his way down the path of life to a peaceful and humble grave."
Henry Havelock Ellis. The Dance of Life. 1923

CHAPTER TWELVE

Hammond didn't bother to shower until midday and cut his toiletry routine by not shaving. He studied his reflection in the mirror and wondered what information his features gave away. He was frowning and attempted to relax the brow muscles but found the more he studied himself, the more tense his features became. Is this what others see? He tried to remember the last time he had bellowed with laughter, he couldn't. The possibility that he was entering a depression was frightening. He couldn't understand what was happening, why Beech couldn't trust him to do his job. He rubbed himself dry with the towel that hung off the back of the bathroom door. Could it be that I am getting old before my time? The previous evening's conversation with Kathleen had brought back memories of his mother. Towards the end of her life, she had seemed frail, yet she had only been three years older than he was now when she died. Perhaps it is hereditary, maybe I take after her; I am disintegrating away, piece by piece. He returned to the mirror reflection and told it to stop being so ridiculous before searching for the toothpaste.

He went back to his bedroom and looked for a clean pair of socks. Only one sock was found, he searched the drawer contents looking for the other when his mobile beeped. He saw that he had three missed calls. He pressed call back. Edwards answered, his voice sounded more refined on the phone than face to face. "Sir, I've got good news and bad news, which do you want first?"

Impatiently, Hammond replied he'd rather the information be given without games. Edwards delivered as requested. "DS Dunn has been reassigned to a rape case, so Galvin and I are pretty much the only two here sealing the Robert's case."

"Damn!" Hammond knew Beech was doing his upmost to close the case, having Hammond and now Dunn out of the way meant that less time and resources would be spent on what Beech considered to be a completed investigation.

"Forensics have completed their report. The soil found in the nostrils of Graham Roberts has been identified as being native soil from where he was found so he died after the fall. Secondly, toxicology came back, there were traces of Beta-Blockers, Statins, Angiotensin and Calcium Channel Blockers but negative for Aspirin or Nitrates so the original time of death still stands."

"What about the bike? Can it be proven that it was Thomas' bike that hit Roberts?"

"Yes, there was tissue on it."

Hammond felt defeated, with this evidence there would be no reason not to charge Thomas and hand it to the prosecutor. Edwards allowed the news to be digested before making his offer. "If you want I can hold it back a few hours, give us a chance to look at Robert's house again."

"I don't understand, why go there again?"

There was noise in the background, Hammond recognised Galvin's voice talking to Edwards, there were murmurs between the two men before Edwards came back onto the phone. " Galvin and I were there yesterday, there was no post, not even junk mail. We have checked to see if the mail has been redirected but no official request has been processed. We reckon that the post is being collected by someone."

"The house is still sealed?"

Edwards said that it was, no neighbours had entered the property. A discreet enquiry with the sister had confirmed that she had not been to the property or delegated anyone else to collect the post.

"What do you suggest Edwards?"

"Well, that's why I am calling you Sir. What do you want us to do? Galvin and I searched the house, but we weren't looking for evidence of any one else having been in the property. We didn't notice if the house had been broken into since we were there the first time."

Hammond scratched his head thinking. It wasn't logical that there was no post in Robert's house, he hadn't been absent long enough for bills to be diverted, there would be some mail, even if it were only the pizza takeaway menus that were put through doors on a weekly basis.

"Ok, First look for any evidence of a forced entry, then try the neighbours, it's possible he may have left a spare key with them for whatever reason, then call me. If necessary we can watch the house or check out any CCTV cameras situated nearby. But be discreet, If Beech finds out about this, Thomas will be booked by this evening."

Galvin came onto the phone. "Why don't you come out and look with us? You may see something we haven't and no offence Sir, but time isn't on our side."

"Fine, I'll meet you there in half hour."

The mobile was tossed onto the bed as the lost sock was retrieved and pulled on. He found his car keys and was about to grab his jacket when he remembered he had left the car at the pub. Slipping the keys into his trouser pocket, he called to Jenny. He had a job for her.

The screeching fan belt of the Volkswagen camper van announced Hammond's arrival a few doors away from Robert's house. Hammond wasn't a proud man, but it was easier to be dropped off unseen than have to explain why he had allowed himself to be driven in a vehicle resembling something from the Scooby Doo cartoons.

Galvin and Edwards were waiting in their car on the other side of the road, Hammond thanked Jenny and sprinted across to them, before getting into the back seat of the car.

"If we can do this without the neighbours seeing us, that would be preferable."

Edwards greeted Hammond by offering his packet of Salt and Vinegar crisps. Hammond declined, thinking the loud munching was enough to put anyone off. DC Michael Galvin was sitting in the driver's seat and turned around to Hammond.

"There is the possibility that someone from the media entered the house, they were seen outside a few days ago."

"Either way, we need to see if the entry was forced." The three men split up to look at Robert's house. Edwards took the route towards the front door, Galvin the side window and Hammond around the back. Neither could find any clues that there had been an illegal entry into the house. Galvin produced the front key and the three detectives resumed their search inside the house.

After forty minutes, Hammond gave up. "The only explanation is that someone else had a key to the property."

"We checked with the neighbours, Roberts had never left a key with them and no-one has ever been seen visiting." Edwards confirmed Galvin's statement by nodding his head as he picked out debris from his teeth with his fingernail.

"You think that the house is being watched?"

Hammond shook his head. "Not necessarily, but whoever collects the post has been there daily since Robert's died. We'll have to assume they are looking for something in particular. I reckon we should bait our mystery guest, leave them something worth collecting. If that fails, we'll check the CCTV."

Galvin's eyes widened. "How? Beech is never going to let us."

Hammond was past caring what Beech would or wouldn't allow. He needed to explore all possibilities. If the investigation into Roberts's death wasn't thorough, his murder could easily be seen to be a motiveless crime. Hammond couldn't risk that. If a twelve year old boy was going to be convicted of a crime, it was to be based on an investigation that handled every scrap of evidence possible. Edwards poked a finger at his colleague, "Sure he will, if a neighbour was concerned there had been a break-in."

"But there hasn't been one, we have just established that." Galvin was impatient with Edwards apparent lack of attention but Hammond understood what Edwards was suggesting; if a neighbour was concerned about their security, it would be necessary to reassure them by investigating further. Even if the cause of concern originated from nothing more than a suspicion. The men left the house. Galvin and Hammond watched from the car as Edwards rang the bell of the neighbours doors before addressing himself to an elderly man who looked warily up the road as the Detective Constable spoke. Hammond laid a firm hand on Galvin's shoulder "Galvin, I am your superior officer, you will be following my orders."

It was with some regret that Hammond contemplated the mornings events. Not only had he behaved recklessly by attempting to tease information from a bereaved stranger online. He had just allowed a member of his team to cause deliberate concern to an elderly neighbour of a murder victim and had unburdened himself of his worries onto the shoulders of his son's best friend whom he also now knew was emotionally vulnerable. This was not the man Hammond wanted to be but he knew he was running out of choices as far as the investigations were concerned. Part of him felt responsible for Thomas' fate and he owed his career to Lloyd Harris so his actions, reckless though they were, had some justifiable cause. Hammond had seen a look of disappointment flash across Galvin's face when he had allowed Edwards to behave the way he had done, but he knew the only way of identifying who was taking Robert's post would be by baiting them to collect more post or looking through CCTV recordings taken of Dymchurch Road during the last few days. It was important that this was done as soon as possible before Thomas Taylor was charged. He hoped silently that Galvin would remain co-operative. He admired Galvin, he was enthusiastic and not arrogant like Edwards but he couldn't trust that Galvin wouldn't report on his underhand methods of investigation. Keeping these thoughts to himself, he accepted Galvin's offer of a lift to where he had left his car at Charing. The journey lasted twenty minutes in which time the three men discussed how to continue their investigation. Edwards had had no luck tracing the mobile number called from Robert's home the night before his murder.

"The mobile was switched off when I tried it, but the good news is that Robert's had phoned this number several times in the last month, each call lasted between two to ten minutes each time. That suggests a familiarity between both parties. The bad news is that the number isn't registered so we have no idea to whom the phone belongs."

Galvin had attempted to search for the Mother and son whom had filed a complaint against Roberts in 2001.

"The Mother's name was Gail Lawson. She married a second time in 2003 to Nicholas Ricci and they moved towards the Clapham area. I think they had more children but the information is pretty limited. I'll have to delve a bit deeper. Either way, I couldn't find anything else that suggests Roberts' posed a threat to her son or to any other children. There have been no other reports of him behaving inappropriately, not officially anyway."

Hammond was disappointed. It was beginning to look as if the motive behind the attack on Roberts was nothing more than Thomas losing his temper after being humiliated. However, it still didn't explain the missing wallet. They decided to keep looking although they all felt that time was running out. As Hammond left the car, he agreed to meet them at the station later in the afternoon. Whilst he was in Charing, it may be worth checking in on Lloyd Harris. Hammond did not want to believe that Kathleen had been dishonest regarding her father's state of mind, but it may be worth paying him an unexpected visit.

As Hammond collected his box file from the restaurant office, he was aware of a look of respect by the manager. At first he wondered if it were due to the generous tip he had left but his thoughts were quickly corrected by the other man who made it no secret that he had admired Hammonds choice of dinner guest the previous evening. Despite his slight annoyance at the manager's lack of discretion, Hammond found himself blushing as Kathleen was mentioned. He was reminded again of his cowardly behaviour towards her and it embarrassed him enough to make a hasty exit from the restaurant as he made his way to the car. As Hammond opened the driver's door he was surprised by the musty smell that greeted him. Instinctively he looked up towards the side of the Restaurant building looking for the air vents that could explain the smell but he couldn't see any. He shrugged dismissively and proposed that the smell had been caused by the damp air as the car had been left stationary. The car throbbed in response to the turned ignition, he allowed the engine to idle as he quickly texted a message on his mobile to Paul telling him he intended to call him later that evening. He hoped that Paul wouldn't be waiting for another call like last time. He missed talking to his son and wanted to make an effort to enjoy a real conversation with him. The reply beeped several seconds later. It took Hammond several seconds to translate Pauls' reply which used numbers to abbreviate words but he understood Paul would expect his call at eight in the evening. There was a hint of sarcasm in his son's reply, Paul was probably amused by his Father making an appointment to talk to him, but it satisfied Hammond enough to put the car into gear and exit the car park.

Neither Lloyd or Kathleen Harris were at home when Hammond called there but he felt partly relieved. He wasn't sure how he would face Kathleen after his rejection of her advances the previous evening and he would have been embarrassed if Harris had sensed the discomfort between them. Harris would not have allowed such a situation to pass by without comment. At the same time, Hammond wanted to see for himself how his former colleague was coping with his illness. Every time he had seen him, Lloyd Harris had behaved quite capably, yet Kathleen would have had no reason to exaggerate. The inconsistency didn't make sense to Hammond, and the detective within him wanted to find the answers. Instead he resigned himself to trying later and called Edwards telling him he would be there within the hour. He hung up and instinctively patted the box file lying on the passenger seat beside him. The sooner he had answered Harris' enquiry the better.

The Philadelphia Orchestra had soothed Hammond's mind into a still focus as he headed towards the motorway, The pitch and lows of the Adagio Strings lifted his spirits and eased his responsibilities momentarily until he heard a clunking noise from somewhere underneath him. He switched off the radio and tilted his head towards the floor of the car in an attempt to decipher the cause of the noise which was beginning to cause him alarm. But the noise had gone. Checking his rear view mirror, he was satisfied that he had not driven over an obstacle in the road and increased the radio's volume as he merged with the motorway traffic. Occasionally his right hand lifted with the swell in the music and then lowered gently back onto the steering wheel as he allowed the music to caress him. His attention was drawn momentarily to the rear number plate of the car travelling in front of him. It was obviously a bespoke registration; LUV 31Y. He studied it for several seconds before it dawned on him that the numbers represented similar looking letters. It reminded him of the text messages Paul had sent. Hammond guessed it was known as text language but he personally found it easier to write full English, perhaps it was his age. As he pulled into the middle lane a thought struck him suddenly. A thought so profound he laughed at his stupidity at not realising it before. He knew who Cherry13 was. He slapped his hand back onto the steering wheel with a triumphant gesture. A black BMW shot past him at terrifying speed on the overtaking lane, startling him out of his moment of jubilation. Annoyed, Hammond cursed the reckless driver hoping that they would be caught by a traffic patrol further along but then, as soon as he had made the wish, he regretted it. Seeing a traffic police car parked on the side of the hard shoulder, the black BMW suddenly slammed the brakes and swerved in front of Hammond's car. As Hammond punched his foot down onto the break, he realised too late that the car wasn't responding. A tide of sickness overwhelmed him as he predicted what was about to happen. Instinctively, he allowed his body to go limp and helplessly waited for the blackness that engulfed him.

The bright lights hurt his eyes. He couldn't see anything but blobs that moved in and out of focus and occasionally made mumbling noises. He tried to lift a hand to cover his eyes but instead felt a wave of pain that overtook his senses and sent him back into the blackness.

The threat was particularly vicious. It was more terrifying than anything he had ever sensed in his life, he tried to run but found his legs were paralysed. He found himself wanting to scream but no sound came from him. There were lights flashing around him, he squeezed his eyes closed to block out the luminosity that threatened to burn his mind but even with his eyelids sealed he knew the light would enter his head, it would eradicate all his thoughts and memories. He screamed silently, knowing that he could not be helped, that no one would rescue him.

Wallace Hammond awoke, not knowing where he was or how long he had been there. He knew he felt different, but he couldn't understand where the feeling was coming from. He tried to touch his body but found he couldn't move his arms. He attempted to lift his head but discovered that doing so brought on pain and nausea. There were vague memories but he couldn't make sense of them. He could move his eyes but realised that he was only seeing through his left eye, the right eye was covered in a pink blur. He knew his heart was beating, he could feel it thumping in his eardrums but all other sound was muffled as if he were underwater. The feeling of panic that arose from his gut swept over him, he tried to cry out but instead he could only move his tongue which was dry and swollen. For the first time in years, Wallace Hammond prayed for mercy.

"Wallace?" The voice was indistinguishable but it tugged at him as if there was a connection there that he could trust. He gargled a response and then felt hands over him, he felt his eyelid being lifted and a light shone into his eye. It hurt him but it was over quickly. There was activity around him, hurried movements and he knew his prayer was being answered.

His tongue no longer felt swollen, he found he could move his left hand a bit more and was surprised to discover that his head was elevated slightly. He moved it towards the left side of him where he was aware there was someone seated. The figure moved forward and he felt a hand on his squeezing gently. His eye focused on the woman who had saved him from his nightmare. Lyn. He tried to speak her name but she put a finger on his lips and moved closer.

"You had us worried there for a while". Lyn had moved so close to him that he could smell the scent of apple shampoo in her hair. She looked tired, her eyes were swollen with dark circles underneath.

"You are at the hospital Wallace, you crashed your car. We have been here with you since. Paul was here until an hour ago but he is coming back. The nurses have just phoned him to tell him you are awake." Lyn was talking fast, as if she had to fill the silence with explanations. He wanted to respond, he wanted to be back in the body that moved and functioned but he was restrained somehow. Slowly, he thought about what he wanted to say and formed the words in his mind. After a few moments mouthing the shape of the words he managed to speak. "Bad smell in car." The effort made his head fall back and he slept.

"The promised land lies on the other side of a wilderness."
Henry Havelock Ellis. The Dance of Life. 1923

CHAPTER THIRTEEN

He was told that he had been unconscious in the Intensive Care Unit for a week, Paul had offered this information to his father with an almost accusatory tone. Hammond instinctively mumbled an apology in response and then apologised again when he saw Paul had tears in his eyes. Time had been stolen from Hammond and he felt cheated. He did not remember much about the car crash and his first thought was to wonder if he had been responsible but each time he asked, the question was ignored and the topic of conversation changed. He could now move his head freely and his right eye was not so swollen although he couldn't yet open it fully. He could see that the nurses had collected all his cards and messages from well wishers on a string that was strung over his bed in his private room. His right arm still felt heavy but his left hand was able to move without difficulty. His conversations with the doctors made him realise how lucky he was to be alive. Other than severe concussion caused by head trauma, a cracked rib and a smashed ankle accounted for the pain but he knew from the expressions on his visitor's faces that he wasn't looking particularly handsome. He guessed his blackened eyes and bruised, swollen face had something to do with it. Lyn had visited him several times and he had enjoyed her attention but she visited him less now that she knew he was recovering. Paul and Jenny had been with him every day since he had woken and they passed the time playing chess or cards. Hammond would often question why he had not seen Galvin, Edwards or Dunn, but often this question was ignored until the Doctor explained that Lyn had asked for them to keep away. This had made Hammond angry, even though he knew it had been Lyn's way of caring for him. Even now she couldn't accept that his work was as much part of him as his family. The emotional ties between himself and his colleagues were not endearing but they were necessary. Lyn would only ever see his police career as a sideline, but in reality it wasn't about choice. Being a detective was being Wallace Hammond just as much as it was being a father to Paul. It didn't take long for Hammond to demand Paul phone his team and invite them to the hospital, he ignored Paul's protests but bribed him with the thought that the sooner he could return to work, the sooner he would recover.

Sergeant Lois Dunn was not tactful with her reaction upon seeing Hammond in bed. Later he would describe her actions as almost gagging. Galvin and Edwards just looked sheepish and awkward. They were working with DCI Morris who had closed the Roberts case the day after Hammond had crashed the car. Hammond was not surprised but he was upset. To compensate the team offered to fill him in on the details. Hammond knew they were humouring him; no doubt they knew that he needed a distraction from his ailments. They couldn't talk to him about the cases they were working on although Hammond had kept up to date with the local news and knew there had been a fatal stabbing during a domestic disturbance locally.

"So Thomas has been charged?"

Dunn looked down at her hands as she answered him "As far as I know, they are waiting for the results of the psychiatric evaluation on Thomas. I think the CPS are pushing for Grievous Bodily Harm."

Hammond sighed. "You're going to Robert's inquest?"

Dunn shrugged. "I guess so, although we know what the outcome will be."

"I am not sure what I was going to do that day. I know I was returning to Folkestone, to do something but I can't remember what. I know it was important though."

Hammond had a niggling feeling that there was something else he had meant to do but he couldn't remember. There was a sense of urgency that he couldn't rid himself of.

Galvin spoke up for the first time, he avoided looking at Hammond's face as he did so. "You shouldn't worry about that now Sir, you have got to rest."

Hammond flinched at the suggestion that he was useless. He felt frustrated. He was sick of being an invalid. The team felt the change in atmosphere and tactfully withdrew, offering to visit him again. He nodded, resigned to the fact that he wouldn't be included in any investigation whilst he was a broken man. He attempted to smile as they bid him goodbye and closed his eyes trying to remember what he felt was so important.

Two officers from the Serious Collision Investigation Team visited Hammond in the afternoon. He automatically felt guilty by their presence and demanded to know how many people had been hurt in the accident. Instead of answering his questions, the first officer blinked at him with evident surprise.

"You believe you are responsible for the collision?"

Hammond tried to shuffle his weight slightly, he was in pain and needed more medication but it was important to him that he remain alert. He felt that he was missing something about the crash, it was obvious to him that his earlier visitors had been deliberately evasive as if they knew more about the incident than they wanted to share with him. He suspected that they were ashamed of any mistakes he had made.

"To be honest I don't remember the actual incident but I feel responsible somehow."

The first officer helped himself to a chair and sat opposite Hammond.

"There were traffic patrol officers who witnessed the incident. It is evident that the collision wasn't your fault. The accident couldn't have been prevented, although the severity of the collision is believed to have been exacerbated by the condition of your car."

"I don't understand. You are saying my car wasn't road worthy? It had its MOT a month ago!" Hammond was confused and wished the man wouldn't talk in riddles

"What do you remember?" The question was asked by the second officer, a young slim man.

"Like I said, I don't remember anything."

"You were heard saying to your wife that "the car smelt bad." Do you remember to which car you were referring?"

Hammond was tempted to correct the reference to Lyn as his wife but instead concentrated and then slowly remembered getting into by his car outside the restaurant. He had opened the driver's door and been aware of an unfamiliar smell. He recounted the memory to the officers.

"Can you remember what kind of smell, was it a burning smell for example?"

Hammond replied that it had been more of a musty smell, like a man who hadn't washed recently, he gave a lop-sided smile as if to excuse what he said, aware that such a description wasn't helpful.

The interview was short but left Hammond exhausted. He knew his memory couldn't be rushed but he felt a sense of urgency that wouldn't leave him. He was confused. There were too many gaps. He wanted to talk to Jenny. He knew that she would be honest but he suspected she had been asked to withhold information. There was a telephone above his head but it needed a credit card and he didn't have Jenny's mobile number. Paul had said that he was staying at home with Jenny whilst Hammond was in hospital but he didn't want to phone the house. Paul would be loyal to his mother and therefore it was not a good idea to ask him what Lyn didn't want him to know. But Jenny had her own ideas. If she knew how bothered he was not knowing what was going on she would tell him, he was sure of it. He considered whether his mobile phone was nearby and asked a passing nurse if she could pass him his belongings from the cupboard but her search showed there were no personal belongings in the room. He guessed Lyn had it all.

To Hammond's disappointment he did not receive any visitors the following day other than the Physiotherapist and surgeon. He needed to have surgery to pin his ankle and they talked about the after care. It was becoming increasingly obvious to Hammond that he wouldn't be walking unaided for several months. The thought depressed him and he wondered how he would cope at home alone. The nurses had been busy during the day putting up Christmas decorations along the wards, it was a bitter reminder that Christmas was drawing closer and he didn't relish the idea of being alone unless he was working. Paul would spend Christmas with his mother, and rightfully so. Lyn's teaching job had the advantage of school holidays. Presumably Jenny would join them. He dwelled on the idea that he may be lonely and this lead to more thoughts about Kathleen. He couldn't understand why Kathleen had not visited him at the hospital but then logical thought told him she didn't know about the accident. It was likely that she thought he was avoiding her following the embarrassment at the restaurant weeks ago. Thinking of Kathleen he suddenly remembered what else he had in the car with him during the time of the accident. He had forgotten about the file Lloyd Harris had compiled. With a sickening thought he pressed the button for the nurse's attention and asked to use a phone. It was after some heated persuasion that the phone was to be used for 'police business' that the nurse reluctantly agreed to allow him to use the phone at the nurse's station and delivered him with some aplomb at the desk in his wheelchair. He phoned Ds Lois Dunn and asked her to visit him that afternoon. He stressed the word 'important' more for the nurses benefit than for Dunn's but she agreed to visit him after finding out what had happened to his mobile phone and the file.

As he was wheeled back to his bed, Hammond felt more revived than he had been for the several weeks he had been there.

The surgery on Hammond's ankle was deemed a success, within hours of waking up he was moved to another ward. Somewhat irrationally Hammond felt as if he were now under pressure to get well quickly to allow more beds for other patients. He grumbled mentally thinking how much better off he would be if he had taken the option of private health care through the Police Healthcare Scheme. It had seemed an unnecessary expense at the time, but he now realised how cavalier he had been about his health. As the wheelchair took him along the corridors the mingled wafts of stale air, disinfectant and cafeteria food drifted after him and reminded him of his first hospital stay when he was four years old. It was summer 1962, he had been in hospital with Pneumonia. He remembered being on a ward that was full of children who didn't appear to have any reason for being there. They weren't ill like himself, they would spend the days playing or reading him stories. He remembered one girl in particular, her name was Sarah. She had been sad when he was finally discharged, he remembered her handing him the remaining squares of her Fry's Five Boys chocolate as a leaving present. Hammond found himself smiling at the memory, he remembered the chocolate wrapper even now, a picture of five boys all showing different moods. Sarah had said he had reminded her of the boy called expectation. Many years later, he was told by his mother that the children on his ward had stayed at the hospital whilst their parents were in prison or until there was room at the orphanages. The hospital had provided available beds for them until they found more permanent accommodation. Now, almost five decades later, the hospitals were throwing patients out as quickly as possible. Hammond's stomach responded to the smells of lunch being served and he realised he hadn't eaten properly for several days. Gloomily he wondered what food he would be offered if he were now in a private hospital and apologised to his stomach for depriving it of such promise. No-one had mentioned how long Hammond would stay in hospital, but as he reached his new ward he realised how badly he wanted to leave. His ward companions looked as if they were clinging on to life by a thread. The racking cough of his neighbour from the next bed only ceased for a second as his arrival was noted before it continued its tormenting sound.

It was a welcome relief to see Lyn walk into the ward. She greeted him coolly and sat on the chair next to his bed. He noted she was carrying a large carrier bag and the contents looked heavy. His stomach grumbled loudly and he hoped she had brought some treats but instead she took out a can of shaving cream and a razor blade. The stubble he had ignored the day of the accident had now grown to a thick beard but he hadn't minded, in fact Hammond wondered whether it had added some distinguishing character to his features. The way Lyn looked at him showed him that she didn't agree.

"You look terrible Wallace. Do you wash?"

Hammond flushed slightly wondering if he smelt.

"I get a bed bath...it's difficult with my limbs in plaster."

Lyn sighed heavily and walked to the basin near the end bed. She returned with a pulp kidney dish that she had used as a bowl for warm water. Hammond enjoyed feeling her gentle touch on his face, it made him realise how much he had missed her and wondered how long he had taken her for granted during their marriage. He watched her as she carried out her task with precision. "This brings back memories." He smiled at her and was relieved to see her smile in return.

"That was years ago."

He felt reassured that she remembered shaving him during their first year together. It had been an intimate moment between them that had led to hysteria as she had nicked him several times leaving him with cuts all over his face. "What happened to us Lyn?" A wave of regret swept over him as he realised yet again that he had lost her. Lyn didn't reply until he touched her hand. "There is no point crying over spilt milk Wallace."

"So that is what we are; spilt milk?"

"Wallace, there is no point going over the past. Our marriage didn't work. We just have to accept it and move on."

"Have you?" It was a question he had wanted to ask her for a long time but now he needed to know.

Lyn didn't respond for several minutes, she busied herself rinsing the razor and dabbing his face with a towel before she looked into his eyes and gave him the answer he dreaded. "Yes, I have."

"Who is he?"

"Does it matter?" She looked at him unsure whether to give him all the information. Eventually she sat down on the chair and faced him directly. Her voice was firm when she replied.

"His name is Cameron. He is a solicitor. We have been dating for six months now and yes, before you ask, Paul knows. There is nothing more to tell."

Hammond was hurt. His son had known his mother had found someone else and had given nothing away. He shouldn't be surprised, Paul was loyal to his mother and always had been but he had wished Paul had warned him.

"I suppose I thought we would sort it out eventually. Silly really, but you were my wife Lyn. That counted for something didn't it?"

Lyn sighed making it evident she was frustrated by the topic of conversation. She shrugged her shoulders, wondering why he was being so obstinate.

"Wallace, let's be honest. We didn't have a marriage, we co-existed. When we met we were young and naive. We married because that was the logical next step."

Hammond stared with disbelief at the woman with whom he had shared almost three decades of his life.

"We married because we were in love and wanted to spend our lives together. Or have you forgotten that bit?"

Lyn studied his face for several seconds silently, then she leaned forward, resting her hand on his.

"Were we in love? I loved you Wallace, but was I *in* love? I don't think I was. I don't remember feeling the ache from wanting you, the euphoria after you had called, the excitement at the prospect of building a future with you, the thrill of being in love. Did you?"

She waited for him to answer but instead he was mute. He found her words hard to digest, yet he needed her to tell him more. He couldn't believe she had never spoken to him about the way she had felt before. He swallowed hard, unsure what to say so simply nodded to show he was listening.

"I know you loved me Wallace. I know you were faithful as I was to you. But had we been in love with each other,

I don't think I would have been so resentful that your mind was always occupied with your work. Even when you were in the same room with me, your mind was elsewhere."

"How do you know you weren't in love? What would you compare it to? The stuff you read in women's magazines, the nonsense you watch in chick-flicks? Lyn, this is real life. The thrill, the euphoria you are talking about. That's not love, it's infatuation."

Lyn smiled suddenly as if she couldn't help herself. Watching her Hammond realised her radiance came from something else other than her finding humour in his words. He felt nausea rising at the back of his throat.

"So, this Cameron guy. You are in love with him, is that what you are saying? How do you know Lyn that it isn't some middle age crises, an infatuation?"

"Because he makes me want to be the best person I can be. Not for his approval, but because being with him makes me see how life could be if we allow ourselves to relax and accept what life brings."

"And I didn't? You achieved all the things you wanted Lyn when we were together. It's true my mind was often occupied, but you and Paul were my priority. You got your career, you became a mother, what is the best that you can be?"

Lyn met his eyes. "Do you remember lending me your Tolstoy book?"

Hammond nodded, he had been an avid reader of classical literature during his youth, when time had been a luxury he could afford.

"The truth was I didn't understand much of it. I liked Jackie Collins and David Bowie, you liked the Classics. My simple tastes couldn't compare to your intellectual and cultured interests. I became a teacher because it was a practical career choice, not because I wanted to be. I wanted to be an air steward, to travel the world. So no, I didn't get the career I wanted and although I love Paul more than anything, I would have preferred to have had children when I was older, after I had experimented with life first. Wallace, we compromised to fit with each other."

"I didn't force you to do any of those things Lyn. You gave the impression of being happy."

"I was, at first. But then you got the career you wanted and I became second best. It wasn't enough for me. I suppose I wanted you to be my hero, not a hero to all those victims of crime but me. I needed you Wallace. I needed a friend and a lover and instead I had to share you with complete strangers who could have you looking after them any time of day or night whilst I was left at home raising our son and wishing I could do something else." Lyn had spoken the last sentences rapidly as if it were flooding out of her mouth before she could stop the words from being heard. Suddenly she paused for breath and her shoulders sank. The silence lingered between them before she lifted her chin proudly and left the side of his bed to empty the bowl of used water.

As she left his bed, she picked up the carrier bag and placed it on his bed closer to him.

"I think this is what you wanted. Lois Dunn asked me to make sure you got it, she said she was meant to visit you but something came up."

He looked inside the bag and saw the battered edge of the box file Lloyd Harris had given him. He smiled and thanked her with sincere appreciation. Lyn looked at him silently as she watched him struggle to release the file from the bag with one hand. "It is not your fault Wallace, but this illustrates my point exactly."

He raised his head and sent her a questioning look.

"The only time I have seen you smile since your accident is when you have had something to work on."

Lyn left him soon after. He had thanked her for her visit rather formally. He knew Lyn wouldn't visit him at the hospital again. As he listened to the fading sound of her heels clicking down the corridor, he called the nurse and demanded more painkillers, but even as the pills were dispensed, Hammond knew the only cure for the pain in his chest was time.

"We can never solve the so-called world riddle
because what seem riddles to us are merely
the contradictions we have ourselves created."
Henry Havelock Ellis. The Dance of Life. 1923

CHAPTER FOURTEEN

Despite the complaints by the nurses, Hammond was using his hospital bed as an office desk. The box file was emptied of its contents. Photographs and jotted notes were organised in piles using every available space. Each photograph was examined closely first. Some looked like random pictures of various people of different ages. One was of a group of children seated on steps outside a large house. None of the children were smiling but they looked relaxed and comfortable. One girl, the darker of the five, had long plaits that brushed down her upper arms. She looked about fourteen years old and was particularly striking to look at. Another girl with lighter strawberry blonde hair sat beside her squinting in the sun light that shone from behind the photographer causing their shadow to rest on the steps by the children's feet. Hammond couldn't tell if the shadow depicted a male or female, the figure was slight and had their arm raised to their face as they held the camera to their eye. Behind the second girl stood a boy, Hammond guessed he was no older than fourteen. He was skinny and dressed in a tee-shirt that was too small for him and pinched him under the arms. He wasn't looking toward the camera but instead had his head turned slightly as his eyes stayed on the strawberry blonde haired girl seated in front of him. To the right of the boy was a slightly dumpy girl with mousey coloured curly hair. She wore glasses with thick frames that didn't flatter her. She had her arms crossed across her chest and was frowning. Her long blue skirt brushed the steps and hid her feet. An older boy, possibly late teens, Hammond guessed, was standing apart from the group. He had his head raised slightly and turned to the camera with an arrogant expression. His right hand rested on his hip whilst the other held a burning cigarette. Hammond studied each figure intently and turned the photograph hoping for their names to be written on the back. Instead he read 1987 scribbled in pencil. Hammond leafed through the other photographs until he recognised a single photograph of the girl with the plaits. The picture was in black and white and wasn't posed, suggesting that the photographer had caught her unawares. The scene suggested they were at a party. She looked slightly older with her hair tied back in a chignon. The person she was talking to was evidently male and broad shouldered but was unidentifiable with their back to the camera. Hammond studied the girl, trying to read her expression. It was neutral, she wasn't smiling neither did she look sad. It was as if the girl was listening politely. Hammond found another photograph of the same girl, taken at the same time. Only this time the photographer had caught her from a side angle and showed her at full length wearing a long black shoulder-less dress that flattered her figure. She stood next to a long mirror. The mirror's reflection showed several people standing beside her in formal attire within a large room decorated with chandeliers and flowers. Hammond studied the scene and considered that the room may have been in a hotel. Then he looked again, he thought he saw a mark on the girls shoulder-blade, it was small and not easy to decipher without magnifying the picture. He looked at the back of the photo, but there was no writing.

He placed the photograph back onto the bed and sorted through the other photographs. There was a small picture that surprised him. He recognised Lloyd Harris immediately despite the fact that the picture had been taken at least thirty years previously. The youthful Harris was slimmer with thicker hair but he didn't look much different than when Hammond had first known him. The younger Lloyd Harris was posing with a tall, elegant woman in a bright yellow dress. Her poise reminded Hammond of a young Sophia Loren. Her lips were wide and full and she was leaning on Harris arm as if they were sharing a private joke. Hammond pondered the identity of the woman in the picture. He hadn't known Harris' wife Elisabeth as she had died only a year after he had met Harris but there was no doubt that the woman in the picture was Kathleen's mother. They were almost identical. Hammond gazed at the picture for several moments before placing the picture on his bedside cabinet. Harris had obviously misplaced the picture in the wrong file, he made a mental note to return the photograph to Lloyd.

Hammond turned his attention onto the jotted notes handwritten in a large untidy scrawl but it was easily decipherable. Hammond skimmed the content and was disappointed to discover the notes referred to a social worker by the name of Raphael Turner who had worked for the Kent County Council's Child Care Services in the 1980's. There was no reference to any of the names he hoped to find or to any police business. He tried another page, which detailed an Offstead report on the same Child Care Services written in 1989, the content was equally irrelevant. With frustration, Hammond threw the notes back onto the bed. His ankle was itchy under the plaster and he searched for something scratchy. He found a paperclip in the bottom of the file and unravelled it into a straight tool. He moaned with pleasure as he scratched at the skin under the dressing.

"Sounds dubious."

Jenny had pulled back the curtain surrounding his bed without warning. He sat up guiltily feeling like a school boy caught sneaking a smoke by the bike sheds. Despite being annoyed by her intrusion, he was also pleased to see her and even more so to discover she had brought his mobile phone with her. He accepted it gratefully from her outstretched hand and wondered how she had got the phone. She explained that Lyn had kept it since the car's surviving contents had been handed to her for safekeeping but Lyn had since left to return home and had returned the items to Paul to pass to his father.

Hammond was disappointed to hear that Lyn had left, but he wasn't surprised. He had hoped that Lyn would stay to see him recover fully but he knew it was unreasonable to expect her to do so. That would have been a wife's duty, not an ex-wife's. He sighed heavily ignoring Jenny's raised eyebrow and gestured for her to close the curtain. She did so before plonking herself onto his bed heavily. The sudden movement caused him to cry out in pain as his ankle and rib were disturbed and she held a hand to her mouth with an aghast expression, voicing her regret that she had caused him pain yet a faint smile appeared behind her hand and he enjoyed the humour with her.

"I need to get out of here Jenny, I am going mad."

Jenny looked at him with genuine sympathy. "I meant to give you a message. DS Dunn called round the house and said that she wanted to visit you at the hospital but she won't be able to yet."

"That was all?"

Jenny nodded before helping herself to the grapes that sat sweating in their plastic bag beside his bed. She made an attempt to view the photographs strewn on the bed but was stopped by Hammond. He felt he were being disloyal to Harris by allowing her to see them. He hastily collected the papers and replaced them in the folder.

"It's a bit unusual for Dunn to come to the house. Did she explain why?"

Jenny tried to answer through a mouthful of grapes. The attempt made her dribble grape juice down her jumper. She wiped her mouth with the back of her hand and shrugged her ignorance. She left him moments later wondering what had caused Dunn to make a personal visit. He had an inexplicable feeling Dunn had wanted to deliver some bad news personally although he couldn't imagine what the bad news could be.

Wallace Hammond spent the next four days enduring physiotherapy and looking through the contents of the box file. It had been an exhaustive progress but he was now able to recognise all the children pictured in several of the photographs. The quality and colouring of the photographs suggested they had been taken within the last thirty years. To his surprise there were several photographs of Lloyd Harris which made him realise the inclusion of the first photograph had not been accidental. One picture in particular aroused Hammond's interest. It showed a middle-aged Harris seated around a table with four men who were toasting the unseen photographer with raised glasses. There was no inscription on the back of the photograph but Hammond presumed the picture had been taken during the 1980's, he recognised the subdued coloured suits and narrow neck ties they typically wore during that era. He looked closely at each man in the photograph and wondered if they had been police officers whom had been betrayed by Harris. He could imagine their disbelief that he himself had felt during Harris' confession. The inclusion of the photographs alerted Hammond to the realisation that Harris was involved with this case more directly than he had been led to believe.

Hammond had been in hospital for almost four weeks when he decided he couldn't stand it anymore. His hand and rib were healing well, his headaches were easing although he suspected the bright lights in the ward were responsible for most of them. It was four days before Christmas when Paul came to visit him bringing a box of chocolate liqueurs and Mary's homemade cookies. It was at that moment Hammond made up his mind to discharge himself. His mind was sluggish and needed to be revived by a few home comforts. Jenny received this news with what looked like relief. They discussed the practicalities of him returning home. It wouldn't be easy since he couldn't manage to do much with a broken rib and a leg in plaster but they both agreed he would recover quicker with his mind occupied.

It was only after Jenny and Paul had left that he wondered why Jenny had looked so relieved by his decision. Was she lonely at the house with only Paul for company? It didn't seem plausible yet he hadn't imagined the look that had flashed across her face when he had told her of his decision. Thinking back, he realised that she didn't look as carefree as she usually did, she had looked tense and the way she scoffed the chocolates had suggested more nervous energy than hunger. He hoped she wasn't still suffering from the breakup with her girlfriend. It would probably do her as much good as it will do me to be at home he thought and managed a smile imagining the chaos that was to come.

Two days later Wallace Hammond was relishing the thought of going home, he had signed the discharge form with ill disguised glee despite the evident disapproval from the consultant. He didn't even complain when he discovered that his front door was partially blocked by the treadmill he had ordered and subsequently had forgotten to cancel. The enormous parcel had been pushed into the hallway during a joint effort by Paul and Jenny whom had both decided early on that it was too heavy for them to move anywhere else. So Hammond had returned home with a grin and a sideways hop through the front door. He took a long look at the home he had missed. Trails of tinsel hang down from the stair banisters. A small Christmas tree, bedecked with garish baubles and blinking fairy lights had been wedged between the arm chair and the sofa bed in the living room. Hammond thought his house had never looked worse but he thanked his son and Jenny with heartfelt appreciation for his welcome home.

It quickly became evident that all was not well within the house. Jenny was behaving particularly oddly. She was constantly fussing over him, offering him blankets or attempting to move furniture to ease his access. He was managing well on crutches in spite of the discomfort to his sore ribs, but despite appreciating her efforts, her bustling only achieved in making him short tempered and irritable. For the fourth time since he had entered the house, Hammond found Jenny looking out of the window in a furtive manner. During his absence she had started to bite her nails. Hammond had become familiar with her daily routine of sitting on the steps outside the front door to smoke a cigarette but he now noticed she went to the back garden. Paul was also behaving differently; Hammond saw the way his son had snapped at any question directed his way, as if he were in defence mode.

Finally, when he caught Paul and Jenny mouthing silently to each other over the dining table, he had enough and demanded an explanation.

Paul did his best to reassure his father that everything was normal, but he failed to convince his Father whose temper threatened to escalate. It was Jenny who eventually relented by explaining that the house had been broken into during Hammond's absence.

"Did you report it?"

Paul spoke up; he was obviously prepared for an argument.

"No, Dad. Nothing was taken, I expect we disturbed them."

"You were in the house?" Hammond was aware his voice was getting louder; he was beginning to fear the worst.

"No, we were at the hospital, visiting you. We came home and found the house disturbed."

Hammond questioned them why they had not reported the break in. Nothing had been taken, there was no evidence of having had an intruder break into the house other than a broken lock on the back door and a house left in greater disarray than it usually was.

"Tell me everything."

"The drawers were pulled out and emptied but that was all. We checked everything and were sure that nothing was taken."

Hammond pushed Jenny's offering of fish fingers and peas away from him, he was uneasy. It would have been common sense to have called the Police, they could have checked for fingerprints.

"The thing is Dad. Jenny is a bit paranoid. She thinks it has something to do with you, that someone was looking for you or something."

Hammond looked sharply at Jenny who flushed. "That's absurd. Why would anyone want to find me? They are not going to find me in a drawer!"

Jenny threw her fork down onto the table with such force, it surprised Hammond into muteness.

"I am not being paranoid Paul! Why ransack the house without taking anything of value? Of course they were looking for something in particular! And I know I was followed that day, I know it!"

Hammond felt stress form a hard ball in the pit of his stomach. He repeated his request to be told everything, warning them not to try and keep anything back.

Eventually Jenny sat down and leaned her arms on the table as she looked at him.

"Ok. Two days before the break in, Paul was at the hospital with Lyn, I went to get some supplies from the corner shop. As I left the house, a silver car pulled up beside me really slowly and then drove up the road. I didn't think anything of it at the time but on the way back, my bag split and I was bending down picking everything up when I saw the car again pointing back the way it had come. I noticed that the driver was watching me through his side mirror."

"That's nothing Jenny! He probably fancied you or something!"

Jenny's reply to Paul was spoken equally vehemently." No! I saw the same car the next day outside the house and then again when we were on the way to the hospital."

Hammond was watching Jenny closely. He questioned whether it could simply be a neighbour's car. Could she identify what car it was? Jenny answered with certainty; a silver 2005 reg Citröen Picasso. The driver had been of large build. Mary had been sure that the car was not owned or used by the neighbours. Hammond believed that Jenny was genuinely concerned but it was possible that the break in had nothing to do with the silver car that Jenny described.

"Why didn't you tell me before?"

"I told Sergeant Dunn the day she came, she told me not to concern you and that she will look into it."

"So, that's why she wanted to see me?"

"No, not entirely anyway. I think it had something to do with a case you had worked on together."

Hammond shook his head. It didn't make sense. The only case he had worked on with Dunn recently was the

Robert's case which had been taken over and consequently sealed by DCI Morris. If it was necessary, Dunn had plenty of opportunity to visit him at the hospital, yet as far as he knew she had made no effort to see him during the last fortnight. If she had known he was still at the hospital, why did she come to the house? It was peculiar and he was too impatient to wait for her to contact him. He pulled himself out of the chair, grimacing as his tender rib protested at the exertion. Impatiently he left a message, telling Dunn he was now at home and that she must call him as soon as possible. Hammond replaced the telephone receiver back onto the wall mount but remained leaning against the kitchen counter. Behind him he could hear Paul and Jenny clearing away the dishes and he shouted at them to stop. He wanted to be left alone. He needed to be quiet and still, his head was consumed with tangled thoughts. He had thought that coming home would help him to think but instead he found it suffocating.

Ten minutes after the front door slammed behind Jenny and Paul, Hammond allowed himself to breathe slowly. He knew he was being irrational but his distemper had got the better of him. He was angry with himself for being weak. He was angry with his failed memory for not allowing him to understand why he was carrying a sense of urgency for reasons he still couldn't identify. He was angry at Paul for not telling him Lyn had a new boyfriend and he was angry at Lyn for not loving him. Lastly, he reasoned, he had a right to be angry at Dunn for not answering her phone.

Hammond ignored the dirty dishes on the table and shuffled his way towards the living room with the almost-empty bottle of Brandy. He couldn't be bothered to find a glass and swigged the liquid enjoying the sensation of warmth creeping down inside his body. It took him several attempts to make himself comfortable on the sofa bed but eventually discovered that if he piled the pillows underneath his right knee, the pain in his ankle eased enough to allow him to relax. He laid back as much as he was able without disturbing the bandages wrapped around his chest and closed his eyes. For the first time in over a month he found peace.

When he awoke, it was dark outside. He had no idea what the time was. He pulled himself into an upright position and listened to the sounds in the house. It was silent apart from the ticking of the grand-daughter clock in the hallway and the letterbox flapping gently from the draught that came in around the front door. He heard no sound to indicate that Paul or Jenny had returned home. He laid back again and tried to go back to sleep but his mind was too alert so he opened his eyes and allowed them to become accustomed to the shapes of furniture in the darkened room.

He thought about Lloyd Harris and wondered if he was going through a worse torment than what Hammond felt, his memories were teetering at the tip of his brain; within reach yet irretrievable. He tried to focus on each thought, one at a time, but found that one thought quickly became overlapped by another more consuming until he was barraged with thought after thought that had no ending. Eventually he sat up and fumbled his way to where the light switch was by the living room door, cursing every obstacle that caused him to lean too heavily on his damaged ankle. He blinked quickly forcing his eyes to adjust to the brightness in the room and made his way towards the sideboard beneath the CD Player. It took him several minutes to find what he was looking for; a box of twelve shot glasses given to him one Christmas by a friend of his mothers. He took each glass out of the box and laid them upside down, then he positioned them at different corners of the table. One glass represented Lloyd, another Kathleen, he placed both glasses beside each other and then identified other glasses with each thought. One glass represented Thomas that was placed beside the glass representing Graham Roberts. Beside them, he placed another glass, the one without any name. This glass represented the unknown person who had collected the post from Robert's home. On the far side of the table he placed five glasses, Mark Callum, Theresa Davenport, Claire Bennet, Fiona Nwasu and Lucas Dean. Near to them he used a glass to represent Salima Abitboul and another underneath. He did this without knowing who this last glass represented but he knew he had forgotten someone. One by one Hammond positioned each glass in a separate area on the table until he was able to consider each topic of thought individually. The box file had been wedged underneath the Christmas tree, he hadn't known where else to place it but now he pulled it out and returned to the chair where he opened the box and reviewed its contents for what felt like the hundredth time. He looked again at the photographs of the children seated on the steps looking towards the shadow of the unknown photographer. He studied the girl with the plaits again and thought how beautiful she was. Her eyes were dark and arresting, her skin dusky, her limbs long and lean. She didn't look European or Asian. Could she be Moroccan? Could she be Salima?

When Hammond had met Harris at the Golf Club, Harris had said that Salima had come to England to be a model. Later Harris confessed to having suspected Salima had worked for Pattie as an escort. He looked again at the date of the back of the picture. 1987. Salima, (if that is who the girl in the picture was) looked no older than fourteen. Salima had been nineteen at the time of her disappearance in 1991. It made sense, it was plausible. Hammond reconsidered Harris' information that girls had been brought over to London from Africa and Europe for prostitution. Could Salima have experienced the same or was she approached after her modelling contract had expired? The late 1980's had brought changes to the Migration Laws. Hammond's parents were the few who had agreed with Margaret Thatcher's claim that British people feared being 'swamped' by immigrants. It would have been difficult for a young Moroccan to have been granted entry to the UK as anything other than a tourist but not impossible, particularly if she had relatives resident in the UK. If Salima had wanted to remain in England after her visa had expired, it would have been difficult to have had a new work permit granted so marrying a British citizen may have been an attempt to settle in Britain. Hammond read through the notes again. He still couldn't understand the relevance of the Offstead report or the notes about Rachel Turner, the social worker.

Hammond sat still and breathed slowly, trying to ignore the wave of frustration that threatened to overwhelm him. He was bored with this case, all the possibilities could easily amount to absolutely nothing at all, yet he couldn't rid himself of the sense of duty he owed to Harris. There was still a nagging feeling in him that Harris could be right. There was something odd, but he couldn't pinpoint exactly what. He tried to remember the first time he had the uneasy feeling. It had been when he had been looking at the photographs of Lucas Dean's apartment. Perhaps it would be worth looking at them again, but to see what? He had looked at the police investigation pictures carefully, if there had been anything unusual he would have seen it, even if he didn't the investigating officers at the scene would have. So why this burning feeling that he was missing something? The clock ticked monotonously in the hall, the minutes slid past and the stress gradually left him. He thought about Paul and wondered where he was, whether he was angry. The Christmas tree stood like an unwelcome guest in the corner of the room and he realised he hadn't even bought any gifts for anyone. He had been so preoccupied with his own mess that he hadn't even considered how his son was feeling. He had left his studies to be near me and in return I am behaving as if he isn't here. Hammond looked around the room, noting the decorations and the tracks in the carpet left by the vacuum cleaner. He swallowed with guilt. I am a rotten father he thought. I should appreciate my family instead of shouting at them. Then it dawned on him what he had failed to notice before. Mark Callum had no family. Fiona Nwasu and Claire Bennet had no family. Lucas Dean had been in foster care throughout his childhood. Theresa Davenport was described as a loner, with no known family, but she was an exception. Someone had cared enough about her to have written about her on a forum for bereaved family and friends of people who had committed suicide. And then Hammond remembered. He allowed himself a gleeful chuckle before clutching his ribs to stop them hurting. He remembered Cherry13, and he knew their identity. He had found the connection between the five decedents and Salima Abitboul. They had known each other during their younger years, had possibly lived together or had been fostered by an unknown carer. This explained why Mark Callum had kept Salima's hairbrush. It had been a memento, something to remember her by; an item no-one would notice missing.

Hammond was relieved to have found a lead but at the same time, was infuriated by the slow progress. There were still unanswered questions. What was their connection to Pattie? Salima had possibly been employed by her, but what relevance was Pattie to the others? Were they working for her also? If so, in what way? Nausea welled up in his throat with the thought that the children had been used as prostitutes. It wouldn't be the first time that lone children had slipped through the welfare system. What Hammond didn't know was whether Rachel Turner had been their social worker at the time, if so, she would have known each person individually and would possibly be able to shed light on the five people. Harris had been correct in his assumption that the deaths had been linked, but this wasn't enough to warrant any more attention on the deaths themselves if all people had died by their own hand. The only conclusion that Hammond could make, at this point, was that there was a possibility that the five people had all agreed to end their lives or perhaps more rationally, they were affected by the death of their friends and had decided to follow by example. There wasn't enough to suggest anything suspicious although

Hammond was aware that he was beginning to feel increasingly concerned about Harris' involvement. Obviously there was more to his story than he had admitted, no doubt involving the woman Harris had referred to as Pattie. However, it didn't explain why Harris had initiated the investigation. His research had been thorough, the amount of notes he had written confirmed this, but what wasn't apparent was why Harris had felt the need to delve deeper for more information. The only rational thought was that Harris had been unaware of what had been going on at the time of his involvement. Perhaps he had been used somehow. Following Harris' confession during their last meeting, it would be easy to assume that Harris wanted to free himself of guilt before it was too late, but even as he thought it, Hammond knew such a theory didn't make sense, because Harris had only suggested being guilty of taking bribes and coercing confessions. There would be a time when Harris wouldn't remember his own involvement so surely it didn't matter? Unless, Harris was guilty of a lot more but was too ashamed to say. But why willingly expose himself when it otherwise would not be discovered? Hammond studied the photograph of his former colleague, he searched the eyes in a foolish attempt to understand the man behind the image. Suddenly he realised why his friend had asked for his help. He had already known there were more to the deaths than simply suicidal people ending their misery, Harris wanted the truth of their deaths investigated by someone he trusted because in some way he felt responsible.

*"No reasonable moral being may draw breath in the
world without an open-eyed freedom of choice."*
Henry Havelock Ellis. The Dance of Life. 1923

CHAPTER FIFTEEN

The call from Dunn came just before seven in the
morning. Hammond was wide awake having spent
several hours reviewing Harris' notes.

"I couldn't get back to you any earlier, we had multiple
stabbings outside a nightclub."

"'Tis the season for it."

"Too many drunk people getting out of control isn't
exactly my idea of Christmas celebrations. Anyway, your
message sounded urgent."

"You have a lot to tell me, and I want to hear it. Sooner
rather than later."

He could hear her hesitation at the other end of the line,
and it annoyed him. It was obvious she wanted to tell
him something but was holding back. Hammond didn't
want to play games. He prodded her for information.
There was a pause and then a sigh as Dunn decided to be
co-operative.

"Beech is hauling us all in about the Robert's case.
It seems that DCI Morris has made a formal complaint."

"Against whom?"

"You."

The conversation was limited, since Dunn had been taken off the case before Hammond, she was unable to provide much information.

"All I know is that I was called in to go over my report. Edwards and Galvin had to do the same. I don't know for sure what the complaint is although I suspect Edwards and Galvin had more to answer than myself."

"What kind of questions were you asked?"

There was a heavy sigh before Dunn replied.

"Mainly about whether I thought you were capable of doing your job."

Paul was sulking and Hammond was doing his best pretending not to notice. He knew he owed his son an apology but decided it could wait until they all had a chance to sit down and talk properly that evening. He made an effort to act cheerful and suggested they go Christmas shopping in the afternoon. It was Christmas Eve and therefore probably too late to buy a turkey but there was only the three of them, roast chicken would be just as good. Jenny nodded politely to Hammond's suggestion but her eyes focused on Paul who had thrown himself into the arm chair and deliberately drowned out his Father's words by increasing the television's volume. Tempted though he was to leave Paul to sulk alone, Hammond found himself hobbling towards the sofa bed where he sat and faced his son. He waited for several moments until Paul granted his attention by switching the television off.

"I've let you down Paul. Christmas has come too quick and I guess I wasn't organised enough. It is not too late to go to spend it with your Mum if you prefer."

Paul looked petulant. "You need me here, you can hardly walk."

Hammond denied this, realising his son preferred to be elsewhere. He wasn't surprised although he was disappointed.

"We've hardly seen each other Dad. Mum thought you would be lonely here on your own."

Hammond felt annoyed at Lyn, he knew it was her guilty conscience that was responsible for Paul being where he didn't want to be. Either that or she wanted to be alone with her new lover without Paul. But whatever the reason, Hammond felt she had manipulated the situation and a burn of resentment towards her flared up in his gut. With restraint, he managed to reassure his son that he wouldn't be lonely. They arranged to meet in town for a festive meal before Paul and Jenny depart for Lyn's house that afternoon. First he needed a lift to the Police Headquarters.

The Police Station looked as if it had been subjected to a brawl between tinsel and foil garlands. As Hammond walked into the reception area, he smelt traces of vomit and disinfectant. He wondered what Christmas would be like if all alcohol was banned for a week and then realised it was the kind of thought his mother would have spoken aloud. He saw Dunn immediately upon entering the Serious Crime Unit. She looked tired, her eyes sunken and dark, but she smiled as she saw him and waited patiently as he made slow progress down the corridor, leaning heavily on his crutches and wincing as each movement reminded him of his healing rib.

"I told them all you were coming in today, I wanted to talk to you but it is a bit hectic at the moment. Galvin and I are occupied on a baby shaking case, the last time I saw Edwards he was about to interview a husband arrested for slashing his wife's face with a broken bottle. There's no rest for the wicked."

"Or the ones left to clear their mess."

Dunn smiled wearily as they made their way inch by inch towards Detective Superintendent Beech's office, she knocked on the door and left before Hammond hobbled into the office. DCI Brian Morris was evidently waiting for Hammond's arrival; his face was set and looked as if he were attempting to restrain an outburst. Beech stood up as Hammond entered and made a performance of moving a chair closer towards Hammond gesturing for him to be seated. He gave the expected polite greeting of welcoming Hammond back before Hammond interrupted and cut to the chase.

"I understand you wanted to see me regarding the Robert's case?"

Morris turned towards Hammond; he was a good looking man in his early forties. Lean and fit he was often in the newspapers for running marathons and fundraising for numerous charities. Hammond felt in awe of the man's physique but managed to hide his inner thoughts behind a deliberate open expression.

"DCI Morris has asked me to make some enquiries regarding your involvement in the investigation Wallace. It seems that there have been some details not included in the original report which should have been."

"Oh?" Hammond's expression was one of innocent enquiry. He raised an eyebrow at Morris who had leaned back in his chair, the back of his hand rested against his mouth as he allowed Beech to do the talking.

"A neighbour of the late Mr Roberts phoned to enquire

whether we had caught the intruder that had been prowling around the neighbourhood. In particular he was most keen to know how long Dymchurch Road was going to be under surveillance."

Hammond's eyebrows rose up further; he turned to Morris and shrugged slightly as if he was as confused as the others. Morris appraised Hammond, his eyes narrowed.

"Cut the crap Hammond! You knew Edwards had been conducting his own surveillance without authorisation and you know why. He had been watching the house for days before he caught Samuel Lawson letting himself in to the house last night!"

This was news to Hammond whose ears immediately switched to selective hearing mode. He failed to hear Morris' continued ranting as he acknowledged DC Edwards's success. Samuel Lawson. That was a surprise, but then as Hammond digested the information, he realised it wasn't a surprise, it was the exact opposite. Especially since Lawson was seen letting himself in, presumably with a spare set of keys since there had been no sign of forced entry into Robert's house. The answer had been staring them all in the face since the beginning. He wasn't aware that he smiled until Morris's voice increased in volume.

"...You wanted to stir things up from the very beginning! Everyone knows you wanted to delay the arrest of Thomas Taylor. You've handled this case as badly as you handled your team, only now it's down to us to sort your mess out!"

Hammond leaned forward, ignoring Beech who had sat up ready to take control of the situation. He kept his voice deliberately calm.

"If my team and I had been allowed to investigate Robert's murder proficiently, I wouldn't have had to go behind anyone's back. My team knew that there were too many unanswered questions. Unlike you, they are not so concerned with their case solving ratings as they are doing their jobs efficiently."

"Damn it Hammond, you always have been a pedantic bastard! You had a confession and substantiating forensic evidence! You had everything you needed! The case was solved."

"No. It wasn't, it still isn't. Not until you can account for the several phone calls to the mobile number or missing wallet, the missing mail or the large cash transactions. Where did the money go? Was Robert's being blackmailed? If so, you have an alternative motive."

Morris swore, he found Hammond old fashioned and stubborn; a dinosaur whose methods were outdated and lacking.

"No wonder you haven't made it past Detective Inspector! The boy gave a motive. The fact that Roberts was a pervert was backed up by Schaffer's statement. Thomas Taylor lied about training with the other boys, he probably lied about forgetting what he had done with the wood he used to strike Roberts. Either way, his confession and the evidence was good enough for the CPS, anything else will come up in court if it needs to..."

Hammond interrupted. "Did it not occur to you that the woman who made the complaint in 2001 against Roberts shared the same surname as Samuel Lawson? I will bet that Samuel Lawson was the boy approached by Roberts all those years ago in the public toilets. I am also willing to bet that Samuel Lawson recognised Roberts and blackmailed him, and I am sure you will no doubt discover that the money given to him by Roberts was spent on expensive bike components, all of which were paid for online by a credit card under Robert's name. Moreover, it wouldn't surprise me if the missing post was collected by Lawson in an attempt to hide the credit card statements. As Lawson is an arrogant little git, it is likely he has held onto the credit card which was probably in Robert's wallet when it was taken either before or after his death, and I am sure will be found in Lawson's possession when you have conducted a search." Hammond paused. He felt liberated. He tried not to show his pleasure at having sussed out what should have been obvious at the beginning but he couldn't help it and eventually allowed himself to face Beech whilst still grinning.

Beech coughed "It's nothing but supposition Wallace. However, it won't take long to check it out if it is as you say, but what about Lawson's statement? He had an alibi for the time of the attack."

Hammond shook his head. "He said he was at home, it is hard to disprove but if he did travel up to Saltwood, he would have cycled or would have taken the train like he usually did. I reckon he would have travelled to Saltwood by train, but possibly, if he was worried about being seen later would have cycled back. Either way, it is easy enough to check."

DCI Morris spoke up "Lawson gave us a DNA sample, it didn't match anything found at the scene."

"I am not suggesting that he attacked Graham Roberts. I believe Thomas is responsible for that. But I reckon Lawson has something to do with this. At the very least he withheld information about Schaffer warning him about Roberts. Why would he do that unless he was hiding something? He may have witnessed the attack or he may have come across Roberts afterwards as he lay injured. It could have been Lawson who had covered the body with the logs or even taken the wallet and the nitrates."

"What about fingerprints? There weren't any on those logs."

"Lawson wears bike gloves. There would be no fingerprints."

"The bank statements showed cash withdrawals, not credit transfer."

Hammond shrugged. "It is still possible that Roberts withdrew cash from his current account to pay the credit card bills in full each time. It's a complicated way of doing it but not out of the ordinary."

"And the mobile?"

"It could or could not be Lawson's number, but it shouldn't be hard to check."

There was a pause as the three men considered the next plan of action. Eventually Beech spoke.

"Well, if you are right, it does give a different perspective on things. It is possible that Lawson could have called emergency services and saved Roberts or even have intervened and prevented his attack which means he will have to face charges. Also, we have a substantiated motive behind Thomas's attack on Roberts, two witnesses who can back up the theory that Roberts was a sexual deviant." He sighed. "Of course, the media will get the public behind the boys once they get a sniff he was a threat to kids." Beech turned to DCI Morris.

"You are going to have to find the wallet, check if there is a credit card. Find the statements and any receipts for the bike parts. It is worth finding out how Lawson let himself into the house. There wasn't a forced entry so he could have had a spare key which suggests he had known Roberts better than he led us to believe. Confirm whether he was the boy approached in 2001, the names could be a co-incidence."

Beech waited until DCI Morris left the office. He scratched his head as he looked at Hammond, positioned like a rag doll in the chair opposite him.

"Wallace, you are a pain in the arse sometimes. I bloody well hope you are right. What the hell was Edwards thinking? I presume he was acting on your orders?"

He acknowledged Hammonds shaken head as denial.

"The media are going to have a field day with this one. I blame you entirely, the whole investigation has been a catastrophe but hopefully it can be turned on its head and be seen to have a successful outcome. It goes without saying that you are not to be involved in this case any further."

Hammond sat up straighter in the chair. His ankle was throbbing but he was trying to wean himself off the painkillers.

"You think I am a weak link in the chain, is that it?"

Beech looked surprised by Hammond's directness. "No. Not at all. But I think you have been behaving less like a police officer and more of an independent investigator lately and I struggle to understand why."

Hammond was about to answer, his satisfaction with the way the Robert's case was turning out was making him feel bold. There was plenty he wanted to say but he never got the chance to speak his mind. Beech came around the table and sat in the chair Morris had just vacated. He looked at Hammond for several moments before speaking.

"You need to be interviewed again about the car accident. What do you know about the crash Wallace?"

The question was asked not by an interested colleague but as a police officer about to embark on an interrogation. It surprised Hammond enough to be quiet for several moments as he wondered why Beech was interested. It was inevitable that he was to be questioned again. His memory hadn't returned wholly yet but Hammond had presumed that the investigation would be handled in the normal channels by the Serious Collision Investigation Team.

"A car swerved in front of me and caused me to crash into it." The answer was simple, it was all Hammond knew but he trusted the information he had been given by the young officer had been true.

Beech looked down at the floor as if he were thinking what to say next and then met Hammond's eyes.

"No. Not quite. Your car has been examined. You crashed into the car in front because your car's brake calliper bolts had been cut then loosely refitted, causing them to shear under heavy breaking."

Hammond was unsure how to respond. Beech's words were ridiculous. It was impossible that anyone would have had the chance to sabotage his car or even have any reason to do so. Yet he could see Beech was serious. As he sat in stunned silence, Beech collected a folder from his desk and handed it to Hammond, encouraging him to open it. Inside there were photographs showing multiple angles of twisted metal and vehicle carnage scattered across three lanes of a motorway.

From what Hammond could tell, there had been several cars that had been destroyed. He found himself gulping, his mouth and throat had become dry.

"How many...?"

Even as he asked the question, Hammond knew the answer was going to be worse than he could possibly have hoped for.

"Two died, another was in hospital for two weeks. You are not to blame Hammond. That is clear from the witness reports, however, your car wasn't roadworthy so you will be held partially accountable."

Hammond nodded. His mind was fogged. None of what Beech was telling him made any sense. He questioned how it was possible that anyone could have cut his brake calliper bolts without anyone noticing. Surely it would have taken time and skill to have done such a thing?

"Is there anything I should know?" Beech was offering Hammond an opportunity to explain why someone would want him dead but Hammond was as confused as his superior officer. He didn't know anyone who could have done such a thing or would have had any reason to do so. He had received death threats before, it was part of his job to piss criminals off by incarcerating them but less threats were made with the actual promise of being fulfilled.

"DS Dunn suggested you were re-investigating an old case?"

Hammond looked at Beech surprised. What had Dunn told him? Surely she wouldn't have told Beech about Lloyd Harris? He didn't answer, preferring to wait until he knew how much Dunn had shared.

"She didn't tell me anything as such, just a comment that she spoke without thinking before she clammed up. So, I did some checking of my own. It seemed you did some research into a murder from 1991 and checked the computer records on suicides that have happened within the last two years."

Hammond said nothing. Each computer search was logged, telling the date, time and the searchers identity, he knew this but hadn't thought anyone would check up on his movements.

Beech was waiting for an explanation but he wasn't going to get one. He looked at his watch impatiently before getting up and returning to his desk.

"It's Christmas Wallace and I have a family to go to. I can't be bothered to sit around playing mind games but I will say this; Providing you maintain the lifestyle of a law-abiding citizen, what you do in your own time is your business. But if you are going to investigate a case in a non-official capacity, you do it in your own time and with your own resources. Keep a day book and log everything. Is that understood? If there is a crime to investigate, by all means, present me with the facts and we'll consider it but otherwise, leave it outside of this office." Hammond interpreted Beech's tone as an opportunity to leave. He shuffled his way out of the chair by leaning heavily on his crutches.

"How long are you going to be on sick leave?"

Hammond turned his attention back to Beech. "Six weeks."

"Use the time wisely Wallace. Don't come back until you are fully operational. Hopefully by then this car crash business will be resolved."

Hammond shared the thought. He looked up at the foil arrangement resembling a star hanging above him and wished on it hard.

Chapter Sixteen

As Wallace Hammond threw the dregs of cognac down his throat, he realised he was feeling tipsy and very nearly overbalanced off his stool. The bar attendant was a bald headed Irish man who enjoyed having an audience and caused Hammond to laugh at everything he said even if it wasn't particularly funny. He refilled the glass that Hammond slammed back onto the bar whilst telling a joke about a nymphomaniac nun. The punch line lacked lustre but caused Hammond to laugh loudly, attracting the attention of fellow diners in the restaurant next door. Hammond raised his glass and toasted the onlookers with a wide grin before tossing back the liquid in an extravagant display of Christmas joviality. They responded with cold stares of disapproval before turning their gaze away from him. He shrugged and muttered to his new Irish friend that people had no humour nowadays. The barman suggested that maybe he should go and celebrate Christmas with his family. In reply Hammond pushed his glass forward to be refilled.

"I have just finished celebrating with my family, now they have gone to celebrate with the ex-wife."

The barman made an "ah" noise as if he now understood the reasoning behind Hammond's wish to get drunk. Hammond was aware of the other man's presumption but didn't bother to contradict him. He was feeling as if he should celebrate his freedom whilst he could. For the next few hours, there would be no expectations to fulfil, there would be no emergency call outs, no son to disappoint (something he had regretted to notice he was becoming quite good at.) No boss to piss off. He was under no obligation to do anything but please himself. His stool was jolted slightly as a group of women, Hammond guessed they were in their mid-thirties, clustered around the bar, all talking at once and giggling amongst themselves. Hammond smelt their perfume mingling as one, it made his nose itch and threatened to make him sneeze but he managed to contain it and watched them as they deliberated their drink orders. He found the scene being played out in front of him fascinating. The women were constantly playing with their hair as they spoke or adjusting their busts. It was like watching a mating ritual being played out on a wildlife documentary. He caught the eye of a large breasted woman and raised his glass as a toast. She smiled at Hammond. He smiled back. She walked with her companions to a free table at the far end of the room but sat at the table in a place that allowed her to maintain eye contact with him. The women sat talking animatedly amongst themselves, the laughter becoming screeches as the wine flowed amongst them. It was entertaining to watch them and Hammond did so without attempting to be discreet in his surveillance.

At midnight, the barman wished them all loudly a happy Christmas and was invited to their table for a Christmas kiss from each woman. They stroked his bald head and covered it in lipstick kisses which he must have enjoyed because he went back a second time carrying another tray of drinks. The atmosphere within the restaurant bar was happy and manic. Hammond was tired, he wanted to leave and get to bed but he couldn't face going home alone. He found himself thinking of Lyn and wondering if she were giving Cameron a Christmas kiss, then he wondered if Cameron was bald like the barman. For a second he was tempted to phone her but pressed Kathleen's number instead and waited whilst it rang unanswered. He hang on for several rings before his courage failed him and he disconnected the call. When he looked up, the woman with the large breasts was standing next to him, she offered him a drink. He accepted.

Hammond awoke feeling sick. He made it to the bathroom just in time before his stomach emptied itself with force into the toilet. He groaned and wondered why he had been so stupid as to drink too much. He hadn't felt this ill for a long time. He sprawled on the bathroom floor, not wanting to return to bed. He knew the woman would be there, she had probably woken from the noise of his retching. He didn't want to face her again, and wished his clothes were nearer the bathroom so he could escape discreetly. He had been drunk but not so drunk that he had forgotten what they had done. She had been a demanding lover, urging him on by whispering filthy suggestions into his ear that to his surprise had overwhelmed him with desire. He heard her calling him back into the bedroom and decided he had no choice but to leave her in a non-chivalrous manner. He hobbled back into the bedroom, realising he looked ridiculous naked apart from his ankle in plaster and bandaged ribs. The woman had sat up in the bed, she made no effort to cover herself. Her breasts were heavy and full and for a split second he was tempted to return to their cushioned warmth but instead begun to dress himself without uttering a word. He left her shouting obscenities at his retreating back.

The taxi driver had offered to help Hammond up the steps to his front door but Hammond declined. The smell he carried on him was a potent mixture of alcohol, sex and vomit. He paid the driver a large tip and returned a happy Christmas wish before attempting each step one at a time, leaning on the concrete wall and dragging the crutches under his arm. As he opened the front door, he had an idea and managed to shout to the Taxi Driver who had left the engine running whilst talking on the radio. It took several minutes of persuasion but after the promise of a triple fare, the man agreed. With the help of a passing neighbour, the taxi driver loaded the treadmill into the car. With the back seats folded down, it stuck out the open boot which was secured with rope. Hammond handed the taxi driver Lyn's address before scrawling a message onto a post-it note and stuck it onto the package; "*Dear Paul. Happy Christmas. Love Dad.*"

Hammond spent Christmas Day nursing a hangover. He lay on the sofa bed feeling sorry for himself and watching the Queen's Speech. A tradition his Mother, who had been a loyal Royalist, had installed in him from the days of sitting around the radio tuning in to the BBC at three o' clock on every Christmas day afternoon. Hammond watched her Royal Highness as she talked about the importance of sport and how it could be used to create harmony. He mumbled that in his case, it was too late for sport and possibly for her too, before returning her Seasons greetings and switching onto another channel. The day passed mindlessly and quietly. The telephone didn't ring once and he wondered whether Paul or Jenny had thought about him at all. He sent a text message to Paul wishing him an enjoyable day and then forwarded the same message to Jenny's phone. His mobile vibrated in his hand alerting him that both messages had been received. For a moment he wondered how the woman from the previous night was. He felt guilty at leaving her the way he did but justified his behaviour as that of a free thinking adult. A one night stand was no big deal, she hadn't wanted anything apart from one thing in particular which he had granted and from what he remembered, she hadn't been disappointed.

Christmas passed as quickly as it had arrived and Hammond was relieved when the street outside resumed its normal activity; car engines left running whilst commuters scraped their windscreens at seven in the morning. The paced footsteps of joggers burning off the Christmas excess. During the last two days he had worked out a plan, his investigation into Harris' enquiry was to be resumed with enthusiasm and renewed perception. Hammond felt revived knowing that any niggling doubts he had over the Graham Roberts murder could soon be explained and more importantly, proven. Even though he had officially been taken off the investigation over a month ago, his mind would not have allowed himself to forget the questions left unanswered. But now, thanks to Edwards, he could relax knowing that the investigation had been thorough after all. He smiled as he thought of his younger colleague. Arrogant and crude though he was, he was also reliable. He knew that Edwards would help him find the information he needed, and scrolled down in his phone menu to call his number. After a few rings, a small child, he couldn't tell whether they were male or female, answered the phone. Patiently Hammond asked to speak to Tom, the child giggled and said she didn't know a Tom. For a moment, Hammond thought he had phoned the wrong number before asking the child if he could speak to their Father. Edwards came onto the phone, he sounded breathless.

"Apologies, I was in the middle of washing up." Household chores was the last thing Hammond imagined his colleague doing, he played with the image in his mind before getting to the point. His colleague agreed to his request without asking any questions and agreed to call back with the information as soon as he could. They wished each other a prosperous New Year before ending the call. It was hard to imagine that it would soon be 2011. Hammond sighed; it was as if time slipped past without him noticing anymore. In April he would be fifty-three. Only four months left of his fifty-second year. Whether he chose to admit it to himself or not, he was now on the wrong side of middle age.

The address Edwards gave was thirty miles away in Winchelsea. It wouldn't be a problem if Hammond had a car, but he didn't and even if he did, he wouldn't be able to drive with an ankle in plaster. It would be presumptuous, not to mention downright arrogant to ask any of the team to act as his chauffer. They were busy investigating cases that demanded their priority. There was no choice but to travel by bus. It had been years since Hammond had travelled by bus and at first, he enjoyed sitting back and letting someone else have the stress of rush hour traffic. After thirty minutes, his enthusiasm flagged and he found himself screaming silently as the elderly women from the nursing home took their time to find their bus passes. They took turns to arrange their shopping trolleys on the baggage rack before the lengthy decision process of choosing their seats whilst Hammond, feeling less than charitable, mentally urged the bus to get a move on. The journey took seventy minutes, by which time Hammond had made the decision to travel homeward by taxi. He knew it was an expense he couldn't really afford, especially after his Christmas drinking binge, but he figured that if there was a choice between lashing an old woman to the baggage rack or having to use cheaper toilet roll for the next month, there was no contest.

*"It has always been difficult for Man to
realise that his life is all an art."*
Henry Havelock Ellis. The Dance of Life. 1923

CHAPTER SEVENTEEN

Cheryl Bailey's house was a detached property at the end
of a cul-de-sac. It stood out from the neighbouring
houses with their uniformed tidy gardens and clean
windows. The garden was a jungle of overgrown weeds
and vigorous ivy that reached out to pedestrians on
the pavement causing them to tilt their heads sideways
or walk in the road. Hammond was exhausted and
feeling irritable. The lame walk from the bus stop had
taken longer than he expected and his ankle was
protesting at the activity. For the first time that morning
he wondered whether he had done the right thing
coming here. He had not forewarned of his visit. If
Salima Abitboul's former flatmate had gone away for
Christmas, it would have been a wasted journey. He
stood at the end of the narrow path that lead to her
front door and tried to ignore the pain by forcing
himself to breathe slowly, he massaged his hands
aching from the crutches handle then hobbled slowly
towards the front door and pressed the bell with a determined finger.

The door was opened and Hammond saw a mass of dark curly hair and flushed cheeks of a woman in her mid forties. She looked at him and surveyed him for several seconds.

"I don't like Charity calls. If you want a donation, please just leave an envelope through the door."

Hammond spoke quickly aware that the door was about to be shut in his face. He gave his name and showed her his id badge.

The eyes that were hidden under the thick fringe of hair were suspicious. Hammond quickly explained the reason for his visit.

"Ms Bailey, you may not recognise my name, but you and I recently were corresponding via e-mail. I am here about your concerns regarding the death of Theresa Davenport."

Cheryl Bailey looked aghast, Hammond had imagined that she would have deny all knowledge of Theresa Davenport but her surprise at his words had left her vulnerable and unprepared. He could see she was panicked by his revelation, he spoke with a deliberately reassuring tone explaining that he was there to offer his help. They were distracted momentarily by a group of children who were watching them unabashedly from the end of the garden path. She looked at them before her gaze returned to Hammond. Conscious of their spectators, she reluctantly invited Hammond indoors.

"Just so you know, if you try anything I know how to defend myself."

Hammond replied that this was reassuring news. It took several minutes before her face relaxed. She showed him into a small living room that was neat and homely and sat down, waiting for him to do the same. Her posture was rigid and tense, her hands clasped so tightly in her lap that Hammond could see white circles appearing under her finger's pressure.

"You are Inspector Gadget?"

Hammond winced with acute embarrassment at his alias name being spoken aloud and wished Jenny had used a better name but he nodded and repeated his true identity. "How did you know who I was?"

"After my many attempts to translate my son's text language I finally realised that 13 could also be seen as the letter B, and Cherry is recognised as being a derivative of Cheryl."

She nodded and glanced down at her hands, unfolding them and studying the marks where her nails had left an impression in the skin of her hands.

"Not very imaginative I suppose. I have never been very creative. I am more a matter-of-fact girl."

Hammond smiled gently. "I should say Ms Bailey that I am here on a non-official basis. I really want to ask you some questions but I should say that you are under no obligation to answer anything or indeed, give me your time, but I confess that I feel you could help me enormously."

Her gaze returned to his face as his words were considered. He guessed that she had decided to trust him by the readiness of her reply.

"What do you want to know?"

"I understand you were a friend of Salima Abitboul?"

He was replied by a sharp nod of her head which caused her fringe to fall back over her eyes.

"You also knew Theresa Davenport?"

"Yes, I knew Theresa through Salima. They were fostered together before Salima and I shared a flat. Theresa was a young girl then, I didn't know her very well to be honest but Salima treated her like a little sister."

"Who fostered them?"

Cheryl Bailey hesitated. It was obvious she was nervous to continue talking, she asked to see Hammond's id again and studied his card meticulously before handing it back to him apparently reassured.

"I don't know the woman's full name, Salima used to call her Mrs Goodchild. That was what they all called her."

"They all? There were others?" Hammond was tempted to produce the photograph of the group of children taken from the file but held back for confirmation.

"Yes, there were quite a few. Some stayed for only a few days, others stayed longer. When Salima was there, there must have been about six children all living there."

"Do you remember their names?"

"Not really..why are you asking? You said I could help you but how? Salima is dead now, Theresa is dead too. Why do you want to know about them?"

The volume and pitch of her voice had risen with anxiety, Hammond realised he was about to lose his opportunity. Very quickly he explained his interest in the suicides of Theresa, Lucas Dean, Claire Bennet and Mark Callum. He told her that he believed the deaths were connected somehow and that this made him suspicious. She listened carefully whilst studying his face and he knew she was looking for tell-tell signs of deceit. Hammond deliberately spoke as honestly as he could whilst withholding any information on Lloyd Harris.

"I didn't know Claire. Mark Callum, yes, I remember him. He was very skinny, used to be frightened of everything. Salima was very concerned about him, she always talked about him and said that she wanted to help him but all her attempts were refused. He wouldn't have hurt her. I think it is more likely that he kept her hairbrush as a reminder. She became his only comfort after Katie went."

"Katie?"

"Mrs Goodchild's daughter. She and Mark were very close, inseparable for most of the time. Whenever Katie wasn't around, he was inconsolable. I didn't spend much time at the house, Salima used to sneak me in sometimes when Goodchild wasn't around but I hated being there anyway. I was always terrified of getting caught. Goodchild was an absolute bitch."

Hammond produced the photograph and asked Cheryl to identify the faces of the children. She studied the picture for a while and traced Salima's face with a gentle forefinger.

"That's Salima. Beautiful wasn't she? Poor Theresa was very dowdy in comparison. That's Katie with Mark staring at her as usual. And Lucas..I had a crush on him for a while."

"Cheryl, what can you tell me about the children? What happened there?"

She looked at him surprised. "I am not sure what you mean. I don't think anything happened there as such but I can tell you that I always felt very uneasy. Goodchild was very controlling, the kids were very much under her thumb. There was one occasion that I remember. It unsettled me so much I never went back. I think that was several months before Salima moved in with me."

"What happened?"

"I was upstairs with Salima, I had sneaked in as usual and had brought her my personal stereo for her to listen to. The kids weren't allowed radios or stereos and Salima missed listening to music so I would sneak it in and we would hide in one of the rooms with an ear-piece each. Anyway, we heard shouting from downstairs and I panicked because I was terrified of getting caught so Salima told me to wait outside on the window ledge! We were in a room on the first floor so it wasn't too high up and the ledge was quite broad so it wasn't as scary as it sounds but anyway, from where I stood I could see downstairs into the porch where Goodchild was with this man. He was shouting at her, obviously furious. Goodchild was doing nothing, just standing there poised and quiet as he was screaming at her. I don't remember what he was shouting about to be honest but I do remember that Katie appeared and he suddenly grabbed her arm and starting to pull her towards him, telling her that she had to go and live with him. Katie started crying, then Mark appeared and started to pull Katie back. Goodchild slapped Mark across the face telling him to let Katie go, that he was never to see her again. The man left with Katie. I don't think Katie ever went back there."

"You said that Katie was Goodchild's daughter?"

"Yes, there was no doubt about that. They looked so alike."

"Yet she was willing to allow this man to take Katie away?"

"Like I said, Goodchild was a bitch. I don't understand why she fostered the kids anyway, she didn't care for them, she ruled them."

"How? Was she violent?"

"No, I mean, she slapped Mark but in those days it wasn't seen as abuse to slap your children if they misbehaved. But Goodchild was a very devious woman.

She controlled them through mind games. I didn't understand it at the time, I was too young, but looking back, yes, I would say that Goodchild was psychologically violent."

"She abused them emotionally?"

Cheryl looked at Hammond intently before answering. Her posture had relaxed but her eyes remained alert, her body leaned forwards towards Hammond.

"She controlled them not by making them fear her, but by making them fear the outside world. She offered them protection from the big bad world outside."

"I don't understand, how would she do that?"

"By taking away their sense of self, their sense of belonging. All the children had rooms exactly the same as each other. They were constantly moved from one room to another so that they didn't have their own space, or a sense of privacy. The house was enormous, I think there were about twelve bedrooms, but all of them were identical. Everything was bare, there were no pictures, no brightly coloured walls, nothing to give any indication of the characters that lived there. You couldn't tell which room was which. The kids would never sleep in the same room on any consecutive night. This was a rule. I remember this particularly because I never knew where to find Salima."

"But how did this make them fear the outside world?"

"Apart from Salima and Katie. All the children were there because they were either delinquent, like Lucas, or deprived in some way of paternal care. Mark's mother was neglectful, Lucas's mother, I think, had died of a drug overdose. Theresa's history was hazy, but I know she had been to numerous foster placements before going to Goodchild. Each one of them had a reason to feel hard done by, and Goodchild never let them forget it. Salima would tell me how Goodchild would lecture them all on how they had to reverse their own fortunes by striking back. We used to laugh about it at first but now I realise it was quite mad."

Cheryl paused speaking whilst she stood up and walked to the window. The children were still outside the house, she watched them for several minutes before turning around and facing him.

"After Salima disappeared, I tried to look after Theresa, I thought it was what Salima would want me to do. Theresa was highly intelligent but also a difficult girl. I think she was as affected by losing Salima as I was. We used to meet in private, just to talk. There were times when I was seriously concerned that Theresa was growing up to be disturbed. Cruel even."

Cheryl stopped talking. She returned to the chair but kept her eyes turned away from Hammond's. "There was a young girl who stayed at the house for a week or so. It was after Salima's disappearance, I can't remember the new girl's name but I do know that Lucas had taken an interest in her. I remember because I was jealous." She paused as though she was about to divulge a guilty secret.

"I confess I hated the girl even though I never met her. I suppose you could say that I was so obsessed with Lucas that I didn't think rationally. When Theresa told me about this girl and how Lucas had taken a shine to her, well, I just saw red. I said that I hated the girl, that we should do something, get rid of her, that kind of thing. It was a jealous rage, Of course I never meant it but, well, Theresa thought that I did."

"She did something to the girl?"

"In a way, yes. Theresa used to give me updates, possibly to reassure me that nothing was happening that I didn't know about, then one day Theresa came running over to the flat telling me that the girl had been rushed into hospital with some ailment or other. I am not sure what it was now, but it turned out that she had to return to hospital needing surgery. Theresa, in her misguided way, encouraged the girl to take Ginkgo Bilbao herbal tablets prior to the surgery..."

Hammond was confused. He felt that Cheryl had told him something relevant by the way she avoided looking at him, but he wasn't sure what she was telling him. He murmured aloud his ignorance.

"Gingko Bilbao counteracts aesthetic actions."

"You mean, Theresa wanted the girl to wake up..." The thought was too malicious to comprehend. He left the sentence unfinished.

"to wake up during surgery. Yes. That is what Theresa intended."

"Jeez...But how was it discovered?"

"The girl very nearly bled to death. Theresa didn't know, at least, she claimed not to know, that Ginkgo Bilbao is also an anti-coagulant."

"But surely the social services intervened?"

Cheryl shrugged, "Possibly, I don't know. The girl left, but Theresa stayed. She was very proud of what she had accomplished, but I unfortunately didn't offer my thanks. I think I had since realised that Lucas wasn't for me anyway."

"But you stayed in contact?"

"Not at first, no. Salima's body had been found soon after and our relationship became strained. But then I recognised Theresa several years later and I approached her. She was very withdrawn, very nervous. She was polite and obviously eager to remember our times with Salima but at the same time, it was very difficult to get to know her. I found her very odd, but at the same time, her new personality intrigued me. I followed her home one day. Nothing had changed as far as how she had lived. Her flat was completely free of personality, there were no pictures, no television, absolutely no trace of the person Theresa was, and then of course I realised."

"Realised what?"

"That Goodchild had brainwashed her so much that her sense of self had completely vanished. Her flat had replaced one of the rooms at the foster home; She had deliberately removed the number on the door of her own apartment! Can you believe that?"

Her words hit Hammond straight between the eyes. He had missed it before, but now he understood the uneasy feeling he had had when looking at the photographs of Lucas Dean's apartment. He remembered the WPC from Ashford saying she had gone to the wrong apartment because Mark Callum had no number on his door. All scenes had been identical apart from the method of death.

"Are you saying that Goodchild manipulated the foster children using some kind of sensory deprivation?"

Cheryl nodded.

"Do you have any idea why?"

Cheryl uttered a sound that resembled a short laugh, yet her tense body language betrayed her lack of amusement. "Like I said, she was a bitch. I guess it was to enjoy having control over them. I can't explain evil, can you?"

Hammond ignored the question."Do you know if Theresa maintained contact with Mrs Goodchild?"

Cheryl shook her head. "I don't know. But I do know that she was desperate for Goodchild's approval, it is unlikely that she would have walked away willingly from her. Theresa told me that it had been Goodchild who had told her about the Ginkgo Bilbao in the first place but I don't know whether this was true, although it wouldn't surprise me if she did. I know that Goodchild liked to know people's weaknesses and she would play to them. For example, Salima's weakness was that she was caring and loving. Goodchild kept telling her to toughen up, she said that Salima should learn that emotion was nothing more than chemicals in the brain."

Hammond was interested in what he was being told, but he couldn't understand why Cheryl had written about Theresa's death on a bereavement forum.

"Theresa was terrified of heights, really terrified. I read about her death in the paper and I knew that somehow her death wasn't as clear cut as it was reported. Theresa was odd, but she wasn't depressed. She wouldn't have killed herself."

"But you said yourself she wasn't the same person as she was when you had been friends."

"I don't think you can eradicate fear. Manage it, yes, but sacrifice yourself to the fear itself? I don't find that plausible."

"Do you suspect who was responsible? You wrote in your forum. "the bastards", plural. There were people rather than one person you suspected of foul play?"

"Inspector Hammond, what I wrote is immaterial, I cannot prove anything. I wouldn't be surprised if Goodchild is behind it somehow. When Theresa died, I tried to track down the others but I found absolutely no trace of them which I considered odd, especially now it is so easy to find people with the social networking sites and information so readily available on the internet. I kept playing over in my mind the last time I had seen Theresa. She was a shell, and I believed that Goodchild had created this.." Her hands moved in synchronised circular motions as if turning a cog in her mind, searching for the appropriate word.

"... vacant human being with her manipulation. I blamed her for Theresa's death. And the social workers, all the people who had turned away and done nothing to help. I wanted to find those people and draw them out of their closets. If any of the others had wanted to find her, all they would have had to do is a search on her name and my entry would have come up. I wanted them to read about her, to know that what happened to Theresa, that it wasn't right. Effectively, Goodchild had murdered her the second she had taken her into her home, the girl had no chance of living a normal life. Now of course, there is no one left. I don't believe any of it is a coincidence. Mark was frightened of life but he would have never had the courage to kill himself either."

Cheryl was becoming agitated, her voice became louder, her speech more rapid. Hammond felt his time with her was running out, he knew he had to be quick in maintaining her attention. He took out the few remaining photographs he had brought with him and laid one on the coffee table beside her. She followed his direction and picked up the photograph showing Salima at a party, her back to a large mirror that reflected a room decorated by flowers and chandeliers.

"I haven't seen this picture before. That is one regret I have, that I have nothing to remember her by."

Hammond leaned forward, his eyes deliberately met hers.

"Cheryl, do you know if Salima knew a woman called Pattie? Did she work for her?"

"I don't know anyone with the name Pattie. Salima never mentioned anyone of that name but I think she did some work other than the modelling."

"What kind of work?"

Hammond tried to keep his voice as neutral as possible but the way Cheryl looked at him made him realise his enthusiasm had betrayed his intention.

"Salima told me that Goodchild had chosen each child for their own individual gifts. She liked them to be useful, to earn their keep I suppose. Theresa was highly intelligent, Lucas was charming and devious. Mark was subservient. Salima's gift was her beauty, her ability to attract wealthy suitors which Goodchild encouraged but Salima was not a whore, Mr Hammond. She would never have sold herself that way."

He was losing her co-operation. He held up a hand in a mute apology.

"You have been really helpful Cheryl and I really appreciate your candour but I need to ask you just one more question...Do you have any idea why Salima was killed?"

Cheryl shook her head slowly. "Salima wasn't just beautiful to look at, she had a purity about her that was unique. Men wanted her, but not to have their fun with, they wanted to claim her as their own. She was frightened by it, she would ask me what to do and of course, being the plainer of the two I thought she was lucky! It was Goodchild who taught her to use men for her own needs. To tempt them into giving her whatever she wanted.

I don't think that Salima was comfortable with it though. I always presumed that maybe Salima gave the wrong impression, that she was available but then changed her mind at the last moment causing the man to lose control." Cheryl stopped talking, she looked drained. Hammond took his cue to leave but then had a thought and presented the photograph of Lloyd Harris standing next to the attractive woman in the yellow dress.

"Do you recognise this woman? Is this Mrs Goodchild?" The answer was the one he wanted. "Yes, that's her." Her voice trailed off as she continued to stare at the photograph, she bit her lip in concentration for the next few seconds before looking up at Hammond suddenly with widened eyes. "That's him! The man who took Katie!" She pointed to Lloyd Harris. And then Hammond knew. Goodchild's daughter Katie had grown up to become Kathleen Harris.

The taxi driver was looking in the rear view mirror hoping to catch Hammond's eye and resume his one sided conversation that he had initiated as soon as Hammond had sat down on the rear passenger seat but Hammond ignored him. His mind was occupied. He realised he should feel reassured that his suspicions had been proven correct but instead he felt even more frustrated. It was becoming increasingly apparent that all despondents had known each other, although Hammond wondered why Cheryl had not mentioned Fiona Nwasu. It was logical to presume that Fiona had been fostered by Pattie Goodchild at a different time to Salima, so Cheryl would not have had any reason to have known about her, yet, this fact was inconsistent and therefore possibly relevant in some way. Not knowing how it was relevant was already infuriating him. Looking at the information he had gathered so far, no conclusion could be reached to prove that Lloyd Harris had been justified in asking Hammond to investigate the deaths further. Hammond was angry, there was no doubt he had been used. But he couldn't understand why. Lloyd Harris had known the people that had committed suicide, he must have known that the woman he had known as Pattie had fostered Mark, Claire and Lucas, and possibly also Fiona, as well as being the mother of his daughter so why hadn't Harris simply given this information at the start? The more information Hammond discovered, the less sense it made. Hammond was being sent on a wild goose chase but the geese were turning out to be tame ducks.

When he had seen the policeman at the bus stop, he had decided on impulse to wait with him. It was amusing to stand there beside him, knowing the other man was completely unaware that he was in the company of his killer. He couldn't help but smile at the thought. It hadn't been necessary to board the bus and sit behind him, it would have been just as simple, and certainly more discreet, to have followed the bus by car and wait for the policemen to disembark, but his enjoyment at watching the man's ignorance amused him too much. He sat behind the policeman and waited. Occasionally the policeman would utter a discontent sigh as he rubbed his right leg and it gave him a perverse satisfaction to witness that his handiwork had caused the man pain. His plan was to have killed him but even though the plan had failed, he realised it was more enjoyable to watch him suffer. For a while at least.

The bus journey had been monotonous but his patience was soon rewarded. He waited for the policeman to limp towards the front of the bus before he left his seat and did the same. He crossed the road and watched from a safe distance as the policeman found his bearings and then begin a slow shuffle down the road. He waited and watched until the policeman disappeared from sight and then he sprinted after him.

The children playing on the pavement were excited by their mission. He had promised them two pounds each if they were successful in eavesdropping on the policeman's conversation with the woman standing in the doorway of the end house. The children were willing spies and fulfilled their duties as well as he could have expected. The information they brought back wasn't enlightening. The chubbiest of the group said he had heard the fat man saying he was there to send the curly haired woman an e-mail. His information was instantly contradicted by a girl wearing a Hannah Montana t-shirt who protested that the man had called the woman Mrs Bailey and that he was there to talk to her about Theresa.

The money was handed over to the children and they ran off excitedly, pleased with their accomplished task. He stood there for several moments and took a note of the address, then, as he walked away back towards the bus stop, he made a call on his mobile.

"It is not the attainment of the goal that matters,
it is the things that are met with along the way."
Henry Havelock Ellis. The Dance of Life. 1923

CHAPTER EIGHTEEN

Dunn had parked her car directly opposite Hammond's living room window. He saw her sitting in the driving seat as he opened the curtains and checked to see if it had snowed overnight. It hadn't. He was surprised to see her there and attempted to get her attention by waving to her from the window, but she didn't see him, so he shuffled to the front door and whistled until she looked up and noticed him. She exited the car immediately and sprinted towards the house, entering his premises somewhat hesitantly.

"You should have rung the bell, Have you been waiting long?"

Hammond led her to the kitchen at a snails' pace along the hallway. She followed him patiently as he struggled to open the kitchen door with his crutch.

"The house was in darkness, I assumed you were in bed."

Hammond smiled. It was 6.30am, whatever the reason for Dunn being there, it was obvious it couldn't wait, although it was unusual for her to come to his house, normally she would phone. She sat down at the kitchen table and accepted his offer of coffee with a quiet nod of her head. He leaned his back against the countertop waiting for the coffee to filter and watched her, waiting for her to speak.

"I didn't mean to disturb you but I wanted to see you rather than phone. I owe you a confession."

Hammond raised an eyebrow out of curiosity but didn't question her, instead he held out a mug of coffee until she accepted it, wrapping both hands around the warmth as if she was in need of comfort.

"I inadvertently told Beech that you were investigating a case on your own. I didn't give details but it was enough for him to get the gist of what you are doing in your own time."

"Yes, I know, Beech has spoken to me. Is that the reason why you are here? An apology isn't necessary."

Dunn watched him and then looked down at her coffee as if studying it.

"Actually no, that is not the reason why I am here, it is a bit delicate but I wanted to tell you that I am considering requesting a transfer."

Hammond was surprised but didn't say anything; instead he busied himself with leaning his crutches against the table whilst he lowered himself into a chair opposite her.

"You are not going to ask me why?"

"Should I? I presumed you would tell me if you needed to."

"Well, half of it is personal, I broke up with my partner and I think distance will help with the aftermath but the other half is because of you Hammond. I can't work with you anymore."

Hammond's eyebrows rose, he looked at her and waited.

"You've been...difficult lately. My skills, my experience, I guess you could say my expertise, is not being valued enough for my liking. There is no point me standing around waiting for someone to recognise what I have to offer, basically, I feel useless."

Hammond was surprised, he believed Dunn to be an asset to his team. For a start, she was a woman and her gender was a valuable resource when it came to interviewing vulnerable or overly sensitive victims. Sexist as it seemed, it was well known that young people often responded to a female rather than a male. The fact that she was a woman without responsibilities at home meant that her mind was always on the job. Secondly, he could trust her. He had often chosen her to work with him knowing she was thorough and persistent, confident that she wouldn't let him or the team down.

"I am not sure what to say Dunn, I am not the kind of man that enthuses about my colleagues to their faces, however, I thought we had an understanding that we appreciated what the other could offer. We work well together, your brains, and brawn and my..well, my..." He paused, trying to think of a positive attribute he could claim as his own.

"Your stubbornness, your conceitedness, your arrogance, shall I go on?"

Dunn's face had reddened slightly, she obviously wasn't joking. Hammond appraised her and nodded.

"Yes, I guess that too...Don't hold back Dunn, please, say what you really think."

Dunn leaned towards Hammond across the table.

"When Beech asked me why I hadn't contributed more to the investigation, I felt humiliated and cheated.

I give my all Hammond, and the Robert's case was no exemption, yet you took over on a one man's crusade without even questioning what I thought was or wasn't relevant. You were the senior officer so what you say goes, but at no point did you consult me on the investigation other than to give orders."

She waited whilst he blustered a reply, before asking her what she would have done differently. Dunn's reply surprised him, not because she offered any other approach than the one he had already taken, but by offering the perspective of an outsider which was, she reflected, exactly what she had been made to feel.

"Mrs Taylor's behaviour during Thomas's questioning, it seemed rather over dramatic to me. I mean, she was obviously worried for her son but her reaction to Thomas' account was odd."

Hammond didn't reply, he was remembering the interview. He waited for Dunn to elaborate and refilled her cup as he did so.

"I thought about it afterwards, even replayed the video of the interview and there is definitely something that caught my interest. Her body language was contradictory."

"She's his mother, it's natural that she feels guilty that she didn't protect him, she was under stress."

"Yes, but protect him from what? Thomas admitted that Roberts didn't do anything as such. During the interview, she was using up as much space as possible, she spread her elbows wide on the table, and the next minute she has her hands under the table. It was as if one minute she wanted to take charge of the situation, the next she was occupied with trying to hide something."

Hammond looked across at Dunn quizzically. It was unlike Dunn to read too much into things yet her words did make sense to him. Reading body language was a part of the job, a skill that came with experience, but he felt as if he were missing what Dunn was trying to say. He encouraged her to continue.

"I felt we were missing something. Thomas' confession explained the evidence but it didn't explain the motive, at least not well enough. My instinct is that Thomas' mother knows something that she is not telling us, something that may explain why Thomas behaved the way he did." Dunn looked at Hammond directly as she spoke, her brow was furrowed as if she were trying to explain as well as she could yet was finding it difficult to convey her reasoning.

"So, what are you saying exactly? It is possible that she was trying to stop Thomas from admitting the assault, that's natural."

Dunn nodded but her eyes averted Hammond's gaze, then she looked up at him directly." No, I think she was frightened of saying anything more than was necessary, it was as if she knew what he was going to say and she wanted to stop him."

"So, you think she knew about the attack?"

"Maybe, I wondered whether she had found Robert's wallet or his tablets in Thomas's room and disposed of them after you questioned Thomas the first time, although, she did seem genuinely shocked that you had reason to bring Thomas in for questioning, I think that initial reaction was genuine. Maybe I am just splitting hairs, seeing stuff that isn't there, but personally I would have spent more time with her, without Thomas being present. It's too late now, but we failed to pick up all the signs. You said yourself that there were too many questions left unanswered."

"Dunn. I never stopped you from doing what you felt was necessary."

"Your approach wasn't objective, it was obvious you were more sympathetic to the young assailant than you were to the victim, who had suffered a terrifying ordeal. He was beaten, then he was left to die, alone. Regardless of whether he was or was not a threat to children, you never considered that it was anyone else other than Thomas Taylor who needed a compassionate response. We can't afford to take sides Hammond. You were responsible for heading a thorough and impartial investigation, and personally I do not feel that you did."

Dunn leaned back in her chair and studied his face for a response. Hammond was silent for several minutes, digesting her words. He found himself agreeing with her. It was true that he had felt protective of Thomas, even though it was apparent that Thomas' attack on Graham Roberts wasn't an act of self defence. He sighed and faced Dunn.

"You are not the first to offer me criticism Dunn, and you will not be the last. I failed you and the team miserably, yet we got a result. In that sense the investigation had an almost satisfactory outcome. At least, we made an arrest and Thomas has been charged. However, I go by my gut, that is what has guided me throughout my career and my instinct is my most valued tool. Call it arrogance if you wish. As for the Roberts case I do not believe that it is closed. Not until everything is accounted for. Thomas Taylor was charged with Robert's assault with the risk that other factors were being ignored."

"You've changed Wallace. Over the last year you've become this semi-retired PC, you've lost the drive, the ambition that I used to admire in you."

Hammond appreciated her honesty, he knew she believed what she was saying and felt himself comparing her words to Beech's criticism. Her honesty showed she had some respect for him which he was grateful for. He said so, offering a lop-sided smile to show her that her opinion was valued, no matter how hard it was to listen to.

Dunn acknowledged his thanks with a slow nod. "This case you are working on for your friend. I offered you my discretion and my free time, but you didn't accept my offer. Why?"

"To be honest Dunn, I haven't exactly known what the hell I was supposed to be investigating in the first place. I guess I was just attempting to make sense of why Harris had asked me to look at his suspicions. It didn't seem rational to ask anyone to investigate with me."

Dunn seemed surprised by Hammond's admission, she sipped her coffee and her posture relaxed. "Yet you asked your lodger...what's her name? Jenny?"

"Jenny? She's my son's friend who needed a distraction and a place to stay. I didn't ask her to do anything really; she simply enabled me to make contact with a potential witness."

"A witness? To what, the suicides?"

Hammond waved a hand to dismiss the idea.

"No. The witness was a former flatmate of a girl who was murdered in ninety-one. The murdered girl had been fostered by the same woman and at the same time as all the despondents who have committed suicide within the last two years."

Dunn raised her eyebrows. "You found a link, which is what you were looking for."

Hammond updated her on the details of the investigation. He felt as if he owed her, he wanted to make her feel included, to reassure her that her opinion mattered. Which it did, he valued Dunn's ability to think concisely and objectively.

"You may need to take me up on my offer Hammond. You can't go everywhere by bus or taxi. Even if you use me as your own transport services, at least I know you are not acting like a one-man band. You should realise you are getting yourself a reputation as being too single minded for your own good."

Hammond retorted that she was beginning to sound like Beech to which she replied it was Beech's words she was simply reiterating. They bickered good humouredly before Dunn became serious.

"I got the feeling that this accident of yours is being investigated further."

Hammond was embarrassed by the idea that his car had been sabotaged. He had tried to push the thought to the back of his mind since Beech had spoken the thought aloud. Someone had wanted to kill him. It seemed too dramatic to accept despite all other explanations being less reasonable. He was surprised by Dunn's reaction when he told her.

"You are a crazy fool! You didn't tell anyone? Why?"

"There is, there was, nothing to tell! As far as I know, the car is still being examined; until it is official I cannot go around assuming I am a potential victim. There is no reason why someone would go to such lengths to kill me. Scare me, maybe, but I don't know who or why so I am not going to start getting paranoid until I am sure the attempt was a serious one."

Dunn stood up from her chair so abruptly, her coffee mug wobbled, causing its contents to slosh onto the table. She walked around the table and leaned over Hammond, her face inches from his.

"Damn you Wallace! Why do you insist on behaving as if you know all the answers! You are being naive. Of course someone wants to kill you! Right now I am tempted myself! You wander around, ambling from one chaotic scene to the next without looking over your shoulder and seeing the mess you have created! Someone wants you harmed Hammond, you need to think who that person is fast! Otherwise, they will succeed next time and it won't be just innocent drivers on a motorway who suffer, it could be your colleagues, it could be your family! Don't be such a bloody martyr!"

Dunn's eyes were staring at Hammond with such anger; he was taken aback and unsure how to respond. At the reminder of the people who had died at the scene of the motorway crash, he felt humbled and sickened that his arrogance had allowed him to forget them for one second. He felt responsible for their deaths; even though he knew he had done everything right. He hadn't driven with recklessness, he had maintained the car safely yet lives had ended because he had antagonised someone so much that they had resorted to sabotaging his car with the intention of harming him. His head lowered, he felt his eyes stinging but didn't want Dunn to see him weak. He knew she was right to be angry but his pride wouldn't allow him to acknowledge it openly. He waited until she had backed away before he raised his head and continued drinking his coffee in silence.

"Has it not occurred to you that the car accident and the break-in are connected?"

Dunn's voice was quiet and calm, she was standing behind him so he couldn't look at her but he knew she was thinking, trying to make sense of what he had told her.

"I guess it crossed my mind for a moment, but it could be simply co-incidence. There is the possibility that the burglar was looking for Christmas presents and didn't find any so left."

"You didn't get your family any presents?" Her tone was incredulous.

Hammond ignored her question, he wasn't oblivious to the fact that she wasn't behaving as his subordinate, if anything she was showing her disapproval like a frustrated wife.

There was an awkward silence before Dunn resumed her seat at the table.

"Ok, let's consider the possibility that whoever broke in was looking for something other than Christmas presents...let's also consider that there is a possibility that the same person was responsible for the car damage. They sabotaged your car, maybe not to kill you, maybe it was a warning or an attempt to handicap your progress with an investigation. Whilst you are out of action, they break in to your house looking for something..."

"Jenny thought the house was being watched."

Dunn nodded as if she was aware of this already. "It is a possibility, I looked for a silver Citroen when I arrived this morning but there wasn't one fitting the description she gave me. I guess we will have to keep an eye open. Where are Jenny and Paul now?"

She listened to Hammond's answer impatiently. "Allow yourself the luxury of being paranoid, look out for yourself Hammond. Think about what it is you have discovered that would make someone want to stop you delving deeper. Do you think it could be something you've uncovered about the girl who was murdered in 1991?"

They discussed the possibility but couldn't produce any theory that would make sense. For a brief second Hammond considered the contents of the box file. He had the file with him at the time of the accident, it was plausible that the same person had wanted to find the file whilst he was in hospital.

Dunn asked to look at the file. Rather than limping to where he had left it, he directed her into the other room and waited for her to return into the kitchen. They browsed through the contents together whilst Hammond identified the faces in each photograph.

"It's unlikely someone was looking for this, there isn't anything incriminating here surely."

Hammond agreed. He pulled out the Offstead report and notes on Rachel Turner, the social worker.

"You've investigated her yet?"

"No, that was my next point of call."

"Well, if I get a move on I may be able to do a discreet check."

Hammond smiled at her "Are you offering your skills, expertise and valued experience?"

Dunn returned his smile." You may as well make the most of it now in order to appreciate what you will miss later."

For some time after Dunn had left, Hammond found himself thinking about what they had discussed. It was the first time he had allowed himself to think about the cause of the car accident. He couldn't agree that the sabotaged car was an attempt on his life yet at the same time, he could find no other reasonable explanation. He had been selfish to have ignored the warning. What if Paul had been in the car? The idea was too awful to think about. He wondered whether Lyn had been told or whether she had assumed he had been to blame. He hoped not. Her opinion about him still mattered, it always would.

The house had been ransacked whilst he had been away in hospital, someone had been looking for something and had used this time to explore the house. This meant that they had known they wouldn't be disturbed. Jenny may have been right, the house had been watched. But for how long? Hammond was relieved that Jenny and Paul were away, at least he was reassured that they were safe. There was a possibility that the same person was responsible for the car damage and the break-in which was a chilling thought. If they had wanted to hurt him, would they have been willing to have hurt Paul or Jenny if they had been at home when they broke in? The thoughts swam around Hammond's mind and he knew Dunn was right. He had to work out who was responsible and why, before anyone else got hurt. He sat at the kitchen table and wrote a list of people from whom he had received violent threats, all those he had arrested in his career, people who had reason to feel angry enough to strike back at him. Then he read the list. There were thirty three people, all of whom had threatened him with violence or revenge at some point in his career. Then he considered what each person would benefit from his death and drew a blank. There was no benefit to any of them with him being dead. Maybe a perverse satisfaction that he had been taught a lesson, but otherwise there was no reason for them to have taken the trouble to have sabotaged his car. It would have been easier to have killed him with a passing shot or a knife in the back whilst he was unprepared. It didn't make sense, none of it did. Hammond sighed and crumbled the list before throwing it in the recycling bin. He got up from his chair and looked in the fridge, even though he knew it was empty. He hadn't shopped since before Christmas and he needed to eat, it was the only thing that brought him comfort when his mind was occupied with answering riddles he had no hope of solving.

The phone rang as Hammond was debating whether to order a pizza.

"So far I haven't found anyone registered as a foster carer under the name of Goodchild but I think I've found something else." Dunn didn't wait for Hammond to answer before she launched herself into an explanation for the call.

"Rachel Turner was registered with the Social Care Council in 1984, she worked with the Kent Social Services for twelve years, until she disappeared in 1999. I found a missing persons file on her. I am certain it is the same woman as the Rachel Turner mentioned in the Offstead report you have in the file."

"There's no other information?"

"Well, only the obvious, the notes of the police investigation into her disappearance. You want me to pick you up? I can leave now."

Rachel Turner's husband was a slim, intelligent looking man in his late fifties. He ushered the two officers into his home with a welcoming air, and immediately offered Hammond a chair to rest his plastered leg upon. He listened politely as Dunn explained the reason for their visit. They were investigating the background of several people who possibly had been fostered under his wife's supervision as a social worker. Dunn made no promises to investigate his wife's whereabouts but she gave no reason for him to believe that the police investigation into his wife's disappearance had been forgotten.

Mr Turner seemed nervous of their presence but made it clear he wanted to help with their enquiries.

"We understand Rachel was working for Child Protection Services at the time of her disappearance?"

Mr Turner nodded affirmatively.

"Did she ever talk to you about her work?"

"No, not much. Rachel was a very discreet person, she took her work very seriously. There were occasions when I could see she wanted to tell me about certain cases she was working on, but she was a stickler for protocol, she would never have broken confidentiality."

"It says in the Police report that you suspected Rachel had left with another man? Do you still believe that?"

Mr Turner sighed heavily and removed his glasses, he drew a hand across his forehead massaging the temples for several quiet seconds before replacing his glasses.

"To be honest, I don't know what to believe. Rachel was a good wife, she was a great mother to our daughter Heather who was only four when she left. When it happened I was convinced that Rachel would come back in the door at any moment telling me she had made a mistake, but she never did. The police had traced her movements throughout that day. She told me she was going shopping, but apparently, she had met some man at a local motel. It didn't seem plausible but I was shown the security film footage from the motel lobby, it was definitely her. The Rachel I knew would never have left our daughter, she was devoted to Heather."

Mr Turners words were spoken hurried and without care, it was as if he was still trying to rationalise the incident.

Dunn was silent for several moments, Hammond was aware that she shot a sideways glance at him before plunging in with her question.

"Rachel had been beaten shortly before her disappearance? I understand that you were questioned by the Police about her injuries?"

Dunn maintained eye contact with him, willing him to answer.

"I never harmed a hair on her head. Never! Two weeks before Rachel left, she came home later than usual with a black eye and a broken nose. When I asked her about it, she said she had been mugged, and that she had spent the afternoon at the police station. I had no reason to disbelieve her. As for the police...they didn't question me Sergeant Dunn, they accused me of abusing my wife. At one point, they suggested I had something to do with her disappearance. When I told them that Rachel had reported a mugging only weeks earlier, they accused me of lying. Apparently there was no such report."

Hammond spoke up, he realised a man to man talk may seem less accusatory.

"The details that the police uncovered during their investigation into Rachel's disappearance, it must have been a shock to you. You said that the Rachel they portrayed was not the same woman you had known. Is it possible Mr Turner that your wife had led a double life?"

Mr Turner looked at Hammond for several seconds, studying his face before answering.

"I don't want to believe that Inspector Hammond. Rachel was a gentle, honest woman. We were a close and loving family. I cannot think of one reason why she would have left, yet I cannot understand why she met that man. I don't believe she was having an affair, at least it didn't look like that from the motel's security video. I don't know who she met, but she knew him, it looked like they were in a heated discussion, at one point he had his hand on her shoulder and was looking directly at her which isn't the kind of thing you would do with a stranger."

"Had her behaviour changed in any way leading up to that day?"

"Yes, I did say this to the police because I thought it was relevant. Rachel became very withdrawn and secretive about her work for about a year before she left. She wouldn't discuss any individual cases with me anyway but I discovered that she stopped bringing her paperwork home with her, like she used to."

"Do you think she suspected you of reading her work?"

"I cannot imagine why, I respected my wife's work. It was none of my business what her charges were going through, I never had any desire to know about her work other than what she would tell me."

"Do you think someone else looked at her private papers, hence her being more security conscious?"

Mr Turner looked with surprise towards Dunn, he obviously found her question ridiculous.

"Who would look at her private papers here? It was only ever me and our daughter, who was an infant!"

Hammond interjected, he leaned across and helped himself to a custard cream and smiled as he did so, hoping to ease the atmosphere.

"The fact is this Mr Turner, your wife suddenly left one day and didn't come home. The police could find nothing suspicious other than an injury to her face that she didn't report. Your wife was a conscientious worker, good at her job, and for some reason, she becomes over protective of her business papers. Then she lies to you about going shopping and instead meets a man who you do not know before disappearing. There isn't much in this account that suggests a crime had been committed, which means that Rachel's background would have been investigated. Is there anything, no matter how trivial it may seem, that would have been of interest to the people investigating her disappearance?"

Dunn sipped her tea casually, she knew what Hammond was suggesting, that maybe Mr Turner hadn't known his wife as well as he thought.

"Soon after Rachel and I married, she was desperate to have a family, this would often cause arguments because I wanted us to enjoy a relationship before we had children. At one point we had an awful row about it, and she confessed that she had had a child when she was seventeen, a son that she had given up for adoption. She regretted it ever since. When she left, I wondered if she had managed to trace him which is why I didn't report her missing until forty eight hours after she failed to come home. I wanted to respect her wishes to keep her son a private matter."

"Did she tell you she had attempted to trace her son?"

Mr Turner shook his head. "No, but I thought she may have worried about telling me in case I disapproved. You see, when she mentioned the idea of tracing her son, I told her that I didn't think it was a good idea to look for him, I suggested she leave her details with the adoption contact agencies so that, if her son wanted to trace her, he could. That way it would be his decision. I wanted to protect her from being rejected by him. But, perhaps she thought my motives were selfish."

"You didn't mention any of this to the police. Why?"

Mr Turner looked exasperated by Dunn's question but he answered her calmly and simply.

"The police were quick to presume that I was a wife beater, they didn't listen to my concerns, instead they saw it as an act of guilt, that I was in some way responsible for her disappearance. I didn't want them stampeding into an investigation of Rachel's background. Her character would have been blackened. Becoming a mother at seventeen years of age wasn't unusual but to Rachel, it was something to be ashamed of and I had no right to humiliate her by telling all and sundry."

"But you are telling us now. Why?"

"Because eleven years have passed. If Rachel had contacted her son during this time, he would have had enough time to get to know his mother and trust that she didn't abandon him. Heather is now fifteen years of age, she has forgotten her Mother. Also, I believe that if Rachel is alive, she is happy doing what she wants and that she has left her life with me and Heather behind. It doesn't make a difference anymore. Rachel isn't the same person now, she probably has a new identity and a new life. One where she has no secret to be ashamed of."

"Rachel's son, did she offer you any information about him at all?"

"None. But I do know that Rachel left home when she discovered she was pregnant. She moved into a hostel near Dartford which is where we eventually met. It is likely that she gave birth in a hospital near there, sometime in summer 1970."

Dunn gave an encouraging smile. "It should be easy enough to check out."

Mr Turner ignored her comment and looked at Hammond. "If you find her, tell her I am here. I won't move house, it's important she knows that there will always be a home here for her. Everything she left here is untouched, ready for her. I won't throw anything anyway."

Hammond stood up and looked at the other man. "You have Rachel's belongings here?"

Turner nodded. "Of course."

Hammond looked quickly towards Dunn and caught her eye. She knew what he was thinking, she came away from the door and ventured to her original spot in the living room.

"May I borrow something of Rachel's?" He hoped Turner wouldn't question why but was prepared to be truthful if it was necessary.

Turner studied both his visitors hesitantly. "You promise to return them?"

Hammond nodded and told him he would write a receipt for anything Turner could offer. Turner nodded and lead them into a back room. Hammond cast his eyes over the room in a cursory glance. It was evidently Rachel's former working area. A small mahogany desk was positioned in the far corner of what appeared to be a spare bedroom. A small wardrobe stood facing the window; Turner opened it and gestured to the clothes hanging above rows of shoes lined up at the bottom.

"There is not much in the desk, a notebook and her diary with her appointments. The police looked through it but found nothing that was of any help so it is doubtful that it will help you either. As for her clothes, well, take your pick.

"Do you remember what she wore on the day she...
left?" Dunn deliberately used the term Turner had used
rather than referring to Rachel's missing status.

"Yes, a blue short sleeved blouse, grey skirt, matching
jacket and navy heeled shoes. A faux pearl necklace and
matching earrings, a tortoiseshell hair clip and a silver
watch with clasp fastening."

Dunn's eyebrows raised with the detailed description, a
quick glance in the wardrobe showed her that the clothing
he had listed was not in the wardrobe. Hammond moved
over to the desk and pulled open a shallow drawer. The
diary was on top of a jotter pad; he removed both items
and flicked through them. There wasn't much to see but
he asked to borrow them anyway and wrote a receipt for
both items.

As they bid Turner a farewell, Hammond shook the
other man's outstretched hand with sincerity. He
found himself pitying the man whom he knew would be
waiting in vain for his wife to return.

Dunn turned to Hammond as soon as he had settled
himself into the passenger seat.

"Well, did you find him convincing?"

"If you mean do I think he is responsible for his wife's
disappearance. No, I don't. He is innocent, I am sure
of it. In fact I think he is deluding himself that Rachel is
still alive."

Dunn nodded as she turned the ignition. "I agree. He
couldn't even refer to his wife having had disappeared,
he kept insisting she had left. Although I find that rather
strange. One minute he refers to her as being a devoted
mother and wife, the next he is convincing himself and
us, that she chose to leave him, even though they were a

close and loving family? I am willing to bet he knows a lot more than he is saying."

Hammond looked at her, noting her self-assurance. He was tempted to place a bet but decided against it.

It was almost dark by the time Dunn's car left him outside his house. She walked him to the front door, offering an arm as he hobbled up the porch steps. He ignored her gesture, he was embarrassed by his disability, and would have preferred she had left him on the pavement. He dismissed her offer to accompany him inside.

"I'm going to look through the diary, you never know there may be something that proves helpful."

"Phone me if you find anything. I'm in court in the morning, but I'll get back to you if you leave a message." They said their goodbyes and he waved to her with his crutch before letting himself into the house.

From the moment he entered his hallway, Hammond knew something wasn't right. The house felt different as if something was not as he had left it earlier that day. He paused by the coat rack, listening for any sound that would explain his unease. It was silent. He turned on the light and made his way slowly through the rooms downstairs. The living room and kitchen looked no different than usual yet he felt an inexplicable build up of nervous tension, goose bumps formed on his neck and arms. He started talking to himself out loud, telling himself he was being ridiculous but the feeling didn't go away. For a moment he considered calling Dunn and asking her to return, but he couldn't risk appearing a fool, a grown man scared of his own shadow. Eventually he forced himself to venture back into the living room and turned on all the lights and the television hoping the noise would distract him from his anxiety.

Only when he reached for the television remote control did he notice the twelve shot glasses he had left on the coffee table had been moved. Each glass had been left in their individual groups, yet the glasses he had used to represent the thoughts of Thomas and Graham Roberts had been moved across to the corner he had used to represent Lloyd and Kathleen Harris. He had no doubts. Someone had been in the house whilst he had been away, and whoever had been there had been looking for something. He moved towards where he had left the file. It was gone. His mind was racing, did it matter that the file had gone? He could remember everything that was in it but the idea that someone had entered his home and gone rooting through his belongings made him nervous. Whomever had broken into the house had known he would be away which meant he had been watched. He forced himself to think calmly. It was possible that the intruder had left, that they had got what they had wanted and had no reason to stick around, yet he wanted to make sure.

When they had moved into the house over ten years ago, Paul used to play in what he had called the 'secret chamber'. In reality it was the old larder next to the kitchen that backed onto the wall of the old outside toilet. In time, the plaster and the brick work had disintegrated leaving a small gap between the walls. The forty-four year old Hammond had promised to re-plaster the walls to stop the draughts but he had never got around to doing it so Lyn had resorted to blocking it with the pine dresser that she had filled with Portmerion and Wedgewood collector pieces. Lyn's china collection had since left with her so the dresser was easier to move. Hammond discarded his crutches and pushed himself against the dresser edging it away from the wall until he made a space to crawl behind. He cursed aloud at putting himself in such a pathetic situation as he made his way through the gap until he was in the old toilet room. The air was damp and heavy, his throat and nostrils filled with dust causing him to choke. Using one hand to cover his mouth, he crawled on his knees until he could raise himself to his full height. He was surprised to find Paul's long-forgotten plastic Indian figures lined up on the wooden board that covered the old toilet bowl but refused to allow himself to be distracted by sentimentality as he concentrated on loosening the nailed boards that blocked the exterior door. It was an easy job and reminded him of his earlier half hearted attempts at D.I.Y. From his position, he could see into the back garden but was far enough away from the back door so he couldn't be seen if the back of the house was under surveillance. He studied the footpath that lead around the back of the houses. He couldn't see or hear anyone.

It would have been possible to have simply looked out the front window to have seen anyone watching the house from the main road at the front but it wasn't dark enough to be unseen and he wanted to be discreet. The side passage that ran alongside the house would exit further down the road. He shuffled his way out of the outside toilet and edged his way along the side passage, confident he wouldn't be seen in the shadows. At the end of the alley way he kneeled down and peered around the corner of the next house. The car was parked two houses away. The engine wasn't running and the lights were turned off but Hammond distinguished it as being alien to his neighbours cars, someone was seated in the driver's seat. From his position it was difficult to tell if the driver was male or female. He stayed in the shadows for several moments wondering what to do. Then he made up his mind. He scrolled down his mobile's contact list.

"Edwards, are you free?"

Hammond was whispering, it was unlikely he would be heard from where he stood but he wasn't going to take any chances.

"Yeah, what's going on?"

"I need you. Do you think you could drive to my place? When you arrive, don't stop, keep on driving slowly until you see a car parked on the right with the driver inside. Check to see if anyone else is in the car and take a note of the registration number."

There was a hesitation on the other end of the line. Hammond guessed that Edwards was confused as to why he was being asked to drive there when all Hammond had to do was walk down the road.

"Can you do that for me Edwards?"

"Sure. I'm on my way. You want me to phone you when I am there?"

"No, drive past, and then wait when you are out of sight and I will call you."

Edwards muttered a response and the call ended.

Hammond's ankle was throbbing but he resisted the temptation to move. He wanted the person watching to think Hammond was still in the house, ignorant of the fact that he was the subject of scrutiny.

"Life must always be a great adventure,
with risks on every hand."
Henry Havelock Ellis. The Dance of Life. 1923

CHAPTER NINETEEN

The twenty minutes that passed as Hammond waited for his colleague felt like an age. Hammond was uncomfortable, he wished he had brought his crutches to lean on, but he couldn't risk leaving his hiding place so resorted to gritting his teeth and accepting his discomfort like the man he wanted to be. He leaned against the wall of the next house and kept checking to see if the car was there. The driver hadn't moved from their position. Occasionally car lights would sweep past and cause Hammond to step further back into the passage once he had checked it wasn't Edwards.

Eventually Hammond heard heavy breathing accompanied by rapid footsteps as a man hidden under a hooded top and scarf jogged past with a bull dog on a leash. The man didn't seem at ease with running, he lifted his knees too high with each stride as if he were attempting dressage. Hammond watched them and caught his breath as the man stopped by the car with the driver inside. He saw him bend down to the pavement and heard muffled words before the jogger continued with his awkward practise. More minutes past and then Hammond recognised Edwards' car crawl past slowly and continue down the road. Hammond waited five minutes then called Edward's mobile.

"It was just the one person in the car. We've got the registration. You want us to check it?"

"If you can. Anything else?"

Hammond heard a voice in the background. "Yep. We've got a full description of the driver. Caucasian Male, mid fifties, heavy build. Dark hair with a small bald patch. Does that sound familiar?"

Hammond thought hard. "No, not at all. How did you manage to get that good a look?"

There were muffled noises coming from the other end of the line before Hammond recognised Galvin's voice. "Sir? There's two things I am bad at, one is cooking and the other is running. But I am good at dog training sir, so when I say 'pee' my old boy cocks his leg and does the job on cue."

Despite his predicament, Hammond smiled and congratulated the men on their observation, Edwards returned to the line. "Are you going to tell us what this is all about? Do you want us to make an arrest?"

"There's no need. My house has been broken into and is being watched. I want whoever it is to think I haven't noticed them and am still inside. But I want to know who they are."

Edwards promised to get back with the information as soon as he could. Hammond thanked them and arranged to talk in the morning.

When he returned indoors, he pushed the dresser back into position and checked the locks on the doors. He knew it was pointless since the intruder had managed to get into the house undetected before, it was likely they would again. He wondered why the car had remained there. It must be that they are waiting for me to go to bed, to be unprepared. For the first time, Hammond acknowledged that he was scared. He resolved to staying awake all night, maybe even wait for whoever it was to enter the house and surprise them.

The night passed peacefully and without disturbance. Occasionally Hammond would peep through a gap in the upstairs curtains to check that the car was still there. He had made a performance of turning on alternate lights around the house, giving the impression he was blissfully unaware of being watched until all lights were turned off at 11pm. Since then he had waited but nothing had happened. At 3.30am he checked again. The car had left.

Hammond woke himself up by snorting loudly. He sat up in the armchair and checked the room. Nothing had moved. The clock told him it was 6am. Since his voyeur had left, He had tried to occupy his mind by looking at Rachel Turner's diary and jotter pad but found the pages full of meaningless squiggles he couldn't decipher. Occasionally he would find stars on the top right of several dates suggesting some significance but there was no star added on the day of her disappearance which he deduced if a meeting had taken place, it was probably unexpected.

The rest of the time had been spent dozing, although his mind wouldn't allow him to rest. Any sound or movement caused him to over-react. He kept a hold of his crutches at all times, it was the only weapon he was prepared to use if the need warranted it. He updated his log book, and made descriptive notes of everything that had happened during his investigation so far. From time to time he would stop and mutter to himself that doing such a thing was pointless, no conclusion could be reached with what he had uncovered so far. A family of foster children had grown up to become reclusive and withdrawn from society until they eventually killed themselves. The only evidence he had that any criminal activity had taken place was that someone had taken the file by forcibly entering his house. But as Hammond wrote down the facts, he knew that someone was getting nervous and wanted to stop him investigating further, even if it meant harming him. It caused him to feel apprehensive yet at the same time, he felt a glimmer of excitement for it meant he was getting closer to finding out the truth.

Hammond had washed and dressed by the time his doorbell rang, he hobbled towards the door expecting to see Dunn but was irritated to see DCI Brain Morris accompanied by an uniformed officer .

An hour later and Hammond was feeling more than irritated, he was in a rage and Morris looked as if he were enjoying being the instigator of Hammond's discomfort.

"Hammond, you have a temper, we've all seen it. You can't help it, I know. Sometimes the stress gets too much to cope with and you go 'pop', it makes you human. But what did Cheryl Bailey do to make you go pop, Hammond? What did she do that was so bad, you wanted to hurt her?"

Hammond's head was swimming with confusion. For the last hour he had been seated across a table with

Morris in the interview room explaining his visit to Cheryl Bailey. He couldn't believe that the woman he had spoken to thirty six hours ago was dead. What was more unbelievable was that he was a suspect in her murder.

"I told you, when I left her house she was alive and well. The taxi driver collected me from the end of her road, talk to him."

"We have. He said you were distant and unresponsive to his friendly chatter. You looked as if you were troubled. His statement doesn't give the impression you left her house with a smile on your face."

Hammond swore with impatience. He was bored and frustrated with Morris' game-play. It was one thing to enjoy making Hammond feel belittled but quite another to accuse a fellow officer of murder. He sat quietly for several moments before deciding to sacrifice his pride.

"Morris, you know that I am not the one guilty of murder. I've answered your questions, now let me go and find the real culprit."

Morris continued to sit with his back straight against the back of his chair. He laughed and wagged a playful finger at Hammond before allowing his face to set straight and serious. He searched Hammond's face for several seconds before answering.

"You're right Hammond. I don't want to believe that a colleague is capable of murdering a defenceless woman. Yet here you are, and it is not for the pleasure of your company. You are here because your fingerprints were found at the scene, and on the knife that stabbed her. We have a sole impression from your trainer at the scene. Witnesses saw you at the woman's house."

"I haven't denied being there! My fingerprints were at the scene because I was interviewing her earlier! As for the knife, look at my hands! If I had stabbed Cheryl Bailey, I would have a cut on my hand from where my hand slipped down the handle onto the blade from the impact, but I haven't."

"You're a detective who has dealt with this kind of investigation before Hammond. You would know how to avoid leaving behind that evidence."

"In that case, why have I supposedly left a knife at the scene with my fingerprints on it?!"

Morris smiled and opened his arms wide as if to invite further conversation.

"I don't know Hammond. You tell me."

Hammond didn't blame Morris for not telling him at what time Cheryl Bailey had died. It was enough to question why Hammond's contact details had been left beside her body and as well as the other so-called evidence that had been planted at the scene. It was his sacrificed pride that helped him. By admitting he had asked for help from Edwards and Galvin following the break in at his home, he had inadvertantly provided himself with an alibi for the time of her death and a good enough reason to eliminate himself as a suspect. Yet Hammond felt humiliated and found it difficult to face his colleagues who were waiting for him in the briefing room.

Beech nodded at Hammond, silently acknowledging his presence and continued debriefing the team that had assembled. "I have asked Inspector Hammond to give us details on the investigation that he worked independently on until now. He will debrief us all on his findings because it is possible that what he has discovered is connected to Cheryl Bailey's murder."

Beech signalled to Hammond to take his place. Hammond made his way to where Beech had stood, suddenly feeling self-conscious. He scanned the faces in the room noting several familiar faces, people he had worked with over the years and wondered how many of them had thought him capable of murder.

"My business card and kitchen knife were found at the scene of crime. An impression from my training shoe was also at the scene. This is relevant, because it indicates that the same person or people had entered my home and removed the kitchen knife, shoe and my research before going to Ms Bailey's house.

Last night, my house was watched by an unknown male. He was seen by my two colleagues, his car registration was a duplicate and therefore untraceable but an e-fit of him will be handed out in a moment. He may not be the person responsible for stabbing Cheryl but it is likely he is connected. Whether he ensured I was at home alone whilst the murder took place to guarantee I would be a suspect in her murder is a plausible theory. The motive for killing Cheryl is one of two possibilities; to stop her sharing information about Salima Abitboul or simply to prevent my investigation from continuing through my incarceration. It is also relevant to note that it is possible my car was sabotaged several months ago for the same reason. This means we are looking at people or a person related to my investigation."

Hammond paused, he couldn't decide how much information to give. Lloyd Harris had not been entirely straightforward with the truth when he had asked Hammond for his help, yet Hammond had discovered Harris' true involvement during his investigation. On impulse he decided to follow by example and withheld information about Kathleen's background and Harris' involvement with her mother. He did not mention that Harris had worked as an informer for the Home Office. It was possible that no-one would find out, which was preferable. For some reason he felt protective of Harris, and didn't want to give the team any reason to be prejudiced. He told them about the murder of Salima Abitboul, hinting that her killer may not have been found as was believed two decades previously. He explained about the hairbrush of Salima's found at Mark Callum's apartment and the relationship between Salima and Cheryl Bailey. The connections between the suicides of Salima's fellow foster children were highlighted before Hammond focused on Rachel Turner, the missing social worker.

"Her disappearance does not suggest a crime, there has been no body found answering to her description, no witnesses to any violent act towards her, no evidence found that suggests her disappearance wasn't voluntary. However, she is connected to these suicides. She knew all these people as they grew up and was familiar with their routines and home life as did Cheryl Bailey. Cheryl indicated that Mrs Goodchild, as she was known, had fostered the children with the intention of using them. For what purpose, I couldn't ascertain but Cheryl did give details of the type of care the children received whilst they were in Goodchild's care. Whilst it wasn't neglectful, there is a strong suggestion that the children underwent sensory deprivation. They were not allowed to listen to music, to watch television, or sleep in the same room on any consecutive night. Cheryl described the house as being bare of any visual stimulation. Our suicide victims all showed signs of being socially inept as adults, reclusive and lived in similar environments to their former home." Hammond realised he was bombarding his audience with too much information. He stopped speaking and allowed his words to be digested. There was the sound of rustling paper as the e-fit of the his voyeur was handed out. Hammond waited patiently before proceeding.

"The name that seems to link all the incidents together is Mrs Goodchild. It is possible her first name is Pattie. It is believed that she worked as a prostitute during the 1980's and then worked up the ladder to become a madam with her own brothel. I stress that, so far, there is no indication that Goodchild used the children to work in the sex trade. However, it is possible that Salima Abitboul had worked with Goodchild before her death. It had been my intention to find out about Goodchild, especially since there is no-one registered under this name as being a foster parent. I did have photographs but unfortunately they were stolen from my house last night so instead I have given a description, you will see her likeness on the pages you have just been handed. The description you have in front of you is from a photo-graph that is almost thirty years old, so we are looking for a woman who is now in her late fifties to mid sixties." Hammond ceased his deliberations and stood quietly. He was relieved to note that all faces turned towards him were engaged. Some faces were confused, others looked neutral as they contemplated the information he had given. He welcomed any questions but was interrupted by Beech who had resumed his original place in front of the team.

"Cheryl Bailey's death is our priority. Whilst the information Inspector Hammond has given us may be relevant, it is important to focus on what Cheryl was doing before she died. We may have a motive, but it has to be proven. We know that Cheryl met Inspector Hammond. We do not know what happened afterwards and that is what we must concentrate on before we get sidetracked by psychopathic foster carers or missing social workers."

Beech's sarcasm hung heavily in the air whilst he surveyed the faces turned towards him. He gestured to DCI Morris who stood with his back against the door, standing tall with his arms crossed. He had watched Hammond throughout the debriefing, his tongue poking his inside cheek like an infant dismissing its mother's breast. His dismissal of Hammond's blundering was equally blatant. He spoke across the heads of Beech's audience causing people to turn around in their chairs to face him.

"I will be your Senior Investigator. All of you will be giving this your priority. There is a strong possibility that the person or people responsible for Cheryl Bailey's death has also attempted to harm one of our officers. So, we will work through until we get a result. Door to door enquiries are being made with Cheryl's neighbours as we speak. As well as Cheryl's house, Hammonds house is also a crime scene therefore SOCO's will be at his house dusting for fingerprints. Inspector Hammond will be distributing copies of his investigation notes. I want the man watching Hammond's house to be identified and found."

Morris barked orders to individual faces until the room was dispersed. After a while, he approached Hammond who sat on a chair with his forehead leaning against his crutches.

"You are giving us everything, right?"

Hammond looked up, he wondered how much information his features were giving away. After a stress filled night and morning, it was becoming difficult to hold things back. "I have given you all my notes, I have opened up my home to forensics. What more is there to give?"

Morris sat down on the chair beside Hammond. "Let's start with the truth. Why did you start questioning suicides that had been investigated previously with a satisfactory conclusion?"

Hammond hesitated. He knew Morris wasn't stupid, there seemed no point in trying to justify his actions any more. He was exhausted, physically and mentally. Fulfilling Harris' request had caused him more stress than any case he had worked on. Maybe it was the emotional ties of his friendship with Harris that had added burden. Most police investigations were ruled by the monotony of writing reports and following protocol but there were times when solving seemingly impossible puzzles became thrilling and compulsive. Admittedly he had enjoyed feeling challenged, but now he was the subject of ridicule amongst colleagues whose professional opinion mattered.

"Off the record?"

Morris studied Hammond. "Don't play games Hammond. I haven't the patience. If you are withholding information, you will lose more than your reputation when I am through with you."

Hammond nodded slowly. "Ok, but I need something to eat first. I haven't had a decent meal in days."

CHAPTER TWENTY

Hammond's immediate reaction upon entering DCI Morris' office was distaste. Everywhere he looked there were framed photographs of Morris and his family. It took an ego-maniac to take delight in his own image and Morris was certainly not shy to show off his attributes at every opportunity. Hammond had no problem working with ambitious people, but Morris took it one step further and it irked him. He fought the urge to remark on the pictures which one couldn't miss even if they wanted to and sat down at the desk. Morris seated himself beside Hammond rather than at the desk before him.

Hammond felt defeated, he knew the time had come to explain about Lloyd Harris' request and he spoke frankly but only repeated the information he had offered during his earlier interrogation. He stopped speaking expecting Morris to conclude the meeting, but he didn't. Instead the younger man sat and waited, his pen hovering above the notepad. Reluctantly Hammond gave further details, he mentioned the relationship between Harris and the woman he had known as Pattie, later identified as Mrs Goodchild. Then he mentioned Kathleen. Several moments passed until Morris put down his pen and turned to face Hammond directly.

"Your loyalty to your former colleague is admirable but I fear it is misplaced. Lloyd Harris was a bad advertisement

of the police force Hammond. I confess I already knew that it was on his request you initiated your investigation."
Hammond went to interrupt. How did Morris know? But instead he backed down and allowed the man his turn to speak.

"I should warn you Hammond, you may not like what I am about to say but it helps to have the truth even if we don't always want to hear it. Lloyd Harris was not known to be a trustworthy colleague, you are probably already aware that he was an informer to the Home Office, asked to spy on his work colleagues during the scandal in the 1980's?" Morris ignored Hammond's widened eyes and continued.

"What you may not know was that Harris was suspected of deliberately giving false information by accusing the wrong people of coercion. His statements gave names of officers that were later found to have had no dealings with Harris, yet he had given detailed accounts of conversations between himself and them, based on lies and supposition. However, I am digressing.." Morris could see he was going too far for Hammonds' liking. His tone changed to a lighter note.

"I urge you to think about this Wallace; How did Harris know that the hairbrush in Callum's apartment had, not only foreign hairs, but those of Salima Abitboul's? The presence of her passport could have been a clue to whom it belonged to, but there was no forensic investigation warranted on Mark Callum's apartment following the post-mortem since everything pointed to suicide. The hairbrush wasn't analysed."

Hammond's back felt clammy, so he shuffled forward allowing air to move between him and the back of the chair. "It was included on the inventory."

Morris inclined his head in acknowledgement. "Yes, I saw that. But how could Harris had known that? Even if he had found out somehow, the hairbrush wasn't dusted for fingerprints and I doubt that the hairs were tested. For a start I doubt whether there was any DNA sample of Salima's to match the hairs to, although I don't think it would surprise me if the hairs did belong to Salima Abitboul."

Hammond felt impatient, he had the feeling that Morris was trying to suggest something and preferred the man spoke in plain English rather than waiting for Hammond to take a hint. It was as if Hammond's intelligence was being tested, and he had no patience for mind games.

"Wallace, you are a good detective. I've read your file, I am confident that the reports about you are all true. You are thorough, persistent, intuitive and fair minded. I admire your work ethics. You are like a dog with a bone, you don't let go until you get to the truth. I like that. However, you know what they say about old dogs learning new tricks..." Morris paused, he smiled at Hammond, seemingly unperturbed he had just insulted him with his patronising air and offensive words.

Hammond sat still. He knew if he answered the words that would emit from his mouth would be vulgar. He studied his hands on his lap, concentrating on the calluses on his palm. He should use hand cream.

"Wallace. Please understand what I am trying to tell you. Like you I read the file on Salima's murder, but unlike you I considered the possibility that Harris himself coerced a confession out of the man accused to save his own back. Harris could have solved the case with time and professionalism just like we have to. From what I read in the reports, Salima's death was not premeditated, it was an impulsive act, one that would have left a trail of evidence yet Harris picked on the first person available at the scene. Why so desperate?" Morris stood up from his chair and circled around Hammonds, eventually resting his hands on the back of Hammond's chair and leaned forward to Hammond's ear.

"I think I know why and I think you do too. Harris was guilty of killing the girl and was desperate to cover his tracks."

Hammond reacted. He bellowed with rage at the upstart who enjoyed tormenting with innuendos and a superior attitude. Yet he didn't leave. Much as he wanted to. There was some sense in what Morris was suggesting, much as he hated to admit it. During the last few months he had learnt things about Harris that he would never had thought possible. His voice was becoming high pitched so he spared himself any more humiliation and gestured for Morris to continue.

"Harris was deeply involved with vice, he was a regular at the brothels, how else did he get to know this Pattie woman? He knew Pattie Goodchild (if that is her name), he would have doubtlessly had the opportunity to meet Salima. I have nothing against men satisfying their God given urges Hammond, but Harris was not the ideal copper you believed him to be. Think about that, that is all I am saying. I know you feel obligated to protect his interests but don't risk your career for his sake."

The cheese sandwich Hammond had eaten moments earlier was destined to ferment, it was unlikely any food would be digested now. Hammond was too stressed, too churned up. He felt an anger in his belly flare up as he thought about Harris. How Harris had made Hammond run around in circles, just to find out connections that Harris had already known. What had been the point?

"So, what do you propose to do now?"

Morris returned to his chair. "There's been five suicides, an attempted murder, two deaths as a result of that attempt, two break ins at an officers' home and now a murder. The one recurrent theme linking all the incidents isn't just this Goodchild woman, Hammond. It's Lloyd Harris. I want Harris brought in for questioning."

Hammond nodded. He said the only words left to say. "I agree."

*"What we call "morals" is simply blind
obedience to words of command."*
Henry Havelock Ellis. The Dance of Life. 1923

CHAPTER TWENTY-ONE

The screaming fan belt belonging to Jenny's Volkswagen
camper heralded her return. He heard the approach
from the kitchen where he was occupied with scraping
the last of the Marmite from the jar and spreading it on
stale crackers he had found at the back of the food
cupboard. He put down his knife and went to the front
door to greet her. He waited whilst she parked the van
and then called to her as sprinted towards him up
the porch steps, a look of concern across her face from
having seen the police tape cordoning off the house from
the pavement.

"Don't panic, but don't ask questions either." He
embraced her gently and on a moment's impulse
slammed the door shut behind him and headed towards
her van. "Come on, you're driving."

They parked the Volkswagen by the sea front, the air
was chilly but Hammond sat in the passenger seat with
his window wound down, enjoying the salty taste of the
breeze. It was quiet in the van. Hammond preferred to
relax by listening to the waves crashing against the beach

and the sound of shingle being dragged back into the foam but the seagulls were screaming loudly to each other as they dive-bombed the overfilled rubbish bins. He had updated Jenny about the break-in but wanted her to be reassured he wasn't in danger. Even as he had spoken the words, he wondered whether he should be concerned, but he pushed the thought to the back of his mind and helped himself to another chip from the dashboard.

"Pleased though I am to see you, I am not so sure it is a good idea for you to be here, Jenny."

"Oh, right, because I am a feeble woman, is that it? You can stay on your own waiting for some bully to attack you but I can't. I never put you down as a sexist, Wally." Hammond threw his chip at her. "Calm down, that's not what I meant at all, and you know it. I would feel responsible if anything happened."

Jenny broke off some battered fish and shoved it in her mouth as if she were ravenous. Without waiting until her food had been swallowed she continued to talk with her mouth full.

"No offence Wally, but you are not in the best physical shape. If something did happen, I am more likely to be able to put up a fight. Either way, two people are better than one in the house. So, thanks, but I'm staying."

Hammond watched a young gull drag a crisp packet around the pavement with its beak. He didn't protest anymore, there was no point in trying to change her mind. He asked her if Paul intended to come home. He tried to keep his voice casual although his disappointment in not seeing his son belied his indifferent manner.

"He went back to college, said he had course work to complete before the beginning of next term, although personally I think it has more to do with the new lady in his life."

Jenny sucked the salt off her fingers before reaching for the can of drink wedged in the door pocket beside her.

"Paul has a girlfriend? I never knew." Hammond said these words with sadness, he had no idea what was happening in his son's life anymore. He wondered how much Lyn knew.

"Who knows, he wouldn't tell me. But he has been really sulky lately. Bound to be signs of love sickness."

Hammond sighed heavily and helped himself to another chip.

They returned to the house just before 9pm. Jenny brought in her bags from the van and heaped them on the bottom of the stairs, then they sat in front of the television and watched a Channel Four documentary about an obese man preparing for Bariatric surgery. Hammond noticed his stomach protruding over his waistband and sat up straighter in his chair. He was simply overweight he told himself, no need to compare yourself to the man on the screen. He got up from his chair within twenty minutes of the programme starting and begun sorting through his laundry. Despite his effort in trying to keep himself distracted from thinking about Lloyd Harris, he wasn't succeeding. Eventually he gave up trying and considered whether he had done the right thing in telling Morris everything. Then he decided he had. Harris should have been honest at the start, he should have explained what he wanted Hammond to investigate instead of using the local suicides as a ruse. What did he really want to learn? None of what Harris had asked him to do made sense anymore. He wondered whether Morris was having any luck in getting the truth.

Maybe he should have persisted earlier and insisted he be the one to question Harris, instead of meekly accepting Beech's insistence otherwise. The thoughts churned within his mind on a never ending cycle until he couldn't stand it anymore. He groaned aloud and gave in to the temptation to phone DCI Morris.

"I thought I told you to go home and leave us to do our job." Hammond refused to be put off by Morris' patronising manner, he had every right to question any progress.

"Actually, Hammond. I'm glad you called. Officially you are still on sick leave but truth be told I was tempted to ask you to come in. Lloyd Harris is missing, his daughter refuses to co-operate unless she speaks to you first."

Hammond didn't hesitate. He hung up and looked at the time. It was half past ten.

Hammond arrived at the police station within twenty minutes. He made a point of retaining the taxi receipt and filling in an expenses form before putting it in the admin tray. He found Morris seated behind a stack of files on his desk. The man looked dishevelled, his tie had been loosened, his shirt sleeves rolled up casually above his slim wrists. For a split second Hammond felt empathy for the man who was obviously fatigued, but reminded himself that this was what ambition did to you. It forced you into situations where you had to earn recognition. Even if Morris would have preferred to spend the evening with his young family, he had to prove his worth by wading through statements and past case histories. By convincing Beech that Hammond was incapable of heading the investigation into Cheryl Bailey's murder, the pressure was now on him to unravel the web that Lloyd Harris had created.

Morris looked up as Hammond tapped lightly on the door, he waved Hammond to enter the room and watched as Hammond settled himself into a chair.

"I'm glad you called Wallace, the truth is we need your input. This case seems complicated." Morris spoke wearily, he ran his hand through his hair, causing it to spike upwards from his forehead. "I've taken the common approach to look at Cheryl's intimate relationships first. The ex-husband obliged with the formal identification, he seemed genuinely devastated. Apparently the two of them remained good friends following their divorce. He has an alibi which has been proven. They have a daughter who emigrated to New Zealand a year ago. On the face of it, Cheryl's murder seems an unprovoked random attack, but what gets me is the effort the killer took to frame you. We've got a witness statement that some kids who lived near Cheryl were approached by a male they didn't recognise as being local. He paid them to eavesdrop on a conversation Cheryl had with a man answering your description. That is what makes me think that it is more to do with you then it is about Cheryl."

"I think it's likely that someone was worried Cheryl was going to tell us something." Hammond said. "Framing me was part of a game."

Morris frowned. "A game?"

Hammond spread his hands wide, he imagined the twelve shot glasses he had arranged on his sideboard.

"So far, my investigation has been a game of cat and mouse with an unknown opponent. My car was vandalised, then my house was broken into. Whenever I learnt anything new, something happened to distract me. I was targeted because I was the person Harris approached for help."

"But his appeal for help was based on a fictitious reason. He lied to you."

"I still think that Lloyd Harris meant me to satisfy his need to know. What he needed to know I can't say but the suicides were the starting point. He may not be the innocent party but he isn't a murderer, I am sure of that. Cheryl was a major part of the investigation, she was more than willing to share her knowledge about Salima Abitboul and the people who committed suicide recently. She knew Goodchild and Harris by sight. It is possible that she knew more than what she told me. She may have been killed to stop her from telling me more which means someone else out there is trying to stop me from finding out what Harris wants to know." Hammond spoke slowly, he knew he was talking in riddles but he was trying to make sense out of a situation he didn't understand.

"I spoke to Harris' G.P; he confirmed that Harris is showing signs of dementia. It is possible that Harris was confused and didn't know what he was asking."

Hammond agreed. "Yet by the time I knew this, I had already started looking into the suicides. I didn't find anything suspicious about the deaths themselves but it is strange that a family of foster children grow up to become reclusive and lead such private lives before killing themselves within weeks of each other. Apart from Theresa Davenport, there are no explanations how they earned a living, they weren't employed, there's no record that they were on social benefits so how did they support themselves? None of them had bank accounts. They weren't in debt, their bills were paid in full; rent, utilities, everything. Something else that is odd; apart from Fiona Nwasu, they all left suicide notes with almost identical messages, suggesting they had no choice but to end their lives. Who were they writing to? Why bother justifying your actions if there is no-one in your life to answer to? Only Theresa had a funeral, most of the guests were work colleagues from the library but there was no family mentioned. Neither have I discovered who paid for the funeral expenses. Cheryl said that they were chosen because they were useful somehow. Who is this Goodchild woman? Why isn't she registered as a foster carer? There must be something, social services wouldn't have just allowed these kids to go to a perfect stranger, she must have been checked out...but under what name? We can't find any trace of their guardianship documents. What if they worked for Goodchild throughout their lives? In which case, they must have been in contact with her yet she didn't come forward at the time of their deaths. In my mind, that is peculiar."

Morris leant forward, his elbows resting on the table. "Illegal earnings perhaps? It would explain why nothing was declared."

The two men pondered in silence before Morris sighed heavily. "But this is all conjecture. Harris must know more than he let on at the beginning. There is a reason why he asked for your help Hammond, we need to know what the real reason was. You said his daughter tried to dissuade you from helping him?

"She was protective of him. That's understandable, considering his diagnosis."

"I'm keen to talk to her about her Father but she has refused to speak to anyone other than yourself Hammond so if you could help us by talking to her that is a start. It doesn't help that her Father has gone wandering.

There's a team searching for him and we sent her home in case he returns there."

Hammond agreed to co-operate but he was unsure how to proceed. He didn't know how much Kathleen knew about her past. If she had spent her earlier years with Goodchild and the foster children, it would explain why Harris didn't want her to know Hammond was investigating their suicides. It was possible that Kathleen had been taken away by Harris as a child because he had tried to protect her from a life of neglect or it could be that he wanted custody of his own daughter. Either way, Hammond knew he would have to tread carefully. The last thing he wanted to do would be to unleash suppressed memories.

He left Morris alone in the office. He had done his best avoiding Kathleen but she was obviously expecting to hear from him. He debated whether it was too late to phone her, but decided he had no choice. She picked up the phone immediately.

"I apologise for bothering you." He said. "I'm calling because I need to speak to you."

Kathleen didn't seem surprised by his call, but she was obviously upset.

"Can you come over?"

He agreed. It would take a while, he was unable to drive he explained.

"Get a taxi. I'll pay. Just get here as soon as you can, please Wallace."

Hammond made his way downstairs to wait for the taxi and decided to call Jenny to tell her he would be home late. He didn't want her alone in the house and suggested she stay at Mary's until he got back. Jenny's response was negative, but she promised to call him if she saw anyone hovering outside. It wasn't what he wanted to hear but he accepted it. Jenny wasn't his daughter; there was no reason for her to respect his wishes. She was old enough to make her own decisions, even if her stubbornness threatened to be her own downfall.

The taxi drove him up to the porch where Kathleen stood waiting for him. She watched Hammond's clumsy exit from the back seat but showed no surprise on seeing his plastered ankle. Instead she paid the driver and led him into the house. A uniformed officer was seated on a chair inside the hallway. He acknowledged Hammond with a smile before the sound of his radio crackled and beeped. He excused himself and walked towards the back room to answer his colleagues enquiries.

"No news?" Hammond declined Kathleen's offer of a hot drink.

Kathleen shook her head and stopped mid way to the kitchen to light a cigarette. Her hands were shaking and it took several attempts before the flame caught. She took a deep drag and turned her head away from Hammond to exhale.

"Nothing. I was going to drive around but they told me to stay here in case he comes back." She inhaled more smoke. "Damn it! I feel so useless!"

Hammond placed a reassuring hand on her shoulder. "I know, but believe me, staying here is the best thing you can do. There's people looking for your Dad, they know what they're doing. You have to have faith."

Kathleen's eyes met his and she gave a nod before stubbing her cigarette. She repeated her offer of a drink and excused herself as he reminded her of his earlier refusal.

"What happened?" he asked.

"I left Dad alone this afternoon, I needed to go to town and he was sleeping in his armchair. I was gone about an hour or so, when I got back around four, Dad was agitated, he was in his office..."

She stopped talking and exited the kitchen where they had just walked and instead turned back towards Harris' office. They entered the small room, where only a few weeks previously Hammond had sat whilst Harris had reminisced. Harris' office looked as if it had been turned over, papers and books were on the floor. The photo-frames that had been left face down were also on the floor, devoid of pictures. Pieces of shattered glass lay by their feet inside the door where one of the picture frames had been thrown.

"Did you leave a window open when you left? Had someone broken in?"

Kathleen looked at him surprised by his presumption. "No. Dad did this. He was throwing everything around, shouting and slamming things about. I don't know what got into him. I tried reasoning with him, tried to calm him, but he screamed at me to leave him alone so I called the Doctor."

Hammond looked enquiringly at her. Morris hadn't mentioned this when he had told of his earlier conversation with Harris' G.P.

"I thought Dad was having some kind of episode, I didn't know what to do. Anyway, whilst I was distracted on the phone, Dad walked out."

"You haven't seen him since?"

"Of course not! Why do you think there is a search team looking for him!" She quickly apologised for snapping at him before lighting another cigarette.

"Kathleen, are you aware that the Police want to question him?"

Kathleen looked at him squarely in the eye. "Yes. I do. I don't know why but I guess you have something to do with it. Why the hell would you send the police round to question a man with a mental impairment?"

Hammond was aware that standing in the doorway of Harris' ransacked office wasn't the best place to have the conversation he had in mind. He suggested they move to the living room. She followed him meekly and sat herself on the sofa. Hammond looked at his watch, it was past midnight. Harris had been missing for seven hours.

"Kathleen..." Hammond paused. He was about to question her about her time with Goodchild when he had an idea. He changed direction in his conversation. "Do you have a recent photo of your Dad? Something that can be used to show people and ask whether they have seen him?"

Kathleen nodded. "Yes, I gave the Search team one earlier."

"Do you mind if I take a look?"

Kathleen handed him a photo album. He pretended to look at the later photos but then deliberately turned to the front of the book where the earlier photographs were. He found a photograph of a younger Harris with a white haired woman. She wore a blue evening gown that brought out the blue in her eyes. Hammond looked up at Kathleen. It was no surprise to him that there was no physical resemblance between the two women, but it helped to turn the conversation around to the topic he wanted to discuss. "This is Elizabeth?"

Kathleen nodded. "Yes, it was taken three years before she died."

Hammond pretended to admire the picture. "I never met your mother. I worked with your Dad when she was ill but she died soon after."

Kathleen didn't take the bait. Instead she smiled politely and took the photo-album from his lap.

"I'm sorry Wallace, I can't think straight." Unexpectedly, Kathleen started to cry. Hammond didn't know how to comfort her. Much as he would have liked to have persisted with his questioning, he knew it wasn't the right time. Instead he waited whilst she composed herself. "I should go, you're exhausted. I'll come back in the morning."

Kathleen grabbed his arm. "No! Wallace, please don't go. I really need some company."

She leaned forward until her body pressed against him. He automatically put his hands around her back. He hesitated for a second, he sensed they were heading for uncharted waters. At this point a wise man would have firmly said his goodbyes. But Hammond wasn't thinking rationally. Whether it was his exhaustion or simply a moment of weakness, he couldn't decide but he found himself agreeing to her request.

"He who would gain his life must be willing to lose it."
Henry Havelock Ellis. The Dance of Life. 1923

CHAPTER TWENTY-TWO

Making love to Kathleen was different to how Hammond would have expected it to be. She was a beautiful woman, there was no denying it. She could not have lived thirty eight years without recognising the effect she had on the opposite sex, yet she revealed herself to him with hesitation and nervousness. As he held her he was aware that despite the intimacy of their embrace, there was a sense of separation, as if her mind was elsewhere. Her head was turned away from him as he kissed her neck and stroked her limbs but she uttered no sound. Her lack of response gave him the impression that she had no sensation, or worse, that she wasn't pleasured by him and the thought made him feel pressured and unable to perform. Eventually she straddled him and he came quickly, but he was aware that she had not climaxed with him. Afterwards she lay with her back to him as his arm rested over her breasts. They were disturbed by the sound of discreet knocking on the bedroom door. Kathleen wrapped herself in a bathrobe slung over a chair and left Hammond alone. He heard mumbled conversation from the other side of the door and wondered what to do. He should leave, He knew he had made a mistake staying. He started to get dressed as Kathleen re-entered the room. She looked surprised to see he wasn't in bed and asked him why he was dressed. He changed the subject by asking her if there was any news on her Father.

"They're calling off the search until the morning, it's getting too cold for the search team to stay out there."

Hammond studied her expression. He didn't want to leave her in a state of anxiety.

"Kathleen, you need to sleep. The search will continue in a while." He sat on the bed and collected his shoes that had been kicked off earlier.

"So that's it. You've had your fun and now you leave." Kathleen's voice was steely. She turned her back towards him as she walked towards the en-suite bathroom. Hammond took a stride towards her and reached out what he intended to be a reassuring hand but then stopped. Her robe was loose around her neck and exposed the top of her shoulder. Before he could stop himself, he pulled the robe further away from her back to take a closer look. On her shoulder blade was a small mark that seemed familiar. As he drew his finger over the scar, Kathleen jerked herself around angrily and saw the expression on his face that registered shock. She realised her mistake, and pushed his hand away, but it was too late. He had first seen the mark on Mark Callum's autopsy pictures and again on the photo of Salima Abitboul. It couldn't be a co-incidence. The scar on Kathleen's shoulder was the same size and shape as the one he had seen on Salima's shoulder as she had stood with her back to the mirror in the picture. The only difference with Mark Callum's scar was that his hadn't healed after his mark was inflicted, leaving an excess of fibrous tissue.

"Kathleen, what's that mark on your shoulder?"

Kathleen ignored him and began to walk away from him, but he stopped her and forced her to face him.

"I need to know, Katie!" He used her childhood name deliberately; he was tired of walking on eggshells. He needed to know if she remembered her time with Goodchild, if her scar was a reminder.

Kathleen stared back at him, her eyes were wide, her mouth open as if she was trying to think what to say. Eventually her anger took over and she pushed him away from her, pulling her robe tight around her neck.

"If you don't leave me alone Wallace, I swear I will scream rape, it will take one second before the officer outside will come in through my door. How will that look to your buddies at the station?."

Hammond looked at her shocked. In that instant he realised how stupid he had been. She was right. No-one would believe he hadn't forced himself on her, there was nothing to prove she had consented or even instigated their lovemaking.

Hammond took a step back and allowed her to move away. He wondered what would happen if he opened the door. Would the officer see him? Would Kathleen fulfil her threat? He kept watching her as he tried to predict her next move.

As if she sensed his panic, she began to laugh. "You are a fool Wallace, an idiot! You think because you have a badge you have the right to intrude on everyone's lives, that you can rake through people's drawers and uncover their secrets. You don't have that right. You are here because I asked you to be, not because I am willing for you to pry into my life." Kathleen's eyes flashed with fury, she came forward towards him and looked as if she was about to strike him. Impulsively he stepped back quickly. The sudden movement caused him to overbalance on his plastered ankle and he fell.

Kathleen stopped mocking him, instead she reached towards him almost tenderly. He refused her outstretched hand and managed to get himself up. It was only a matter of time before the officer outside would come to check on the noise and Hammond still didn't know if Kathleen would carry out her threat.

Seeing his bewilderment made Kathleen calm down. She sat on the bed and looked at him silently. She reached out her hand and offered it to him as a truce. He gingerly accepted it, unsure what to do.

"I'm sorry Wallace. I'm stressed, worried about Dad."

"I know, I am too."

She encouraged him to sit on the bed beside her. They sat in an awkward silence.

"No-one has called me Katie for years." Her voice was quiet, her head remained low as she looked at the floor.

"Do you remember who used to call you that?" He asked her with genuine interest.

"Of course. Mark was my only friend, he was like a brother. My shadow." She smiled sadly and Hammond saw the tears roll down the side of her nose.

"I know you want to know all about my dark secret Wallace, but the truth is, there's not much to tell. I lived with my mother and the children she fostered until I was twelve. My natural mother is not what you would call the maternal type, my father was around but he didn't know how to relate to children. Lloyd offered to take me in, he and Elizabeth couldn't have children so they offered to adopt me as their own."

"So he is not your natural father?"

Kathleen shook her head. "No, but I called him Dad, he was the nearest thing to a Father figure after all."

Hammond nodded carefully. "The scar. Mark and Salima had an identical one."

Kathleen wiped her eyes dry with the back of her hand and lifted her chin with renewed dignity. "Yes, all the children did. It was our way of knowing who we belonged to. Our brand if you like."

Hammond stared at Kathleen in disbelief. "You mean... your mother did that to you?"

"She used to say that it was for our own good, a way of ensuring that we wouldn't get lost." She gave a short laugh. "I guess it is a bit like marking your pencil case at school. Putting your initials on it so no other kid would steal it. My Mother did it to all those she wanted to keep as her own."

"But that's abuse! It's sick!"

Kathleen's eyes searched his face before answering. "I think Lloyd thought that too. Hence him taking me away."

"Did you see any of them again? Did you see Mark again?"

Kathleen nodded but didn't say anymore. She had clammed up. Hammond wanted to push her to telling him more. He moved closer towards her, noticing she didn't move away.

"Your father asked me to investigate the deaths of the other foster children. Did you know they had committed suicide?"

Kathleen nodded, but her eyes remained lowered. "Yes. But there is nothing to investigate Wallace, this is what

I have been trying to tell you. There is no great mystery, no sordid secret. My Father probably wanted to protect me, maybe he felt guilty that he couldn't protect the others, but in his confusion he saw things as being more significant than they really were. I don't know why they killed themselves. Mark was a very sensitive boy, he couldn't cope with life as we know it, he probably just had enough."

Hammond knew the subject was closed. Kathleen's shoulders became hunched as if her body was closing in on itself. An unconscious attempt to become invisible. He knew she was exhausted. He got up to leave. Suddenly she pulled at him.

"Wallace, don't go! Please stay here, just until the morning!" Her voice had taken on a sudden urgency. The dramatic change in her behaviour un-nerved him.

"Kathleen, I can't stay. I've got to go."

She stood up suddenly and walked towards the door, placing her back against it so that he couldn't exit. He was confused. She was irrational. He tried to be firm with her, to gently encourage her away from the door but she wouldn't co-operate.

"Why are you being like this? I'll come back."

Suddenly Kathleen pulled off her robe and stood before him naked. "Make love to me again Wallace."

This time Hammond decided to be the wise man he should have been earlier. He picked up her robe and attempted to cover her whilst gently urging her away from the door. From the other side of the door, Hammond heard the uniformed officer calling Kathleen's name. He sounded concerned. Alarmed, Hammond remembered Kathleen's threat and found himself unable to speak. He waited whilst she decided what to do.

It seemed as if minutes passed before she called back to the officer, telling him she was fine. The sound of footsteps filtered off down the corridor. Kathleen looked at Hammond, she was breathing heavily, anger darkened her face.

"I thought you of all people would enjoy a bit of attention. But obviously you are out of your depth."

Hammond was perplexed by Kathleen's sudden change of mood. He declined to answer and instead reached for the door handle, pulling the door open.

He heard her sneer. "Don't take it all so seriously Wallace, it's just a game."

Hammond looked over his shoulder at her. Kathleen was standing clutching her robe tightly against her. "That's just it, Kathleen. You play too rough."

He closed the door before she could answer.

The early hours of Friday 7th January would forever stay in Hammond's mind as a bad memory. He arrived home at 2.30 am. His body coursed with unspent anger flooding through his veins that made him feel shaky and out of control. His mind was distracted and he forgot his pin number for his credit card much to the irritation of the taxi driver who demanded Hammond pay him in cash instead. Despite the urge to clout the driver in the face, Hammond remembered his pin number in time and punched it into the machine, before snatching the receipt and marching as much as he was able to with an ankle in plaster towards his porch steps.

He slammed the front door shut before remembering Jenny would be asleep upstairs and for the first time since the Forensic team had left, he entered the living room. Traces of white fingerprint powder could still be seen on the mahogany sideboard; furniture had been moved, including the sofa bed. He surveyed the room and reminded himself to dispose of the Christmas decorations first thing in the morning. Out of habit he checked his phone messages, Lyn had left a terse warning not to send any unwanted furniture to her home again unless he wanted to see it smashed on his front lawn, the other message was from Paul, thanking him for the treadmill. Hearing his son's voice made Hammond want to return Paul's call. He felt the need to warn Paul not to fall in love. No woman was worth the heartache, but remembered Paul was probably asleep so resorted to texting it from his mobile phone instead. He tried to remember where he had left the Brandy but failed so climbed onto the sofa bed and allowed himself to drift off to sleep.

In his dream, Kathleen was standing over him. She was smoking a cigarette and exhaled clouds of smoke over his face. It caused him to choke, and he turned his face away from her, but she got closer to him and tried to kiss him. She touched his face but her hands were hot and burnt him. He yelled at her to get away but instead she began to climb over him. Her skin scalded his thighs. Burning smoke bellowed from her mouth and nose, circling him in a devil's pit of fire. He couldn't breathe. Kathleen started to laugh, her mocking was shrill. The noise woke him up and he discovered he wasn't dreaming. The smoke alarm was heckling. The room was on fire.

For a second his mind was paralysed, he couldn't think what to do. The smoke drenched the room in darkness. He was blind and already disorientated, but then he remembered Jenny. He clambered off the bed and crawled his way towards where he thought the door was only to discover that he was heading into a wall. His ears filled with the sound of hissing and popping as trapped air escaped around him. The heat began to sear his lungs. He covered his nose and mouth with his shirt and lowered himself onto his belly. Desperate to find his way to the door he began to pull himself along on the carpet, the thought of Jenny upstairs driving him forwards. One arm stretched outwards as he attempted to identify any obstacle with the back of his hand. His mind became foggy, he found himself wanting to sleep but fought the urge to close his eyes. He knew his hands were burnt, the skin was tight and unable to grip his shirt against his face for much longer. His fingers from his outstretched hand grasped a lead of some kind and he knew he was now in the hallway at the bottom of the stairs. The temptation was to go to his right where the front door was but he couldn't leave Jenny, even if it meant leaving this sorry life with her. He wriggled towards the left where the stairs were and found the bottom step but exhaustion had claimed him. He knew he wouldn't make it. A sob clasped his throat, his eyes streamed, his chest was burning from within.

 Suddenly he noticed all noise had stopped, his head was clear of sound, his mind numb of fear as if he were out of the fire and in a bubble of absolute clarity. He realised none of it mattered anymore. Life would go on without him as if he had never been born. The thought calmed him and he allowed his eyes to close.

He would have liked to have watched the house burn down. He hated to start something without knowing how it would end but he would return later, he would admire his handiwork when it was safe to do so. He had chosen the flames because they were his favourite. He had chosen a beautiful death for the policeman, because in some way he respected the man's refusal to be scared or back down. She considered the policeman to be stupid, an idiot. He didn't share her opinion, although he would never say. But he chose the flames for this reason; to share beauty as a sign of respect. And he knew the flames would be beautiful, they always were. It wasn't just that they were hypnotic or unpredictable, although he liked that. It was his relationship with fire. The attraction to something that was unattainable, that would never love you back. The promise that no matter how much you admired it's power or mystery, it would hurt you. That was why he loved her of course, she was his fire. Her heart was cold and unfeeling but she burned with such intensity, it made him want her more. She was his paradox. No-one would or could ever understand her, It made her a mystery. And no one would ever be able to claim her as their own. That made her powerful, but also deadly. She was his fire. He looked at the house and wished again that he could stay. The thrill of what was to come excited him, but he was prepared, just this once, to let the policeman have the pleasure for himself. The policeman had no idea how lucky he was.

"One must win one's own place in the spiritual world painfully and alone. There is no other way to salvation."
Henry Havelock Ellis. The Dance of Life. 1923

CHAPTER TWENTY-THREE

Hammond woke up choking, He felt coolness on his face and drank in the air greedily. The sudden intake made him vomit. The hands that were pumping on his chest ceased as the figure that had sat astride him rolled off. His eyes were stinging, he couldn't see anything but blur as he lay. Gradually his vision returned. All around him he could sense heat. He had no sense of smell but he could hear. The crackle of flames were deafening. Slowly he moved his head and saw an elfin like figure kneeling beside him. Hammond recognised Jenny and tried to speak her name. She couldn't hear his whisper so he reached to touch her and then she looked down at him. Through the blur he could see her blackened face, streaked with the tears that rolled down her cheeks and dripped off her chin. As he moved to a seated position, he saw the smoke that bellowed from the door and then he realised. He shouted to Jenny but found his throat had tightened and he couldn't speak. He moved quickly, grabbing her arm and gesturing wildly. The sudden movement made him dizzy and he almost fell but he recovered and grasped Jenny again, pushing her towards the front of the house. He mouthed the words he wanted her to understand. "Mary!" He pointed to the next house and she gaped in horror before joining him. He half ran, half limped his way to the next house, desperate to find something that could smash the window. Eventually he found a plant pot and threw it at Mary's living room window. Smoke seeped through the broken glass and he knew he had to get into the house quickly. He held his breath as he tried to stop himself from inhaling more smoke. Neighbours had started to run into the street, a man saw Hammond and realised what he was trying to do, he ran over to where Hammond was and helped him to remove the glass from the window frame. The man leaped into the house through the opening. Jenny was shouting at the man, he didn't hear her so she vaulted in after him. People were surrounding Hammond, they tried to pull him away from Mary's house but he resisted. He waited, feeling powerless. He shouted for Jenny to come out but he couldn't see her. By now the smoke was pouring from both houses, ashes rained down onto the street like snow. The street was a blur of activity as people gathered watching the scene before them with helpless horror. He saw the lights flashing from the approaching fire engines and found himself praying a mantra. "Please get her out safely."

"We make our own world."
Henry Havelock Ellis. The Dance of Life. 1923

CHAPTER TWENTY-FOUR

Later Jenny would say that it was Hammond's temper that had saved them. He had awoken her when he had slammed the front door closed. She had tried to get back to sleep but had smelt burning before the smoke alarm had alerted her to hurry downstairs. The fire had taken less than four minutes to take hold before she found Hammond at the foot of the steps. Somehow she had dragged him to the door and pulled him down the front steps by wrapping her arms around his chest and struggling backwards. He never would understand how she had managed it. She had not only saved his life, but also Mary's. Mary hadn't smelt the smoke that seeped through the walls of the terraced house or heard the roar of the flames on the other side of the wall, but she understood Jenny's signing as the girl and the man jostled her awake from her bed. All three had escaped the house before the poisonous gases had polluted the air enough to have rendered them unconscious.

Hammond rested his head on his bandaged hands and waited for the nurse to complete her tasks. He had

328

waited over an hour whilst she attended to Jenny and during that time he found he couldn't get the image of his blazing house out of his mind. It was hard to believe that there would be no home to return to. The smell of burning lingered on his body and clothes so that even the slightest movement was enough to overwhelm him with the stench of destruction. He tried to doze but every time he closed his eyes he envisioned flames devouring his possessions. He couldn't care less about the furniture or even his prized collection of vinyl records, it was the lost photo-albums that caused him to feel despair. The albums with his wedding pictures, images of Paul growing from a wrinkled baby into a young man. They were irreplaceable. The thought made him catch his breath and he found himself weeping silently into his cocooned hands.

Eventually the nurse pulled back the curtains around Jenny's bed and beckoned him to approach. She occupied herself ticking boxes on the forms attached on a clipboard but he was aware of her sympathetic gaze whilst watching his disabled advance. The nurse replaced the clipboard onto the foot of Jenny's bed and looked at him directly as she replaced her pen into her top left breast pocket of her uniform.

"My, you have been in the wars." Hammond looked at her unsure how to reply so instead he gave a polite smile. The nurse took the hint and left the two survivors alone.

"What an appropriate choice of words." Jenny wasn't looking her best. Without a trace of her usual black eyeliner, she looked incredibly young. Withheld emotion hiccupped in his throat.

"You could have been killed Jenny."

She looked at him then and offered her hand, which he covered with his bandaged paw as he sat beside her bed. "Right bunch of weirdo's aren't we?" Despite the solemnity of their situation, Hammond uttered a sound resembling a chuckle. It was true their appearance attracted attention. Jenny with her singed hair and reddened eyes, Hammond with bandaged limbs that made him look more like a teddy bear than a man.

"Can I do anything for you?" Hammond felt helpless seeing her looking so vulnerable, he felt responsible for her having been in danger.

Have they called your family yet, do you want them here?" It was an awkward question since Jenny had never spoken of her family but Hammond believed it was necessary to approach the subject.

Instead of replying, Jenny looked at him with a serious expression. "You are already here, Wally."

Whilst Jenny slept, Hammond located Mary on the ward further down the corridor. She was obviously pleased to see him and kept stroking his bandaged hands as if administering healing powers. Her gentle manner was humbling and for a moment he was reminded of his mother stroking his forehead when he was tired as a boy. Through gestures he reassured her Jenny was going to be fine. Her eyes glistened and she mouthed to him her joy at hearing the news. Watching her delight that his reassurance brought to her, Hammond felt a touch of envy as he was reminded of Jenny's friendship with the woman who was at least forty years Jenny's senior. His fear at losing Jenny in the fire reminded him that, although he wouldn't admit it, he had grown to love Jenny as a daughter, but even he would not be able to relate to Jenny the way Mary could. He would never be able to communicate in their silent language or be able to understand what made them smile and giggle. Their friendship was exclusive, and omitted even him. He stayed with Mary until her breakfast was served before making his excuses and headed down to the newsagent stall on the ground floor. He considered buying Jenny some magazines and leafed through several but wasn't confident that she would be interested in articles instructing her how to get the man of her dreams or reading 2011's horoscope forecast. He checked his watch and decided to catch a bus into town. Once there he found a second hand bookstore and was delighted to find a copy of Havelock Ellis' 'The Dance of Life'. Only hours earlier He had had a copy on his own bookshelf but now it was just a pile of ashes. He allowed self pity to sweep over him momentarily before he leafed through the copy in his hand. He began to smile as he relived the quotations he had learnt to love as a young man. The book wasn't an original but it had retained the musty smell of antique pages and he pressed his nose into the edges of the book inhaling deeply. He paid using the credit card he had thankfully retained in his pocket the previous evening and pretended not to notice as the salesman gazed sympathetically at his bandaged hands. On leaving the shop, the sky seemed bright with a gentle breeze that seemed out of place for the season. Hammond realised he still smelt of smoke and entered the first clothes store he came across. He changed into a new white shirt and chose a pair of dark trousers and matching jacket before settling on a striped tie. He was surprised to discover he was two sizes smaller than usual. The labels were torn off and handed over at the till to be scanned with the new underwear and socks.

Accepting the offer of a carrier bag, he shoved the old clothes into it before disposing of it as soon as he got outside. On the way back towards the bus stop, Hammond bought toiletries, food and several bottles of mineral water from the supermarket and headed back to the hospital.

Jenny was awake, she had sat herself up and was fiddling with her IV drip with an irritated expression as Hammond entered the ward.

Without speaking, Hammond handed her the book and watched as she fluttered through the pages for several minutes before glancing back at him with an enquiring look.

"It's a late Christmas present. I thought it might give you some guidance." Hammond smiled sheepishly. For him gift offering was an embarrassing act for it was only ever meant as a display of endearment. Jenny replied with a polite curve of the lips, she looked back at the book and made a display of reading the first pages. Impatiently Hammond pulled up a chair and sat down beside the bed, he leaned across her slightly, his enthusiasm for the subject now ignited. "Havelock Ellis is the personification of irony. He is the kind of guy you would like; Known to be the foremost sexual psychologist of his time, he was a virgin until his thirties, married a lesbian and was impotent before he realised, in his sixties, that he got turned on by watching women go for a wee!"

Hammond's description of the author was a humorous attempt to divert Jenny's attention away from what his offering meant. In truth, Hammond wanted to share with her an enlightening that Ellis' musings had offered the younger Hammond.

"So you're saying that I will like him because he was obsessed with sex?" There was a hint of annoyance in her tone. He was quick to set her straight.

"No. I was just explaining why he was so famous.." His tone changed into one of sobriety. "You know Jenny...it is so easy to fall into a routine and live each day out of habit. It is more comfortable to live our lives without stopping to observe our patterns of behaviour or even consider why we think or behave the way we do. If we paused for a moment, we may see that one word we utter or one action we perform can have consequences for ourselves or others that we cannot measure if we do not allow ourselves to notice..." Jenny was looking at Hammond with an expression of confusion etched into her brow. "Occasionally there will be one person who takes the time to observe and teach us what he or she has learned and when they do, the lessons are the same...we learn that life really is quite simple, that we do not have to make it so complicated. Life is a continuum, there is no reason to feel fear at the prospect of change..." Hammond realised he was gabbling. He was lost in his words as if hearing himself from far away. Despite his wish to share wisdom with Jenny, he realised it was himself he was talking to. What did I do to make all this happen? But there was no self-pity in his question, instead a sense of complacency overcame him. I have to move on, he thought. Most of what I loved has now gone, my marriage is over, my home is destroyed. The mementos of a past life gone with it, but I have a future. The thought humbled him. He became aware of Jenny watching him so intently he felt as if he were naked, allowing his inner thoughts to become visible. He corrected his posture and tone back into reserved mode and pointed to the book in Jenny's lap. "...Ellis is one of those people who took the time to observe." Hammond found his voice faltering; he wasn't sure how to continue so ended the topic by leaning back away from where his elbows had rested on the bed.

"To be honest, Wally. I've never heard of him, but he sounds a cool guy. I'll read it, thanks."

"Do you know the expression; "Making a mountain out of a molehill?" Hammond chose the one he figured she would be most familiar with. He acknowledged her nod before pointing to the book. "Ellis wrote that!"

Hammond left Jenny after gently but firmly persuading her to return to her studies in London. All her protests were ignored as he reminded her that not only had she escaped from a burning building, but that she had saved the lives of two others. That fact alone should act as evidence that she was emotionally strong enough to face an ex-girlfriend. In reality he wasn't sure whether what he said was true. He worried that the trauma of the fire would leave Jenny more reluctant to face another emotional ordeal, but his words seemed to inspire her for she agreed to join Paul within the week ready for the new term. Hammond stayed whilst she gave her statement to the visiting investigators before submitting his own. His mind was switched onto automatic mode as he answered each question with as much detail as he could remember, but even as he offered the information they requested, he couldn't make any sense of what had happened. The Christmas tree lights had not been turned on. He did not smoke, neither had he used any accelerant in the house. His instinct told him that the fire had been started deliberately and he had said so, noting the look that passed between the two officers. It gave him a sense of foreboding which he forced to the back of his mind. Afterwards he dialled Paul's number and did his best to sound as reassuring as possible.

The police station was the closest thing to home for Hammond, which is why he automatically ventured there when remembering he had no home to go to. He went downstairs and showered, making an effort to shampoo his hair several times to rid himself of the stench of smoke that seemed to seep through every pore. He dried himself using his old socks and redressed in his new garments. After several failed attempts to zip up his trousers, he removed the bandages that had covered his hands and surveyed them, realising with relief that despite the sting, they were not as badly burned as he had feared.

News of the fire spread as rapidly as the fire itself. By ten o' clock, images of his burning home were in the local newspapers and on television. He watched the news report on the internet but found it difficult to view. His mind swayed between feeling sorry for himself and worrying about Harris. He still had no idea whether Harris had simply got lost or whether he had left the house in a rage and was sulking somewhere but whatever the explanation, it wasn't the typical behaviour of the man Hammond had known. But maybe he never was, he thought. Maybe I never knew him. He pushed the thought away and phoned Kathleen from the office, her mobile was switched off. After several attempts to phone the house and failing, he left a message on her answer-phone to call his mobile and began searching for an update on the Graham Robert's murder investigation. He still hadn't heard whether his suspicions on Samuel Lawson had been correct. There was a need to know and he had no confidence that Morris had any intention of informing him on his findings. He had no home to go to, there was no point going to a hotel until the evening so in the meantime, it made sense to stay where he was and be useful. Hammond was aware that he was forming a justifiable excuse for being at the station whilst on sick-leave but the truth was, Hammond needed to be occupied. Other than Paul and Jenny, who didn't need him, work was all he had left.

"Oh good, they said you were here!"
Hammond switched off the computer somewhat guiltily, he would prefer his search to be discreet.
"He was there! We got the bastard!" Galvin was waving something at Hammond who was having trouble seeing what the object was. He held up a hand wearily hoping that Galvin would calm down enough to allow him to examine the e-fit that Galvin was holding.
"I watched the news report about your fire on the TV, and he was there!" Galvin hesitated as he noted Hammond's look of confusion.
"The guy who was watching your house on the night Cheryl Bailey was murdered!"
Hammond returned to the computer and connected to the news report he had just abandoned, he waved Galvin over to his side of the desk to watch over his shoulder. The images Hammond had earlier avoided were now enlarged onto full screen; Hammond studied the images with concentration, doing his best to pretend they weren't depicting the smouldering remains of his

own home. The camera panned from the reporter as she described how a neighbour had seen a young girl pulling an unconscious man from his burning home.

Galvin was poking a finger at the screen. "There! That's him! In the crowd, can you see?"

Hammond pressed pause and peered closer. His heart was palpitating; he unconsciously rubbed his chest as he examined the scene on the screen. The figure Galvin's finger was pointing to was standing in front of the destroyed building amongst a group of about ten other spectators but he was alienating himself from the crowd. Whilst some were watching the reporter or were distracted by the sight of the investigating officers, the man stood staring at the smouldering debris as if he were admiring a piece of artwork. He was in profile, but it was possible to see the man's face. His mouth was open slightly as if he were entranced by what he was seeing. Hammond recognised the expression on the man's face. It was pride. He felt a jolt of jubilation as he realised Galvin was right. They had the arsonist in their sight, but then he felt an indescribable flare of anger wrench itself free from his stomach as he imagined what could have happened.

"They never learn, do they Sir? They always return to the scene of the crime!" Galvin's voice was excited. "You want me to print the picture?"

Hammond nodded silently and swallowed the bile that had risen to the back of his throat.

At first glance, the blackened shape could easily have been mistaken for a pile of burnt rubble which was why the fire investigation officers passed by the charred body several times without recognising it as being human remains. On closer inspection the hands and limbs were more easily recognisable. The fingers were hooked like claws, the legs flexed at the hips and knees, the arms held away from the body. The skin, camouflaged in the blackened environment, was dry and wrinkled. It wasn't possible to identify the gender of the corpse nor have any idea of the age of the body but the reaction upon seeing it was reflected on all the faces that gathered around it as photographs and video clips were taken. The preliminary investigation into suspected arson had just likely become another murder enquiry.

CHAPTER TWENTY-FIVE

Hammond's headache was getting worse by the minute, he found the glare of the computer screen intolerable and found himself squinting with discomfort. Galvin, who was whispering earnestly into his mobile phone, mistook Hammonds facial expression as disapproval and ended his call quickly, snapping his phone shut with an apologetic smile.

"Sorry Sir, my wife has been having Braxton Hicks all day, Panic over now though." Hammond gazed at the younger man, wondering why the sudden explanation and realised how tired Galvin looked. He had lost weight, not much, but his trousers were evidently loose around the legs and seat. He realised Galvin's situation wasn't an easy one. Becoming a Father for the first time was exhausting, more emotionally than physically but nonetheless it was a forecast for the disturbed routine that was to come. Despite a quarter of a century having passed since Hammond had anticipated Paul's arrival, he remembered the time as being wildly conflicting. He had played the game of appearing obliging and patient with Lyn's increasing demands. He had fetched the cushions, massaged the swollen ankles, erected the nursery furniture. Even painted the walls pink at Lyn's insistence that the baby was going to be a girl before repainting yellow, just in case the baby wasn't a girl and then blue when Lyn decided that the kicking inside her womb indicated a future footballer. He had felt the obligatory guilt at having put Lyn into such a uncomfortable situation, and he had fought the urge to tell the truth and agree she did look fat. But he also remembered the good times, the anticipation of what their baby would look like, what name they would choose, what school the child would attend. He recalled the times when he thought Lyn couldn't have been more beautiful and also when he thought she couldn't look any worse. The sex he relived with vivid imagination. It had been incredible during the first few months of her pregnancy, her raging hormones had created an insatiable and adventurous seductress until the day she looked at herself in the mirror and compared herself to a whale in a dress. And then of course, when she did lose the excess weight, the bed was used for nothing more than dropping onto it unconscious with exhaustion. Hammond was lost in his reminiscing before he realised that Galvin had been waiting for Hammond to reply. He wondered whether his facial features had given any clues to what he had just been thinking.

"It will be all worth it, Galvin. Not long to wait now is it?" Galvin looked at Hammond with an expression of appreciation for having been given the opportunity to share his concern.

"Her due date is three weeks away but I think it wants to come early. My wife is at the nesting phase. Every time I get home, the house looks even cleaner. I reckon by this evening there will be no carpet on the floor she's vacuuming it that much."

Suddenly Hammond felt the urge to steer the conversation away from Galvin's wife before the subject of hormones became the next topic. He wondered whether he could sneak away and continue looking for the update on Samuel Lawson, but was distracted by Edwards who had come into the office carrying several manila envelopes. Edwards offered his hand to shake Hammond's before slapping Hammond hard on the upper arm. "Good to see you are almost in one piece Sir."

Hammond rubbed his arm. He felt a wimp doing so but Edwards was evidently stronger than he looked. He mumbled words of thanks to Edwards but his reply was unnoticed as Edwards committed himself to Galvin's conversation.

"Trust me Galvin, you'll look back at these days and consider them as the happiest. Make the most of your wife before you become second best." Edwards winked at Hammond as if inviting him to join in the banter but Hammond was having none of it, he slowly headed towards the door.

"Is it that bad?" Hammond could feel Galvin's eyes directed at him and attempted to increase his pace.

"Nah, only kidding with you. To be honest the day my first came along was the day when everything made sense. I never loved my wife more and as for the kids, well, I have three now and would quite happily settle for three more!"

Despite his eagerness to get away from the conversation, Hammond found himself faltering at the door, he couldn't resist the urge to turn around and judge whether Edwards was joking. When he did so, he found himself mimicking the expression of Galvin; complete and utter stupefaction as Edwards grinned with pride. My God, Hammond thought. He's serious. He left the room quickly before his contribution was due.

If Hammond's ignorance of the discovery at his former home was bliss, his time at the coffee machine were the last few seconds he would be spared before the full weight of the morning's drama came crashing down upon him. From where he stood, stirring the third spoonful of sugar into the creamed liquid, he could hear dribbles of conversation filtering through open doors. The scraping of chairs was immediately followed by hurried footsteps as if activity had suddenly heightened in the offices surrounding him. He leaned back on the heel of his good foot glancing up and down the corridor and wondered what was going on. Replacing the spoon onto the countertop he made his way back to the office when his mobile rang.

"Hammond. Where are you?"

Hammond was irritated by Morris' tone, it would have been nice to have heard the polite "Glad to hear you are Ok" comment, even if it were untrue, yet Hammond's preferred retort remained unspoken and he confirmed his whereabouts.

"Good. Stay there. We need to talk to you. Don't go anywhere." Morris ended the call before Hammond had the chance to reply. As if expecting an explanation from the phone itself, Hammond studied it in his hand. He hadn't been mistaken, something was going on.

Detective chief Inspector Morris had taken charge of the briefing room, he now stood with his usual stance, feet spaced apart at hip width, his hands rested on his haunches, his back straight. His voice was firm and concise.

"Firstly, the investigation into the cause of the fire is suspected arson. The source of ignition appeared to be from a cracked lighter and burning cigarette. The girl staying at Hammond's is a smoker but both Inspector Hammond and the girl insist that she does not smoke in the house. The living room window and the letterbox on the front door were both wedged open which makes me inclined to believe that someone intended to increase the oxygen content to fuel the flames. At the moment I am intending to investigate both the fire and the body found in the house as connected incidents. Let's suppose that the fire was intended to dispose of the body with the added bonus of causing danger to Inspector Hammond. Remember this is not the first attempt to harm him although we cannot presume this is all about him."

Morris held the attention of everyone in the room. His manner was authoritative and firm, there was no questioning his determination to have all questions answered. A hand was raised at the back of the room, but whomever it belonged to was stopped from asking any questions by Morris who continued with his briefing. "For the time being, let's assume that the body found after the fire was connected; on the preliminary pathology examination, no soot was found in the airways of the deceased so we know our victim was not breathing when the fire started. They were lying under the kitchen table, but there were no obstacles between where they lay and the nearest exit, suggesting that they made no attempt to escape when the fire took hold. Therefore, we can presume that the person was already unconscious or that they were already deceased before the fire was started. It's going to take longer for the anthropological examination obviously, so as yet we cannot confirm ethnicity or age of our victim but we have an idea of how they died. Our victim has the typical lesions and fractures that you would expect from being in a burning building but it is significant to note that the skull fractures seen on our victim's temporal bones terminated at the suture lines rather than run across them, which suggests that the injury was incurred before the fire. So…"

Morris slapped his hands together in an optimistic gesture. "Our victim was possibly killed by a blow to the head, accidental or otherwise. The e-fit you see before you was taken from media footage of the fire. This man was also seen watching Hammond's house the night of Cheryl Bailey's murder. We cannot assume that Inspector Hammond is innocent of starting the fire or for burning the body but we can allow ourselves to think logically; What would he have to gain by knocking someone unconscious and leaving them there or by placing a body in his own kitchen? I want to know more about the girl that is staying with him. Jenny. What do we known about her? I want to know everything about her, could she be the one out to harm our Inspector? Does she know this man?" His eyes swept over his audience. Dunn was standing to the right of him having been called in an hour earlier.

"Or could it be that this guy is trying to get to Jenny? Either way, Inspector Hammond won't find it easy to accept we intend to check her out. He is very protective of her." Dunn bit her bottom lip, she had an uneasy feeling that one way or other the nightmare wasn't over for Hammond. Morris glanced at Dunn before his eyes returned to the rest of the group.

"All the more reason to suspect her. Hammond is downstairs, he doesn't know what we are talking about here so there is no need for him to know what or who we intend to investigate at this time." Dunn answered by tilting her head slightly to one side as she contemplated that maybe it wouldn't hurt just to do a check on Jenny, if only to eliminate her. There was no doubt that the trouble had started almost the same time as Jenny had appeared.

"What about Cheryl Bailey? Do you think that the arson and the body are connected to her murder?"

The question was raised from the back of the room. Morris shook his head slightly.

"It is possible, but so far the only link between the two is Hammond. Preferably I would prefer to treat both as separate incidents. The problem of course is that we are now pushed to our limit. The media are aware of the house fire, so the pressure is on but there is no reason for them to know it is anything other than it is being treated as suspicious for the time being. As yet they do not know about the discovery of the body, and I do not want them to know. It is likely that they know Hammond survived the fire because he was witnessed helping the neighbour. The problem is that if there is a potential killer out there, they will know their plan failed and they may try again." Morris paused, he took a sip of water from the bottle beside him and surveyed his audience. "For now, I want to know what information we have gathered on Cheryl Bailey, if there is another link between her and Hammond's fire, we will find it. So, what have you got?"

There was a rustle of papers and files as information was slowly offered by all members of the investigating team.

"The door to door enquiries have proved slightly helpful. Three people have confirmed that a man was seen talking to a group of children from the neighbourhood. The same children have given a description. The only problem is, their descriptions are slightly contradictory. The only detail they agreed on was that he was of heavy build."

"Do we know how our man travelled to the scene?"

Edwards looked up at Morris and confirmed that this had been checked. "It couldn't be definite but the all the statements we gathered indicated he had walked from an easterly direction towards the Cul-de-Sac where Cheryl Bailey lived. It is possible that, like Hammond, he arrived by bus. We are collecting the security footage from the bus company after this meeting."

Dunn glanced at Morris as if unsure how he would receive her information, he had a habit of dismissing her input sometimes, but she persisted regardless and handed over photocopies of Rachel Turner's diary that she had produced earlier.

"I managed to decipher Rachel Turner's notes. Basically she wrote everything in Pitman's shorthand only normally there are diacritical marks added to indicate vowels but these were omitted, probably for speed. Anyway, the notes mention the name 'Brad' quite often. It looks as if she were compiling a report about this Brad, suggesting he was unsuitable to be working with children. She had issues with the way he ignored the children in his care, avoided eye contact and suggested he had an intimidating manner. Then, further up..." Dunn shuffled a few pages until she found the one she was looking for.

"This one is the most interesting. She had written about a married couple under the name of Dean, according to her notes, the husband left the wife soon after they adopted a baby boy, she turned to drugs and she lost custody of the boy before taking an overdose." Dunn stopped speaking and suddenly her face reddened. She looked up from her notes and paused as if were suddenly distracted.

"What if...?" She walked over to the stack of files that had been brought in and placed to the side before rummaging through them. Morris called to her and asked the relevance of the notes on Rachel Turner, how was it connected to Cheryl Bailey?

Dunn turned around to face him. "I am not sure yet, it may be nothing, I need more time." Her mouth opened again as if to speak some more but she was interrupted by Beech who had come into the room.

"We don't have the luxury of time Sergeant Dunn. So, we need to stick to what we can prove is relevant." He turned to Morris. "I want you in my office as soon as you are finished here." Morris waited for Beech to leave. "Like I said, there is pressure on all sides so let's pull together on this. We'll meet this evening and I want the following; the security footage from the bus. I want information on Hammond's friend, Jenny what's-her-name. Also, no matter how back stabbing you may believe this to be we need to check Hammond's expenses. Is he in debt? Does he have a house insurance policy? Has he been threatened by any debt collectors lately? Any items of significant value taken out of the house before the fire? Also, Hammond has been rather vague about where he was last night. I want an alibi from when he left me here at eleven last night. He was going to question Lloyd Harris's daughter. What time did he leave her? He said he came home about two thirty in the morning by taxi. He paid by credit card so it shouldn't be difficult to check that out. I want this information no matter how rotten you may feel getting it. If Hammond is as innocent as we all believe him to be, he will understand that we are simply doing our jobs. But first, I want everyone to dig deep into their pockets and put a donation in that tin over there. Hammond needs all the help he can get right now, the least we can do is buy him a comfortable night at a hotel and a good meal."

The team dribbled out the door with their tasks to complete. Dunn watched as Morris checked his mobile phone, he stood looking crestfallen at his phone for several moments. Then, as if snapping himself out of his reverie, he paused by the collection tin at the door before leaving the room and heading for Beech's office.

"The place where optimism most
flourishes is the lunatic asylum."
Henry Havelock Ellis. The Dance of Life.1923

CHAPTER TWENTY-SIX

The hotel room was basic but comfortable with twin beds placed on either side of a three drawer cabinet. Hammond dumped the carrier bag of groceries beside the desk and sat on the bed nearest the window. Despite his headache and the need to sleep, he spent several minutes surveying the room that was to be his home indefinitely. He opened the top drawer of the cabinet and found a bible. It wasn't his choice of reading matter but he opened the book anyway and flicked through the pages. Hammond did not consider himself to be a man of faith. He did not believe in one God, a master of divine providence, but he did have faith that life was set on a path on some kind, that there was always a way ahead, a way around obstacles. Why he believed this he couldn't explain, perhaps it was simply a method that allowed him to keep looking ahead towards a future. He wondered whether his belief stemmed from his Father. A man who had thrived on optimism and inner strength. He had raised Hammond with a firm hand but had guided him with the gentle philosophy.

"To climb a mountain, you just have to put one foot in front of the other until you reach the summit." Thinking of his Father now made Hammond wonder what he would have said if he could see his son now. Would he be disappointed? Hammond knew his mother wouldn't be, she had never shown anything other than motherly pride. He sat there, slouched on the single bed, lost in his musings. He could afford to dwell on sentimentality, he needed to remind himself of his good fortune despite the overwhelming feeling of loss that threatened to anchor him in the one spot where he sat. If he give in to despair, he knew he wouldn't leave the room at all. He allowed himself to lay back and stared at the ceiling for several moments feeling his eyelids get heavier until his eyes closed and he slept.

Hammond awoke at five feeling hungry, his headache had gone leaving his neck and shoulders tender. He rummaged through his groceries trying to find something that looked appetising before deciding he would walk over to the hotel restaurant. The waitress was a young woman whose ponytail swung like a pendulum as she walked towards him with the menu. He ordered the Mushroom risotto and allowed himself to view the other diners, realising he was the only single one there. He wished he had sat by the window, at least he could observe activity without seeming to be a voyeur.

His mobile rang and he answered it quickly, aware that the noise had disturbed the couple at the next table, he offered an apologetic smile in response to the elderly man's scowl.

"I can't believe you're being kept away." Dunn's voice was sympathetic which was unnecessary. He understood why Beech had decided it was for the best, although he had no intention of abiding by the decision. He said so, becoming aware that the waitress had returned with his meal. He declined her offer of black pepper with a shake of his hand and waited for her to leave the table before resuming his conversation with Dunn.

"We are making progress here, but...I want to see you if that's ok. I think I have found something but I don't want to run it by Morris until I'm sure."

"What's it about?"

"Rachel Turner, the social worker; I think I have sussed out why she was so protective over her case papers."

Hammond took in a forkful of risotto realising too late that it was hotter than he expected; he blew over his scalded tongue, and took a gulp of his cola before answering.

"You'll have to come here; I can't be at the station until I am deemed innocent."

Dunn pretended not to hear the sarcasm in his tone. She agreed to visit him within the hour. He ended the call and allowed himself to smile with optimism. He knew his faith in Dunn wasn't misplaced. Her imaginative approach may not be appreciated by those who preferred the methodical and exacting methods of deduction, but if anyone was going to make improbable or even peculiar connections in a case, it would be her. Dunn arrived on time but Hammond was surprised she was accompanied by Galvin, who looked flushed as if he had rushed there. Without any word of greeting, Galvin sprang over to the chairs where Hammond was waiting in the Hotel lobby and thrust some papers onto Hammond's lap like a child showing his parents an award he'd earned from school. Taken aback by his younger colleague's apparent enthusiasm, Hammond looked down at Galvin's offering. The pages he now held were still photographs taken from a bus' security camera. He recognised a profile view of himself standing beside the driver as he accepted his bus ticket. The next image showed Hammond about to exit the bus, and another with a man standing behind him. The man was balding with a heavy build. It was difficult to tell his age as the camera was positioned so that it looked down towards the door of the bus but Hammond recognised him. It had been the man Galvin had pictured in the e-fit, the one who had watched Hammond's house on the night Cheryl Bailey was killed, the same man who had stood watching Hammond's house smouldering with an expression of pride. Hammond looked up at Galvin who was still standing before him, practically hopping from one foot to another in his excitement.

"Wait, there's more.." Galvin helped himself to the pages on Hammond's lap and pulled out the last few from the bottom of the pile.

"This was taken from the Oak restaurant in Charing, the camera is positioned by the kitchen exit, so you can't see much but if you look to the far left, you can just about make out your car in the car park."

Hammond followed Galvin's direction. He couldn't see what Galvin was so excited about, he recognised his car as he had left it the night he had dined with Kathleen. It was the only car in the car park. He looked up enquiring at Galvin.

"What is there to see?"

Galvin leaned over Hammond. "Look carefully, in the back window of your car, you can just about make out a reflection."

Hammond looked closer, he could see what Galvin meant, there was a definite image of another car, parked behind his own, away from the camera.

"Explain to me what it is you're trying to tell me, Galvin." Galvin sat down on the arm of Hammond's chair and continued to poke at the images he was holding in front of Hammond's chest.

"It took them a while, but they were able to maximise the image, it is blurry but you can make out some of the registration and also the silhouette of the driver, it's the same guy."

Hammond concentrated his gaze so much, he was now squinting, His eyesight wasn't as good as the younger constable's, but he could just about make out the image now he had some direction. "Question is Galvin, who is he?"

Galvin practically clapped his hands together with glee at his own ingenuity. "I looked at the media footage of the fire again, and for a split second, he held onto the plastic tape that was used to cordon your house off. I managed to get the tape and get fingerprints off it. You'd be surprised how many fingerprints were all over it despite our guys wearing gloves..."

Hammond interrupted. "Get on with it Galvin, you got fingerprints?"

"Almost, a partial thumb print that was matched on the database."

"Did it match any prints taken from my house?"

Noting the negative response, Hammond shuffled his weight forward on his chair, he was aware that Galvin was enjoying his moment of revelation. For a second he was reminded of Poirot addressing a room of suspects about to point the finger at the guilty suspect.

"The thumb print belonged to a Bradley Kelsey."

Hammond pondered for several moments, the name was familiar but he couldn't place it. He shook his head hesitantly, slightly disappointed that the name didn't mean anything to him. He looked at Dunn, hoping she could help to clarify his confusion. She had sat quietly beside him throughout Galvin's presentation, but now, having Hammond's attention, she spoke up.

"The name is significant to the case you were working on. Rachel Turner's diary mentioned a Brad having been involved with the care of adopted children, she was about to write a report on him, complaining that he was an unsuitable warden."

"You've presented this to Morris?" Hammond was aware that the information they had gathered was lacking in evidence, so far it was all circumstantial.

"We're going to the briefing later this evening, but like I said, I've got an idea that I wanted to consult you first."

Hammond held up a hand. "Hang on, this could be important. Morris is the senior investigator on this case now, not me. He needs to know. If Brad is responsible for cutting my car's calliper bolts, there could be evidence on the wreckage, in which case that could be enough evidence to bring him in for questioning but otherwise all you have is a man who was photographed following me on a bus and then is seen outside my burning house. That's not evidence of arson, neither is it evidence of him killing Cheryl Bailey, you only have him being near the scene of the crime committed earlier in the day. So far, you have no motive and more importantly, no evidence. It's not enough."

Dunn eye's focused on Hammond. "But, it's a start. We've got a few hours, then we'll present what we have, but what is the harm in looking at what we have in the meantime? You should be aware that Morris is investigating you, your ex-wife and Jenny, he will be less interested in anything I have to give him until you three have been cleared."

Hammond looked at Dunn surprised. "Jenny? But she has nothing to do with this! She's a witness, that's all!"

Dunn shrugged. "If it was the other way round, you would investigate her yourself."

Hammond knew she was right, so he released the thought temporarily and allowed himself to focus on the information to hand. He looked at Dunn as she leant forward, her body bridging the gap between the chairs they were sitting on.

"Rachel Turner's diary mentions a family with the names Dean. I think she was researching Lucas Dean. So I looked into it, he was born in August 1970 in Bexley Hospital, which is strange because it was a psychiatric hospital and therefore did not have a maternity ward. The hospital isn't there anymore but some records exist..."

Hammond watched her as she spoke, her tone was calm but contradicted the enthusiasm shown in her stare as she shared the information she had gathered.

"It was confirmed that a baby boy was born 24th August 1970 to a Raquel Burchett, aged seventeen. I looked into the Deed poll archives but it doesn't seem as if the name change was enrolled so it wasn't included on any central register."

Dunn stopped and looked at Hammond whose blank expression showed he couldn't see the significance of what she was telling him.

"Don't you see? Rachel Turner was Lucus Dean's mother! Her husband said that she had given a baby up for adoption when she was seventeen. She probably changed her name to Rachel instead of Raquel before they married. She became a social worker, maybe she was trying to find her son and when she did, she not only discovered that the adopted mother had become a drug addict and that the child was put into care, but also his foster carers were unsuitable, hence her writing a report on this Brad guy."

Whilst Dunn had been talking, Hammond had restrained himself from interrupting. Dunn's theories were plausible, but again, they couldn't be proved and he knew that it was unlikely any evidence could be provided to support her claims. Instead, he nodded encouragingly.

"I guess it's possible. We've presumed that she gave up her son for adoption by choice, but maybe it wasn't. If she were in a psychiatric hospital, it's probable she was considered mentally unfit to take parental responsibility so the baby was taken from her by Social Services, in which case she would have been unable to trace the child."

Dunn was biting her lower lip, a sure sign she was deep in thought. "So the only way of finding her son was to become a social worker herself. It explains the change of name. Rachel's husband said that she had a sense of shame about being pregnant at seventeen, but maybe the shame was from having her child taken from her."

Hammond scanned his memory. Rachel Turner's husband had been co-operative but it was possible he had known about the circumstances of the adoption. Dunn's instinct had told her he had known more than he let on, it was possible he had known about the circumstances behind the adoption of Rachel's child. He shifted in his seat as he weighed up the options and asked her what she intended to do with her findings.

Dunn looked at him surprised. "We find the autopsy report on Lucas Dean, compare any samples with samples taken from Rachel Turner's house.." Her eyes were widened with surprise at Hammond's lack of enthusiasm. "We can't do that Dunn; there is not enough reason to do so. Lucas Dean's parentage isn't relevant to the investigation, although I agree that it does provide us with a link. It could also explain Rachel Turner's disappearance if she had confronted Bradley, he could have tried to scare her into submission hence her injuries before she went missing or he is the person seen with her on the hotel security footage that her husband told us about. But, we can't prove this. The best we can do is find this Brad guy and take it from there."

Dunn sighed and leaned back into her chair. She looked at Galvin and then Hammond before lifting a shoulder in resignation. "So, you want me to give this to Morris?" Hammond nodded. "I can't be the one who gives the orders Dunn, I probably shouldn't even be talking to you about this but I have to admit, it is beginning to make sense..." Hammond stopped short, his memory was ignited suddenly. "What was the name again? Brad what?"

Dunn looked at him blankly "Kelsey."

Hammond slapped his hand down on his knee and swore so loudly that the hotel receptionist looked across in astonishment.

"Dammit! Kelsey is the name of the guy who found Mark Callum's body! That explains the missing pen and paper!"

Dunn and Galvin looked at one another perplexed. They had no idea what Hammond was talking about. They watched as Hammond struggled to his feet from the chair and made a hasty exit towards Galvin's car.

*"The sun, the moon and the stars would have
disappeared long ago, had they happened to
be within reach of predatory human hands."*
Henry Havelock Ellis. The Dance of Life. 1923

CHAPTER TWENTY-SEVEN

Bradley Kelsey's details had been on the database since ten years previously when he had been arrested and charged for assaulting a police officer during a drugs raid at a party he had attended. Galvin was happy to give these details to Hammond but Hammond was not so keen to receive them, he kept interrupting with a barrage of self abuse. He was angry at his own stupidity not to check out a witness. Dunn offered the reassurance that the officers investigating Mark Callum's death hadn't either, and even if they had, there would be no reason to have investigated him as a potential murderer but Hammond wasn't listening. He knew that he had accepted Harris' challenge half-heartedly. Had he been more willing to believe Harris had reason to be suspicious of the suicides he would have been more thorough.

The car swerved sharply as Galvin miscalculated a corner and Hammond swore loudly. He felt the nervous tension in his body increasing as he anticipated his meeting with Morris. Hammond's contribution had been refused already but this time, he wasn't going to sit back and let the investigation continue without him. If the team were going to busy themselves investigating his finances and his relationship with Jenny, then their time would be wasted. There was a sense of urgency that stirred within him, He wanted Bradley Kelsey to be found quickly.

Morris looked at Hammond obligingly which was better than Hammond had hoped for.

"This is the best lead we've got so far." Hammond said. "But you haven't given me anything, we are no further along in the investigation than we were the last time we met, all the material we've got and still we have reached no conclusions. Even if you bring in Kelsey for questioning, we are going to have a snowball's chance in hell of proving he was directly or indirectly involved with Cheryl's murder ,the arson attack on your home or the body found inside. We've got a distorted photo image of him parked behind your car, video footage of him outside your house after the fire and on a bus the same time as yourself. It's odd, it's coincidence, but all it gives us is a link to scenes of crimes. It doesn't count as concrete evidence of his involvement in criminal activity."

"He found Mark Callum's body. I became a target as soon as I started looking into Callum's death, there has to be a connection! Let's question him. See how he copes under stress, he can't be sure that he didn't leave any trace evidence at my house or on the car and then see where it takes us. We can arrange an i.d line up, if the kids recognise him as the man who asked them to eavesdrop on my conversation with Cheryl Bailey, it will be enough to keep him a little while. I'm sure we are on the right track. If we show we have reason to suspect him, it may be enough to convince him that we know more than we are letting on."

Morris studied Hammond for a minute then shrugged with resignation. "I think we should stick with splitting the team and look from different angles. I don't even know for sure which incident should take precedence. Cheryl Bailey's murder has to be treated as an unrelated crime to the body found in your house, we have a link but it isn't strong enough to treat it as a related case."

Hammond tried to keep his impatience under wraps. "There isn't enough time or resources. If they are connected, and Kelsey's involvement suggests there is, we don't know who else may be a possible victim here, there has already been two attempted murders as well as the death of three innocents, it is now looking as if Kelsey is more involved in the suicide of Mark Callum, there could be more deaths to come. What other angle is there? We have some evidence that Kelsey is linked between all incidents."

Morris was quick to correct Hammond. "He's not the only link."

Hammond ignored the implication, instead he waited for Morris to see sense. Eventually Morris sighed heavily. "Fine. I want a background search on Kelsey, and I want to see what the others can give me tonight. We'll question him in the morning. Against my better judgement I will allow you to stick around, if he sees you alive and well despite his attempts to harm you, he may react strongly enough to implicate himself."

The unmarked car with Morris and Edwards inside was parked on the other side of the street from Kelsey's apartment block. Hammond settled into the back passenger seat, breathing in the welcoming smell of bacon and coffee that lingered from their takeaway breakfast. He thought of all the hours he had spent in cars like this one, surviving the monotony of surveillance through the relief of takeaways and chewing gum. They exchanged greetings before Edwards turned to face him from the front passenger seat.

"He returned from work about ninety minutes ago. He went inside for a while but then re-emerged and walked around the block, before heading down London Road."

"When did he return?"

Morris replied from the driver's seat, his face still turned upwards towards the windows of the flat they were surveying.

"Just before you turned up. There's been no movement since, it's probably best to go in soon before he makes a move again."

"Did you learn anything useful last night?" Hammond asked with an air of innocence. Inwardly he doubted whether the wait had been fruitful. If the man had been confident enough to break into the home of a police officer twice in daylight, it was likely he believed there was nothing on him to raise suspicion.

Edwards looked at Morris as if waiting for permission to speak but turned back to Hammond when no response had been granted. "Nothing dodgy. Not married, no kids. He has lived here for the last twelve years. No criminal record other than hitting a uniformed officer at a party. The party's host was growing Cannabis plants in his loft. Kelsey wasn't part of it, just took offence to the police interrupting a good time."

"So, he's aggressive, we know that at least. Do you think he knows you're here?"

"He slowed down when he passed us on his way back the first time in his car, but he didn't stop, it's hard to tell."

Hammond sighed. "It's possible he was suspicious of having two men seated in a car observing the area, especially when he recognised the GN prefix to your car registration, in most cases it indicates a Kent Police vehicle."

Morris snorted. "I doubt he would even consider that Hammond. You're giving him credit for being more intelligent than he probably is."

Morris' tone was devoid of inflection. He evidently believed he was wasting his time being there. His comment irritated Hammond.

"Yet he walked around the apartment block afterwards, it could be he was checking you out."

Morris interrupted Hammond by turning around to face him abruptly, The car wobbled slightly with the sudden movement.

"You and your theories Hammond, it's a pity you don't spend as much time exercising your body as you do your brain. What the hell are we doing here anyway? This whole case is a bloody waste of time! If you hadn't poked your nose into suicides that were not even suspicious, we wouldn't be here twiddling our thumbs for no good reason. Instead I would be at home, playing Mario Kart with my son like I promised."

Hammond was about to reply, even though he was unsure how to, before Edwards pointed a finger up at the window on the third floor of the building."He looked out the window! You think he is checking us out after all?"

Hammond moved his body closer to the back exit as Morris opened the driver's door. He got out, then bent down sticking his head into the car and faced Hammond for the first time since he had arrived.

"You can come, just stay out of the way. Let him see you, but that's all. Edwards, stay with the car for the meantime but get ready to join us. We don't know how he will react."

The ride in the elevator to the third floor of the building was stifling and awkward. The stench of stale urine contaminated the small enclosure. As soon as the doors closed, Hammond felt he was suffocating. He refused to open his mouth for fear of tasting the air. Pressed against the steel walls, Morris was making no effort to hide his displeasure in being there. He sighed loudly and tapped his foot until the doors opened and Hammond allowed himself to breathe. They found Kelsey's door at the end of a long quiet corridor. The silence was interrupted by Morris' knock on Kelsey's door which echoed around them. From somewhere above them, Hammond heard a baby crying and then the sound died as quickly as it had begun. It was quiet again. There was no sound emerging from behind the door. Morris knocked again, harder this time and motioned for Hammond to stand to the other side of the door. They braced themselves expecting sudden movement but nothing happened. Hammond moved towards the window at the end of the corridor and looked down, he could see the back of Morris' car but it was impossible to see if Edwards was still there. He wondered what Kelsey could see from the window in his flat, it was unlikely he was prepared for their visit so why didn't he answer the door? He frowned at Morris and found himself becoming increasingly irritated.

"For God's sake! Give it a kick!"

Morris scowled back at Hammond. "I'll pretend I didn't hear that.. We need to bait him somehow."

Hammond groaned inwardly. He motioned silently to Morris pretending he could hear movement, he ushered Morris back a step and then leant his head towards the door as if trying to get his ear closer to the imagined sound.

"I think I can hear a cry for help." He said seriously before suddenly flicking his good leg up and threw muscle behind a kick at the door lock. The wooden frame splintered as the door swung open immediately. Hammond couldn't resist a grin, he expected it to be more difficult, the door looked as if it had needed three good kicks at least.

Morris' face inflamed with fury but he had no chance to reprimand Hammond for his stupidity before the full weight of Kelsey came flying towards him through the doorway. Morris' legs buckled as his body was caught up and thrown towards the opposite wall of the corridor. From his position beside Kelsey's exit, Hammond registered a blur that was Morris and his attacker joined together in a ball of motion before Morris' head slammed against the wall. His limp body slid down to the floor, his eyes glazed and open in surprise. Kelsey righted himself but Hammond reacted quickly and leaped forward, delivering a blow to the man's right kidney. Kelsey whirled around, his left arm flying in an arc directed towards Hammond's chest. Without thinking, Hammond lifted his right knee and made contact with Kelsey's genitals. There was a loud gasp as Kelsey lost his breath but he recovered quickly and managed to grab Hammond's leg, twisting it and causing Hammond to lose his balance. The two men fell, Kelsey on top of

Hammond, the full force of his weight lay on Hammond's chest. The pain from the impact on his injured rib shot through Hammond's body, circles of light danced before his eyes before nausea welled up within him. Choking, Hammond pulled himself to the side as Kelsey tried to stand. Hammond used his free hand to clasp Kelsey's foot, holding him down with the full strength of his arm but it wasn't enough. It took a microsecond for Kelsey to free his foot and kick at Hammond's arm, before wriggling out of his grasp. He sprung with surprising agility to his feet and turned as if to leave but then stopped as he registered Hammond on the floor. At that moment Hammond realised that he had been recognised, but instead of the fury he would have expected. Kelsey grinned, looking down at him. Lying on his back on the floor at his attacker's feet made him more vulnerable than he had ever been. Hammond's eyes turned towards the wall where Morris had laid but saw nothing. Kelsey's foot stamped down towards his chest, but he missed his aim as Hammond rolled sideways, The force of Kelsey's foot slammed down onto the hard floor, impacting his heel before he raised his leg again, this time his foot aimed for Hammond's head. Hammond dared himself to look up, he tensed his stomach and neck muscles ready to shoot his upper body towards the man's groin, but instead he saw Kelsey suddenly teeter to the side as Morris' arms enclosed Kelsey in a bear hug from behind. Kelsey's leg faltered in mid-air for a second. It gave Hammond the opportunity he needed to wriggle towards the wall and heave himself onto his feet. By now Morris was shouting, his arms pinned Kelsey's to his sides but he wasn't able to hold the man for long. With a burst of energy, Kelsey threw his head backwards and connected with Morris' chin. Morris grunted and tumbled backwards, his back slammed against the wall. Seizing his chance, Kelsey pushed himself away and managed to get himself free. He ran towards the fire exit. Morris stunned by the sudden impact against the wall, didn't recover in time to halt Kelsey's progress but by now, Hammond was on his feet and ready to pursue. He was oblivious to pain in his ankle as he propelled his body after Kelsey. Behind him, he could hear Morris shouting in his radio at Edwards.

Neither Edwards nor Hammond reacted in time to prevent Kelsey's escape, by the time Hammond had made his way down the stairs of the fire exit, Kelsey had got to his car and roared off in a dramatic display of screeching tyres and blowing exhaust. Hammond reached Edwards whom had attempted to block Kelsey's exit from the car park. His eyes were widened in partial disbelief.

"I didn't expect that."

All of Hammond's energy was concentrated on breathing. His lungs were on fire, he felt shaky from the adrenaline that was coursing through him. There was no sensation or pain but he knew it was only a matter of time before his body reminded him it was still in the process of recovering from a car crash. It couldn't cope with the extra demands of fighting with a man heavier than himself. He bent over coughing as his lungs attempted to correct their intake of oxygen and he waved a hand at Edwards gesturing to rejoin Morris at the apartment where Hammond had left him moments before.

He hadn't noticed before that Morris' head was bleeding but now, in the aftermath of battle, the injury to the back of Morris' skull was evident. His hair was matted with the blood that seeped a steady stream onto the collar of his shirt. Morris seemed dazed and Hammond was concerned. He told him to sit down as he attempted to stem the bleeding by grabbing his jacket and rolled it to a ball, pressing firmly against the wound. Morris was groggy but resilient, he made attempts to get up but his concussion caused him to overbalance before he vomited onto the floor. Hammond barked at Edwards to call an ambulance.

With Morris safely despatched to hospital, Hammond and Edwards were free to examine inside Kelsey's apartment. The living room was confined but furniture had been placed to ensure maximum comfort. A wing-backed armchair faced two televisions connected to several DVD players. Edwards went straight to the players, looking for any DVD's whilst Hammond checked out the bedroom. A double bed and a wardrobe were the only items of furniture. The wardrobe housed several shirts, a pair of jeans and some trainers. Hammond prodded the items with his pen, part of him expected to see his one trainer that Kelsey had stolen from his house but it wasn't there. It disappointed him, having Hammond's trainer in Kelsey's wardrobe would act as evidence that Kelsey had been at his house as well as at the scene of Cheryl Bailey's murder. He continued to look under the bed and behind the wardrobe, eventually giving up and checking the bathroom. He met Edwards in the hallway.

"Anything?"

Edwards shook his head. "So far, nothing, the DVD's are copies of Disney Films!"

Hammond frowned. "You checked them all?"

Edwards nodded. "I didn't go through them all but so far, there's nothing incriminating."

Hammond sighed, he ignored the twinges that were beginning to spread across his back and thighs. "What about the kitchen?"

The two men went towards the kitchen, Hammond looked in the washing machine for laundry. There was none. He checked the fridge-freezer. It was empty.

"That's odd. Why is the fridge switched on if there is no food in it?"

Edwards looked across from where he was looking in the cupboards. "He hasn't got much in the way of utensils. Maybe he doesn't live here full-time."

Hammond agreed with the possibility but remained standing in front of the fridge. He checked the drawers of the freezer and noted scratch marks and indents in the frost as if something had recently been removed.

"It's too clean. Do you think he was prepared for us?"

Edwards slammed the cupboard door closed and scratched his head with a gloved finger.

"There's no smell of burning or anything to suggest he has destroyed any evidence."

Hammond looked up. "He left the apartment and walked around the building, do you think he could have deposited anything outside?"

Edward's features set as he concentrated. "No, he wasn't carrying anything. The only time he could have deposited anything was if he took anything away in the car and that would have been before he knew we were there."

"In which case, any evidence he had was either left in the car, or was small enough to have been secreted on his person." Hammond swore, he knew in his gut that Kelsey was guilty but without any proof, he was helpless.

Worse still, he would have trouble justifying his search to Beech. The frustration mounted within him, he wanted to shout out his rage but instead he tried to rationalise.

"Ok, Think back to where Kelsey walked. You say he went down London Road. We have to re-trace his steps. Presuming he did see you waiting in the car, maybe he was clever enough not to leave anything in his car with the presumption, that, like his flat, his car may also be searched. So, what would he do? Probably take whatever it was to another place where he could return later and collect it."

Edward's nodded hesitantly. "No offence, but we are grasping at straws here. We don't even know what evidence we are looking for, there may not be anything. What are we trying to prove anyway?"

Hammond met Edward's eyes and stared him silent. "We need to seal this apartment, get uniform to block the doorway just in case Kelsey comes back. In the meantime, walk me to where you saw him earlier this morning. It's worth checking."

Hammond ignored Edward's sigh as he made his way back out the apartment.

It was luck that the elevator was stuck on the fifth floor. Hammond didn't believe it at the time, his healing ankle was resisting any weight and the pain was now coming in waves but he couldn't rid himself of the feeling that time was precious. He made for the fire exit where he had chased Kelsey earlier and leaned heavily on the banister to take some of the weight of his ankle. They had descended the stairs to the first floor when Hammond saw the mobile phone lying face down on the step. He picked it up, it could be anyone's but nonetheless he felt excited at the find. The back of the mobile had cracked so that the battery compartment was exposed; it had fallen with some force, possibly whilst running down steps as had Kelsey. Hammond held his breath, and used his pen to select the menu. First he checked for any photos in the media album. There were pictures of children. Head and shoulder portraits of children of various ages and ethnicity. He passed the phone to Edwards and raised his eyebrows. Edwards scanned the photos one by one.

"They are not incriminating photos, there is nothing here to suggest foul play, it could be quite innocent."

He returned the phone to Hammond. "Bag it. Check out the contents later, just in case."

Hammond nodded, but remained staring at the phone. He looked at the call lists and scrolled down. There were only two numbers. One of them was vaguely familiar but he couldn't work out why. He took his own mobile out of his pocket with the intention of scanning his own contacts list but checked the found phone for any text messages first.

There was a text message alerting a message in voice-mail. He dialled the number instructed, selecting the loudspeaker option to avoid putting it against his ear.

"Don't do it tonight. I tried to keep him here as long as I could. I really tried but he was difficult...please don't do it tonight."

The message ended. Hammond felt a shudder run through his body, he felt paralysed on the spot where he stood. Edwards was confused, the message told him nothing. But to Hammond it told him everything. The voice message had been left by Kathleen two nights ago. The night his house had been burnt down.

"The artist is one who sees life as beauty"
Henry Havelock Ellis. The Dance of Life. 1923

CHAPTER TWENTY-EIGHT

Bradley Kelsey hoped she had watched the news report on the television, that she had seen his artwork, had admired his mastery. She wouldn't tell him in words or actions but he knew she would be pleased. Deep down he knew there was an appreciation for him and the work he did. He had never declined her requests, he never would. The television was switched on in the sorting office when he returned to the depot. The shift supervisor was standing in front of the television whilst dipping a Garibaldi biscuit into his mug of tea. He nodded a greeting before his eyes returned to the screen, transfixed by the drama that was unfolding. The noise of the machines drowned out the words spoken by the anchorwoman, but it didn't matter. For a while, Kelsey pretended to be occupied with sorting out the parcels but the temptation to watch his own work was too great. His eyes kept returning to the screen. The flames reminded him of a blazing snake that writhed and licked at the air before contaminating it with its venom.

As soon as his shift ended he returned to the site. He couldn't help it, he was drawn there. He wanted to relive the experience, breath in the smell of smouldering debris, savour the moment for as long as he could. That was the problem with great works of beauty; most of them were temporary, like the chalk drawings on the pavements or the sand sculptures that were admired for no more than a few hours before the waves took them. Kelsey wasn't alone standing there. There were others watching. The ignorant few who were more interested in being captured by the television cameras so that they could point at their images during the evening news and prove they had been witnessed the drama. He didn't mind so much, although he envied their freedom to declare their involvement openly. More than anything he wanted to say "I did that." But of course, he couldn't. Only to her.

There had been no news on the Policeman, he read that someone had been pulled out of the burning building. The possibility that the policeman had survived again didn't disappoint him as much as he thought it would. He was beginning to admire the man who couldn't be defeated although it would mean she would demand him to do things her way from now on. He knew she would enjoy making the policeman suffer, he had caused too much interference with his meddling. She had reason to be angry, there was a lot to lose if the Policeman discovered everything. He had spoken to her about the possibility of using Katie, even though he had concerns. Katie was weak, he didn't know how far she would be prepared to go and he suspected she was beginning to like the Policeman more than she let on. He obeyed the instructions and kept his head down during the day that followed. He occupied himself preparing copies of the DVD's and checked on Katie as he promised he would and then returned to the depot for the night shift. In the morning he returned home to discover the unmarked car parked near the apartment block. He looked casually as he drove past, and saw the two men dressed in shirts and ties. He knew they weren't covert but his gut churned at the prospect that they were there to watch him, to surprise him with a visit no doubt. He parked the car as usual and went to his flat where he looked down from his window. They were still there. Luckily he was prepared for this eventuality. She had always told him that there was a risk he would be traced, but there was no reason to suspect him of anything as long as he got rid of the evidence before they found it. The package hidden under the wardrobe was removed first, then the frozen bags from the freezer, he wrapped them several times in plastic bags, worried they would defrost. He needed to find somewhere cold to hide them. If he was being surveyed, he couldn't take the car, they might follow him and he couldn't be sure that he wouldn't be picked up by the street cameras. He had to carry the packages under his clothing and walk to the hiding place. There was no other way. He left the apartment and made a performance of walking around the building, occasionally he would check the reflection in the windows to see if the car was still there behind him. Satisfied it was, he ambled his way towards the road. His pace changed to a brisk walk as he approached the cafe. The proprietor smiled at him as he entered, she recognised him from the deliveries he had fulfilled there several times previously. He returned her smile politely and asked her how she was, hoping she would reply by redirecting his question. She did, and he made a performance of acting frustrated with the explanation that his freezer had broken down and he was worried about his prized fishing trophies defrosting too quickly. The cafe proprietor took the bait immediately and offered to store his package in her freezer which he accepted gratefully. He kissed her on the cheek, wondering if his display of gratitude was over acted. He smiled as he left the cafe; all he had to do now was to find somewhere safe to store the passports.

He returned to the flat, feeling self-conscious as he re-entered the building. Whilst he was there he spent time cleaning all the rooms. He couldn't take the chance that he hadn't left some trace evidence on anything. He had watched enough Forensic science programmes on television to learn you could never be too careful. At regular intervals, he checked out the window. It looked as if there was a third person in the back seat of the car but it was too far away to tell. It was possible that he was simply being watched for now, if the Police were going to come to his flat, they would have done so by now but he couldn't think of a reason why they would. He stood in the middle of the room weighing up the options. He could leave right now, he could make it down the back stairs and out the fire exit on the ground floor or he could stay where he was and carry on as usual. They would get bored eventually. His thoughts were interrupted by the knocking on his door. He froze in the spot where he stood. The knocking became more persistent but he ignored it until the door caved in at the lock.

He didn't notice he had lost his mobile until he went to phone her. He had driven only a short distance before abandoning the car and making for the bus stop, where he stood, his hands flapping against the sides of his pockets with the futile hope that he would find the phone caught in the folds of his jacket. People were looking at him suspiciously and he knew he looked bloodied from the altercation with the policeman. The Policeman had fought better than he had expected him too, the man was out of shape but he knew how to react quickly and dodge the blows. The policeman wasn't a boxer, he couldn't concentrate enough energy behind his fists but Kelsey shouldn't have underestimated him. He wouldn't do so again. From now on, there would be no subtlety behind his attacks. He was going to finish the Policeman for good. He turned away from the bus stop until he found a public telephone in the entrance porch of a supermarket. He told her all the details of the mornings' events, including where he had deposited the frozen bags and passports. Then he told her about his mobile phone. He didn't know where he had lost it, it was possible it had dropped during the fight. Her voice was calm, but then it always was. There was no way of predicting the consequences of his mistake but he knew it wouldn't be just him who suffered.

CHAPTER TWENTY-NINE

The bitter taste in Hammond's mouth was still there. He bent over the basin with his head cocked at an angle to allow the water to flow from the tap directly into his mouth. He gargled several times in an effort to rid himself of the resentment that filled him. The mirror above the basin taunted him with the face of a cuckolded fool. An old man who had allowed his vanity to cloud his instincts. A man who had allowed himself to believe that a beautiful woman had wanted him. Or had he believed it? Even now, as he stared back at his reflection he knew he hadn't been convinced by Kathleen's attention, he had known she wasn't to be trusted but his loneliness had over-ridden his need to be cautious. He cursed loudly and head-butted the mirror causing it to crack. A red blotch appeared immediately on his forehead. He was really stupid. Not only for letting himself be fooled into bed, now he had to resort to punishing himself. He was tempted to leave the men's bathroom, to head straight for the interview room where he knew Kathleen had been brought. He understood why he wasn't allowed to be there, but the anger within him threatened to disregard all protocol and retaliate against his humiliation by storming in and pinning her against the wall until she told him everything. This wasn't about the suicides of her former foster brothers and sisters anymore, this was bigger than that. He knew it, he had been right not to have trusted her in the beginning. Kathleen had lied from the start. The bitterness rose up again in the back of his throat and he spat out his disgust watching it crawl its way to the plughole. It wouldn't drain away, not on its' own anyway, it needed a force greater than itself to wash its putridity away.

Dunn was waiting for him outside the door, she looked at him concerned when she noticed the bruise forming on his forehead but didn't refer to it. Instead she updated him on the team's findings as she accompanied him back towards the office.

"The photos on the mobile phone are being looked at to see if any of the children can be identified. Uniform are searching around Kelsey's apartment block to see if they can find anything that Kelsey may have hidden outside." Hammond was surprised that the search had been warranted but said nothing. He was distracted by the thought of what Kathleen might be saying in the interview room. He had many reasons to be concerned. She had threatened to report he had raped her, he didn't know whether she would fulfil her threat. It was possible she had planned it from the beginning, he didn't know what she was capable of.

"Who's interviewing her?" His voice was unjustly curt, but his directness towards Dunn was not taken personally. He didn't need to explain himself to Dunn, not like with most women.

"Morris, he came back an hour ago. Claims he is fit enough."

Dunn was interrupted by Galvin who was walking down the corridor towards them.

"They've got a positive identification on the body."
Galvin looked awkward as Hammond stopped and
waited expectantly.

"I'm sorry. It's Lloyd Harris. It was his body they found
in your house."

The wait for Morris to emerge from the interview room
was short but Hammond had no concept of time. His
desperation to know what was being said on the other
side of the door threatened to make him incapable of
waiting calmly.

Morris came out the door, and closed it quietly behind
him. He seemed surprised to see Hammond outside and
frowned slightly as if expecting a confrontation.

"The body has been identified as Lloyd Harris."

Morris' features gave nothing away, instead his eyes
scrutinised Hammond's face as if trying to gauge how
Hammond had taken the news, but there was nothing
to see. Hammond felt numb, he couldn't decide how
he felt. He wondered what feelings he should be
experiencing now. Possibly grief that a friend had
died suddenly, dismay that his friend's body had been
cremated in his house, or complacent. Acceptant of the
fact that his life was being ruled by forces he couldn't
comprehend.

"I know. I was told moments ago. I've just left her to get
used to the idea." Morris moved his head towards the
interview room.

"How did she take the news?"

Morris corrected his posture as he settled into the topic
of conversation.

"She behaved as if in shock, she asked me to repeat
myself, then she sobbed..but..."

Morris' brow was furrowed as he described Kathleen's behaviour.

"I felt as if she were playing for time. It was hard to tell whether she was in genuine disbelief. She suggested that Harris may have wandered to your home in his confusion and got trapped in the fire."

"What impression did she give you?"

Morris pondered Hammond's question before answering. "She was prepared for some of the questions. Her speech was rapid when answering although occasionally I would change direction and then her answers were slow and carefully worded. She was giving herself time to think, but so far she's stuck to her story that Harris was confused and obsessive, that he had left the house in a kind of rage and that she hadn't seen him since."

Hammond shifted all his weight onto his good leg. "Do you believe her?"

"She's only contradicted herself once, but it was enough to raise my suspicions. I asked her how her Father would have travelled from their home in Charing to your place in Stanford and she couldn't explain how he would have managed the journey. I told her we had checked all bus routes and with the taxi's; that the only logical possibility was that he had driven himself, in which case, where was the car that he used? She couldn't give me an answer. She said her Father hadn't driven since he had been diagnosed with dementia. So then I asked her to offer me an alternative suggestion. I asked it as if I genuinely wanted her opinion and that's when she slipped up."

Morris' arms were folded across his chest with a renewed air of confidence.

"She suggested that someone had taken him to your house. When I asked who, she said she didn't know but that they must have tried to help. That whoever the person could have been, they probably did what they thought was for the best. That was odd. She offered a sympathetic explanation for someone she supposedly knows nothing about. So, I suggested Kelsey, maybe it had been him who had offered Harris a lift."

Hammond leant with his back against the wall. His hands had found their way to his trouser pockets. He now stood in a completely opposite pose to his colleague. Morris the confident one, Hammond portraying a confused and insecure thinker.

"How did she react to Kelsey's name?"

"Not a flinch, nothing. She expected it. I asked her how she knew Kelsey and she said she knew him as an acquaintance, that she didn't have much to do with him but the next moment she is talking as if it would not surprise her if Harris had accepted a lift from Kelsey to your house. Now, this is where it got interesting.." Morris' finger shot forward in a poking motion.

"I asked Kathleen if Kelsey had known where you lived, if so how did he know and why would he be willing to travel to your house? She said that she had known that Kelsey had taken an unhealthy interest in you, that he probably offered to take Harris with the hope that he could confront you."

"Why?"

"She claimed she didn't know for sure but suggested he was jealous of your relationship with her." Morris raised one eyebrow as if questioning the significance of what he was saying.

Hammond felt his forehead tighten in a frown. "But that doesn't explain how Harris ended up in my kitchen.

I wasn't there to let him in and Jenny would have asked him in if he had called round."

Morris grinned. "Exactly, her story doesn't make sense. There's something else that doesn't add up. I offered no explanation for her Father's death. All I told her was that her Father had been found in the remains of your house, that it had not been possible to identify him earlier due to the damage caused by the fire. Not once did she ask me if I thought he would have suffered. Most people would imagine burning to death to be an agonising, frightening death, they need reassurance that their loved ones died quickly or painlessly. Why didn't she?"

Hammond nodded slowly. "Because she knew he didn't die in the fire." He was struck by a thought that seemed relevant. "On the night Lloyd went missing, I was asking her about him and she said. Quote. I called him Dad. Unquote. She used past tense. She must have already known he was dead."

Morris sucked in his cheek. "Maybe. I think she is involved somehow but I am not convinced that she is guilty of causing Harris' death or that she knew what Kelsey was up to."

"What about the phone message?"

Morris shrugged. "Apparently, she can't remember what she had phoned him about. She paused for a long time as if trying to remember but that is how she protects herself, she gives herself time to think what to say. She's very controlled with her answers. We can't say for sure that she was referring to you when she said she tried to make 'him' stay. It could have been anyone at any given time."

Hammond suddenly felt the urge to come clean. "There's something you should know." He was about to commit career suicide but it was necessary. Without being forthcoming, there was lesser chance of getting to the truth. Kathleen's secret would remain hidden and he was sick of playing her games.

"Me and Kathleen..." Hammond could feel the heat rising up his neck towards his face, he glanced up the corridor to make sure he couldn't be heard by anyone else.

"The other night when you asked me to speak to Kathleen. I didn't explain why I was there so long. I did try to find out more information but I got sidetracked. We have a history, not much of one, but well, we've known each other for years and ..."

Morris leant forward towards Hammond accusingly. "You slept with her?"

Hammond quelled the impulse to step back but waited until Morris did so instead. There was an uneasy silence as Morris massaged the back of his neck, not speaking for several moments before addressing Hammond.

"You'll have to include it in your report. Your reckless-ness may have compromised the investigation although I doubt it did. She hasn't said anything and she could have done, she has had plenty of opportunity. I suggested that her phone message to Kelsey was to prevent him from committing arson. She claims she didn't know he intended to set fire to the place but she was worried."

"Yet she did nothing?"

Morris looked at Hammond sharply. "Apparently she said she had tried to persuade you to stay with her rather than go home. Now I understand how." Morris' voice trailed off as he continued to study Hammond's face.

Hammond realised she had told the truth. Kathleen had tried to persuade him to stay that night. She had tried to block his exit from the bedroom door, when that failed, she attempted to seduce him into staying before her attempts to antagonise him enough so that he could easily have turned back into the room to vent out his rage. He remembered her behaviour as being erratic; maybe it had been her desperation to ensure

he didn't go home. She hadn't known about Jenny, that Jenny was at the house alone that night.

"But that just substantiates the content of the phone message. What are you going to do?"

Morris sucked in air through his mouth and then released it as a heavy sigh.

"Her story doesn't add up so I am going to keep on for a little longer and see where it takes us. We need to prove that she is working with Kelsey and why. I can't think of a motive. She claims she has no idea who Cheryl Bailey was and for the moment I am inclined to believe her."

"What about this Goodchild woman? She's Kathleen's mother. Could she be the missing link? Harris knew her so that could be how he knew Kelsey, maybe they are connected."

Morris nodded as his hand returned to the door handle.

"I'll give it a go. I'll keep you posted."

The door swung shut behind him.

All of Hammond's energy was rapidly draining away, but his stubbornness kept him at the station. He was in the throes of one of the most complicated cases he had worked on, he had been almost killed twice and humiliated several times yet he knew he was closer to understanding why it had all happened. He just had to concentrate. He sat at one of the desks and rummaged through a drawer until he found a pad of post-it notes.

He used them in the same way he had done with the shot glasses, he wrote each idea on a different note until the desk was littered with yellow paper. The first note listed the murders of Cheryl Bailey, Salima Abitboul and possibly Lloyd Harris that he suspected were all connected to the suicides of Mark Callum, Lucas Dean, Claire Bennet and Theresa Davenport. He studied the names, and the information he had gathered on all of them. Then he added Rachel Turner to the list with a question mark. His gut told him that Rachel Turner's disappearance was not a co-incidence. On the second note he added Kathleen. He suspected that Kathleen's role was to end his enquiries. He listed all the occasions they had spoken. She had tried to dissuade him for helping Harris at the start, then she had resorted to flirting with him. He remembered the evening when he had taken her to dinner, how at first she had seemed withdrawn and non-responsive then she had left him whilst he had parked the car. Her attitude had completely changed when he joined her inside the restaurant. Kathleen had deliberately encouraged him to drink knowing he wouldn't be able to drive home. She had attempted to seduce him, which he knew had been planned because she had known there was an available room, all her efforts had been so that his car would be left in the car park, allowing Kelsey the opportunity to disable it. It made him sick to realise how gullible he had been. But what was her motive other than to stop him investigating Mark Callum's death? He wondered what she had done when she had left him in the car park. She had used the excuse of needing to use the ladies room but maybe she had needed the opportunity to make a phone call, in which case it may be possible to check Kelsey's call lists on his mobile and match the date and time with any outgoing calls from her phone.

On the third note he drew a square with Kathleen, Mrs Goodchild, Kelsey and Harris at each corner and a question mark in the centre. He needed to know in what way they were all related. Next he drew a map of Kelsey's apartment and noted where he had looked, where Edwards had looked and what they had found. He knew this process would be repeated later but he needed to do it with the benefit of a fresh memory. The photographs of the children taken on Kelsey's camera phone were not enough to suggest that Kelsey had acted inappropriately but it rang alarm bells. He inserted the first DVD into the CD rom drive of the laptop and waited whilst it loaded. He ignored the option to play the movie but instead selected the special features menu. The images that appeared were not what Hammond had feared but he understood the significance of what he was seeing. Children were lined up looking at the camera, boys and girls ranging from pre-teens to young adults. They didn't smile, their expressions were blank as they approached the camera one at a time. Hammond swallowed, but found his throat had gone dry, the motion caused him to cough.

He ignored the phone ringing on the desk opposite and ejected the DVD, replacing it in the evidence bag. Dunn leaned over him with exaggerated impatience to answer the phone, she greeted the caller then covered the mouthpiece and enquired where Galvin was. Hammond looked up and shrugged before returning to his brainstorming.

The receiver was replaced but Dunn continued to stand close to him. "That was Galvin's mother in law, she doesn't sound happy, apparently he's not answering his mobile."

Hammond didn't look up. "I expect he needs a breather, poor guy is probably surrounded by nagging women and raging hormones at home."

He heard Dunn's sharp intake of breath and automatically tensed his shoulders as if expecting a recrimination.

"Well, apparently his wife thinks the baby is coming soon so I am going to find him. If you see him, make sure you tell him to phone home."

She waited until he grunted a reply before walking off at a brisk pace. Hammond looked up as she left. He contemplated on the irony of how women expected the world to slow to a stop when a baby was due yet insist of moving on following a death. His eyes were tired, he allowed the eyelids to close over them momentarily whilst he rubbed his face with both palms. He thought about Lloyd Harris and for the first time felt a wave of sadness wash over him.

He was still at the desk half an hour later, trying to unravel the weave he had inherited from Harris when Galvin came in. He sat on the nearest chair to Hammond and told him he was terrified of what the next twenty four hours would bring. Hammond, lost in his own brooding, presumed Galvin was referring to the investigation and asked why the next twenty-four hours were particularly relevant, had Beech given a deadline? Galvin shook his head and explained he was talking about his impending role as a father. Hammond sighed and resisted the temptation to tell Galvin to concentrate on the job in hand. Instead he asked what was so terrifying about having a baby, it was part of human existence, perfectly normal.

Galvin studied Hammond's face for a moment, possibly aware that he was the cause of Hammond's irritation, but his need to be counselled was greater than Hammond's need for peace. "I haven't a clue what I am supposed to be doing. Already I feel as if I am in the way, that I am a nuisance. Does it get any easier? What if I don't feel anything for the baby?"

"Galvin, the sad fact is that no first time parent has a clue what to do, it's all guesswork. There will be times when your child will think you are their hero and then they grow up to consider you are an embarrassment, but during the time in-between, there will be moments that remind you of why you even considered the idea of having a baby in the first place. I have been a Father twenty-four years and I still don't know how to be a good parent, but what matters is that you love your child and that they know it."

Hammond finished his speech and bent his head back over his notes. The air filled with silence that was only interrupted by Galvin's sigh. He looked back up again at the younger man who had remained in his chair and was now biting his lower lip deep in thought. "Do you need to leave?"

Galvin looked surprised. "No, my wife said it would be best if I stay here just in case it is another false alarm, but I've set my phone to have a particular ring tone so that I will know when she goes into labour."

Hammond got up from the chair. "In that case, you need a distraction. Come with me."

Obeying Hammond's instruction, Galvin parked by the Kelsey's apartment block and together they retraced Kelsey's steps around the perimeter of the building. Hammond was finding the rest at the office had benefited his ankle and he was able to bear weight without discomfort. His pace equalled Galvin's. They searched the undergrowth on either side of the path and compared their findings. A cigarette packet, plastic bottles and crisp packets were the only evidence of previous human activity.

"Maybe Kelsey wasn't dumping anything, you can easily see the road where you were parked in the window's reflection. It's possible he was just toying with you."

"Only a guilty conscience would make him think he was the one under scrutiny in the first place. The flat was too clean, it felt as if something was missing, We'll continue."

The two men continued down London Road on either side and examined any possible hiding places. It became evident that they were wasting their time.

"Kelsey came this way and was gone several minutes before his return to the flat. He wasn't carrying anything on him on the way or on the return journey. Yet, I am sure he came down this way deliberately, so where would he have gone?

"Visiting a friend?" Galvin's voice was quiet but carried a hint of negativity. He had doubts that Hammond had interpreted Kelsey's actions correctly. The man had probably just taken a walk, the only person who suspected Kelsey of hiding anything was Hammond and his suspicion was based purely on instinct.

Hammond wasn't listening. He glanced up and down the road, and forced himself to banish all self doubt. His gut told him that Kelsey had brought something from the flat to deposit somewhere. He had to listen to what his instinct was telling him. Galvin was standing waiting for instructions, his hand remained in his trouser pocket, no doubt clasped around his phone waiting for the call from home. Hammond's stare caused the younger man to feel uncomfortable before he realised that Hammond was looking at the post office behind him.

"To hide something of value, you need to ensure that you will get it back without running the risk of damage or discovery." Hammond entered the post office and waited for the customers in the queue to be served before showing his identity card to the clerk.

"Were you working here at nine this morning?" he asked with a smile.

The clerk nodded affirmatively. "Did you serve this gentleman around the time you opened? He may have been your first customer." Whilst he spoke, Hammond slid Kelsey's e-fit under the glass division.

The Clerk nodded, then called out to his female colleague who was occupied arranging sacks of mail ready for the next collection.

"Yes, I remember him, I wouldn't normally but Sarah asked me to run out and try to find him after he left."

"You did? Why?"

The clerk didn't answer Hammond, instead he called to his colleague who walked towards him with an enquiring expression. She returned Hammond's smile as he bent down, directing his voice towards the microphone that allowed communication on either side of the glass window. He pointed to the e-fit and repeated his question. She studied the paper and then nodded, gesturing she would come around and talk to him at the front. She did so and they walked to the side of the shop where they wouldn't be overheard.

"Yes, this is the man from this morning. He seemed pleasant enough, very polite."

"Did he buy postage for a parcel at all?" Hammond noticed she was wearing a black bra that was evident under her white blouse and averted his eyes.

The woman nodded positively. "Yes. He asked for postage for printed papers, but of course, we have the new postage system in place now so we can only charge for weight, rather than size. I explained this and he put it on the scales, I told him how much he owed and he gave me the exact money before sliding the parcel underneath. Then he left."

"Could you describe the package for me?" Even as he spoke it, Hammond was not sure what kind of answer he expected but her response exceeded anything he would have wished for.

"I've got it at the back. The package didn't have a complete address on the front and no sender's address. I got Stuart..." She pointed to the other clerk "..to run after him so that he could correct it and include it in the twelve o'clock collection, but he had gone. I was waiting to hear what I should do from my supervisor but in the meantime, a woman came in and tried to claim it on his behalf."

Hammond felt exhilaration rise within his chest. "Why didn't you give it to her?"

"Well, I couldn't prove that she had the right to. I told her to get the gentleman who had tried to send it to come back and write the recipient's address in full."

"The woman that came in. Did she say who she was?"

The clerk shook her head. "No, but I can describe her." Her eyes looked up toward the ceiling as she engaged her memory. "Tall, slim, very attractive. Dark hair tied back in a elegant fashion. I reckon she must have been fifty or so."

Hammond handed her the e-fit of Goodchild. "Is this her?"

The clerk smiled and nodded before looking at both men in turn. "Why? What have they done?"

Hammond ignored the question and instead asked to see the parcel.

Hammond returned to the office triumphant. He now saw that until that moment, he had followed a trail laid by assumption rather than looking at reality. He had believed Harris had wanted him to investigate suicides because he had found a murder victim's hairbrush in a despondent's apartment. This had been a ludicrous reason to start another enquiry, yet Hammond had done so because he had assumed Harris had good reason to. The reality of that situation was that no-one else would have bothered without more evidence of Mark Callum committing murder twenty years previously. From the moment he had agreed to help Harris, he had assumed that the suicides had been suspicious deaths which he now realised were not. All despondents had died by their own hand. Yet, their deaths had lead to an unexpected explanation, one that Hammond only now realised. He gathered up all the post-it notes from the desks and went in search for Morris.

He found Morris in the canteen, he was texting on his mobile phone but quickly stopped as Hammond approached and held up a hand as if to ward off any enquiry.

"Before you ask, I released her. There wasn't enough to hold her."

Hammond paused before seating himself beside his colleague. "I'm not surprised. I think you are right. I don't think Kathleen understands what this is all about either."

Morris looked at Hammond sharply. "You've changed your tune. Missing her already?"

The sarcasm was lost on Hammond, he sat forward eagerly. "We were assuming that this was all to cover up deaths made to look like suicides, but that didn't make sense. Harris wanted to discover something, but we didn't know what. He used me to find out on his behalf, something that he believed he was unwittingly involved in."

Morris was watching Hammond with an annoyed expression, his fingers remained on the keypad of his phone as if waiting for the opportunity to continue his text message.

"You said yourself that all those previously fostered by Goodchild may have been involved with illicit earnings, they survived on an income that we cannot trace. What if they were all involved with organised crime? Cheryl Bailey said that Goodchild chose her charges with a specific requisite, that they had a skill or ability that could be used somehow. Until now, I presumed that Rachel Turner had been investigating Goodchild for the purpose of tracing her biological son, Lucas Dean. But could Turner have been working with Goodchild, she chose each child on Goodchild's behalf? That it was she who arranged for each of them to be referred to Goodchild's care so that they could be used. Goodchild wasn't registered as a foster carer, which meant that they were practically untraceable, and easily managed. Cheryl said that Goodchild would remind the children that they had to reverse their fortunes by striking back, she brainwashed them into compliance. But, it went wrong when Turner discovered that one of those she had referred to Goodchild was her own son. So she tries to undo the damage by reporting Bradley Kelsey as an unsuitable guardian hoping that her actions would expose the organisation."

Hammond's mind was racing and he was finding his speech was becoming rushed. Morris watched him incredulously. "But that would expose herself to scrutiny. If what you say is true then Rachel Turner was equally guilty of child exploitation and would have faced charges."

Hammond shrugged. "She loved her son enough to take the chance ."

"Do you think she was killed?"

They both were silent with the knowledge that it was unlikely they would discover Rachel Turner, alive or dead.

Morris eventually spoke. "What has this got to do with Cheryl Bailey?"

"She knew too much. She brought attention to Theresa Davenport's death, with the accusation that Theresa was manipulated into taking her own life. I looked into her death as a result of Cheryl writing on a public forum. Cheryl told me about Goodchild, about the connection between Harris, Goodchild and Kathleen."

"But that still doesn't explain her murder."

"Yes, it does. Cheryl suspected Goodchild had caused Theresa to be depressed and reclusive but what she didn't realise was that she had witnessed first-hand the workings of a criminal organisation. Even Salima was involved, she was used as bait to attract wealthy suitors who could then be manipulated into parting with their cash. A honey-trap I think you call it, but it went wrong when Salima was killed by a potential mark."

Morris had now leaned forward, he was dubious about Hammond's theories but interested enough to listen further.

"So Harris, what relevance has he to all of this?"

There was a disturbance at the next table as an officer in tactical wear spilled his tea and yelped as the hot liquid scalded his hand. The two men looked over distracted for a moment before Hammond resumed voicing his thoughts.

"I think Harris covered up Salima's murder to protect Goodchild. Cheryl said that Harris had confronted Goodchild before taking Kathleen into his care. At first I thought it was because he wanted parental custody but he must have been aware that Kathleen was being used in some way by her mother. I know that the children in Goodchild's care were all scarred; a marking left by Goodchild on their bodies to remind them that they belonged to her. (Those were Kathleen's words.) If Harris suspected abuse then that would explain why he took Kathleen away from that harmful environment, but it doesn't explain why he didn't report Goodchild or even arrest her in his capacity as a Police Officer and attempt to protect the others. He must have been involved to a certain point, but was ignorant of the full extent of Goodchild's crimes. When Mark Callum died, he became suspicious. The manner of death was peculiar as were the others. He wanted me to discover what she was up to and act accordingly."

Morris shook his head. "That doesn't seem right to me. Why didn't he just tell us everything himself?"

"He was losing his memory, anything he would have said to us would have been invalidated by his mental impairment."

"His office was ransacked before he disappeared. You saw it. If Kathleen was telling the truth, Harris was in a rage when he left. Otherwise, it was staged for our benefit. You haven't explained why."

"Harris was desperate to know the truth behind the suicides and I think he discovered it the night he disappeared. I just haven't worked out how."

Hammond listed the items found in Kelsey's flat. "The DVD's found were filmed for the benefit of potential buyers of cheap labour. The photographs found on Kelsey's phone were probably intended to be downloaded onto the internet. We now have a confirmed link between Kelsey and Goodchild. " He went on to explain to Morris about the package Kelsey had attempted to send back to himself at the post office. Kelsey had probably rushed and in his haste, didn't notice he had written an incomplete address. When he realised his mistake he sent Goodchild to collect the package on his behalf but the post office wouldn't hand anything over without permission. The package had contained seventeen passports from minors. Kids from Eastern Europe, Africa and Asia. Morris' eyes' widened.

"So the motive behind Cheryl's murder and the attempted murder on you was to cover up child trafficking?"

Hammond nodded. "I'm sure of it."

CHAPTER THIRTY

"The kids were probably brought in via Eurostar. They can travel unaccompanied and there are no specialist police patrols in Ashford so they could easily have been brought over here from across Europe without too many questions being asked." Morris' left hand had abandoned its task of trying to continue texting on his mobile, instead he returned the phone to his trouser pocket as he stood up from the table, indicating Hammond do the same. They walked from the canteen, their heads bowed, as they attempted to compile a plan of action between them.

"We need to find Kelsey. I was hoping that Traffic had picked him up but his trail went cold five miles from his flat. The car was abandoned and I doubt that any vehicle search will prove fruitful." Morris stopped walking suddenly and stood in the middle of the corridor, ignoring other pedestrians who attempted to get past him by shuffling sideways against the wall. Feeling it was necessary to apologise on his colleagues behalf, Hammond smiled at the irritated faces and stepped back to allow access.

"You know Kathleen better than I. Are you convinced she knows nothing about this? If she is involved..." Morris's voice trailed off.

Hammond faced the other man directly. "Harris was adamant that Kathleen was kept in the dark about what he asked me to do. I presumed it was because he didn't want her to remember about her childhood with Goodchild, but now I wonder whether it was to protect her from knowing what they were involved in."

"Harris must have known that Goodchild was involved in trafficking. He told you about the girls brought in for prostitution, he was probably part of it."

"No, I think Harris was a grass eater, not a meat eater." He spoke the thoughts aloud but he was reassuring himself rather than Morris. He had wondered before how corrupt Harris had been but now he realised that Harris had simply pretended not to notice what was going on, rather than being directly involved.

"I hardly think his vegetarian preferences are relevant." Morris scoffed as he resumed his walk down the corridor. His strides had lengthened and now he directed his speech over his shoulder. "Kathleen could have mentioned you sleeping with her the other night. She must have known that your indiscretion would compromise any court case later on which makes me wonder whether she values her friendship with you more than her desire to protect herself or Kelsey. That gives us something to work on."

Hammond guessed what was coming next. "You want me to talk to her?"

Morris stopped outside the office door and turned around to face him. "It's worth a try. Right now we need all the help we can get. If she knows anything that she wasn't prepared to tell me in the interview, she may open up to you if you give her the opportunity."

Kathleen was nervous, Hammond couldn't tell whether it was her guilty conscience showing or whether it was his direct manner that was making her so hesitant but she welcomed him into the house. Galvin stood in the doorway, unsure whether to follow them into the hallway, he knew he was needed as a witness but that didn't mean he needed to make it obvious he was listening to the conversation being played out in front of him. He stood by the front door, his hand wrapped around his mobile phone, just in case his wife called.

"Wallace, I.."

Hammond interrupted Kathleen before she attempted to explain herself. He wasn't there to listen to her excuses, he needed facts.

"Kathleen, I need you to help us. We need to know where Bradley Kelsey and your Mother are. Can you tell us?" He knew his manner was short but enough time had been wasted.

Kathleen looked up at him, she looked bewildered by his tone. "No, I don't know. Why should I?"

Hammond stepped closer to her, he wanted to appear intimidating. "Because it is only a matter of time before you contact them or they contact you. They are going to want to know what you told us in the interview. Am I right?"

Kathleen's left hand released its hold where it had rested on her right shoulder. She was still in defence mode but wanted to appear willing to co-operate.

"Bradley sometimes comes here, I don't know if he intends to come back. I don't even know whether he knows I have been questioned, but if he asks I will tell him the truth, just like I told your Detective Chief Inspector. I don't know anything!"

"But you didn't tell us the truth Kathleen, you said that Kelsey was an acquaintance, you never mentioned he was your biological father."

Kathleen's face betrayed her astonishment. Hammond was surprised he hadn't worked it out earlier, but when the thought had popped into his head it had made sense, enough to have voiced it aloud without fear of sounding as if he were bluffing, which of course he was. She hesitated for a second and glanced at Galvin who pretended to be studying his phone.

"I don't know him, that much is true. Like I said, Lloyd was my Father. Bradley is more of an acquaintance who just happens to share my DNA. We only met a few years ago and we don't see each other often. When we do, we don't talk much. There is no relationship to speak of."

"Yet you are protecting him by not telling us where to find him."

"Because I don't know! I only know his mobile number. What is going on? Why won't you tell me what this is all about? I swear Wallace, that I am as confused as you!"

Her eyes were open wide but Hammond wouldn't allow himself to be fooled again. "We need to find him Kathleen, if you don't know where he is, then give us something you do know. When did you meet last? What did you say? Anything at all."

"The last time I saw him was when Dad had his episode. I lied when I said that I had called the Doctor. I called Bradley."

"Why?"

"I had left the daily newspapers for Dad to read when he woke up before I left to go to town. When I returned, he was shouting, kept waving the newspaper at me and bellowing. He was saying things that didn't make sense to me. I tried to reason with him but he went crazy. So I phoned Bradley, I asked him to help me."

"Why him? Why not the Doctor like you said?"

"Bradley had told me that if I needed help with Dad to call him first."

"Did he help?"

"He came to the house. When he got here Dad was still ranting and raving. I was told to leave, to give Dad some time to calm down." She looked at Hammond for reassurance. "I was upset, I didn't know what to do. Bradley said that I needed to take a breather, that I would be more helpful if I gave Dad some space, so I waited outside on the drive until the shouting stopped."

Hammond prompted her to tell more. "When you got back inside, where was your Dad?"

"I don't know, I guess he was in the office. The door was open, but I didn't see him. I only saw Bradley."

"What was he doing?"

"He was collecting the papers that Dad had been waving about. When he saw me, he told me that Dad had hit his head accidently. He was unconscious and Bradley was going to take him to the hospital."

"So why the secrecy? Why didn't you mention this when you knew the Police wanted to talk to your Father?"

Kathleen's voice caught in her throat. "Because I knew he was dead, I could see from Bradley's expression that something was wrong. I tried to get to my Dad but he stopped me, told me that I shouldn't look."

Hammond studied Kathleen's face for several moments, She was telling the truth, either that or she was a better actress than he had given her credit for.

"How could I tell the police? I didn't know where Bradley had taken Dad, I was told to report Dad missing, to say that he had wandered off. I didn't know that Bradley had taken Dad to your house, how could I have known?"

"Yet you tried to keep me from going there..it doesn't add up Kathleen, you are not telling me everything." Hammond resisted the temptation to continue questioning her, there was so much he didn't understand but time was of the essence.

"We'll talk about that later, in the meantime, I want to find Kelsey and I need to know where he is. Think Kathleen, this is important, we need to find him."

Kathleen shook her head. "I have never been to his house. He approached me, never the other way round, but I do remember seeing an address in Aldington. I presumed it was where he lived."

"Aldington? Where did you see the address?"

"He had written his mobile number on a scrap of paper that had been torn off an invoice for building renovations. It was addressed to him and I don't remember the address, just that it was in Aldington."

"What was the name of the building company?"

Kathleen shook her head as if trying but failing to remember.

"Think Kathleen!" Hammond was infuriated by the slow progress he was making. He resisted the urge to shake her by the shoulders. Whether it was his wounded pride that had got the better of him or whether it was the need to have the answers in one go, Hammond felt desperate. He could feel Galvin's eyes fixed on him from behind and forced himself to breath slowly through the nose.

"The name was written in orange lettering. Champion. I think the name was Champion. Or was it Chapman? Yes, I think it was Chapman and Son's."

"And the renovation work was definitely for an address in Aldington?"

Hammond turned away from her, he directed Galvin to forward the information to the station. Kathleen's reached out her hand hesitantly until it rested on his forearm.

"Wallace, that night.. I want to explain."

He removed her hand from his arm firmly. "Kathleen. I want you to go back to the Station, speak to DCI Morris and tell him everything you just told me and anything you didn't. Everything." He met her eyes and retained the gaze until she nodded in agreement.

"I know you think I can't be trusted Wallace but..."

Hammond interrupted her again. "The newspaper article that agitated your Dad, do you remember what it was about?"

"It was about benefit fraud."

Hammond turned towards the exit, but stopped as Kathleen called his name. Her voice had a renewed confidence in the tone, it caused him to take notice and turn back around to face her.

"They knew her as Goodchild, but really her name is Gutkin."

He nodded his thanks, reminded her to return to the station and left the house as abruptly as he had arrived.

As Galvin steered the car southbound. Hammond updated Dunn over the phone and explained they were heading towards Aldington. He knew that it would be sensible to return to the station and debrief Morris but he didn't know how he could convince his colleagues that he had found a lead worth concentrating all their attention on. By debating the plausibility of his theories, they would be losing time and enable Kelsey to get away. Dunn ended the call promising to call back with any update on her enquiries with the building company.

Galvin kept silent. He was concentrating on driving but occasionally his head would turn towards Hammond with a perplexed expression. Hammond felt the heaviness of Galvin's lack of faith in his actions rather than heard it but he pretended not to notice. He knew he was acting as a one man band again but reckoned this time, he had justifiable reason to do so. During the twenty minute journey the light had faded and Galvin turned on the main beam of the headlights as he navigated the car through narrow country roads. They parked the car in front of an entrance to a field just outside the village awaiting Dunn's call. Minutes passed during which time Galvin made several checks on his mobile.

"Why don't you call her?" Hammond motioned to the phone.

"We agreed it was easier if Anne called me when the time came, otherwise she'll have to keep answering the phone every time I call to check." The car was silent for several minutes before the pressure of Galvin's thoughts forced themselves out of his mouth.

"Where you there, with your wife?"

Hammond looked at Galvin unsure what the other man meant. He raised his eyebrows enquiringly.

"At your son's birth."

"Ah." Hammond wasn't sure how to answer. He knew the man needed reassurance but he couldn't give it to him. If he said he was there the moment Paul was born, Hammond would be asked to describe the scene which he had forced to the back of his mind as soon as it had happened, but if he lied and said Lyn had given birth before he had got to the hospital in time, Galvin's desperation to know what he should expect would present itself with more questions which Hammond would be expected to answer. He decided not to answer at all.

"Look Galvin, if necessary, just leave me here and get home if you need to. Don't worry about me, I will find my own way back."

Galvin smiled and shook his head. "That's not necessary, if it happens I will drop you back on the way."

The conversation stalled and the car was quiet. Hammond wondered why Dunn hadn't called and said so. He felt stifled in the car, his body was riddled with nervous energy, part apprehension that Galvin would ask more questions about Paul's birth. He wound down the passenger window and leaned his elbow over the edge of the door frame. The waft of farmland manure seeped into the car.

"Don't you think it would have been better to have organised surveillance on the place first? You don't intend to go and confront him if this is where Kelsey is staying do you?"

Hammond didn't answer, he was embarrassed to admit he hadn't thought that far ahead.

The wait for Dunn's call was too long. He suggested they drive the car through the village and look for evidence of building work. Satisfied with the distraction, Galvin drove through the village, they found nothing to encourage them. Hammond decided he was thirsty, the village shop was still open. He left the car and entered the shop, selected a bottle of mineral water from the chiller cabinet, paid for it and left the shop just in time to see Galvin's car headlights flashing intermittently for his attention. Presuming it was to tell him Galvin's wife had gone into labour, Hammond gestured for Galvin to leave but Galvin didn't. Instead he continued to flash the car lights. Hammond stood at the entrance of the shop for several seconds before he realised what Galvin was trying to communicate. Kelsey was on the other side of the road exiting the Butchers. He was walking casually, swinging a red and white striped carrier bag in his hand as if he hadn't a care in the world. Hammond glanced quickly at Galvin in the car and weighed up his options. He could run after Kelsey and take him there and then or he could follow him and see where Kelsey would lead him. He decided on the latter and gestured to Galvin to pull the car up. He got in the car.

"Follow him, but stay back as much as you dare, if necessary I will get out and walk."

The car crept forward . Kelsey turned right at a bus stop and crossed a stile leading into a field of darkness. Hammond made a move to open the passenger door. Galvin looked across at him nervously.

"You're not following him in there! What if it is trick?"

Hammond shook his head. "I doubt he knows we are here. I will keep in contact with you, only start to panic if you don't hear from me in ten minutes."

He left the car and shuffled across the road towards the foot-stile. The grass was long and wet, the dampness sucked at his trousers as soon as his foot trod down on the soft earth on the other side of the stile. The field stretched downwards away from the pavement he had just left. Despite the urge to stay close to the reassurance of the street lights, Hammond trod further into the field. He couldn't see Kelsey. There was silence apart from the faint drone of traffic that was audible even though the main road was a distance away.

Hammond inched his way further, his eyes slowly became accustomed to the darkness and he could make out a faint line where grass had been trodden down to make a path. He followed the trail. The path went around a sharp corner towards the left. As Hammond made his way round, he saw a glimmer of light beckoning to him through the cluster of trees. A small gate was visible, obviously disused, the shadow of overgrown vegetation was woven around it. Light seeped from underneath a boarded window reflecting off scaffolding poles that had been left lying in a heap against the cottage walls. Hammond moved closer, he was beginning to question himself as to what he intended to do next but whilst deliberating he continued to move forward, leaving him less choice but to continue edging towards the wall of the building. He pressed his ear against the cold wall, hoping to get a better idea of how much activity there was inside the house but he could only hear the sound of his own blood being pumped around his head, the sound he had once believed had been the sound of the sea when he pressed a sea-shell against his ear. His eyes were now fully accustomed to the dark and he could see there was too much vegetation to allow him to get any closer to the boarded window without stepping on twigs and alerting his presence. He stood still whilst he debated what to do, conscious that the longer he stood there, the more his feet sank into the ploughed earth. He thought about what he was doing, how yet again he was acting alone, rebelling against the most fundamental rule of police work; to never go into a potentially dangerous situation alone. Swiftly he made a decision and turned around to head back towards Galvin and the car. His feet were caked in mud. As he placed his foot down to walk forward, the soul of the rubber sandal slipped under the added weight of his plastered ankle and slid forward causing his back leg to bend and throw his weight forward. He landed on his hands with both legs stuck behind him and he remained in the pose of a wheelbarrow whilst he attempted to pull his other leg out of the mud. As he eased his body upwards, he felt the rush of air on his upturned face as the pole came crashing down towards the back of his neck. Everything went dark.

*"When the Gods, to ruin a man,
first make him mad, they do it, almost invariably,
by making him an optimist."*
Henry Havelock Ellis. The Dance of Life. 1923

CHAPTER THIRTY-ONE

When Hammond came to, he did not know where he was. He was lying on his stomach, his arms were outstretched above his head. The ground beneath him was cold and hard. His shoulders and neck ached. He moved his head stiffly trying to see where he was but it was pitch black, he couldn't see his own hands as he drew them closer to his body. The air was heavy and warm which told him he was no longer outside. He groped the floor in the dark with the tips of his fingers, feeling the smoothness of ground that was interrupted by occasional gritty furrows. He detected he was lying on ceramic tiles. He must be in a bathroom. There was a lingering smell of disinfectant. He managed to sit up and strained his ears to pick up any sound but it was quiet. Slowly he willed his body to move and he got to his feet, shuffling to the side until his progress was hindered by a wall. He allowed his hands to explore the wall searching for a light switch. He continued this activity for a while before he heard sounds of someone approaching. The sound of a door opening was heard before light blinded him.

The person by the door was quiet, and made no movement towards him. Hammond blinked to restore his vision and recognised Kelsey standing a few meters away from him. The two men stared at one another, neither spoke. Automatically Hammond looked to see if Kelsey had a weapon but the man's hands hang limply by his sides with the assurance that Hammond wasn't going anywhere. With the light now on, Hammond could see he was in an empty room. The floor was tiled, the walls bare apart from occasional hooks that poked out intermittently. The pain in his neck caused him to refrain from moving his head unless it was necessary. Then he heard the sound of heels tapping an approach before a voice he did not recognise addressed him.

"I must confess, I didn't expect to meet you like this." She spoke clearly, articulating every vowel.

Hammond studied the woman who now stood before him. He recognised her immediately. She was even more beautiful than her daughter, she walked with a confidence that Kathleen lacked. Her tall, lean figure was complimented by a fitted woollen skirt and matching jacket that she wore. It looked expensive, the kind of suit that his mother would have dreamed to have owned in her lifetime but never had.

"I knew we would meet eventually" He said.

She inclined her head with a graceful movement as if to acknowledge his words before handing him his mobile phone. "A few minutes ago, someone tried to call you. I assume there is a person or people waiting for you to reassure them you are well. I would appreciate it if you call them and tell them that you do not need assistance.

I am sure you will agree that enough people have been hurt already."

He took the phone from her silently. He knew Galvin would be worried, that he would have raised the alarm after ten minutes of Hammond leaving him. He had no idea what the time was, how long he had been unconscious, he hoped that Galvin hadn't followed him here. He pressed call back. Galvin answered immediately.

"I'm OK." Hammond said. "I just lost my footing and dropped the phone in the mud."

"Have you found Kelsey?"

Hammond hesitated. He was tempted to give an indication of his predicament but couldn't afford Galvin to get involved.

"No, not yet, But I think I am going to hang around a little longer. Why don't you go home, I will make my own way back."

Goodchild nodded at him encouragingly.

There was a pause as if Galvin was thinking about the possibility. Hammond could feel his hesitation on the other end so he repeated the suggestion. "I will you call you later, let you know of any progress. Just get back home, there's nothing to do here." Goodchild took the phone from him and disconnected the call before removing the battery from the casing.

"I am guessing your colleague is in the vicinity, I hope that he takes your advice, Inspector, but I will send Bradley out to have a look, just in case." She motioned with a hand towards the man who stood silent in the doorway, he nodded and left the room. Hammond prayed that Galvin had left.

"I won't ask you how you knew I was here, Inspector. It seems I underestimated your investigative skills, but it doesn't matter. I have no intention of staying here for very long. However, I must admit I am intrigued as to why you are here."

Hammond tensed his jaw and he stretched himself to his full height. He debated whether to throw himself at her, to throw her to the floor and make an escape. She must be half his weight, it would be possible. As if reading his thoughts she stepped back and smiled again. "You wouldn't be able to get past the security door, Inspector, it requires a password with every entry and exit. I think you should allow yourself to relax rather than fantasise about overpowering me."

Hammond decided to play for time. "I came to question you about your involvement with a number of serious crimes including the exploitation of children. I believe that you took over the guardianship of Salima Abitboul for the intention of encouraging her into prostitution and that you enlisted the help of your former lover Lloyd Harris to cover up her murder in 1991."

"You seem very confident. I assume that you have proof to back up your suspicions?"

"You took over the care of Mark Callum, Theresa Davenport, Fiona Nwasu, Lucas Dean and Claire Bennet illegally. You were not registered as a legal guardian to any of these children. You are suspected of harbouring them under false pretences and encouraging them to partake in criminal activities. Furthermore, I suspect you of being an accessory to the murders of Cheryl Bailey and Lloyd Harris as well as the attempted murder of myself."

"You haven't answered my question, Inspector. What proof do you have?"

"Your daughter's witness statement."

Goodchild laughed with rich amusement. "You are very humorous. I am beginning to enjoy your company, but forgive me for saying that you appear to be deluded. You do not have any such witness statement. I know you have nothing on me that acts as evidence that I have any involvement with the crimes you suspect me of."

Hammond knew he was floundering, he wanted to give the impression of confidence behind what he was saying but she was right, he couldn't prove anything.

"You are keeping me here against my will, that is enough for the time being."

Her laugh echoed around the room, she clapped her hands with childish delight at his words before stepping closer to him. "You are welcome to try to leave, I cannot physically stop you." She stepped away from him again and watched him as he deliberated what to do.

She had mentioned the security door. "You will need to give me the password." He said.

She shook her head. "No, I won't do that. I have no intention of helping you walk out of here. You have caused me too much of an inconvenience already. I did not invite you here so technically, you are trespassing. Look at it from my point of view; A vulnerable woman is at home alone on a dark winter's evening when an intruder breaks into her home. In her panic, she shuts the man in her basement and leaves to get help...what happens next?"

She walked back over to him and laid her finger under his chin, moving his head so that their eyes met. "Like I said, I do not intend to stay here for very long. You however..well, let's just see what happens shall we?"

She winked at him and opened the door. Hammond took his chance, he threw his whole weight towards the opening. Goodchild, startled by the sudden movement, skidded to the side but Hammond wasn't prepared for Kelsey standing on the other side of the door. As Hammond slammed into him, Kelsey grunted and toppled backward but was able to correct himself in time and stop himself from falling backward. He gripped Hammond in a bear hug and pushed him back into the room before kicking him in the ribs. The pain shot through Hammond like a hot spear and he fell onto the floor gasping. Goodchild followed Kelsey back into the room and looked down at Hammond.

"I realise what it is that I like about you. You are an optimist like me. Even though I have already explained to you that you will not be able to get away, you still try. However, after a while your stubborn behaviour will become tedious so please do not continue with your efforts."

"Is that what you said to Mark and the others?"

Hammond stayed on the floor, the fall had knocked all air out of his body. He knew he had been defeated. Goodchild watched him attentively and Hammond knew she was trying to decipher how much he knew. He decided to continue bluffing, it would give Dunn time to get there. She must have found the address by now and would start wondering why he hadn't called.

"There was no need. Mark was very compliant from the start. He understood that I was simply trying to show him that the world outside was not meant for the likes of him. The others saw this too. Their parents had abandoned them in their hours of need, and then society had shunned them. Their voices were ignored. I simply showed them how to take back control."

"You controlled them with your sick games and twisted logic. They were vulnerable and you exploited them."

Hammond heard the faint note of irritation in Goodchild's voice when she answered him. "On the contrary, I showed them that it was the world outside that should be exploited. Society provides for those who play by the rules dictated by a Christian religion that was founded on hearsay and manipulated to suit those in power. And you Inspector have been exploited and brainwashed into believing that by forcing others to abide by those rules, you are doing the greater good. Your moral intelligence is no more superior to mine. The only difference is that I do not wish to be a part of the community to which you belong. I created my own with its own rules; to take what is rightfully ours."

"By selling children?"

For a split second, Goodchild's body tensed, she recovered quickly but it was enough for Hammond to have noticed. He was encouraged, it meant she was surprised by how much he knew.

"In order to create a culture of like minded people, it is necessary to work together, to do what we can to finance ourselves. In that sense, I am a business woman and as such I accept business deals wherever I can find them. There has, and always will be, a market for sex, drugs and cheap labour. I simply act as the distributor, providing what is wanted to the highest bidder. It is often the parents who sell their unwanted daughters or sons. They cannot afford to keep them. They do what they can to survive and I enable that."

Her articulated speech was too controlled, the woman was deranged. It wouldn't take much to provoke her. The fear started to creep in and spread over Hammond's body as if poison had been injected into his veins and was slowing paralysing him. He knew he had to play for time, to keep her talking. There was still so much that he didn't know. "You enable the violation of innocent people and condemn them to a living hell."

"What happens to the children before or after the sale is not my concern."

"You are not human, you are a sick and perverted bitch!"

Goodchild crouched down to face Hammond. "You call me perverted yet you didn't pass the opportunity to use my daughter to satisfy your own urges. You used her to get what you wanted, a cheap thrill. Although I expect you were disappointed. Kathleen has always been frigid. She has the beauty but not the intelligence to know what to do with it."

"You prostituted your own daughter just like you did Salima."

"Salima wanted a lifestyle of glamour and luxury. Such things have to be earned one way or another."

"By sacrificing her life?"

"I was not responsible for her murder. No, I am afraid that Theresa's jealousy was the instigator. She told the client that Salima liked autoerotic-asphyxia. A lie of course. Salima panicked, struggled and it went wrong."

"How was Lloyd involved?"

Goodchild's eyes narrowed, She straightened her back in a defensive stance.

"It was he who recommended Salima's services to the client, therefore it was seen to be Lloyd's responsibility when it went wrong."

"So he framed an innocent man for her murder?"

She opened her arms wide. "Of course. The client was extremely influential. To expose him would be catastrophic for everyone concerned."

"You mean for yourself?"

"Inspector. I do not believe you are so naive as to think that this is all about me. I offer an exclusive service. There are many that appreciate my discretion. If it wasn't profitable, I wouldn't be doing it, yet business is booming. That should tell you something."

Hammond was distracted by Kelsey venturing further into the room, the man stood by Hammond's feet, his eyes rested on Hammond's plastered ankle. The smile that played around his lips caused Hammond to feel under threat of considerable pain. He used his hands to slide his body further away from Kelsey and tried to play for more time by asking questions.

"What about Rachel Turner? Did you send your boyfriend to kill her like you did with Cheryl?"

Goodchild looked at Kelsey for several moments. She began to smile, but this time her smile looked as if she were genuinely amused.

"Bradley does what I ask him to do, just like I do what is asked of me. Like I said Inspector, I have very influential clients who do not want their private lives made public. Some will do anything to prevent that from happening. Rachel proved she couldn't be trusted and that made people nervous. As for Cheryl, I admit that that wasn't planned, but it seemed the best way to get rid of two nuisances, especially as the first attempt to get rid of you failed miserably."

Goodchild's eyes had stayed on Kelsey as she spoke but now she turned her gaze back towards Hammond. "You must excuse Bradley, he is keen to show me that he has no intention of making the same mistake again. Personally I abhor violence, but I have to admit that it can serve a purpose."

Hammond knew she intended him to die, that she wanted him to beg for his life. The panic began to seep into his heart, ballooning it against his ribs. He was finding it hard to breathe. Desperately he tried to think, to keep Goodchild there for as long as he could. he was playing for time that he knew he had little of.

"But you destroyed what you created. Your culture, as you call it, now ceases to exist."

Goodchild looked bewildered, her features arranged themselves to look at him with wide eyed mysticism. She raised a hand to Kelsey and he took a step back from Hammond but his eyes stayed focused on his prey at his feet.

"Whatever do you mean?"

"Mark and the others, they killed themselves to get away from you."

Goodchild stepped back sharply, the heel of her shoe made a cracking sound on the tile.

"No, you got that wrong. It was Fiona's decision. A client wanted to ensure his stay in Britain would not be questioned and I obliged by providing him a wife for which he paid good money. Unfortunately Fiona took exception to his methods and decided to leave him stranded. It caused the client and I a great deal of embarrassment. Bradley followed her to Dover where he intended to remind her of her obligations. She chose another alternative, one that I didn't expect."

"You gave her no choice but to kill herself."

"She chose freedom when she knew there was no going back. You cannot undo a mistake in this business. Compliance is paramount. When Fiona left, she unsettled the others, they started to question their own choices and it caused disruption. Clients became nervous, and when that happens it is necessary to regain control by making the workforce redundant, by making them understand that unless they are willing to commit, they have only one choice open to them. It became necessary for me to start afresh."

The woman is mad, Hammond thought.

"I can see you judging me, but really I think you understand. If you do not play by the rules, your society will reject you. It is necessary to have order. When rules are not respected, it is necessary to abandon those that do not adhere. Lucas understood this better than anyone. He knew his role was to ensure safe delivery of the merchandise, instead he stole and sampled the goods. His love of drugs superseded his respect for the rules and I couldn't trust him, he wasn't useful anymore. Theresa's loyalty was unquestionable yet she was a nuisance. She was manipulative and insecure and believed that she could belong to both societies at the same time. Her desire to belong was her weakness. In the end she realised that she did not belong to either world. I simply suggested going to another place where we all go eventually."

"But they all died within months of each other."

Goodchild sighed as if she were now bored with explaining. "That was more to do with convenience. I intended moving the business elsewhere but as with any business, it takes time to organise and I wanted to start with a clean slate, get rid of any ties that could weigh me down."

"And the notes? Who were they left for?"

"I would have thought that was pretty obvious, they were persuaded to write the notes so that their predecessors would learn if they did not comply, the same would be expected of them."

Hammond was appalled by her cold-blooded indifference. The woman was a sociopath, she had no empathy for anyone. Human life is insignificant to her thought Hammond.

"You speak of death as if it is part of a game."

"Because that is exactly what it is. We all die. It never ceases to amaze me of how surprised people are when they are reminded that death is inevitable. Yet even though they can see there is no way out, they cling to the hope that somehow their fate will be spared. I have no doubt that you will do the same." Goodchild circled around Hammond's slumped body on the floor. "Originally we intended this room to be a vault. It was designed to be air tight and sound proof. When Bradley has satisfied his primitive urges, he will lock this door and when that happens the lights and the air supply will be switched off. You will have several hours alone to reflect on what we have discussed. I am confident that when you have mulled over what I have told you, you will realise that you and I share similar beliefs. You intend to punish me by incarcerating me. I am doing the same to you, only I am ensuring that your prison sentence is limited."

She crouched down behind Hammond's head and gently rested her hands on either side of his face. "I bid you good-bye Inspector. We have played a fair game and I commend your efforts, but I cannot stay any longer. There are people expecting me."

"I should warn you, it is unlikely you will get far Ms Gutkin." Hammond's attempt to un-nerve her with his knowledge did not have the effect he had hoped for. Instead she simply raised her eyebrows in surprise and drew herself up to a standing position.

Kelsey moved back into position at Hammond's feet. "You have made Bradley jealous, he hates other men having my attention."

As she headed towards the door, Hammond knew that the second she disappeared, he was going to experience pain. He swallowed and began to shuffle backwards, a hopeless gesture he knew, but his survival instinct wasn't exhausted. As Kelsey followed Hammond's slow progress, Hammond realised that Goodchild was right. Despite the hopelessness of his situation, he still hoped that he could fight his way out of there. Kelsey smiled as Hammond backed against the wall, there was no-where to go. Hammond closed his eyes and held his breath waiting for the impact and at that moment his fear dissipated into resignation. The panic subsided as rapidly as it had risen, and it gave him strength. Hammond's leg shot forward and impacted on Kelsey's right knee. It caused the man to fall forward. Hammond rolled his body to the side and expected retaliation but nothing happened. He rolled back and was astonished to see Kelsey lying on the floor. He wasn't moving. Galvin hauled Hammond to his feet.

They half dragged Kelsey from the basement up into the main body of the house. In the kitchen they seated him on a wooden chair and stood over him, waiting for the patrol cars to arrive. Galvin updated the station whilst Hammond observed Kelsey. He was conscious, his eyes were open but he was silent and still, his hands restrained in handcuffs behind his back.

"A move like that, you could have rendered him brain dead." Hammond gazed at the angry red weal on the side of Kelsey's neck.

"It was a three second squeeze. Anyway, the man was about to kill you. I had to stop him."

Hammond nodded his appreciation, he felt as if words were insufficient somehow. The adrenaline was still pumping throughout his body but despite the sense of urgency, Hammond knew that it was pointless looking outside for Goodchild. She had no intention of waiting for Kelsey to join her. A woman that cunning would have known that Kelsey would have wanted to prove himself to her at the last minute and she had used the opportunity to get away. Hammond looked down at Kelsey and spoke to him for the first time.

"You do realise that she had no intention of taking you with her? She didn't wait for you."

Kelsey said nothing, his stare communicated his hate and defiance but Hammond was pleased with the response. He knew he had planted a seed in the man's mind that could only flourish into all consuming doubt.

Hammond allowed the man to stew over the thought as he ventured outside to wave to the patrol cars. From where he stood, he could see the blue lights flashing through the darkness and wondered how far Goodchild would get before she was apprehended. He hoped that he would have the opportunity to see her again. She had been so sure that Hammond will no longer be a nuisance that he could imagine the exhilaration he would feel proving her wrong.

He heard the sound almost instinctively. They had been awaiting the call for so long that when it came, he knew instantly what it meant. He turned to go back indoors, and saw Galvin approach him halfway, his face was flushed, his eyes large, he shone with jubilance. "I'm about to be a Dad!" he said.

The moment of excitement was shattered in an instant. Galvin, lost in his euphoria, had turned his back on Kelsey. It was a mistake. As Hammond saw what was about to happen, he lost all speech. As if in slow motion, Hammond flung his body forward in an attempt to shield Galvin from the force of the attack. Galvin's expression turned from joy into confusion before the back of his skull shattered and he fell forwards.

"The more rapidly a civilisation progresses,
the sooner it dies for another to rise in its place."
Henry Havelock Ellis. The Dance of Life.1923

CHAPTER THIRTY-TWO

There are some images that once seen, cannot be unseen. No matter how much effort is spent to cover the sight with imaginings, the condemned vision remains fixed, it burns holes through the pages of memories so that whenever the eyes close, all that is seen is the scalding moment that wants to be forgotten. The event repeats itself in slow motion on perpetual playback with agonising precision. This is how Hammond would remember Galvin.

Galvin had fallen seconds before the officers rushed into the house and had tackled Kelsey to the ground. Suddenly the house was filled with the sound of shouting but Hammond was lost in a silent world. He turned Galvin over gently and cradled Galvin's shattered head, attempting to plug the holes that seeped blood and brain matter, but it wouldn't stop, the stream spilled through his fingers, onto his lap soaking the floor. Galvin's eyes were glazed, the breath that lingered between his lips frothed into oblivion. Hammond rocked him, desperate to circulate the life force that was leaking so forcefully. He shouted Galvin's name repeatedly, telling him not to give up, to hold on, but even as he expelled his appeal, he knew that there was no life left for Galvin to cling to. From somewhere behind him, he heard a scream, then felt hands pulling at his back and shoulders, trying to tear him from his task. Hammond felt Dunn, rather than saw her. She had fallen onto her knees beside him, grasping at Galvin's body. With frantic desperation, she pulled at his listless hands as if to make him acknowledge her, but Galvin was silent and still. Hammond looked up at Dunn, the tears that coursed down his cheeks mingled with the spilt blood on his lap.

"He's gone." There were no more words he could say.

*"In the end, it will be seen we return at
last to the point from which we start."*
Henry Havelock Ellis. The Dance of Life.1923

CHAPTER THIRTY-THREE

On the morning of Monday, January 24th, Hammond's ankle cast was removed. He celebrated his new found freedom by walking along the beach. The breeze felt unseasonably warm as it slapped his face and whipped his hair skywards. He tasted the salt on his lips and marvelled how nature protected itself. She chose her seasons to administer his needs, but she sent constant reminders that he was there as a guest. He couldn't overstay his welcome for his existence was immaterial, an insignificant speck of dust that was carried on the back of a ever turning wind.

Hammond stood on the pebbles and watched the fishing boats shunt further out to sea. Above them the clouds parted to allow a beam of sunlight guide their way. It reminded him of an image he had seen on the cover of a bible when he had been at Sunday School as a young boy, in his innocence he had thought the beam of light was a departed soul's ascension into heaven. Hammond found himself trying to imagine what life was like before birth, whether there was a presence that slowly descended onto the living and became one itself before spending its energy and evaporating into the atmosphere. He wondered about Galvin's newborn son, Michael Junior and the memory of Galvin's death engulfed him, causing him to squeeze his eyes closed. He would never say, but he had identified the second Galvin had died in his arms, he became physically lighter in an instant. Hammond vaguely remembered reading about a physician who had tried to determine the weight of a person's soul. As far as Hammond knew it was never determined, but from his own experience he took some comfort that Galvin's soul hadn't wasted away with his physical remains.

His thoughts turned to Lloyd Harris and he wondered, somewhat absurdly, whether Harris' mental clarity had returned following his death, then he thought of his mother and became lost in his own thoughts for several moments. He continued his walk along the sea front to where he had parked his newly acquired Saab before driving to the police station.

He was back in the office by 9 a.m. He spent the next hour revising his statements and going through the reports on the murder of Cheryl Bailey. He was meeting the team to discuss the investigation he had initiated following Lloyd Harris' request. It seemed as if an age had passed since he had met his former colleague at the Golf Club, since then his life and the life of his team had changed dramatically. He was pleased that Dunn had decided to stay, he valued her contribution.

He greeted them all individually with a handshake before seating himself at the table, the team waited for a few minutes and chatted amongst themselves until Beech joined them.

Hammond's memories of what had happened during the last five months had started to lose its clarity, but the facts that had emerged following Bradley Kelsey's arrest supported his initial theories. Rachel Turner had met Patricia Gutkin during the 1970's. How they met and what had transpired between them was impossible to determine, but they shared a confused belief that society owed them. Rachel Turner had been rejected by her family, her child had been taken from her and she had been left to fend for herself. Gutkin was a young attractive woman who discovered that men would pay for her attention and she exploited their desire to finance her own brothel. During this time she met Bradley Kelsey, a client, with whom she became pregnant. At some point the three of them began a scheme to offer a profitable service to the more discerning clientele. They realised that, to ensure absolute discretion and exclusivity, they would need to use people that had reason to retaliate against the social system like themselves. With Turner's help, they found young people that would not be missed, those with neglectful parents, or delinquents who had been shunned by society. Gutkin changed her name to Goodchild. Hammond considered that it was her own twisted way of making herself appear more trustworthy to the children she took on. Through methods such as sensory deprivation and psychological manipulation, their individual identities were encouraged to be forgotten and this successfully created a secretive and tightly controlled organisation that financed itself through offering specialised services such as drug trafficking and later, people trafficking.

Lloyd Harris, it was presumed, but not confirmed, was a former client of Goodchild, he had referred her services to his colleagues in the Metropolitan Police and had protected them from investigation later on by deflecting blame onto other officers.

Most of the threads had been woven together to provide logical explanations of how the organisation had been founded and how it had progressed to the present day but there were still some questions that remained unsolved. Salima's killer would probably never be identified, just as the client's identities would never be exposed. Bradley Kelsey refused to offer this information during questioning, he maintained that clients never used their real names, although he admitted that several clients were often in the public eye and were therefore easily recognisable. He confirmed that Mark Callum, Theresa Davenport, Claire Bennet and Lucas Dean had been encouraged to believe that without the support of the organisation, they would not be able to continue living, they would not have anywhere to live, no money to survive on. He blamed this on Goodchild's manipulation. Kelsey admitted to having been at Mark Callum's flat the day of his death as he had delivered Goodchild's personal message. It was Goodchild that decided when they were to be 'made redundant'. He refused to clarify his involvement in coercing their deaths, he maintained his innocence by explaining his role was that of a messenger. When asked about the missing pen and notepad, he had explained that he had mistakenly taken them following Callum's death. He had realised his mistake too late. He refused to divulge what had happened to Rachel Turner.

The photographic evidence taken from the bus and the restaurant was enough to encourage Kelsey's confessions regarding his interest in Hammond. He admitted he had killed Cheryl with the intention of framing Hammond. This was, he had explained, on the orders of influential clients. They feared that Hammond's enquiries would expose them. The arson attack on Hammond's home was inspired, Kelsey said, when he saw Jenny smoking. He had intended for it to look as if Jenny had caused the fire accidently. Through several interviews Kelsey dribbled information that proved helpful in establishing why certain events had occurred. But what Hammond could not determine with absolute certainty was Kathleen's involvement. There was no concrete evidence to suggest she was guilty of conspiring to kill Lloyd Harris or Hammond. Kathleen had given the impression of wanting to co-operate fully with the Police. She had answered all questions willingly but Hammond could not be sure that she was telling the truth. She maintained that her contact with Goodchild and Kelsey had been a recent development, following a chance meeting where she had seen Mark Callum in Ashford in September. It had been a shock, she explained, because she had been told by Harris that Callum had died soon after Kathleen had been taken into Harris' care. She had tried to talk to Harris about it but he had refused to disclose any information and subsequently she had attempted to find her biological parents, hoping to re-new contact with Callum. Following her enquiry Kelsey contacted Kathleen and offered to renew their relationship with the agreement that she was not to tell Harris. She had only seen Kelsey a few times, her mother had not wanted any direct contact with her.

Hammond could not satisfactorily conclude what had caused Harris' death. Kelsey refused to claim responsibility, he claimed that Harris had hit his head whilst being in an agitated state, but he did admit to moving the body to Hammond's house with the hope that it would look as if Harris had been visiting Hammond when the fire broke out. Kathleen's statement supported Kelsey's claim, but she insisted she did not know of Kelsey's intention to leave Harris' body or to kill Hammond in the fire. The phone message she had left on Kelsey's phone did not mention names and therefore it was not enough to prove she was lying.

Hammond felt a twinge of guilt as he deliberately failed to mention his fling with Kathleen. The truth was, Hammond could not explain why he had behaved with such recklessness, he saw that Morris had also failed to mention it in his report and wondered whether it had been deliberate

For Hammond and his team, their involvement in the investigation was over. The investigation on the child trafficking was to be handed over to a specialist department. Attempts had been made, but they had not traced Goodchild although the wreckage of her car had been discovered several miles from her home on the evening of her escape. An examination of the car found a considerable amount of blood soaked into the driver's seat. A thorough search of the area had been conducted although her body had not been found.

The meeting concluded after several hours and the file was handed over to the Prosecution Service. It was likely that other charges would be added later but there was enough to indict Bradley Kelsey for multiple murders.

Once the room had cleared, Hammond remained in his chair, lost in space for some time. He felt as if the conclusion to several months of agonising deliberation had been somehow inadequate. Almost like a Greek tragedy ending with a happy ever after. What Hammond would have otherwise wanted, he didn't know but he kept referring back to the same question. Had it all been worth it? If he hadn't accepted Harris's request for help, he would still have a home, Harris would still be alive and more, poignantly, Galvin would probably be seated at the same table, repeatedly asking questions and comparing his infants' progress.

Even with the child trafficking operation now exposed, it was unlikely that it would be stopped. Goodchild had said herself that business was booming. For as long as there was demand, there would be a supply. Hammond wondered again the identities of the clients, he found himself imagining the possibility that it could be people he worked with, people he respected. You could never tell what happened behind closed doors. Friendly faces were a perfect disguise for corrupt thoughts.

The grief that Hammond had been carrying for the last two weeks since Galvin's death drowned him with the unyielding thought that he was as equally responsible for Galvin's death as was Kelsey. The exact circumstances of Galvin's death were yet to be determined, but it was believed that somehow, Kelsey had managed to get out of his handcuffs whilst Galvin had been occupied with his phone call, and had armed himself with a hammer. The murder weapon was easily identified but Hammond was mystified as to how Kelsey had managed to free himself of his restraints. Several theories had been floating around the station. One idea was that Kelsey had carried a universal key with him, but this was, in Hammond's opinion, improbable. Firstly Kelsey would have had to expect an imminent arrest in order to have the key in the first place, secondly, he was taken by surprise by Galvin in the basement, he would not have had a key easily to hand. The other theory was that Kelsey had pushed his hands downwards as Galvin had fastened the cuffs so that they were locked further up his arms. This would have made them looser around his wrists when he had wriggled them down. During the time Galvin was occupied with his phone call, Kelsey may have been able to lubricate his fastenings with kitchen detergent and work his hands loose. Hammond had no confidence in this hypothesis either, there was no residue of any soap on the cuffs when they were examined later. The most probable theory was that Galvin simply hadn't fastened the handcuffs correctly. Nevertheless, how it happened, in Hammond's mind was irrelevant. For it had been his own arrogance that had placed Galvin there in the first place. For the hundredth time, Hammond questioned his own behaviour during the course of the last five months, he had made so many mistakes, mistakes that had risked the lives of his family and his colleagues. He had ignored the warnings offered to him by Dunn and Beech and instead he had headed a one-man crusade. Too many people had suffered as a result.

He eventually pulled himself out of the chair and went to get a cup of coffee. As he exited the room, he bumped into Morris. His despondency must have been evident, for Morris encouraged him into the next office. Over the last few weeks Hammond's opinion of Morris had altered, he wouldn't go so far as to say that he liked him. Morris was too vain in his opinion, but there had grown a sense of camaraderie between them that had strengthened into a mutual respect.

Morris sat down in the chair beside him. His eyes wandered over Hammond, noting the circles under the eyes. "There have been too many mornings when I have walked into this office and asked myself what I am doing here. The criminals will continue their antics no matter what we do, and we continue to pursue them but for what? What difference do we make? Honestly."

He had leaned back in his chair and looked at Hammond with a questioning gaze. For a moment Hammond thought how to answer but he wasn't sure how to respond, so he shrugged mutely. Morris sighed and ran his fingers through his hair. "I seriously considered giving it all up, just walking away..." His arm stretched out to the side of him and pointed to the door to clarify his meaning.

"To do what?" Hammond was genuinely interested.

"I don't know, rent an allotment and grow vegetables at the weekend, maybe try a bit of sport coaching, work for people who show their appreciation."

Hammond uttered a short laugh, he couldn't vision Morris growing vegetables, not unless he was ordering the carrots to un-canker themselves.

"But you haven't, you're still here."

"Yes, and I am glad of it, but it took me to see Galvin die before I realised why I was doing this job in the first place. There are nasty people out there who deserve to be locked up and I want to make their lives as uncomfortable as possible. Galvin was a good man. So young, How old was he? Thirty-two? So much life and enthusiasm wasted. He looked up to you Hammond, did you realise that? He wanted to be like you...poor misguided fool!" Morris smiled as he said the latter words.

The two men sat there quietly, lost in their own thoughts. Hammond looked up at the pictures on the walls and noticed that the photographs of Morris' wife had been removed. The silence was broken as Morris spoke.

"It is going to take a while until the internal investigation is concluded but I want you to know you have my full support. Your methods may be questionable but you succeeded in solving two murders and exposed a criminal organisation. I have to give you credit where it is due. You proved me wrong."

"There's something that has been bugging me." Hammond used the opportunity to his advantage. "You never told me what happened when you questioned Samuel Lawson."

Morris looked surprised. "Nothing to tell. He claimed that he had wanted to look at Graham Robert's house out of curiosity. He hadn't remembered being approached by Roberts as a young boy but he was curious so wanted to look at the man's house. Apparently the front door had been left unlocked, so he had let himself in."

"Did you charge him?"

"What with? He didn't take anything. There was no way of proving that he was lying."

"I was convinced I was right about him." said Hammond. "Unfortunately, some questions don't get resolved in the way we would like."

Hammond slowly nodded his head in resignation.

"Wallace, there is something you should know. We did a check on your friend, Jenny..."

Morris corrected his posture in his seat. "There's something you should know about her..."

Hammond interrupted Morris by standing up quickly. "I don't want to know." He said.

He accepted Morris' outstretched hand and shook it as he went to leave the room.

"Do you think it is worth it?"

Hammond looked down at Morris in the chair. He wasn't sure what Morris was referring to exactly.

"The job. Is it worth sacrificing your pride, your energy, your social life, even your marriage for?"

"Yes." Hammond said simply.

Hammond left the station by 5pm, he went home to his rented apartment in Folkestone and crawled into bed. He slept for twelve hours and awoke with the decision to resolve a question that had plagued his dreams. Later he phoned Mrs Taylor in Saltwood and asked if he could see her. She was surprised but agreed to meet him. When she opened the door, he saw that she had prepared for his visit, the house smelt of furniture polish.

"You said you wanted to talk to me about Thomas, but I don't understand why. He has been charged."

Hammond sat down and smiled reassuringly.

"I know." He said. "But something has been bothering me. You never talked about Thomas' father. I wondered why."

She looked baffled "Why?"

"Sometimes I feel the need to find answers, to get to the bottom of things, otherwise the unknown hangs on and gathers dust. It troubles me."

Her voice carried a hint of sharpness. "I don't understand why you want to know about him. Even if you did, it won't undo what has happened. Knowing the answers won't change anything."

"You're right, but I have the feeling that there is more to Thomas' attack on Mr Roberts than I understand.

He seems a good boy, you are evidently very close. I cannot help but wonder whether Thomas reacted the way he did because he was trying to protect you."

She looked at him with an expression of horror. "I hadn't thought of that. He's a bright boy, he's not cruel, what he did that day...it's not like him."

Hammond waited expectantly.

"My husband and I are separated. He left us two years ago in debt. We were kicked out of our home, Thomas had to leave his school. It was a terrible time." She gazed at the framed photograph of Thomas that stood behind Hammond on the window ledge. "He was a drunk. When he was sober, he was a loving, kind Father but once he had a drink, he was aggressive and controlling towards me. He would come home late and demand sex. For a while I refused him but eventually he wouldn't take no for an answer. On the last occasion, Thomas walked in and saw us. The next day my husband left us."

Hammond nodded slowly. "Do you think Thomas needed counselling?"

She looked at him with an expression of guilt. "I guess so. I didn't think about it, we just got on as if nothing had happened." She started to cry.

Thomas had tried to stop history repeating itself Hammond thought. When Roberts had approached him, Thomas feared losing his home and his family. He had attacked not because he was frightened of being physically harmed, but because he had feared losing his life.

He left the Taylor's house soon after and sat in the car for several minutes. In his rear view mirror he saw William Barnes leave the house with Daisy for their walk. They headed towards the woods.

The service lasted an hour. Hammond stood at the back of the packed chapel as the minister delivered the sermon. He bowed his head as the prayers were read out, he laughed at the humorous memories shared by the family and tried to sing the hymns in tune but all the time his eyes stayed focused on the ceiling. He wouldn't look down, if he did the tears would spill down his cheeks. His throat was tight and painful despite his attempts to exercise the muscles by swallowing. As they filed out the door, he found himself walking beside Galvin's wife. He looked at the baby being carried in her arms and noted the ways its eyes focused on something unseen as all infants did. Hammond wondered whether Galvin had witnessed his son's birth after all.

In February, Hammond made the decision to go away for a few days. He had always intended to visit the Lake District and persuaded Paul to join him, he wanted the opportunity to bond with his son. Hammond felt as if he was losing touch with Paul, and it hurt him to think that his son may not need him anymore.

They stayed at a bed and breakfast in Windermere and spent their first day sightseeing by boat on the lake. The second day they walked from the train station to Orrest Head. It was a gentle walk, but it gave Father and Son the opportunity to talk and enjoy each other's company. By the time they returned back to their room for the evening they were tired but exhilarated. Paul was in high spirits and Hammond felt his son had returned to him again. They toasted their time together, sharing a bottle of cognac that Hammond had bought especially for the occasion.

On their last day in Cumbria they spent the day separately, indulging in their own activities. Whilst Paul depleted his energy partaking in water sports, Hammond spent his morning browsing in an antiquarian bookstore. In the afternoon, he drove to Kendal. He had phoned Eleanor Hayes earlier that day to arrange his visit. She agreed to meet him in a tea shop by the town centre.

She stood out from the other diners with her bright red cardigan and matching beret. She was not as old as she dressed, her skin was clear and taunt. Her eyes bright with an intelligence he found appealing. They sat at a table by the window. Eleanor listened as Hammond explained his visit. Officially the murder of her brother had been solved. Hammond declined to offer too much detail about Thomas, but he explained the circumstances that had surrounded Graham Robert's death. All the while he spoke, she stayed silent. When he finished she thanked him and poured his tea, as if using the opportunity to think what she would say next. When she spoke, she focused her gaze on the spoon that nestled on the saucer.

"My brother and I did not have a close relationship. We did not get on. I confess that I was ashamed of my brother and his ways. Whilst I do not condone the way in which he died, I cannot help but feel that in some way, his death was an end to his suffering. Does that make me sound cruel?"

She looked at Hammond with genuine interest in his opinion. Instead of answering her Hammond asked her to explain.

"My brother was not perverted, but he was disturbed. He was molested when he was twelve years of age. He confided in my Father who beat him and told him never to repeat such filth. It just wasn't talked about, not like it is today."

She ended the conversation by stirring the tea. They drank in silence and watched the world pass by the window.

Hammond had thought about Kathleen several times since he had taken leave. She had attempted to contact Hammond since the night of Galvin's death but he had refused to take her calls, eventually she had left him a message on his phone. She told him that her interest in him had been real. Her voice had sounded genuinely emotional but Hammond couldn't trust her, he would forever doubt her intentions towards him, so he had deleted the message and tried to forget her but often found himself remembering her dimples when she smiled, or the way her hair had brushed against his face when he had kissed her.

He saw her for the last time at Lloyd Harris's funeral. They stood side by side as the coffin was lowered into its resting place. Mentally Hammond bid his friend his farewells. He understood why Harris had asked for his help; he had wanted to see justice served, but whether he had achieved that Hammond couldn't tell.

"You never allowed me to explain."

Hammond looked at Kathleen. He realised that he felt nothing, no anger, no resentment, no residue of his former humiliation.

"I don't think I would understand even if you tried to explain."

Kathleen positioned herself in front of him so that his path was blocked.

"I was attracted to you Wallace because I saw in you someone who I could relate to, someone who I could understand and who would understand me. Whatever you think of me now, you and I are the same. You said you became a police officer to earn your Father's approval. Why am I any different? I tried to earn my parent's respect by doing what they wanted me to do. Just because my parents have a different sense of right and wrong doesn't mean I didn't want them to love me. The only difference is that you were given love Wallace, whilst I strived for it."

"But Harris loved you. He raised you as his own."

"No, Harris loved my mother, and I was the nearest thing he could have."

Hammond did not reply. He walked back to his car and left her standing where he had left her. As he drove away from the church, he noticed the daffodils were about to bloom. Spring was on its way.

Epilogue

"Sunset is the promise of dawn."
Henry Havelock Ellis. The Dance of Life. 1923

The report on Goodchild's car was completed. The driver's seat had been removed and the blood sample had been tested. By weighing the passenger seat and comparing it with the weight of the driver's seat, it was established that over six pints of blood had been in the car, some of it had soaked into the upholstery, most of it had run down and dripped into the foot-well. It would have been impossible for a nine stone woman to have lost such an amount and survived.

The direction of the blood spillage indicated that the source of the bleed had come from a height rather than from an area that had rested against the seat. The driver's seat was covered in blood, the stain had no obvious shape to it so it wasn't easy to determine how the body was seated when the blood loss occurred. There were no puncture marks in the upholstery. Neither were there any drag marks in the blood to show that the body had been moved after the injury had incurred. With this thought in mind, further investigation was warranted.

The blood was screened. The report that was subsequently compiled from the blood analysis was significant. It was confirmed that the blood had come from Goodchild, but the information was limited due to the fact that the blood cells had been destroyed before the sample was taken. The only explanation for this was that the blood must have been previously frozen and had defrosted too quickly.

Author's Note

The background of this novel is based on the work and the dedication of law enforcement officers working for the Kent Police and the Kent and Essex Serious Crime Directorate (SCD) however it is a work of fiction. Whilst some references have been made to actual procedures or investigations conducted by British Law Enforcement or the British Home Office during previous eras, it has not been intended to portray a realistic reproduction of events in Kent Police's History.

I have written what could have happened, not what has happened. Whilst the story takes place in actual locations, the settings and the characters are not real. Not all Police procedures or conductions may be entirely accurate or representative of how Kent Police conduct their investigations in the present day. Since completing this novel in 2011, there have been changes to the organisation of Kent Police so they may differ to the scenarios that have been portrayed in this work of fiction.

I owe my gratitude to everyone who has assisted me in my research whilst writing this book, and my heartfelt appreciation to all those who have shown great patience in helping me with the necessary editing and proof-reading.

The story is entirely my own responsibility and nobody else's.

CD Neill
Kent. July 2013